D0727533

020 8359 1920

Please return/renew this item by the
last date shown to avoid a charge.
Books may also be renewed by phone
and Internet. May not be renewed if
required by another reader.

www.libraries.barnet.gov.uk

BARNET
LONDON BOROUGH

By Christine Feehan

Torpedo Ink series:

Judgment Road
Vengeance Road
Vendetta Road

Shadow series:

Shadow Rider
Shadow Reaper
Shadow Keeper
Shadow Warrior

'Dark' Carpathian series:

Dark Prince
Dark Desire
Dark Gold
Dark Magic
Dark Challenge
Dark Fire
Dark Legend
Dark Guardian
Dark Symphony
Dark Melody
Dark Destiny
Dark Secret
Dark Demon
Dark Celebration
Dark Possession
Dark Curse
Dark Slayer
Dark Peril
Dark Predator
Dark Storm

Dark Lycan
Dark Wolf
Dark Blood
Dark Ghost
Dark Promises
Dark Carousel
Dark Legacy
Dark Sentinel
Dark Illusion

Dark Nights
Darkest at Dawn
(omnibus)

Sea Haven series:

Water Bound
Spirit Bound
Air Bound
Earth Bound
Fire Bound
Bound Together

GhostWalker series:

Shadow Game
Mind Game
Night Game
Conspiracy Game
Deadly Game
Predatory Game
Murder Game
Street Game
Ruthless Game
Samurai Game

Viper Game
Spider Game
Power Game
Covert Game
Toxic Game

Drake Sisters series:

Oceans of Fire
Dangerous Tides
Safe Harbour
Turbulent Sea
Hidden Currents
Magic Before
Christmas

Leopard People series:

Fever
Burning Wild
Wild Fire
Savage Nature
Leopard's Prey
Cat's Lair
Wild Cat
Leopard's Fury
Leopard's Blood
Leopard's Run
Leopard's Wrath

The Scarletti Curse

Lair of the Lion

LEOPARD'S WRATH

CHRISTINE FEEHAN

piatkus

PIATKUS

First published in the US in 2019 by Jove
An imprint of Penguin Random House LLC
First published in Great Britain in 2019 by Piatkus

1 3 5 7 9 10 8 6 4 2

A CIP catalogue record for this book
is available from the British Library.

ISBN: 978-0-349-42325-8

Printed and bound in Great Britain by Clays Ltd, Elcograf S.p.A.

Papers used by Piatkus are from well-managed forests
and other responsible sources.

MIX
Paper from
responsible sources
FSC® C104740

Piatkus
An imprint of
Little, Brown Book Group
Carmelite House
50 Victoria Embankment
London EC4Y 0DZ

An Hachette UK Company
www.hachette.co.uk

www.littlebrown.co.uk

For My Readers

Be sure to go to christinefeehan.com/members/ to sign up for my private book announcement list and download the free ebook of *Dark Desserts*. Join my community and get firsthand news, enter the book discussions, ask your questions and chat with me. Please feel free to email me at Christine@christinefeehan.com. I would love to hear from you.

Acknowledgments

Thanks to Brian for keeping me on task. Thanks to Sheila and Kathie for looking through the pages for all those small mistakes that drive one crazy. Thanks to Domini for always editing, no matter how many times I ask her to go over the same book before we send it for additional editing.

1

MITYA Amurov stared out at the drops of rain running down the window. The town car had tinted glass, adding to the darkness, but it was more his sullen mood that kept him from seeing anything but the endless rain. His body hurt all the time. The bullets had torn into him; not only him, but his leopard as well, nearly killing both of them. He wished they had succeeded.

It wasn't the first time he'd been shot, but the experience had left him doing physical therapy and working out harder than ever to recover—for what, he didn't know. His leopard, always cruel, always clawing for freedom, had become nearly impossible to control. Or it was possible Mitya was just plain tired out from fighting every day of his life to keep his leopard under control. He honestly didn't know or care which it was. He'd gone past the time of hope for any kind of life.

He knew what he was. He'd known from the time he

was born, and his leopard had made him aware of what was in store for him. He'd grown up a criminal. A man who hurt others. A man who destroyed the lives of others. A man who killed. That was who and what he was, and no matter how hard he tried to climb out of that world of blood and treachery, there was no getting out. Never. He didn't have much to live for.

His leopard leapt for the surface, clawing and raking, trying to take him over. As Mitya fought back to stay in control, he thought the cat had responded to his morose thoughts. But then the leopard swung around so abruptly, Mitya's body did as well. He saw headlights beaming from the side of the road.

"Stop. Miron, stop."

His driver instantly hit the brakes. Ahead of them, the car in front did the same. The one behind them did as well.

"Turn around and go back to that car, the one on the side of the road."

They were on a fairly deserted road, one that led to the country home where he resided. It was in the hills above San Antonio, a beautiful estate where he could run his leopard without too much fear of accidentally running into a human being.

"Mitya," Sevastyan cautioned. "What are you doing?" He turned his head to stare out into the darkness at the car. Headlights prevented any of them from actually seeing and identifying the vehicle. His hand slid to his gun, and he sent a quick hand signal to the others in the car to do the same and then spoke into his radio to ensure the other two cars filled with security were ready for anything.

Mitya didn't answer, but the moment the car was parallel with the parked one, he opened his door before Sevastyan, his cousin and bodyguard, could stop him. A woman stood beside the rear of the car, one hand on a tire. The rain poured down on her, but she stood unbending in it, watching him come to her.

The closer he got to the woman, the crazier his leopard acted. Mitya was no longer a young man. Midthirties had caught up with him and he had lived a thousand lifetimes in each of those years, all of them with his leopard, and he didn't recognize this behavior. The cat was still clawing at him, still trying for supremacy, but not in his usual aggressive, "out for blood and mayhem and the taste of human flesh" manner. No, this time he felt almost playful.

Playful? *His* leopard? There was no time; even in childhood, his leopard had never felt playful. They had a relationship, a tight one, and his leopard guarded him as carefully as Mitya watched over his leopard, but that hadn't ever included play.

He was vaguely aware of his bodyguards rushing to surround him, of the furious set to Sevastyan's shoulders that indicated Mitya was in for another one of his cousin's lectures, but he didn't care. He was too busy drinking in the sight of the woman standing there in the rain.

She was on the small side, not at all one of the many tall, svelte models he often fantasized about. He wouldn't be doing that ever again. She wore a suit, a flared skirt that showed off her shapely legs and a short jacket that seemed to shape her waist, ribs and the curve of her breasts to perfection. All white. Not off-color or ivory, but actual white. The buttons were startling in that they were dark and shaped into cars. They made one want to look closer— which he found he didn't mind doing in the least.

She looked vaguely familiar to him, but he knew if he'd ever met her, he would have remembered her. As he got closer to her, he realized the skirt and jacket had images of cars pressed into the material, so the fabric looked embossed. Her boots were the same dark color as the unusual buttons.

Her hair was thick and dark, a glossy pelt shining in the flashlights playing over her. Her eyes were large and for a moment shone back at them almost red, but she blinked several times. Enough that he barked an order to his men.

"Stop shining the light in her face." He was already taking the heavy tire out from under her hand where she steadied it. "You will get dirty. Already you are soaked from the rain."

"Thank you for stopping, but really, it isn't necessary. I have changed tires before."

Her voice made his gut clench hotly. Hell, even his cock reacted. It was the way she sounded. Husky. Like sin in the night. Whispers between two lovers. He wasn't a good talker under the best of circumstances. If she needed someone killed, he was her man, but trying to sound suave and sophisticated was far beyond any ability he had.

Balancing the tire upright, he removed his suit jacket with one hand and tossed it to one of his bodyguards. He didn't even glance up to see who it was. He indicated her car or his. "You should get out of the rain." He tried not to sound like it was an order, but he'd been giving orders for a very long time, so he was pretty certain by the expression on her face that it had come out that way. She looked more amused than angry. Maybe a little confused. "To stay warm," he added gruffly, and turned abruptly away from her.

"Boss," Sevastyan hissed. "Miron can't drive worth shit, but he can change a fuckin' tire. Miron, get over here."

"I can change her tire for her," Mitya snapped, embarrassed that she might think he couldn't. He wanted to stare at her for the rest of the night. He wanted his leopard to keep up the strange behavior. He sensed that this woman, in some way, calmed the dangerous predator in him, and having that respite, if only for a few moments, after a lifetime of sheer hell, was a miracle.

The woman's gaze jumped to Miron and a small smile briefly curved her mouth, drawing his attention to it. She had the kind of mouth he'd fantasized over. Leopards were oral creatures, and he instantly became fixated on that perfect bow. He wanted her lips stretched around his cock, those enormous eyes looking right into his. The predator in his leopard might have turned playful, but that trait in him leapt to the forefront. He wanted to taste her. Bury himself in her. Claim her. Every possessive, jealous trait he hadn't known he had leapt to the forefront.

"I've got it, boss," Miron said and removed the tire from under his hand.

Mitya gestured toward his town car. She hesitated, looking at the force of men surrounding them. Sevastyan, thankfully, had put his gun away. Vikenti and his brother Zinoviy hovered close, but both had also concealed their weapons. The brothers were large and looked exactly like what they were, as did Miron. Sevastyan appeared more civilized than all of them. None seemed as intimidating as Mitya. He looked to be a dangerous man. He carried himself that way without thinking about it. When one had been shaped into a weapon from birth, it didn't go away until one died.

"I'm Mitya Amurov," he said.

Again she hesitated, as if perhaps she'd heard of him. If that were so, he wouldn't have been surprised. It was no secret he'd been shot. The news articles had a field day speculating whether or not he was part of a much larger crime family—and they would have been correct. Or at least, correct as they knew it.

Mitya held the door while Vikenti stupidly held the umbrella over him instead of the woman. He snapped at the man in Russian. "Her, Vikenti, be a gentleman."

Vikenti immediately shoved the umbrella over her head, and she sent Mitya a smile that tightened his belly and put steel in his cock. She was beautiful. Truly beautiful. Up close he could see her skin. It looked so soft he longed to touch it. Her lashes were long and thick, and in the lights spilling from both cars' headlights, even in the rain, her eyes looked more violet than blue. She stepped past Mitya and slid gracefully onto the heated leather seats.

Mitya was certain he detected a little sigh of pleasure when the warmth in the car enveloped her. Before he slipped in with her, he glared at his bodyguards, warning them off. Again, Sevastyan didn't like it, but he nodded curtly. There was going to be another lecture, and Mitya knew he deserved it, but it didn't matter. He needed this. His leopard needed it. It wasn't like this was going to happen ever again, so he was taking it while he could, and consequences be damned. He took his jacket back, slid in beside her and slammed the door closed.

"Your bodyguards aren't going to be very happy with you," she said softly.

She smelled of rain. Of some exotic, spicy flower he couldn't name. She'd been to a restaurant, and she'd been there with a man. He could smell the various scents on her. His leopard didn't like that any more than he did, but he consoled himself with the fact that she had driven home alone. Due to his counterpart, he had an acute sense of smell, and he couldn't detect the faintest scent of sex on her.

"They are bossy," he agreed, deciding it best to just admit he had bodyguards. He was surrounded by them. There was no denying it. "I'm sorry I don't have a towel, but you can use my jacket. That might help."

"I don't want to get it wet." A little shiver went through her in spite of the warmth of the car.

He slipped his jacket around her. "No worries." That was it. The extent of what he had to say. He just fell silent and tried not to stare, feeling as silly as his killer leopard had become.

"I'm Ania," she said. "It's nice to meet you. May I call you Mitya?"

"Yes, yes, of course." He was grateful Sevastyan wasn't

in the vehicle with them. She had a Russian name and pronounced it with the faintest of Russian accents. His cousin would be immediately suspicious she was an assassin come to kill him. He wouldn't have minded so much. His cat was content, and at that moment, so was he. It would have been a good moment to go out.

"I really do know how to change a tire," she said, "but it was miserable out there and I do love this outfit. It would have gotten ruined." Her fingers made a neat crease in the material and then folded it through her fingers as if she might be nervous.

It was a small gesture, but Mitya was trained in noticing the smallest reaction in those he interrogated, so reading her was easy. She was nervous being alone in the car with him.

"Why did you trust me enough to get into this vehicle with me?" he asked, his hand settling gently over hers to still her restless fingers. The silk of her skin was there. In spite of the cold, her touch made him warm all over. She didn't pull her hand out from under his.

"You were nice enough to stop for me," she replied. "No one else did, not that there were many people driving by tonight."

"Where are you heading?"

She turned her head to stare directly into his eyes. He had the feeling he was being studied. He didn't look harmless. If anything, he looked like the very devil. He didn't have a reassuring smile he could send her. If he tried to smile, she'd probably leap from the car in fear. The best he had was the truth.

"Please don't think you have to answer that. It was thoughtless of me to even ask. I'm not used to talking to women."

Her eyebrow went up, lending her the most adorable expression he'd ever seen on a woman. She turned in the seat toward him, continuing to study him feature by feature. Her gaze drifted over the angles and planes of his face, noting every scar. His eyes were darker than most of the Amur leopards. Many had lighter blue-green eyes. His were a darker blue-green, almost a dark cyan. When he shifted, his eyes blended with the darker rosettes in his long, thick fur.

"I would expect that women fawn over you."

He didn't deny what was true. He'd always had his choice of women. "Only because they believe I am someone exciting or that I have money."

"Exciting? You mean as in dangerous?" She gestured toward the bodyguards. "Or famous. Should I know you? Your name sounds familiar."

He sighed. He was tired. Too tired. His body hurt so fucking badly he wanted to stab himself through the heart and get it over with. He was a shifter, and he didn't take pain pills. If he was out of it, his leopard could escape and kill someone. He leaned back on the seat, enjoying the fact that she sat close and his leopard was satisfied just with her near. He was as well.

"I'm no one special, Ania. These women, once they learn this, no longer fawn." He kept his smile to himself. One small trace of his leopard and those women were running for their lives. None wanted him. They wanted what he had. Or what they perceived he had—which was nothing of real value. His cousin Fyodor had something valuable with his wife, Evangeline. Timur, another cousin, had it with his woman, Ashe. He could offer a woman danger. Bullets. Death. He could offer her . . . him. He was no prize. He never would be.

"Everyone is special in their own way, Mitya," she said softly.

"Perhaps. How did you come by the name of Ania? This is Russian, not American."

"It's a family name. My grandmother was named Ania.

She was an amazing woman. She came to the United States as a child with her family, although they only spoke their native language and it took her a while to speak English. She never seemed comfortable speaking it. She spoke only Russian at home, as did my grandfather and parents. I did as well, which explains my accent."

"Did your grandmother know how to change a tire as well?"

She burst out laughing. The sound was melodious rather than jarring. It held that soft, husky pitch he'd come to associate with her, but now it was mixed with something else, some sweet note that wrapped around his heart, shaking him. Women didn't laugh around him. He was used to them wanting him, but not this—not simply finding enjoyment in anything he said.

"I suppose a wagon wheel. I wouldn't have been surprised at anything she could do."

"But you lost her?"

She nodded. "Some years ago in a car accident. My mother, grandmother and grandfather were coming back from a theater production of *The Phantom of the Opera*. It was their absolute favorite. I was supposed to go that night as well, but I ended up sick. I'd grown up going to the theater and had seen it, but I was still disappointed. My father stayed home with me."

"I'm so sorry," he murmured. "I would never want to bring up anything to cause you sorrow." He could hear lies. It was a shifter trait. Something wasn't quite right with what she'd told him, but he couldn't put his finger on it.

"As I said, it was three years ago. I have wonderful memories of my mother and grandparents. Do you like theater?"

A memory surfaced. The theater in Russia. It was a little chilly and very dark. The sound of music was loud. A woman's voice singing, the sound impossibly beautiful, so much so that for a moment he was caught up in the sheer magic of it. Men and women dressed in their finest. The smell of fragrance and cologne. They were there to see the play. He was there to murder four people.

His targets were upstairs in one of the most expensive of boxes. They came often and laughed and cried with each subsequent scene. He had thought for a moment to delay the inevitable, so he could hear the star of the play singing once again, but he knew the longer he stayed, the more people had a chance to catch a glimpse of him. He had killed them fast and silently and walked out without ever hearing that beautiful voice again.

"I do," he replied carefully. "Although I haven't had much chance to go." If he did go, he would forever be dividing his attention between watching the production and his back. The bodyguards of his targets had been too busy watching the play to adequately protect their bosses. He'd killed them first.

She tapped her finger beneath his palm, reminding him he had his hand over hers. He hated removing it, but he had no reason to keep covering her hand, so he immediately lifted his.

"I'm so sorry, Ania. I haven't been around . . ." He forced himself to stop blurting out what a true loser he was with women. "I'm sorry," he reiterated.

"I liked your hand over mine, Mitya. You're unusual. Rare. I don't get to meet men like you very often. I wish we had more time to talk, but I see my tire is back on and your men are standing around in the rain getting soaked. I should go." She scooted across the seat and dropped her hand to the door handle.

He searched for something, anything, to hold her to him a moment longer. "If you are ever in San Antonio, my sister-in-law owns a bakery, The Small Sweet Shoppe. I'm often there." If she said she knew it, he would be there every day just to hope to see her again.

"In the business district?"

"Right on the edge, although the businesses seem to be growing up around it." He found himself holding his breath, his hand on the other door handle.

"I've actually been there once," she admitted. "If I go, I'll look for you. Thank you again for stopping. It was so sweet of you."

Before he could ask for her number, she pushed open the door. In all things he wanted, Mitya was extremely aggressive. He had no problem picking up women when he wanted some quick relief, but this was different. Very different. This woman mattered in some undefined way he didn't fully understand. He wanted to stay in her company. His body wanted her with every breath he drew. His leopard wanted to stay close to her.

He lived in hell. It was that simple. What man subjected a good woman to hell? What kind of a man would he be if he even considered it? He took a deep breath and slowly let go of the door handle, forcing himself to turn away from the sight of her walking back to her car, under the umbrella Vikenti provided.

Sevastyan slid into the car and turned toward him, glaring. Mitya held up his hand. "I know what I did was insane, Sevastyan. I apologize for making your life so difficult. It wasn't done on purpose." It wasn't. He loved his cousin and had placed him in a terrible position. Worse, he'd placed Ania in one. Sevastyan could easily have determined her a threat and shot her.

Sevastyan didn't lay into him the way he should have. Instead, he waited until Vikenti and Zinoviy had gotten back into their cars and Miron was once more behind the wheel. "What made you stop for her?"

Mitya shrugged his broad shoulders. "It was a compulsion. My leopard went wild when we passed her. When we turned back, he acted strange."

"In what way?" Sevastyan pushed.

"Just different. A behavior I'd never seen in him. Not like she was a threat, but more that he was content in her presence. My leopard had to guard me when I was a child. There were conspiracies. I don't know if you remember or not, but Gorya's father, Uncle Filipp, was alive then. He had two sons, Dima and Grisha, much older than Gorya. Lazar and Gorya's older brothers wanted Gorya and his mother dead."

Sevastyan frowned. "How do you know this? You aren't any older than the rest of us."

Mitya felt older, not that the others hadn't gone through hell as well. No one lived in their lairs and had it easy, especially his cousins. Their fathers were cruel and expected their sons to follow in their footsteps. They were expected to torture and kill any who might oppose their fathers' rule.

Mitya's father insisted the toddler be kept with him at all times. He wanted his son to grow up familiar with torture. With seeing women and children killed if their fathers in any way stepped out of line. He wanted his son to be so conditioned to the violence that he would never so much as blink when he had to do the same things. He heard a lot of things as a toddler, things his father planned.

"Mitya? What really happened to Uncle Filipp? Did Uncle Lazar or my father have anything to do with his death?"

Mitya glanced toward the front seat where Miron drove. The man had proved his loyalty to them, and yet he was still reluctant to talk about family business in front of him. Why? Because his father had drilled it into him never to speak of their business in front of non–family members. He had insisted there was no such thing as loyalty. Anyone could betray them, and would for a price—including one's own brothers.

There had been four brothers: Lazar, Rolan, Patva and Filipp. Each had become a *vor* in the *bratya*, the Russian mafia. Each ruled their own lair of shifters. All were very cruel, sadistic men. Talking about them aloud to his cousin was one thing; talking in front of an outsider was something else, but he needed to get over that. He wasn't ruled by his father any longer. In any case, Miron had been raised in the lair. He knew quite a bit about the Amurov brothers.

"Uncle Filipp didn't kill Gorya's mother as everyone has been led to believe," Mitya said. "After Uncle Filipp killed his first wife, he accidentally found the woman who was his true mate. At least my father believed that was what changed him. Filipp suddenly was protesting the bigger plan the family had and he was protecting his wife."

"What plan was that?" Sevastyan asked, frowning. "My father never spoke to me of a bigger plan."

"As a whole, the brothers wanted to take over more territory. I don't think that would have been difficult, but by that time, the leopards were so bloodthirsty they would go into a territory not held by shifters and let their leopards loose on the families of the *vors*. They would kill everyone. Man, woman and child."

Mitya's head was beginning to pound. The moment Ania had slipped out of the car, his leopard had reacted, going crazy, flinging himself toward the surface, demanding to be free. Since then, he hadn't been quiet, not for one second. Mitya's body was already hurting. With his leopard clawing at his insides, as if he could rip his way out of his confines, his body wanted to just lay it all down.

"Mitya, did your father take you along when they invaded other territories?"

Mitya nodded, closing his eyes, but the images were there, stamped forever into his brain. When he tried to sleep at night, those memories looped through his mind, playing out like a horror movie, over and over.

"Every single time. So many nights he let his leopard loose to hunt some unsuspecting tourist who had come to

the nearest town when the ships came in. Because we had
the port right there, it was easy to get one of the women to
lure a man away from the rest of his crowd. Lazar would
let his leopard loose and hunt him. Sometimes it was a
small group of men. He always insisted I accompany him.
In order to keep me from being beaten, my leopard would
come out and he would have to hunt with Lazar."

There was shame in the telling. He'd been too young to
protect his leopard. His father's beatings were brutal. He
would force the leopard to emerge in spite of Mitya fighting to keep him inside. Once the leopard had surfaced,
Lazar would beat the cat until it complied and hunted with
his leopard. Each time, the older, more experienced leopard would force the young cat to defend itself. Mitya knew
his leopard was being taught to be vicious and given
the experience of fighting until the animal was fast and
deadly in a battle. It was one thing to teach a teen, but not
a young boy.

He shoved his hand through his hair, angry with himself when he realized it was trembling. He turned away
from Sevastyan's too-close scrutiny. It was Sevastyan's job
to keep him safe. As head of security, he was the one who
interviewed anyone seeking to come into their employ.
Mitya had taken over a territory in the San Antonio area
that had previously been run by Patrizio Amodeo, a crime
lord who believed in human trafficking.

Like most crime lords in the States, Amodeo was not a
shifter. The man had tried to kill their cousin Fyodor
Amurov and his wife, Evangeline. Evangeline dove off a
counter to cover Fyodor, and Mitya had inserted his body
between the assassins and both Fyodor and Evangeline,
taking the bullets meant for them.

At the time, he'd acted on sheer instinct, but he knew
he had no sense of self-preservation because he was aware
his time was up. He was so tired of the fight with his leopard. More than anything, he loved his leopard counterpart.

Not one thing was the cat's fault. The animal had been subjected to horrific beatings from Lazar and more from Lazar's leopard. Both took delight in their cruelty. He didn't blame the leopard, but he couldn't allow him loose, and that was a constant fight, day and night. At no time could he ever let down his guard. Not when he was tired, sick, alone or in desperate need of a woman.

"Mitya." Sevastyan said his name softly. "You were a boy."

Mitya couldn't remember being a boy. There was no childhood, not with a father like Lazar. He pushed his fingers into the corners of his eyes, wishing there was a way to lay it all down, just for a few minutes. He'd had them, he reminded himself. A few precious minutes. For a moment the need to go back and find the woman was strong, almost overwhelming. Ania. If he took her and kept her, she would give them both peace. God knew, he needed peace.

"I was three or four when he started taking me with him. If I cried, the beatings were worse. I think my first memories were of his fists. The first taste in my mouth was of my own blood."

"And Uncle Filipp?"

"I heard him talking to Lazar. He tried to tell him he had so many sins on his soul. He said it was different when the woman was the right one. His leopard was satisfied and not driving him mad. He saw things with much more clarity."

"Lazar was furious. Really angry. After Uncle Filipp left, Lazar called Filipp's two older sons for a meeting. Dima and Grisha came that evening. They spewed hatred for Gorya's mother and him, although he was just a small baby. Lazar told them to hurt their father first, hurt him so he couldn't move. To wait until he was with Gorya's mother. Until he was lying on top of her, all spent and relaxed, not on guard. He wanted them to realize that their

father had brought this on himself. He had been stupid
enough to fall in love. The woman made him weak, vulnerable. She was really the one to kill him."

"He convinced Dima and Grisha that Filipp deserved
death because he was in love?" Sevastyan didn't sound as
astonished as he should have.

Mitya nodded. "Lazar said Filipp was no longer sharp.
He could easily be overcome. To go into the bedroom,
incapacitate him first, but not kill him until both had torn
apart his woman and her leopard. He was very specific
about needing to be alerted when they were making their
move. He would come to oversee, but not participate. It
had to be all them."

"What was his purpose in going?"

"I think he was furious with Filipp, that he would 'betray' them by falling in love with Gorya's mother. He
wanted to see him punished. Filipp dared to find happiness, something Lazar, Rolan and Patva would never do."
Mitya looked down at his hands. "Something few of us
will ever be able to do."

Sevastyan's breath caught in his throat, an audible reaction. Mitya didn't dare look at him directly. His cousin
definitely saw too much.

"Mitya, there is much to live for. Fyodor and Timur
both found their true mates. This woman you met
tonight . . ."

"I deliberately didn't get her phone number. Or her last
name. It is tempting to believe she could save me, save
Dymka." More than anything he wanted his leopard
saved. *Dymka* meant "smoke," as in fog or mist, and it was
an apt name for his big cat. At times the leopard had been
extraordinary, slipping into places in plain sight, yet never
being seen.

"I would never want to bring a woman into my private
hell. You and I both know Lazar is going to come for me.
If he deliberately had Filipp's two sons kill the woman his

brother loved in front of him and then kill him because of a perceived betrayal, you can imagine what he has in store for me."

Sevastyan was silent for so long Mitya wasn't certain he would respond. When he turned his head to look at him, his cousin was staring out the window into the night.

"She was beautiful," Sevastyan finally murmured. "Your woman. All of us felt her. She's leopard for sure, Mitya. There's no doubt in my mind."

Mitya hadn't given her origins that much thought. "She told me her grandmother was from Russia. She was named after her. Ania."

Sevastyan's head went up. "Seriously? Russian? Mitya, this could be a—" He broke off, frowning. "She looked familiar, and she was on the road leading to our estate. The Dover estate borders ours. I investigated the family before we bought the property. They have Russian connections and a daughter. My guess, she's the daughter. I'll do some checking when we get back to the house."

"That would make sense, her being on this road. She loves the theater."

"It has been many years since I've been to a theater," Sevastyan confessed. "Perhaps we need to do a little more than sit around planning out how to stop criminals such as ourselves." He flashed a small grin at his cousin.

"Once I'm finished with this fucking physical therapy some sadist has planned for me, I think it would be a good idea." Perhaps going to a theater production would help make him interested in life again. Or maybe he could run into Ania there.

"Tell me how Gorya came to live through the slaughter that night," Sevastyan insisted.

Mitya took a deep breath. "My father took me with him. He said he wanted me to see what betrayal looked like. He said he wanted me to see the consequences of betrayal as well. We heard the screams when we entered the house.

Her screams." He still woke up with the sound of his aunt's cries reverberating through his mind.

Sevastyan shook his head. "You had to have been only three or four."

"It was two days before my fifth birthday. My father told me I'd better not cry or make a single sound, or he would let his leopard tear mine apart. To this day, I keep thinking had I tried to call out, maybe Uncle Filipp would still be alive. Of course, her screams meant they had already weakened him in some way, but logic doesn't seem to have much to do with the horror of a child's memories."

"Unfortunately, no, you're right about that. I have a few of my own memories of childhood, and there is no logic in the way I think. Our fathers have a lot to answer for."

Mitya had to agree. "I think all the violence they fed their leopards rotted them from the inside out, Sevastyan. I really do. I think that they began to believe they had the right to choose life or death for others. They came to crave hurting others. Hunting them. They were addicted to killing. What else did they have? Not the love of family. Once Lazar was willing to kill his own brother and Dima and Grisha were willing to kill their own father, there was no such thing as loyalty. Not to family and not to the *bratya*."

Sevastyan nodded his head. The car made a series of turns, a maneuver Miron often made to see if they were being followed. Mitya never could understand why they would be followed back to the estate anyone could find out he owned. He never hid the fact that he was there. He used his own name. Mitya Amurov. If Lazar wanted to come for him, he wasn't going to hide. And there was no doubt that Lazar would come.

"When we entered the room, Filipp lay beside his wife, his head turned toward her. It was easy to see they'd broken his back. He couldn't move. He could only watch as they beat his woman to death. It was sickening the way they took such joy in it. The more they hit her, the more savage they became. I swear it was like watching a transformation from shifters to demonic murderers."

Mitya's stomach lurched at the memories pouring in. His heart pounded alarmingly, acting as a counterpoint to the jackhammer piercing his skull over and over. He wished he could forget, but his leopard couldn't, and that meant neither could he. Every detail was etched into his brain for all time. For just one moment, it was no longer his aunt they were beating. He was lying there broken, looking into Ania's violet eyes.

"When they were finished with her, after beating her to death, the boys took equal delight in doing the same to Uncle Filipp. Gorya started to cry. He was there. In a little crib. He also saw the entire thing. His brothers turned toward him. I think it was their intention all along to kill him. They despised that he was born of a mother who loved him when their mother had never loved them. From everything I once overheard Uncle Filipp telling Lazar, their mother despised their existence."

"I suppose they helped their father kill her." Sevastyan sounded weary.

Mitya glanced at him sharply. "Are you all right, Sevastyan?" He felt selfish, thinking only of himself and the way the painful memories hurt. He hadn't considered that his cousin also had memories, none of which could be very good. "I should have thought about how telling you this would affect you."

Sevastyan shook his head. "I need to know. More, Gorya needs to know. We all thought his father killed his mother and he was too young, so he was sent to Fyodor and Timur's mother to be raised."

Mitya shrugged. "That was the story Lazar decreed everyone tell. He didn't want Rolan or Patva to know he had anything to do with Filipp's death. Dima and Grisha agreed only because they wanted to take over the territory, and if they didn't do as Lazar said, he threatened to expose them to the world as the killers of their own father. After that, he would allow his leopard loose on them. They didn't want that. No one ever wanted to face Lazar's leopard."

Mitya had faced the vicious cat daily. When his father didn't like something he did, toddler or not, boy or not, teen or not, he was subject to the wrath of the animal. He had the scars all over his body to prove it, as did his cat. Now his own leopard was a vicious monster. His father had succeeded in that. He was equally as good a fighter. He was fierce and bloodthirsty. Difficult to control. Wild. Feral, even. His father had seen to that. His father had made absolutely certain that Mitya would forever live in hell.

He shoved his fingers through his hair several times, betraying his agitation. "He claimed Uncle Filipp was killed in a fight to take on neighboring territory, and Dima and Grisha backed up the story. I was a little kid, and no one was going to listen to me, but just in case I thought to tell someone the truth, Lazar beat the shit out of me. By the time I was eight, I didn't even feel him hitting me anymore. It became my normal."

Sevastyan sighed. "I know my father worried Uncle Lazar beat you too much. I would hear him talk to his men, cautioning them that they could do too much damage to a child beating their sons the way you were beaten."

"Lazar didn't beat loyalty into me," Mitya said. "He taught me how to hate. He taught my leopard how to hate. How to feel that terrible burning need for vengeance." He looked down at his open hands and then closed his fingers into tight fists. "I want him to come after me, Sevastyan. This time, I'm not a little boy. This time, I'm prepared to die just to take him with me."

Sevastyan sat up straighter as the vehicle pulled up to the tall gates with the beautiful scrollwork. The code was punched in and the gates swung open, allowing them to continue up the long drive to Mitya's estate. Behind them, after the two other cars with members of the security force—essentially the number of men Sevastyan insisted guard him when he went out—followed through, the gates closed.

"Mitya, you don't throw your life away to kill Lazar."

Mitya didn't respond. He didn't consider that it was throwing his life away. Lazar was evil, a terrible, malevolent presence on the earth. Anything he touched was tainted with a foul, vile energy. He had to go. The problem was—and it was the reason he had followed his cousins to the United States—he didn't fear going up against his father. He knew his every move. Dymka knew his father's leopard's every move. He didn't doubt that they could win in a fight. He had a problem with the morality of killing one's own parent.

He didn't want to say that aloud. Not to Fyodor and Timur, who had killed their father. He didn't judge them. He knew Fyodor had saved both Timur and Gorya from certain death. He didn't want to get into a moral discussion with Sevastyan either. He honestly didn't know where he stood. He had left the country and had joined with Drake Donovan and the others in their plan to rid the world of the worst of the leopards choosing criminal activities in the States. It was the best he could do to make up for the life he'd led before he had gotten out of Russia. There was a price tag on his head. There always would be. There would be no forgiveness from the *bratya*, primarily the leopards running the territories.

"When one welcomes death, one has nothing to lose in a fight," he explained to his cousin. "He always has the advantage. Lazar taught me that, and he's right. I hate that he might be right about anything, but having nothing in this life gives me an advantage."

"This woman . . ."

"I would never bring a woman into my personal hell. I

know Lazar is coming. You know it as well. I would be divided. Need to protect her. Want to live for her." She would be his Achilles' heel. Maybe she already was. He would keep his distance to ensure she would never come to Lazar's attention. "The things he would do to her to punish me—" He broke off, shaking his head. "No. I'll never go there." He said it firmly, meaning it.

2

SHE knew better. She absolutely knew better. She had discipline in all things, but somehow she couldn't control herself. Ania Dover found herself standing in front of The Sweet Shoppe's glass doors. *Again.* How many times had she come in the last few weeks hoping the Russian would be there? Clearly he hadn't been quite as enamored of her as she had been of him.

The second good storm of the season was breaking, the rain driving down so that the air looked as if silvery sheets dropped from above in long waves. She could see the beauty in the storm since she was dry under the roof built over the sidewalk. She was also very warm in her long trench coat with its hood. She often joked to her father that she felt a little bit like Little Red Riding Hood, even if her coat was a deep blue, not red.

Ania stepped inside the welcoming shop. She loved the smells of cinnamon and spice. The shop always felt as if it had arms wide open, calling one home. She noticed every customer who came in seemed to know Evangeline and Ashe, the two women working side by side. They were smooth, in spite of the fact that Evangeline appeared to be pregnant. It was difficult to tell under the apron she wore; if there was a baby bump, it was a small one.

Both women looked up when the little bell over the door rang. Evangeline smiled at her. "Ania, so good to see you again," she greeted.

Evangeline had learned her name within five minutes of the first visit she'd ever made to the shop and remembered her when she returned after her meeting with Mitya. "I'm addicted to your pumpkin spice cakes," Ania admitted, pulling off her gloves.

She took a quick look around, although she already knew he wasn't there. She felt different when she was close to him. Safe. Calm. Just different. In a good way. She would have known if he was in the shop without looking. It didn't matter how many times she told herself he was a criminal and she didn't want any part of that life, she still had come to the shop, driven by a compulsion she didn't understand. She'd done a little research on him the moment she'd gotten home.

Her family home was so very close to his. Just a few miles farther up the same not-very-well-traveled road. She'd been a little worried when he'd stopped, but she'd known, as did all those living on that road, that someone had bought the property bordering their family home. Her father had bid on it, in the hopes of combining the two properties, but he hadn't succeeded in acquiring it. Apparently, Mitya Amurov was the new neighbor.

She'd read all the news reports of how he had been shot, saving his cousin and his cousin's wife, Evangeline. She was a wonderful woman, and no matter how Ania tried to equate her with criminals, it just didn't seem possible. Evangeline was too real. She felt genuine and warm. The way she greeted her customers by name, asked after their families with that same real interest, she just couldn't be anything but innocent.

"Your usual?" Ashe, the barista, asked, turning to smile at her.

Ania nodded. There was Ashe, as sweet as Evangeline, but she moved as if she could handle herself. She saw the world differently than Evangeline. The owner of the bakery, Evangeline clearly looked at everyone as a potential friend. She was interested in them and cared about their lives. Ashe was a bit warier. She was friendly enough, but watchful. She'd noticed Ania's slight Russian accent. The accent was there on just a few words, but she'd noticed and was a bit leery at first, where Evangeline was simply open to friendship.

"Would love it, thanks, Ashe," she said. "The renovations are going to be awesome." The wall between the bakery and the shop next door had come down. It was blocked off during the hours the bakery was open so that customers couldn't go into the construction area, but clearly they planned on making the space larger, and they needed it. Customers packed in looking for Evangeline's baked goods and Ashe's coffee. The two women had a gold mine here.

Deliberately, Ania had chosen to come after the rush rather than during it. Aside from hoping she might run into Mitya again, she liked both women. They didn't know who she was and they didn't want anything from her. They treated her as if she might actually become a friend, and she was hungry for that. Over the last few weeks they'd accepted her more and more into their circle.

Evangeline beamed at her. "I think it's so exciting to see something you dream about come to life. I've always wanted a larger space. Sometimes the customers have standing room only. No one complains, but still, I want everyone to be comfortable."

There it was. Evangeline's true nature coming out. She

really did care about her customers. Ania took a look around the shop while she paid for her latte and the pumpkin spice cake. Already she was eyeing the lemon-raspberry tart as well. She was going to get that to take home to her father. He loved baked goods, and she was usually too tired to get into the kitchen by the time she got home.

There were few people in the shop. Only a couple of men she would peg as bodyguards. They were spread out, at opposite ends of the room, but they couldn't hide what they were, not even when they were idly looking at their phones. She took her latte and the fancy little plate with her cake and sat at one of the tables away from the window.

She wanted to savor every bite. If she was going to be adding all the extra calories by coming in so often, she definitely wasn't going to hurry eating. The latte was perfection and she glanced up, smiling to tell Ashe thank you, only to catch the woman watching her. Ashe immediately flashed a smile and came out from around the counter.

"Do you mind if I sit with you on my break? It's okay to say no. You never look at your phone while you're here, so I thought I might not be disturbing you."

"Of course." Ania waved her toward a chair. "I make it a practice to enjoy every bite, and I don't want to be looking at work while I do."

"Do you work close by?" She seated herself in the chair to Ania's right.

Ania nodded. "I have offices in the Bannaconni building. It's just down the block from here. I don't know why it took me so long to discover you. Once I was told about you, I began hearing the name of the bakery over and over. You have a good reputation."

"That's good to know. Who recommended us?" Ashe leaned closer, her chin on the heel of her hand, her eyes telling Ania she was interested.

Still, Ania wasn't certain if it was a casual question or not. She shrugged. "I got a flat tire on my way home from a date. The date, by the way, was a disaster. And the tire thing worried me. I don't, as a rule, ever get a flat tire because I check them. It's a thing I do. In any case, it was raining, and a gentleman stopped to help me. I was in a white skirt and jacket, a favorite outfit, and he drove up like a knight in shining armor. He was the one who mentioned your shop."

Ashe frowned. "What was wrong with your tire?"

Ania took another sip of the hot latte. The rain continued outside, making her grateful for the warmth of the bakery and the drink she wrapped her hands around. "It was punctured." That much was the truth. It had been punctured. Ania wasn't so certain it was accidental.

"I'm new to San Antonio," Ashe admitted. "Have you lived here long?"

Ania nodded. "All my life. Three generations now. My grandparents, my parents and now me. I think they wanted a son, but alas, I'm an only." She laughed softly because there was no way her parents would have traded her for a son, and she was very secure in that knowledge.

Ashe's eyebrows shot up. "Really? Three generations, that's awesome. I never had the chance to know my grandparents. What's that like?"

"They were wonderful. Very loving. I have to admit, I was spoiled growing up. Our family is all about cars. Anything to do with cars. My grandfather had me working on cars when I was barely in preschool. I handed him all the tools and he'd have me name them. Name the various cars and all parts of the engines. My father was all about teaching me how to drive. I think that started at age three. I couldn't reach the gas pedal, but I was expected to know *how* to drive a stick and an automatic by five."

Ashe laughed. She definitely had relaxed a little. "I love that. I think Timur will be like that with any children we have. He's a man who will want to be a huge part of our child's life."

"I haven't met him. Does he come here often?"

Ashe nodded. "I met him here, actually. He's Evangeline's husband's younger brother. Worked out for me. You said your date didn't go well, so I'm assuming you don't have a significant other in your life."

"No. I have very poor taste in men. I think I'm doomed to be a cat lady."

Ashe burst out laughing. Ania liked her laugh. It was inviting, and she noticed that both of the men she'd deemed bodyguards smiled. Neither looked their way, but they definitely heard Ashe laugh.

"I doubt that with your looks," Ashe denied. "I've never seen anyone with skin like yours. I was going to ask you what products you use, but thought I'd better get to know you a little better or you'd think I was hitting on you."

"Are you?" Ania tried a straight face.

Ashe laughed again. "I'm tempted. You're so lucky."

"Thank you. Seriously." Ania touched her face. She wasn't going to pretend she didn't know she was beautiful. She'd been born with her looks. It wasn't something she'd earned. "My grandmother and mother had gorgeous skin, and I was lucky enough to have those genetics passed on to me. I lost them a couple of years ago in a car accident, and every time I look in the mirror, I see both of them."

"That's beautiful," Ashe said. "They must have been wonderful."

"They were. They laughed all the time. My grandmother used to say, 'Don't frown, Ania, laughter is so much better for the world. Give your family and friends that gift always.' She practiced what she preached. If I frowned, she kissed me over and over until I was laughing. Sometimes I frowned just to get her kisses. Momma did the same."

Telling Ashe brought those memories close and she felt lighter for it, and yet tears were close for the need to see them both.

"I love that. I'm going to remember that, and if I ever

have children, I'll be quoting your grandmother. She sounds as if she was a very wise woman."

"She was. She'd love knowing you were quoting her to your children."

Evangeline slipped into the chair on the other side of Ania. "I need to get off my feet."

"Should you be working?" Ania asked. "I heard a rumor that you're pregnant."

"That rumor is true, and I get very sick sometimes, so if you see me running to the back, you know why."

"Fyodor doesn't want her working at all," Ashe supplied. "He's all grumpy when he comes in to see her."

"I banned him for at least a week," Evangeline added.

"I tried taking over for her," Ashe said piously.

Evangeline burst into laughter. "She nearly burned down the bakery. Don't ever help me again, Ashe, as much as I love you, my beloved bakery wouldn't survive."

Ania raised an eyebrow.

Ashe shrugged. "Can't cook. Can't bake. Timur loves me anyway 'cuz I'm really, really good at other things."

Ania found herself laughing with both women. It felt, for the first time in her life, like she had friends. As if she fit somewhere. She was all about family, and she stayed close to her father, especially now. It had been the two of them for a long time, and he needed her. His health was deteriorating rapidly, and more than ever, she didn't like being away from him for too long.

She'd taken complete control of their business and hired nurses to help, but she oversaw every aspect of his care. She wasn't leaving that in strangers' hands. All of that took up time, leaving little for herself. She hadn't had friends since she was a young girl in school.

"Should you be working, Evangeline?" Ania persisted. "And does your husband actually listen to you when you ban him?"

"I love what I do, but I tried staying home. I promised

him I would while I was pregnant, but it made me so sad, he agreed to let me come to work as long as the doctor signed off on it. I'm careful. If I get too sick, I leave. Fyodor has insisted I have help, so I can call when I need someone to come down. At rush we have a couple of others working. We need more space, though, before that can really happen. As for Fyodor abiding by my decree . . ."

Ashe burst out laughing again, the sound contagious. "Fyodor is a law unto himself. He checks on her about every other second." She looked up toward the door and waved.

Ania followed her line of sight and spotted the camera hidden cleverly in what appeared to be wide molding along the wall.

"Stop that, Ashe," Evangeline said. "He'll take it as an invitation to come and nag me to go home."

Ashe wiggled her eyebrows. "He likes you in his bed."

"Will you stop? You have sex on the brain," Evangeline accused, wadding up a napkin and throwing it at her.

"I have to agree with Evangeline," Ania said. "I just got through telling you my date was an ass, so no sex for me. Lately, I think I'm going out of my mind. Do not believe it when they say men aren't needed. Toys are no substitute for the real deal."

Both women looked sympathetic immediately. Ania realized what she'd said and looked around quickly. She couldn't believe what she'd just revealed to the two women. She'd been coming in for the last few weeks, but she didn't really know them that well yet.

The two bodyguards were suddenly a little more alert. Color began to climb. They were both a distance away, so hopefully neither had heard her.

"There isn't audio on those cameras, is there?" she asked, lowering her voice even more.

Ashe shrugged. "Who knows what that paranoid brother-in-law of mine actually has installed down here."

Evangeline narrowed her eyes at Ashe. "Don't scare her. Fyodor hasn't wired the place."

"Don't act like he wouldn't. If you didn't threaten to hit him over the head with one of your baking pans, he'd have you in a padded room naked, waiting for him."

Evangeline rolled her eyes, but she blushed as well. "Probably true. I'm not saying another word."

Two customers came in and Ashe jumped to her feet, waving Evangeline back into the chair. Immediately, Ania felt the difference in the two women. In the two body-guards. Both men shifted in their seats. They'd looked sprawled out and lazy. Now they looked ready for action. Evangeline and Ashe exchanged a long look that clearly was of concern.

"I can handle them." Ashe hurried to the counter. There was no smile of greeting like there normally was.

For some reason, and Ania had no idea why, she moved her chair just a little, just enough to cut off the two cus-tomers' vision of Evangeline. If they wanted to see her, they would have to step out away from the counter and make it obvious to all occupants in the room.

"Who are they?" Ania asked. It wasn't her business, but already she felt protective of Evangeline. She liked her. She found she was drawn to the bakery not only be-cause she wanted to see Mitya again, and the lattes and baked goods were the best, but because she genuinely liked the two women.

"Cops. They've done things, tried to use me and this shop to find evidence against my husband. They have never found anything, but they won't stop harassing us." Honesty rang in Evangeline's voice. "Those two pretended to be my friends. I've asked them repeatedly not to come back here. The last time it seemed as if the entire police department was here. Clearly they had hoped my brother-in-law Timur would come in before closing so they could make a scene and possibly destroy my business." There was hurt in her voice as well as honesty.

"Should you call your lawyer? If you don't have one, I do," Ania said. "That's not right." She knew better than to jump into something when she didn't have all the facts, especially since she'd met Mitya and there was no doubt that he was a criminal, or at least was very familiar with that world.

"No, it's all right. They wouldn't dare pull anything. They know we have cameras in here."

One of the two cops stepped deliberately from the counter to face Evangeline. He glanced at each of the bodyguards and took a step toward her. Both men stood immediately. The tension in the room ratcheted up significantly.

"Evangeline, now would be a good time to head to the ladies' room." Ania stood up.

Evangeline stood as well.

"Evangeline," the man called out, ignoring the two bodyguards. "I'd like a chance to talk with you."

"Keep walking," Ania said. "Don't even turn around." She fell into step behind Evangeline, not once looking in the direction of the policeman.

Evangeline headed straight to the women's room and threw herself into the wide armchair just inside the door. "I can't believe he would think I would want to talk to him."

Ania was a little disconcerted by her color. Evangeline looked pale. "Are you all right?"

"I have something called hyperemesis gravidarum. I get very sick and can't stop vomiting at times. It's been a little better lately. I'm hoping it goes away. The doctor assured me that it does in most cases after the fourth month or so. I'm not quite there yet, so I still have hope."

"Should I send Ashe in?"

Evangeline shook her head and pulled out her cell phone. "I'm going to text Fyodor. He'll send a car or come himself. Thanks, though, Ania. I'm so glad I was here today and got a chance to visit a little with you."

"Me too. It's been fun. Lately, I haven't had a lot of fun in my life. My father has been very ill, and the business is demanding."

"Business?"

Evangeline was clearly trying not to be sick. Ania detested that she was getting worse right in front of her eyes, and she blamed the two men who had come in and upset her.

"Excuse me," Evangeline said, and rushed into one of the stalls.

Ania stood there for a moment listening to the terrible retching and then she marched out, straight up to the two men just getting their baked goods from Ashe. She was furious. "She's sicker than a dog, and you had no right coming in here and upsetting her. She's asked you several times not to come in here and you don't listen. I swear I'm reporting both of you to your superiors."

Looking like a haughty princess, she ignored both men and turned to Ashe. "She's really sick, and she didn't have a chance to get ahold of anyone."

One of the bodyguards had already stepped to the ladies' room door the moment Ania had vacated, pushing it open and listening as Evangeline got sick. It occurred to Ania he'd made certain that she hadn't done anything to harm Evangeline.

Ashe immediately had her phone out and was texting fast, even as she rounded the counter and hurried back toward the bathroom. As she did, the door to the shop opened and the bodyguard, the one Mitya had called Sevastyan, entered. Ania's heart began to pound. His gaze swept over her, the cops, the bodyguards and Ashe running for the ladies' room. His gaze came back to settle on Ania.

She didn't like the look on his face. He had known she was there. She knew immediately someone had texted him. Evangeline? She doubted it. Ashe? Maybe. One of the bodyguards? How would they know who she was or that she'd met Mitya? She hoped they didn't know she had come so often just looking for him. She'd never chased after a man in her life. Now she felt like a stalker.

She hurried back to the table, ignoring the entire drama. Embarrassed that she'd been so persistent in trying to connect with him when Mitya hadn't felt the same need, she just wanted to go. She had her back to the door, but she knew the moment he entered. He had a presence, and it filled the room. She turned slowly to face him.

He was even more amazing than she remembered. It had been dark, and they'd only had a few minutes there in the small confines of the car, but he'd made a lasting impression. She could see why. He was sheer power. Dangerous. A predator among sheep. He wasn't handsome in the accepted sense of the word. He was too rough-looking. Too scarred, his features too rugged. He looked masculine without one hint of a softer trait.

Her heart pounded harder than ever. From fear or attraction, she didn't know which; she only knew she was in trouble with this man. Something wild in her responded to him. She'd tried so hard to stamp down the wild in herself, now especially when her father needed her to step up for him. Her iron will didn't matter. Her body responded instantly to Mitya's presence, growing damp and hot. Needy. It was crazy.

His gaze took in everything and everyone in the room, then settled on her before moving past to the two policemen who seemed frozen, caught there in the center of the bakery. Behind Mitya, two more bodyguards slipped into the room. She recognized them also from the other night, and then behind them, Miron, the man who had changed her tire. They spread out, boxing the cops in. She was in the direct line of fire. Mitya strode forward, Sevastyan moving with him.

"Evangeline?" Mitya nearly barked the question, still coming at her.

Sevastyan reached her first and stepped aside so Mitya could take her arm firmly and put her behind him so his body blocked hers from the two cops should they pull weapons. Sevastyan stepped in front of them both.

Ania had no idea who the question was meant for, but before she could find her voice, one of Evangeline's bodyguards answered. "In there. She's sick. Ashe called for Fyodor."

Ania tried to loosen Mitya's grip on her arm by subtly pulling back, but that only tightened his fingers so they felt like a shackle on her. She refused to be undignified, especially in front of the cops.

"I was just leaving." She kept her voice low, not wanting to be part of the drama that appeared to be unfolding there in the bakery.

"Now you're staying." Mitya's voice was equally as low but carried the kind of command she recognized as having had complete authority for years.

She'd read Mitya was suspected of taking over the territory of a deceased criminal boss, Patrizio Amodeo, but even if that were true, he'd been in charge years prior to that. No one would dare disobey that voice, least of all her. She never drew attention to herself. It wasn't done. That had been drilled into her at a very early age as well.

"Gentlemen, do I need to call our attorney?" Mitya asked.

"Just came in for the baked goods," one of the cops answered.

"Find another bakery," Mitya suggested. "Evangeline will file a restraining order if it becomes necessary. She doesn't want to have to do that, but she will also bring harassment charges against you. Please leave, gentlemen."

One looked as though he might protest, but the other nudged him, and they both made a move toward the door. Mitya's bodyguards parted to allow them through. "Check on Evangeline," Mitya ordered Sevastyan the moment they were gone.

For a moment she almost wished she was Evangeline. It was made very clear to everyone that she was important and very loved. Mitya had nearly died for her. The others were all concerned for her. Anxious, even.

Ania had always been loved. Always. But she was expected to be strong. To be more like her grandfather and father than her grandmother and mother. They had the protection of the men in her family. She was brought up to be protective and responsible all rolled into one. She didn't mind. But this felt . . . beautiful. And Mitya gave that to Evangeline.

Sevastyan didn't hesitate the way the other bodyguards had. He walked right into the women's room. The moment the door opened, they all could hear Evangeline getting sick.

Mitya kept his fingers wrapped around Ania's arm as he escorted her to a table. This one was at the very back of the room, and he seated her to the right side while he took the chair with his back to the wall, facing the door and plated windows.

"At last. I have found you. You're not getting away this time without giving me your last name and a phone number. I've had my friends looking to see if you came here, and it was reported several times, but I was too far away to get here in time before you left."

That felt better, that he would at least have tried to find her. At the same time, she knew there was a lie or two mixed in with the truth. She'd always been good at hearing lies. Her father and grandfather had insisted that when she thought she heard them, she pay attention, and that had always stood her in good stead.

She smiled at him, giving him her meaningless smile,

the one she used on customers. "While I'd like to believe that, I know it isn't true. You don't have to worry. I did come here hoping to see you again." She wasn't going to lie about it. She wasn't ashamed that she'd been attracted to him. "But the baked goods are amazing, and I'm lucky enough that Evangeline and Ashe both extended friendship to me, and that is worth everything. So, I have you to thank once again."

He regarded her in silence for so long her stomach did a slow roll. His gaze didn't leave her face, and those eyes of his were incredible. The color alone was mesmerizing. The lines in his face were cut deep with pure sensuality. That direct stare spoke volumes of knowledge about secrets she suddenly needed to know. He hadn't said a word, but all she could do was think sex. Sin. Her tongue tracing each of those scars. Seeing if there were more. Finding all of them.

"I am not a good man, Ania, and you're a good woman. A man like me has to think long and hard before he decides to bring a woman like you into his world."

A million butterflies fluttered against the walls of her stomach. It was all she could do not to press her hand there, but that might give too much away. She hadn't expected the truth or the raw longing in his voice, and it touched something deep inside her she hadn't known was there. No man had ever gotten to her the way Mitya did. The attraction was so intense, it scared her enough to make her wary. Yet she wanted him with every breath she drew.

She touched the tip of her tongue to her lip. His eyes followed the action. "Maybe I don't have to be *such* a good woman." She whispered it, meaning it to be humorous, but it didn't come out that way. Not at all. She ducked her head, wishing the floor might open up and swallow her. She *did* have to be a good woman, whether she wanted to or not. "I really have to go, Mitya." Her only recourse to save herself was to run away. Fast.

His fingers around her arm, if anything, tightened. "Hear me out, Ania."

The door to the shop swung open and a man strode in, another who clearly was his brother just edging in front of him. She knew immediately it was Evangeline's husband. It couldn't be anyone else. He looked around the room.

"She's in the ladies' room," one of the bodyguards said. "Ashe and Sevastyan are with her."

Fyodor nodded to the man, and he and Timur went straight into the restroom. Within moments, Timur was striding out fast, Fyodor behind him, Evangeline in his arms. She was still sick, a bowl cradled in her arms. Ania hadn't even realized Ashe had brought one into the room when she'd come in, already prepared, already knowing exactly what Evangeline would need.

Ashe trailed after them, her expression worried. She came straight to the table. "She's going to be all right, Ania. Fyodor will take her home. They have a nurse there, and she'll give her fluids." She glanced at her watch. "I'll take care of the late customers at the end of the business run. Come back when things aren't so crazy so we can visit some more."

Ania nodded, but she knew she wasn't going to come back. Mitya was too much of a temptation, and she'd make a total fool of herself over him. She couldn't afford to lose her heart to him.

When Ashe was back behind the counter making coffee and selling pastries to the newcomers, she turned her attention to Mitya. "Why did you come today? What's changed between when we first met and now?"

His palm slid down her arm, his thumb rubbing over the back of her hand. She knew if she had any sense of self-preservation, she would move it, but she couldn't help herself. She wanted to feel his touch. She wanted the slow burn moving through her body. She'd never felt that way. The butterflies. The somersaults. The dampness like a slow-burning fire building between her legs. Her veins felt as if they were filled with hot molasses. Her skin felt electric. Her breasts were suddenly heavy. Hot. Even her nipples reacted, coming to two tight peaks. Aching. His touch did that. Just that thumb brushing over the back of her hand. She would be in such trouble with this man.

"I realized, looking at every single bit of footage we had of you coming into this shop, over and over, staying up at night watching it, that I am an even worse man than I knew myself to be because I don't want to give you up."

"We don't know if we're even compatible."

"We know."

She couldn't deny that. She also couldn't deny that he was a criminal. He wasn't pretending to be anything else. He just put himself out there, all that raw sexuality, that dominant, commanding personality, and thought she would deal. Could she? She had so much to lose. She knew she did, and the number one thing was her heart.

"You don't even know my last name."

"You would be surprised at what I know about you." His eyes didn't so much as blink, wholly focused on her, almost hypnotic.

"You don't know the first thing about me, and I don't know the first thing about you."

"You know we would burn together."

She considered that. A night? Could she walk away from him after a night? Her heart clenched hard in her chest. It hurt. Just the way it would when she left him. She'd dreamt of a man like him. Reality and fantasy were two very different things. She'd seen Fyodor's face when he'd carried Evangeline out of her bakery. He had the look of a man furious that his woman was anywhere but home. She wouldn't be in the least surprised to read about a fire burning down the shop in the morning.

These were men in control of their lives and everything in them. She would have to live with the bodyguards, at least until the relationship burned itself out. She had her own life. Things she liked to do that she was fairly certain a man like Mitya would try to nix immediately. Things she needed to do she knew he would forbid. There would be fights. If he cared that much. If he didn't, it would be worse than if they fought. Either way, she would be the one to lose.

"You're overthinking."

"I'm an intelligent woman." She gestured toward the bodyguards. "Are they always around you?"

He nodded. "They are necessary."

"If we had a one-night fling . . ."

"One night will never be enough. A thousand nights will never be enough. If you come to me, Ania, it will be a commitment to me. To us. There will be no going back."

"I sat in a car with you for fifteen minutes."

He nodded. "You brought me something beyond any price. I thought to give you your life, but I find I'm not that man. So, I'm asking you to think about sharing your life with me."

"Do you have any idea how unreasonable and insane that is?"

The unreasonable and insane part was that she was considering his ridiculous proposition even for a moment. She didn't know him. She was a little afraid of him. Mitya Amurov was not the kind of man a woman could wrap around her little finger to get her way in all things. He was the kind of man who gave orders and expected them to be obeyed.

"You're shaking your head, Ania, and you haven't given us a chance."

"How would I do that?" The sane, intelligent part of her screamed at her to shut up and walk away. To not listen to another word coming out of his sensual mouth in that sexy, caressing tone that wrapped her up in the need for that mouth on her anywhere.

"Have dinner with me."

Her eyes met his. He would be having her for dinner if she went anywhere near him. Turning him down was going to be the hardest thing she'd ever do. She had few things in her life she could call her own. She'd lost her grandparents and mother. Her father was deteriorating rapidly. She knew it was only a matter of time before she lost him.

This wasn't her time. If she could have had a glorious night with him and walk away unscathed, then she might have gone for it. Okay, she would have. But she knew, looking at him, she would get her heart broken. He was the kind of man she would never be able to resist.

"I would love to say yes, but I know myself, Mitya. This wouldn't end well for me."

"Why are you so certain it would end?"

"We have chemistry." She was determined to be as honest with him as possible because he was laying himself on the line for her. "That's true. Much more chemistry than I knew there could be between a couple, but we're not compatible in other ways. You're . . . you. Don't deny what you're like and say you'll be reasonable. You won't be."

His smile took her breath. It was slow coming, but when it did, it crept into the blue-green of his eyes and softened his harsh, rugged features. "I would never deny what I'm like, but I have to challenge your idea that I'd be unreasonable. Perhaps you would be the unreasonable one and I the voice of reason."

She stared at him a moment, a little awed by his transformation, and then his comment penetrated and she found herself laughing. "Naturally, you'd think you were the reasonable one."

"Have dinner with me, Ania."

She hesitated and then shook her head. "I'll come back to the bakery and see you here. It's safer."

He shook his head. "I know bullshit when I hear it. And

lies when I hear them. You have no intention of coming back here."

She didn't. Self-preservation was winning out. At least for now. She feared Mitya was probably already an addiction and she wouldn't be able to stay away.

"Have dinner with me, Ania. If you are afraid of being alone with me, I will ask Timur and Ashe to come along."

That made her sound like a coward, and she wasn't one. She sighed. "My father isn't in the best of health. I don't like leaving him alone for too long. I'm overseeing the business at the moment, just until it's sold, but it keeps me away from him. If I go out to dinner—"

"I'll bring dinner to you." He was firm.

She was equally as firm. "That's not necessary. Seriously, Mitya, I'll give you my phone number. We can arrange things after I know how my father's doing."

He nodded, and she programmed her phone number into the phone he gave her. She knew he watched her as she left, because she could feel his eyes on her every step of the way. She wanted to run, feeling just a little bit like prey.

3

"EVERYTHING is still quiet, Mitya," Sevastyan reported. "No signs of any Russians trying to come in legally or illegally for the moment. I've got people watching in every place they might slip through."

"Lazar will send his spies first," Mitya said, leaning back in his chair. He sat in front of the fireplace, in his favorite chair. It was big enough to accommodate his size. Solid. He was all roped muscle, a true leopard shifter, larger than most but so well-proportioned that at first one didn't notice how extremely strong he appeared.

Sevastyan nodded. "I have no doubt. There's no way he would come himself unless he was certain you are weak."

Mitya looked up at his cousin, at the expression on his face. "Meaning?"

"The woman. Ania Dover. If you persist in your pursuit of her, Lazar will have found your weakness."

Mitya switched his gaze to the flames dancing in the

fireplace as he pressed a glass to his forehead. Sevastyan was right. He usually was. Mitya's father, Lazar, would never forgive his desertion. He would be forever branded a traitor, and in their world, that was a death sentence. To have his own son desert, the one he'd trained to take over the lair, was the worst crime Mitya could have committed. Lazar was a cruel, vindictive man, and he would never stop until he punished, destroyed and then killed his son in retaliation.

"I'm well aware of this, Sevastyan. I struggled with my decision, but I cannot hold my leopard in check for much longer. I need Ania close to me. I've considered keeping our relationship private, but in the world of leopards, private doesn't work. She has to be leopard or Dymka would never react the way he does. She is most likely getting close to the Han Vol Dan. Her leopard will rise, and Dymka will not tolerate any other male near her."

A woman rarely knew of her leopard's existence until she entered the Han Vol Dan, a time when her cycle matched that of her leopard. That allowed the leopard to rise to the surface and claim their shared form. Dymka, his male, was already enamored with Ania's leopard and she hadn't even shown herself.

Sevastyan sighed, pushed his fingers through his hair and dropped into the chair opposite his cousin. "I was afraid you'd say that. Her family is complicated. As you know, they own the property just bordering yours. About two hundred acres. Most of the hillsides here are planted with grapes, but they aren't in the wine business. They have a very successful business maintaining cars for the wealthiest clients in and around San Antonio. If a driver is needed, they often will drive for the client. They're sought after and are paid top dollar."

Mitya nodded and put his glass down. "The Dover family. I heard of them from Jake Bannaconni. He has a contract with them to maintain his cars. He told me about them. He said there were rumors that the grandfather or father occasionally worked for the Caruso and Anwar families out of Houston years ago."

Sevastyan nodded. "Those rumors would be true. They were both known for their driving skills, and the families hired them as couriers to get packages from one place to another when they knew someone—make that the police— might try to stop them."

"So on the edge of the criminal world but not really in it," Mitya said.

"They knew they were working for criminals," Sevastyan pointed out.

"Who do you have watching Ania?" Mitya asked.

"Kiriil and Matvei. I trust them with my life and yours, so they are watching over her. Not that I like giving up two of my best men."

"I appreciate that you sent them. I need her, Sevastyan. I need her in my life soon. Did you do as I asked?"

"Yes, the dinner will be ready in an hour. We can take it over to her home. She's there now, but Mitya, that isn't the end to the story. That accident she said her grandparents and mother were killed in? That was no accident. Someone ran them off the road. The Dover car was traveling at a high rate of speed, as if it was being chased. Witnesses claim there was another car that appeared to be trying to run them off the road, but a third car was actually what clipped them and sent them into a spin, and the car rolled so many times witnesses lost count. All three occupants were dead."

Mitya was silent a moment, turning the facts over and over in his mind. It sounded like a classic hit. They'd set up the Dover car. While the driver worried about the car chasing him, the other was in position to take him out. "Did they do something to anger either family? Like steal from them? Talk to the cops? Anything?"

Sevastyan shook his head. "I did some digging, but so

far haven't found anything but that the Dovers had an impeccable reputation and no one would ever consider that they would steal from those employing them. Or go to the cops."

"That was how many years ago?"

"Three. Two weeks after they buried Ania's grandparents and mother, her father was robbed on the street just outside of a liquor store. He was shot multiple times. From what I understand, one of the bullets lodged in his brain and they couldn't remove it. He hasn't been seen in public since. He's alive, there was footage of him leaving the hospital, but he no longer works his business. Ania took it over, and a couple of months ago she contacted Jake Bannaconni saying she wanted to sell. He agreed to handle the transaction for her. I've got a call in to Jake to see exactly what his relationship with the Dovers is and what he knows about what transpired between the families in Houston and Ania's family. From what I understand, the business is worth a fortune. She's already independently wealthy and doesn't have to work if she doesn't want to. Jake's in negotiations right now with two different buyers."

Mitya steepled his fingers and continued to stare into the flames. She was selling the business. She'd mentioned that to him.

"Is her property up for sale?"

"No, but there is a rumor that it might be going up. I don't know if that's because she's selling the business or because she contacted a Realtor. Why would you think that?"

"Her grandparents and mother were murdered. Someone tried to kill her father and, in some way, partially succeeded. She told me his health was declining. She's selling a lucrative business that has been in her family for three generations."

Sevastyan sat back in his chair. "Shit. She's getting rid

of all encumbrances. All ties. Anything that would hold her down."

Mitya nodded. "I think I'm going to have to press my suit faster with Ania Dover for more reasons than her leopard rising. I think she's in trouble."

"Maybe not now, but if she messes with either the Caruso or Anwar family, she will be. While the two of you are eating tonight, I'll try to slip in and see her father. That might be the only chance we have.

Mitya frowned. "I'll see if I can get her to have him join us. If he's really bad and can't, then at least she'll talk to me about him and you'll have a better idea of where in the house he is and if anyone is with him.

"What do we know about the two families in Houston? They haven't been on anyone's radar, have they? In all the briefings—and I admit, I'm still not up to speed on all the players—I don't recall Drake or anyone else mentioning either family as a threat."

"Marzio Caruso came up through the ranks with his father in Florida. They ran a port and docks there, very successfully. When the father wanted a change, they relocated to Houston and quickly established themselves as the authorities in the port. They just took over the docks," Sevastyan answered. "Ann is his wife, and they have four children, all boys."

"Great. Are they leopard?"

"According to Elijah, yes, both families. Marzio added a trucking business as well, and the family and their enterprises have thrived. They do business with and get along well with Elijah Lospostos. He says they have always been men of their word. He hadn't heard of a feud between the Dovers and the Carusos."

"And the Anwar family?"

"Bartolo is the head of the family and, from all appearances, is a man of his word. He has two sons, Enrico and Samuele, both, like the Caruso brothers, very involved in the business. The daughter is younger by several years, Giacinta. She's supposed to be very sickly and rarely leaves the house. Again, they do business with Elijah, and he's never had a problem with them. He said even when the Caruso family came to Houston, there wasn't a war or seemingly ill will between the families."

"Elijah is a huge name in the business, not just here but worldwide," Mitya said. "He's an asset. Drake was smart to recruit him."

He tipped the contents of the glass back. He rarely drank. It was never a good idea when one was a shifter, especially when the leopard was as feral and bloodthirsty as Dymka was. His leopard had settled a little knowing Mitya's intention was to see Ania.

"The hit wasn't necessarily put out by either of those families," Mitya finally said. "We're just speculating, Sevastyan. We don't know if a hit was even ordered. The father could have been done by an actual robber. As for the car, that could have been anyone not happy with the family for transporting something successfully for anyone, let alone the families in Houston."

Sevastyan nodded. "Actually, that's true. And it might fit better. If the Dovers had done something against either family, I would think it would be known by most of the other families, but Elijah says there's not a hint of a problem between them. Elijah used their driving services on more than one occasion and he said they always delivered, the reputation was solid."

"If I can, I'll meet with Ania's father. If I get the chance, I'll question him. He won't want his only child to go against a powerful crime family. Even if she succeeded in killing any of the family members, the others would come after her and kill her. He would know that."

Sevastyan shook his head. "Let me question him, Mitya. You concentrate on Ania. She needs to be brought in fast if you really think she's close to the Han Vol Dan.

The last thing you want is for her to go into heat and for every leopard within a hundred miles to go after her."

Mitya pushed down the instant surge of ferocious adrenaline caused by the idea of anyone getting near his woman. His leopard was vicious, raking and clawing, trying to tear his way out. Mitya breathed away the fury and got himself under control. Being a leopard shifter meant absolute control at all times.

"We can make the call when we're there at the house. Get as much information as possible on both families and anyone else who used their services from Elijah. Contact Drake. He seems to be able to acquire intelligence on anyone fast and accurately." Drake Donovan owned a company specializing in the recovery of kidnap victims. His people were renowned as bodyguards, and many were shifters. He had contacts all over the world, and his people were well trained in gathering information.

Sevastyan nodded. "Will do. Be cautious, Mitya. We don't know everything about Ania Dover and her family yet. You have a price on your head, and it's a big one."

Mitya couldn't help but smile. "Do you think Ania is an assassin?"

"I think that family has ties to Russia. I also think something isn't right there. That means you watch yourself and don't get too caught up in her leopard emerging."

Mitya laughed. He couldn't help it. His life was an endless empty fight with a bloodthirsty leopard. He had steel bars on his windows and metal plates on doors so his leopard couldn't break free while he slept. The women he occasionally saw in order to get some relief, he could barely look at or speak to. Interacting with them was dangerous. It was fuck and leave as fast as possible or his leopard would try to tear him apart to get at them. His life was pure hell.

If he were in the least bit a good man, he would stay away from Ania Dover, not drag her down into the mud with him, but she was his only chance at salvation. At life. He'd tried to turn his back on her. He'd resisted going to the bakery so many times, but in the end, he was consumed with the need to see her. Just to sit beside her and feel peace. Calm. Something he hadn't had in all the years he could remember.

Ania Dover had become an obsession. She represented hope. More, she was good. She radiated kindness and compassion. She was everything he wasn't. To have his cousin imply that she might be an assassin hired to kill him was so absurd he actually found himself laughing. Real laughter.

Sevastyan glared at him. "It's not funny, Mitya. You never take precautions with your life. I'm not going to let you just throw it away. I know what's in your head half the time, and it isn't good."

Mitya lifted his head and met his cousin's eyes. He knew Sevastyan could see his leopard because heat banded. He felt every bit as deadly a predator as his cat was. He knew it showed on his face when Sevastyan went still.

"She will be claimed tonight, and there is nothing she can do about it, nothing she can say to stop me. She belongs to me, and I will have her. That makes me a fucking criminal, not her. It wouldn't matter if she was contracted to kill me. She is mine. She'll learn to live with that because she has no choice. Does that make me like my father? Probably. He shaped me into a predator. The only difference is, once I have her, I'll do everything in my power to make her happy, and she'll be protected from any danger. Do you understand, Sevastyan? Her protection will come first."

"I hear you, Mitya."

Mitya heard the resignation in his cousin's voice. There was no denying what Mitya was, what he'd been shaped into. Twisted into. He was a killer, just like his father. He *chose* to wield his power for as much good as possible. It was why he had left the *bratya* and his father's lair to follow his cousins, trying to build a decent life for themselves. That had proven to be impossible. Then Drake Donovan had come along and given them all purpose.

Mitya glanced at his watch. It was time. This was the night he would claim his lady, and hopefully his leopard would be satisfied. He realized that as much as he wanted his leopard to settle and feel contentment, claiming Ania Dover was really for himself. For him. He needed her. He was already addicted to her smile. To her brightness. But it was the way she brought peace to him that he needed. Once he felt that, he knew he couldn't live without it.

THE doorbell pealed. It didn't ring. It was melodious but obnoxious at the same time. Ania sat on the floor, dressed in mint green sweats that dipped low, showing her belly button and the little piercing where the chain hooked around her and danced low on her hips. Her crop top was made of the same mint green material and hugged her breasts but dropped just below them. It was her favorite evening wear. Comfortable. Warm but not too warm so she could enjoy the fire. She was barefoot, and her wild hair was down. The mass tumbled around her face and down her back.

"Melania!" she called out to the housekeeper, but then realized it was late. Melania had gone home. She pushed off the carpet and stalked through the great room to the foyer to pull open the door with a little more force than necessary. Annoyance died on her lips.

He stood there. Mitya. Her heart clenched hard, leapt and then began pounding. Her sex clenched right along with her heart. He was bigger than she remembered. So gorgeous. A rough, rugged, very scary man, and he made her weak with wanting him. He looked unbelievable in his suit. His hair was dark and a little too long, as if he needed a haircut but couldn't be bothered. It didn't detract in the least from his good looks. Neither did the scars on his face.

She just stood there, shocked. No words came out. His gaze moved over her and there was possession stamped plainly into the sensual lines on his face. She tried not to be thrilled by that, but she was. Her entire body responded to him, going electric. Her blood went hot and raced through her veins to pool low and wicked.

She had to say something. "Mitya." That was it. That was all she could get out. She was acutely aware of the fact that she was exposing far too much skin, never a good idea when she wanted a man with every breath she took.

"We have a dinner date."

"We do?" Her voice was faint. She found herself staring up at him. He seemed so . . . invincible. So beautiful. A man. All masculine and . . . She hoped she wasn't saying any of her thoughts aloud.

He put a hand on her belly, his fingers splayed wide. His palm rested on her bare skin, and at once that spot felt so hot she thought she might melt. He applied a little force and she stepped back. He stepped in, crowding her. She gave way again, and the next thing she knew, Sevastyan was in, followed by two more men carrying large bags of something that smelled so delicious her stomach reacted.

She hadn't realized it, but suddenly she was starving. She couldn't remember the last time she'd eaten. She tried to look stern, intending to send Mitya and his crew away, but when she opened her mouth, Mitya leaned down and brushed his lips over hers. A mere touch. Barely there. She felt it all the way to her bones. Her sex fluttered. Her breath caught in her lungs. She grew even hotter, her breasts aching. She could only stare up at him as he took her hand and walked confidently through the house to the kitchen and the large rectangular alcove considered a breakfast nook. It was a much more intimate space than the large formal dining room, which was to the left of the kitchen.

The two men set out plates, silverware, napkins and even glasses. They had a bucket of ice and were chilling a sparkling cider, which was her favorite. How did he know? She just stood there, her hand enveloped in his while the men set the food out. It wasn't just any food. The shrimp were grilled in a ginger-lime sauce and set over jasmine rice with grilled asparagus. Strangely, it was another of her favorite dishes.

She looked up at him. "You've been doing your home-work." She didn't know if she should be creeped out or flattered.

He brought her hand up to his chest and pressed her palm over his heart. "You matter. Of course I'm going to try to find out the things you like."

He was so matter-of-fact, as if it was the most impor-tant thing in the world to research her likes and dislikes, that she almost bought into it. Almost. Instead of protest-ing as she should have and making them leave, she sank into the chair he pulled out for her. The two men who had carried in the food left. Sevastyan followed them to the door, giving them orders as they went, speaking in Rus-sian to them.

Mitya followed her gaze. "I'm sorry, Ania, I can do nothing about my cousin's obsession with watching out for me. They will be outside, though."

"And Sevastyan?" She could see he wasn't going out-side. He seemed to be making himself at home in the great room, right in front of the fire where she'd been all cozy. She picked up her fork. Maybe food was the better deal.

Mitya gave her a faint smile. "I prefer to ignore him. He should answer to me, but it seems I answer to him."

"Did you have me investigated?" She nearly moaned when she put a bite of shrimp in her mouth. It was that good.

"Not me. That was Sevastyan. He would investigate the saints if they came into contact with me. I highly doubt that will ever happen. How is your father doing?"

She blinked, everything in her stilling. "My father?" she echoed, reaching for the chilled glass of sparkling cider.

"You mentioned your father was ill. I wondered how he was doing," Mitya persisted in that same easy tone.

She let her breath out. "He's slipping away. I have a nurse with him during the day and Annalise with him at night. He knows her and is comforted by her presence. I was just with him and he was sleeping. He goes days without speaking and then suddenly rallies." She didn't know why she told him the truth or why she allowed pain and grief to slip into her voice. She didn't share news of her father with anyone. If he was going to die, he was going to do it without aid from an outside source.

"I'm sorry, *kotyonok*, I had no idea he was that bad. Is there anything I can do to help?"

Just the offer of sympathy had her choking up. She didn't have anyone to share her grief with. That burden of her father's care for the last three years. She didn't have family left. Or friends. She'd learned not to trust anyone. She was positive her family had been murdered and her father's death, although slow, was the result of murder.

Ania didn't dare look at Mitya. He'd seen the shine of tears in her eyes, and she didn't do that. She didn't cry in front of other people. She took another bite, mixing the ginger and lime sauce with the rice. It was exquisite. He'd called her *kitten* in his native language, and for some reason that soft endearment sounded like he meant it. That choked her up as well.

"Ania." Mitya waited.

She had no idea why, when she didn't want to look at him, she found his voice so compelling that she had to raise her eyes to his.

"I'm truly sorry. I didn't have any idea, or I would have waited to bring his condition up until after you ate."

No one had shown her kindness or caring in a long time, and it felt good. She hadn't eaten real food in a while. She tended to grab what she could on the run. No one had thought to bring her a meal, nor had anyone ever bothered to find out her likes and dislikes. It was difficult to look away from his mesmerizing eyes. She knew she was falling under his spell, and that was just plain dangerous.

"It's all right, Mitya. I appreciate that you cared enough to ask." Had anyone asked after her father in the last three years? She'd taken over the business, and very few clients had asked about him, though he'd worked for them for so many years. That had taught her something. The clients they had were extremely wealthy. Her family was considered the help, and it was not worth noticing that her father had all but disappeared. They weren't friends and they never would be. It didn't matter that the Dover business was extremely successful, and they were wealthy in their own right; they were still considered outsiders.

"Have you explored every means to help him?"

She nodded, concentrating for a moment on eating another bite of shrimp. This bite didn't just taste exquisite; it tasted like caring. She found herself relaxing, wanting to talk to someone about her father.

"I went to doctor after doctor and surgeon after surgeon. All said the same thing. If they tried to remove the bullet, he would die. Maybe it would have been better to just try it. This has been a slow death for him. And sometimes quite painful. He was robbed . . ."

"I read about it when Sevastyan gave me the report. Do you really believe he was robbed? After what happened to your grandparents and mother, it seems an unlikely coincidence that your father would have been randomly attacked. Sevastyan doesn't believe it, and he's rarely wrong. He has a sense about these things."

Ania desperately wanted someone to talk things over with, but she was cautious. She'd been biding her time for three long years. She might have to wait longer to set her plan in motion. Telling someone she didn't believe that her father was randomly chosen to be robbed might very well ruin everything. Could she trust him? He was a man involved in criminal activity of some kind. She was certain of it. Were the families all connected?

"*Kotyonok.*" He whispered in Russian. Softly. Gently. Almost tenderly.

The way he called her "kitten" twisted at her heart. He definitely used the term as an endearment, his velvet voice wrapping around each separate syllable like a caress. He was a tough, dangerous man, and yet whenever he was around her, he seemed to be gentle and sweet.

"Don't look at me as if you fear me. I would lay down my life for you. If you're in some kind of danger, you need to tell me. I have resources. I was raised a certain way. It wasn't a good way, but it did turn me into a weapon, and I'll be that for you if it is needed." He picked up his glass of sparkling cider and regarded her over the rim. "Some of us can hear the truth or a lie when it is spoken. I hope you are able to hear the truth."

She couldn't look away, mesmerized by him. Every single cell in her body was aware of him. Tuned to him. That thing inside her, wild and feral, was aware of him. Unlike her, the entity wasn't afraid of him. Her body grew hot, her skin feeling too tight. Her jaw ached. Her skull felt as if it might explode.

Mitya rose and held out his hand to her. She could

barely see with the heat banding in front of her eyes. At the same time, the quiet need of him, that smoldering fire deep inside, exploded into a fierce furnace. She gasped and let him pull her out of her chair and into his arms. His mouth came down on hers and the world tilted. Spun. Would never be the same.

Fire poured through her. Hot. Addicting. His taste like no other. It was as if once his mouth was on hers, he planted some spicy aphrodisiac inside her, setting up a craving for life. She closed her eyes and gave herself up to him, letting him take complete control. He took her over, the kisses changing, becoming more aggressive, rougher, more demanding. She followed his lead. Gave him everything he wanted and more. She held nothing back because she couldn't. It was impossible when his mouth was a haven. A sinful temptation. Absolute perfection.

He murmured to her as he moved with her. She felt as if she were floating. His hands stroked her body, and the heat grew so intense she thought she might melt. He turned her away from him, pressing her against the wall, his mouth on her neck.

"Do you feel her rising?" he whispered. His teeth scraped back and forth in a sensual rhythm against the wild pulse beating in her neck. He kissed his way to her nape and then bit down gently on the junction between neck and shoulder, making her shiver with need. His other hand pushed the little crop top up along her back to her neck. "Do you feel her need, Ania? The way she grows so hot?"

Her skin was hot. Scorching. Between her legs, her sex throbbed and burned. Her clit pulsed and pounded. Her breasts ached for his touch. She wanted him with every breath she drew, and she was panting raggedly. Desperate for air. Desperate for him.

He kissed his way up her spine and to her shoulder. "Your skin is like satin. So soft. Softer even than it looks.

Hold still, *kotyonok*, very still. Let them come together just for a moment."

She felt the slide of fur on her bare skin. A blast of hot breath. She tried to turn her head, but his hands refused to allow it. She couldn't move, and her heart thudded hard in her chest. Fear kicked in. She was all primal instinct in that moment, but it was too late, and he had her trapped between his solid, muscular form and the wall.

Teeth clamped down on her shoulder, just below the bone. Pain burst through her body. She cried out, choking with fear and excitement. Deep inside she felt that feral creature rising toward the surface to meet the male leopard. Even though she couldn't see him, Ania knew it was a leopard and he was big. Very large. Very strong. She could feel his power and absolute determination. For a moment she felt the two leopards come together, male and female. Bonding. She knew that was what it was. Her female wholly embraced the male as her mate.

Then her female subsided, sliding away so there was barely a trace of her, leaving Ania alone and afraid. She felt the burn as the leopard released her and then the rough rasp of his tongue over the bite marks. A slide of fur and he was gone, leaving her shaking so hard she was afraid she would have fallen had Mitya not been holding her.

His hands soothed her, moving over her gently, shaping her curves, stroking her skin. He rubbed some kind of ointment into the bites and covered them both with Band-Aids. Clearly he'd come prepared. He kissed his way over her shoulder and down her back, slowly allowing her top to drop back into place. He turned her into his arms and pulled her tight against his chest. Ania did her best to calm her ragged breathing.

"What just happened?" Her voice was muffled, but she didn't care. She needed him to hold her.

"Your female is going into heat, Ania. Were you aware of your leopard?"

Was she? She knew about shifters. Her father was one. Once, he'd showed her how he could shift, and he told her never to be afraid if her leopard suddenly revealed herself. He claimed it was freedom to run in the form of a leopard. It was one of the reasons they had bought so many acres there in the hills rather than having a home in the city.

"I don't know. Sometimes I felt her," she admitted. She ran every evening after she spent time with her father, mostly to rid herself of excess energy and the ever-present grief and anger she felt after seeing the once-vibrant man slowly reduced to a vegetable. When she ran, she was faster than she believed was possible. She could leap distances and could often jump over fallen tree trunks when they were in her way.

"She will be emerging soon." Mitya kissed the top of her head and walked her back to the table. "When she does, my leopard will act on his claim. They are a bonded pair."

Ania sank into the seat and pressed her hand over her eyes. She had always hoped she would have a leopard, that she was born with the shifter genes, but now, she wasn't so certain. When she thought Mitya wanted her for her, it was heady, wonderful and an unexpected gift. She felt so alone all the time. Even if she knew on some level that it wasn't a good idea to give in to her attraction to him, it was amazing to have a sensual man like him want her. She needed to feel as if she was his entire focus. Now she knew it wasn't her at all. It was his leopard and her female.

"I see that your mind is busy setting up barriers between us once again," Mitya said, picking up his knife and fork. He regarded her steadily with his unusual blue-green eyes.

"I don't do that." She could hear the lie. The steady gaze never left her face, and she found herself turning red and squirming. "All right, maybe I do. But in this instance,

I think I need some breathing room to think this entire thing through."

"What's to think about? I'm still here because you are the only woman I want to be with."

"And it just so happens that I have a female your leopard wants."

"When I was a young boy, my father would force my leopard out to protect me and his leopard would viciously rip him to shreds. This happened over and over. I was beaten and sometimes even attacked by his leopard. I have the scars everywhere." He touched one of the slashes on his face and then rubbed his palm over his chest. "The things he did to my leopard were worse than what I suffered."

Ania forgot all about why she was feeling hurt. "Why would he do that?" She was shocked that anyone would treat a child that way. She'd been loved by her grandparents and parents from the moment she was born.

"The lair where I was born belongs to the *bratya*. They believe the *bratya* comes before family, a woman, anyone. To prove loyalty, they take a wife, usually one they buy from another lair, or get as a favor, and breed her for sons. If a female child is born, that child is doomed to the same fate as her mother, if she survives at all. When he gets his sons, to prove loyalty, he murders his wife with his own hands. Often his sons are expected to participate."

She was shocked, and she knew it showed on her face. He spoke matter-of-factly, distancing himself from his childhood, but she could see and hear that he was telling her the truth. "Mitya." She whispered his name, one hand going defensively to her throat.

"The leopards are turned into killing machines. They are always denied their true mates. Eventually, the cats become unmanageable. They are allowed, even encouraged, to hunt human enemies. Sometimes they are taken into another territory and let loose to kill as many as possible. They rage day and night, raking and slashing at their human counterparts, and of course they are extremely strong. Controlling one every second of the day and night becomes more than challenging."

She understood the lines of strain in his face. Sevastyan, his cousin, had them as well. It had to be a horrible way to live. She sat back, the delicious meal suddenly tasting like cardboard. "I'm so sorry, Mitya."

He shrugged his broad shoulders. "Don't be, Ania, not for me. My leopard, but not me. I escaped with cousins, and we came here and have made a life for ourselves."

"You were shot."

His smile was faint, but his eyes had gone a disturbing and very sensual, warm green-blue, pushing the glacier away for just enough time for her stomach to pitch.

"I see you're doing your homework on me."

She couldn't very well deny it. "Naturally. I have my father to look out for and my attraction to you was . . . unexpected. And unsettling. At least I know why it was so strong."

"Why do you think it's so intense?"

There was the slightest touch of amusement in his voice, and that got to her as well, although not in the good way his faint smile had. The chemistry between them *was* intense, but she hadn't gone near that word deliberately.

"Our leopards." She tried to meet his eyes, but she couldn't. She used her fork to push around the rice on her plate.

"Ania, look at me." He went silent.

She knew he was waiting. He could wait until hell froze over. The silence stretched between them, and she felt his eyes on her. Almost as if his gaze was burning right through her. Reaching deep. She tried to resist, but her stomach kept doing those weird slow rolls and she felt him crawling deep inside, right where she didn't want him. She raised her eyes to his. Instantly, she was caught and held. Mesmerized. Unable to look away.

"I've had a lot of women. Fast. Back to me. No time spent. No kissing. Just get relief and send them away. I'm not telling you this because I'm proud of it. I'm not. I'm telling you because I want you to know the moment I saw you, I couldn't stay away. I *had* to be with you."

"For your leopard," she persisted. Her heart was beating far too fast.

"For me. *I* needed you for me. I wanted you for myself. I knew better. You deserve better, but I found I wasn't a good enough man to give you up, not when I knew you were attracted to me." He leaned forward. "We can take this slow. You deserve that, Ania, and I want to give you the world. The problem is our leopards may not give us the time we need."

She bit down on her lower lip, hard. She'd felt the beginnings of her leopard's need, so she couldn't pretend not to understand.

"I don't know, Mitya. I'm responsible for the care of my father. I'm in the middle of trying to sell the family business. This isn't a good time." She forked rice into her mouth. Her food was cold, and she put her fork down again.

"Keep trying to find reasons to push me away."

That was exactly what she was doing because he scared her. Everything about him scared her because everything about him appealed to her.

"I'm not going to say I'm not tempted, because I am, but it's the wrong time right now. I've got responsibilities. A few months from now . . ."

"What will you do when she goes into heat?"

She moistened her lips. She still couldn't look away from him. It was impossible. "I don't know. What do most women do when it happens? Lock themselves away? Find a companion? What?"

"You find a companion other than me and that's a dead man," Mitya said so mildly that for a moment she didn't comprehend.

Footsteps sounded on the tile and Sevastyan was there immediately, stepping between the running woman who had come from down the hallway and Mitya and Ania.

"Miss Ania. You're needed now in your father's room. Hurry."

4

"HE'S having another one of those spells!" the woman shouted. "Hurry, Ania!"

Mitya's gaze had been on Ania's face when the nurse had rushed into the room, calling out to her. He saw the fear in her eyes, in the sudden white beneath her skin, beneath her expression. She tried to hide the trembling of her hands as she put them on the table to leverage herself out of her chair. It wasn't just fear of her father passing; this was much more primal. He was on his feet almost before Ania.

"Stay here, Annalise," Ania commanded. "I'll handle it." She didn't even look at Mitya, almost as if she'd forgotten he was there as she raced out of the room.

Mitya paced along right behind her, Sevastyan at his side. Neither made a sound as they hurried after her. Ania used her leopard's speed whether she knew it or not. A leopard could leap long distances, and she covered the ground at an incredible pace.

Annalise had looked frightened. More than frightened. Terrified. Ania had reacted quickly, without giving her company a thought. When they reached the hall leading to the master bedroom, Mitya heard the chilling sounds coming from the room. He knew immediately what was happening.

"Ania." He tried to stop her, but he'd been hanging back so she wouldn't realize they were right behind her.

Sevastyan increased his speed as well. The two sprinted down the hall and were just able to leap into the bedroom before Ania slammed the door closed and shot multiple bolts. Her eyes were wide with fear. Both could smell it coming off her in waves, but she approached the bed and the contorting man in it.

"Dad. Look at me. I'm here with you."

The man was very far gone. When he swung his head around toward Ania, it was a leopard staring at her. As if that weren't bad enough, the leopard was crazed, in a frenzy of rage, desperate to escape the pain the dying man was in.

Mitya caught Ania by the shoulder and thrust her behind him. She didn't want to go, using her strength to try to get around him.

"Get out of here," she hissed.

Sevastyan caught her by the shoulders. "Hush. You'll trigger the cat."

Mitya moved close to the bed and the thrashing man. Her father's skin rose and fell in waves as if something alive moved beneath it. His muscles contracted and then released. His jaw elongated, his mouth filling with teeth, and then receded back to normal. All the while those eyes tracked Mitya, recognizing the vicious leopard in him.

Her father's name was Antosha Dover and he was in his early sixties. At one time he'd been strong, strong enough to hold back his leopard after he'd been shot multiple times. No one knew he was still fighting, keeping the cat at bay while his brain was slowly shutting down due to the bullet that couldn't be removed. He was still fighting, for his daughter's sake, but the leopard was gaining strength as he lost it.

"Antosha," Mitya said. "I'm your daughter's mate. Look at me. See me. Hold your cat back or I will have no choice but to fight him. My leopard is vicious and very experienced."

The cat's yellow eyes swung around the room, clearly looking for Ania. Mitya had wondered about the deep scratches in her arms. Defense wounds. She had helped her father battle back the cat on more than one occasion. Mitya wanted to shake her. This was dangerous. She needed help and yet to keep her father safe, she had taken on the duty of guarding him from the rest of the world and guarding the world from his leopard. He admired her for doing it, but knew it was far too dangerous for her on her own. Sooner or later the cat would break free and she would be facing a crazed, pain-driven animal looking to kill everyone in its sight.

"Look only at me, Antosha. Your daughter needs to be kept safe at all times. You don't want to be the one to kill her. Have you seen her arms? Your leopard attacked her."

"Stop," Ania hissed. "He feels bad enough. He can't help what is happening."

Mitya heard the unshed tears in her voice, and he wanted to gather her close and hold her to him. How long had she been alone in this fight? He knew from experience that when a man was dying from a brain injury, especially if that injury had occurred violently, the cat was injured as well, and became even more deadly. Her father would have killed her eventually.

"*Kotyonok*, stay quiet and let me handle this." He kept his voice low, but there was no way to keep the command from his voice. He'd been giving orders since he was a child. He was the son of the most vicious *vor* in their homeland. Every other lair knew of Lazar and his son, Mitya. He wanted to be gentle with her, but this wasn't the time.

He shrugged out of his jacket and handed it back to Sevastyan. At the same time, he slid the shiny loafers from his feet. He was always ready for his leopard to emerge. He could shift in seconds, his cat already fighting as the animal emerged. He was a vicious fighter, and he would annihilate a cat that had no experience, as Antosha's leopard clearly wouldn't have.

"Please don't," Ania said. "Let me try."

He didn't want to kill her father. If he did, she would never forgive him. He knew that. He also knew it was going to be necessary. Maybe not this time, but soon.

"Antosha. I know you're there somewhere. Fight him. Don't let your life end with your leopard trying to kill your daughter. You know you don't want that as your legacy to her."

He heard a small sob escape her and then her hand swept down his back. Barely there. Barely felt. But she conveyed so much with that touch. She knew he was trying to save her life. She knew he didn't want to kill her father. She also knew it was going to happen.

"Dad, please." She choked on the plea. "You can do this. You're strong."

"Antosha, do I need to have my cousin take your daughter from this room, or do we talk, man to man? I had hoped to ask for your daughter's hand in marriage. I wanted you to give me advice on how best to give her a home. I want to hear the things you have to say to the man who will spend a lifetime with your little girl."

Mitya tried to appeal to the man fighting his leopard. Say the things that might call to a father. He had used his name repeatedly, knowing Antosha had fought hard to keep his leopard from killing his daughter. Clearly Ania was loved by this man. Mitya knew what it was like fighting back a crazed leopard and he didn't have a bullet in his head that was slowly killing him.

For a moment the cat stared at him. Mitya allowed his cat to stare back. Then the man was there. For the first time, Mitya looked into Antosha's eyes. Ania had those nearly purple eyes. The color was indigo, so dark blue the shade slipped into a dark, gorgeous purple. He looked ravaged by his ordeal, but Mitya could still see traces of what he would have looked like, a handsome man with feminine eyes. Gorgeous eyes.

Ania must have been able to see her father because her hand slid up Mitya's back, beneath his shirt, skin to skin, and he felt her tremble.

"You're a strong man, Antosha. A man to be admired. You have an equally strong daughter. You must be proud of her. Of her accomplishments. Speak with me. Tell me the things you would say to your daughter's man. I need to hear these things."

Antosha renewed his efforts to fight off his leopard. The cat held out, but only for a short time. It was used to following the will of the man. The cat subsided, and the contortions receded. Antosha fell back against his pillows and threw one arm over his eyes, his body shaking. Exhausted.

Mitya stepped back to allow Ania the freedom to get to her father. She flung herself on the bed with him, her arm going around him, her face buried in his chest. Antosha wrapped his arm around her and looked up at Mitya and Sevastyan. There was despair written in every line of his face. Suffering. Determination.

"She can't keep coming in here. I can't hold him back forever." The voice was thin, barely heard. Each word was slurred. The sentences were slow, as if Antosha had to reach for each word, find it and then form it carefully to say it.

Mitya wanted to close his eyes, to turn away from the

plea in Ania's father's eyes. The man wanted him to kill them both, man and cat. The desperation was there. The need. He knew, as did Mitya, that it was only a matter of time before the leopard won. When that happened, the cat would kill anyone it came across—including his daughter and his caretaker.

"How long has this fight been going on?"

"Too long. Can't hold out."

"You can." Ania lifted her head and looked her father in the eye. "You can hold out. You will. If you die, I'll be alone, Dad. I won't have anyone."

Antosha's gaze met Mitya's. "Mate?"

"Her leopard has accepted my leopard's claim. She soothes him. Just being close to her, she brings both of us peace," Mitya assured. "Your daughter will be treasured. I will take care of her."

"Word of honor."

Ania sat up and looked from her father to Mitya as if sensing more was going on in the conversation than just the words.

"You have my word of honor," Mitya agreed.

"Protect her. From me."

Ania shook her head. "Dad. Don't do this."

"Protect her from me."

The words were so slurred and so slow and drawn out that they barely sounded as if they were an actual language. The man was exhausted, and Mitya felt for him.

"I will," Mitya agreed.

"Leopard take mine?"

"No. No, I won't have this. Get out." Ania came off the bed right in front of Mitya and shoved at his chest.

She was strong, but she didn't so much as rock him. Mitya wrapped his arm around her and pulled her into him. She resisted, pushing against him, struggling for a moment. Mitya held her to him, refusing to allow her to escape. It took several minutes before she slumped against him and then began to weep. He wished she would just cry loudly, but she didn't make a sound. He knew she wept because he felt the wet tears on his shirt, and from the way her body shook, but she was absolutely silent.

Mitya rubbed her back and stroked caresses down her hair. He looked at her father over Ania's head. He nodded his answer to the man. His leopard could definitely take Antosha's in a fight. When it came down to it, Dymka would be able to kill Antosha's leopard as humanely as possible.

Antosha regarded the couple for a moment and then mouthed "thank you" before he closed his eyes and was instantly asleep.

"I think it is safe for his nurse to return," Mitya said.

"Annalise was my nanny," Ania corrected, lifting her head from his chest. "Dad's been slowly going downhill. The doctors all said he would. We consulted with the best. It was impossible to remove the bullet without killing him, but over time, the bullet would most likely begin traveling on its own."

"You had three years with him, Ania," Mitya reminded her as gently as possible. "If the bullet had killed him outright, you would have been alone that entire time. How long has this been going on?" He took her arm, pushed up the sleeves and examined the long scratches.

She squirmed, trying to pull her arm away, embarrassed on her father's behalf. "His leopard broke free a few times and I had to contend with it. Not all the way— Dad managed to fight it back—but enough that his claws raked me a few times. I'm lucky that Annalise is so loyal, but I'm afraid to leave her alone in the house with him now."

"You're avoiding the question, *kotyonok*. How long has this been going on?"

She moistened her lips, avoiding his gaze. "The last three months he's been steadily going downhill."

Mitya shook his head, took her hand and strode from the room. He could feel her reluctance with every step they took back to the main part of the house. He went straight through the formal dining room to avoid the kitchen and continued into the great room. He let her go when they neared the fireplace.

"Sevastyan, have Vikenti and Zinoviy pack up the dinner and remove everything from the house. If there is anything we need to know immediately, have them pass the information to you to determine whether or not I need to be interrupted."

Sevastyan knew what he was saying. He wanted all the men to make themselves as scarce as possible while still doing their jobs. The moment they were outside, Vikenti and Zinoviy would use their leopards and the cover of darkness to find out as many things as possible about the Dover family and their estate.

Sevastyan nodded, shot one look at Ania, started to say something and then closed his mouth and moved away.

Mitya went to the bar. "Do you want a drink?"

Ania shook her head and then took a deep breath. "There's water in the small fridge, maybe a bottle of that."

Mitya located one and brought it to her. She sank down onto the thick rug that lay right in front of the long fireplace. The fireplace was very modern, with a long glass window and an abundance of flames leaping and flickering inside.

"I'm sorry about your father, Ania. He's a good man, and very strong to endure the suffering he has."

"He won't use any painkillers because he says the leopard could defeat him."

He kept her gaze captive in his. "Ania. Baby. You know his leopard will eventually defeat him. He's dying. He's in terrible pain."

She leapt up and paced away from him. "Don't you think I know that?"

He watched her, her female close due to her extreme agitation. She was graceful, pacing back and forth like a restless, caged leopard. He didn't reply, because of course he knew. She had to come to terms with her father's dying on her own. She was resisting because she really believed she would be alone. She'd been handling her father's business as well as taking care of him by herself for a long time.

She stopped pacing beside a long leather couch, the color a soft rust. Her fingers dug into the top, gripping it hard. "I don't know what to do."

"You have to let him go, Ania," he said quietly. "You aren't alone anymore, even if you feel you are. You have me to lean on."

She shook her head, rejecting his decree. "I have things I have to do, and I can't do them with you around."

His gut knotted at her disclosure. He'd been afraid all along she was preparing to go to war with a crime lord, one she was certain had set her father up and had killed her grandparents and mother.

"Tell me what those things are."

She got a stubborn look on her face. "I have to do them, not you."

"Ania, you are in my care whether you like it or not. Your father knows me. He knows the kind of man I am—"

"You aren't killing him."

He continued as if she hadn't interrupted him. "He gave his consent and approval to our union. My leopard has claimed yours. We live by shifter law. Look at me, *kotyonok*. Really see me. I am not a man you ever want to fuck with. When I give an order, it is followed. You are my woman, and you will not go behind my back and do anything without my knowledge and my agreement."

She lifted her chin at him, her eyes flashing fire. It wasn't her leopard facing him with fury; her anger was all woman. "You will *not* be dictating to me, nor will you take over my life. I'm not one of your men to be ordered around."

"No, you're not. You're my woman. That means, to me, at least, you will answer to me when I ask something of you. I am asking what these tasks you have to complete are, and you clearly don't want me to know."

"I want you to leave. We're not a couple, and I can assure you, we're not going to be."

"Ania, you're striking out at me because you know your father is dying and it scares you to death. I'm telling you, I'm the man who will stand in front of you every time. You don't have to like me for it, but I'm going to do it. No one else is going to see a man as great as your father lose the battle he has fought so hard to win."

She had opened her mouth to protest but at his declaration, she pressed her lips together and shook her head, tears shining in her eyes again, even dripping on her long, feathery lashes, but she didn't shed them.

"I don't want him to die, Mitya."

"Of course you don't. He's a good man. You have good memories of him. Keep those close. But you will break his heart if you continue to go into that room without aid. He knows his leopard will kill you. One day, you won't win, Ania. His leopard will kill you. Then it will get out and kill Annalise. If it gets out of the house, it could wreak havoc on the neighborhood. It might kill children. Do you want that to be his legacy?"

She pressed her hands to her ears. "Stop talking, I don't want you to say another word."

"You have to hear this."

"I won't let you murder him. That's what it would be, *murder.*" She hurled the accusation at him. "He won't be able to defend himself."

"It wouldn't be murder. It would be self-defense. Or, you could say, a humane end to his brilliant life. What is your plan? You must have one. Once his leopard slips out, what were you planning to do?"

She pressed her fingertips to her face. "I don't know. I just know I'm not going to hurt my own father."

He went still, muscles locked in place. "Tell me you took a gun into that room with you. You are armed, right?"

When her gaze left his and color swept up her neck to her face, he moved. One leap and he was beside her. He caught her arms and gave her a little shake. "Are you out of your fucking mind? You know he's going to lose that battle with his leopard. You know it will kill him to know that he's hurt or killed you, and yet you still went in there without a weapon? Do you have a fucking death wish?"

His fingers bit deep and he shook her again. Abruptly he let her go and began pacing to lose some of the adrenaline rising so fast.

"I'm not going to kill him." She kept her voice pitched low, absolute conviction stamped into her delicate features.

He swung around. "I forbid you to enter that room again. If necessary, I will have Sevastyan lock you in our safe room until this is over. You are not risking your life unnecessarily. Nor will I allow you to throw it away."

She stared at him, shock on her face. "You can't do that."

"I can do it, Ania, and I will. You aren't sacrificing your life because an asshole shot your father and set these last few years in motion. I'll be moving into this house until it's over."

"I'm calling the police and having you arrested."

"You do that. And keep doing it. Each time they come to get me, more men will enter this house and keep you from going into that room. Eventually, Sevastyan will get to you, and he'll do exactly what I say and lock you up. I'm not fucking around with this, Ania. Your life is in danger, and so is that man's soul. He's terrified. Not of dying but of harming you. Can't you see that?"

Ania didn't want to see it, but she did. She wanted to be angry and shout and scream and protest to the heavens, but what would be the point? Mitya was a good target, one she could shoot as many arrows into as possible, but she knew that wasn't fair either. She was being a first-class bitch and bringing out the absolute worst in Mitya—at least she hoped that was his worst.

She swept a hand through her hair and regarded him for a long time while she attempted to get her ragged, labored breathing under control. "I'm sorry, Mitya. I shouldn't be yelling at you. I know you're just trying to help. The thought of him dying is terrifying to me. I keep thinking if I can keep him alive long enough, the doctors will find a way to remove the bullet and he'll be back to normal. I just want him alive."

Mitya regarded her with cold, almost arctic blue eyes. So cold she shivered. "He's suffering, Ania. You have to let him go."

She closed her eyes against the truth. One hand went defensively over her throat, the other over her heart as if it ached so badly, she couldn't take the pain. "I don't know if I can," she whispered. She looked up at him and there was pleading in her eyes. "I don't think I'm that strong."

He curved his palm around the nape of her neck. "You don't have to be that strong, Ania. I am. That's why you have me. I promised him I'd take care of you. That I'd keep you safe. You heard him. You know what he wants. Dymka, my leopard, will make certain his leopard doesn't suffer."

She shook her head. "I don't think I'd ever forgive you."

"I can't pass this duty on to one of my men. First, I respect your father too much for that. I gave him my word, and I'm your man. Not one of them. I trust Sevastyan's leopard, but no other, to make his leopard's death quick and painless. I don't want Sevastyan, who has no anchor, no woman to tame his leopard, to have to control him to that point. This is a debt of honor, Ania. I have no choice. None. I must do this for you, to keep you safe, whether you want it or not. I must do it for your father, to preserve his honor. That means so much to him."

He would not plead with her. He would state facts, but he wouldn't seek forgiveness. If she didn't understand now, he was certain she would eventually. Now, she was emotional and afraid. He didn't blame her. Her father seemed to be a wonderful man. Mitya didn't have that. He knew nothing about the emotional ties between a father and daughter. The fathers he'd known hadn't been good men.

Ania took a deep breath and moved away from him, going to the floor in front of the fireplace again. Just dropping down as if her legs wouldn't hold her another moment.

Mitya followed, bringing the bottle of water for her. He took the chair just behind her so she could rest her back against his legs and put her head in his lap if she wanted to do so. Right now, she remained stiff and upright, holding herself away from him, staring into the flames.

"Tell me about him, *kotyonok*. Clearly, he is a man of integrity. It is obvious he loves you. What did he do for the many crime lords he worked for?"

She was silent for so long he didn't think she would answer him. He moved carefully. His body was still aching and painful from the bullet wounds. One especially still bothered him, and he often eased his position in order to try to remove the chronic pain. He was patient. He knew silence and sorrow often went hand in hand.

"My father was always laughing. Always. He could turn the worst situation into something happy, as if every occasion had some kind of sunshine in it. My mother loved his sense of humor. Every morning they smiled at each other over the breakfast table. We always ate together. They laughed a lot. They were always touching and kissing. I grew up that way, in a house filled with laughter and love." She turned slightly to look at him. "The exact opposite of you."

That was true. She hadn't made it an accusation, but Mitya felt as if she was accusing him, saying without words that he was a killer and always would be. It was true. Even if she had made the allegation aloud, he wouldn't have been able to deny it. He *was* a killer and he always would be. Drake Donovan had given him a purpose, a way to try for redemption, but deep down, he knew he was what he'd been twisted into.

He nodded. "That is true, Ania. The exact opposite." That would be why he could keep her alive. No one, especially her father, was going to harm her.

"He acted as if he likes you. Even respects you."

He couldn't get that from the slow, slurred words, but Ania knew him better than anyone else and her voice rang with truth, so he chose to believe her. That assessment humbled him. Her father was a good man, and to have his respect meant something.

"I knew the moment his leopard saw yours, Dad would ask you to help him. I knew he would." She glanced over her shoulder at him, rubbed her temples and then looked back at the fire.

He caught the despair written into her face. He wanted to comfort her, but he couldn't do that until she came to terms with what he had to do. Shifters couldn't be autopsied. They had to be cremated and only another leopard could handle it. That was their sacred law and all of them, good or bad, abided by it. She was well versed in the lore of the leopards. Her family had allowed her to see their leopards. She knew about a leopard's heat. Her estate was made for leopards. He knew because he'd spent time exploring his property as well as his neighbors', although he hadn't yet known them, or anything about them. The reports were still lying on his desk, just skimmed until he'd met her.

"I know he's suffering, and he needs to be able to let go. I just haven't been able to let him. He's always been so strong. The rock in our family. Without him . . ." She trailed off and removed the cap to the water bottle he'd already loosened. "They stepped out of the alley and shot him so many times. One stood over him and put the bullet in his head."

He heard the sob mixed with her rage. "They were cowards. They knew they couldn't take him any other way. Were they leopard? Do you know those that were there?" If she did, she was the only one. There was no whisper of a hit on Antosha Dover. Not a single rumor.

"My father took jobs for various clients. We take care of their cars, keeping them in top shape. We go to them. We maintain their garages and their car collections. We provide drivers if asked to do so. Anything to do with their cars, we manage. Our family has an affinity for cars, so we often have to turn away new clients." She fell silent again, staring into the flames.

Mitya reached out to stroke a caress down her dark, thick hair. She didn't pull away, so he began a slow massage on her scalp. She leaned into it with a little sigh, so he waited until she leaned back completely, her body between his legs so he could reach her easily.

"Dad was like my grandfather. Very fast reflexes and good eyes. His leopard probably helped, but very few could outdrive him. He cut his teeth on street racing."

Mitya closed his eyes. Sevastyan had wanted to hire a street racer to drive him. There was a young driver no one wanted to race against because no one could beat him. He went by the name of Andi. Pieces clicked into place. Ania was Andi. She was honing her skills against some of the best drivers in the business.

"If one of our clients needed something moved from one city or state to another, and it had to get there fast and safe, they called my grandfather or father. They never failed in a single delivery."

"Did they know what they were transporting?"

"They always knew. They just didn't care. They said it wasn't their business. It was our policy. Dad had contracts with our customers, and if they needed something special done and it was within his power to do it, he would oblige them. After he was shot, there were still a few jobs left undone, and I took them for him." She looked over her shoulder at him. "I'm a very good driver. It's in the genes."

"I imagine you are." He kept his tone neutral. She wouldn't be taking any more special jobs for any of her clients, not once he put the word out that she belonged to him and anyone asking for anything needed to come through him first.

Anià took a sip of water. "I hate being so emotional. My eyes burn and I'm not a pretty crier." She dabbed at her eyes with the water bottle. "I think either he or my grandfather took a job with one of our clients and they didn't want them to see what was being taken."

There was hesitation in her voice. She was skirting the truth. "Ania, I am your mate. I can hear lies. Between us, no matter how painful, there must be truth at all times. Did one of them keep something they shouldn't have? Not complete the drive? Take part of shipment?"

There was silence, but she didn't lift her head away from him. He settled his fingers on her scalp and continued the massage.

"I think but don't know that for whatever reason, whichever one was driving kept the package. I asked my father repeatedly, but he said he had no idea why a hit might be taken out on him or our family. I listened closely, but I didn't hear a lie in his voice. That isn't to say he wouldn't try to deceive me if he thought he was protecting me."

"Who did he work for the last time he drove?"

"Both my grandfather and father went out at the same time. My father drove for the Caruso family. My grandfather drove for the Anwar family. Both are out of Houston.

Both packages originated in New Orleans. They were driving whatever it was to Houston."

"Did you speak to either family after your family was hit?"

"They reached out to me, just as some of our other clients did. Both seemed sincere. I suspected them, but I couldn't catch them in any lies. At the service for my grandparents and mother, my father talked to them. I stood beside him, listening for anything that might indicate they had ordered a hit, but I didn't catch anything wrong. Later, we discussed it. My father claimed he hadn't heard a lie either. Of course, we didn't ask outright if they'd ordered one against our family."

"Have you ever felt threatened, or has anyone tried to kill you?" He couldn't help it. At his questions, which had to be asked, he felt the familiar stillness settle in him—that place he'd been in so many times when he'd been interrogating prisoners for his father. He was more familiar with the ice and the distance than he was the man who continued to try to ease the tension out of his woman by massaging her scalp, neck and shoulders.

Ania hesitated. His hand stilled. He waited. He already knew the answer.

"Yes. Once before my father. I was driving back from the Caruso estate in Houston, where I'd taken care of two of his cars. I was getting close to home and someone tried to run me off the road. It was an ambush. They had a second car waiting, just as they had with my grandparents. I spun my car around at the last second and squeaked between the first vehicle chasing me and the mountainside. I got away."

Mitya closed his eyes. So close. She'd almost died. "The second time?"

"Someone took a shot at me when I was driving home, just about two miles before the entrance to my road. By shot, I mean about seven bullets. Again, my driving skills saved me. That was the day after my father was shot. I was coming home from the hospital to get a change of clothes and a shower."

Mitya swore in his native language. "You should have told me of this, Ania."

"I don't know you, Mitya. You're in that world. I'm not. My father and grandfather may have been, but if so, I knew nothing about it. I'm just trying to maneuver my way and keep my father safe. We've had three attempted break-ins. I'm positive whoever wanted my father dead wanted to finish the job. The alarms were set off and the police called. They ran. Even with an enhanced sense of smell, I didn't know them."

She got to her feet and moved across the room from him, not looking at him.

He studied her averted face for a long time. "Ania. I'm your mate. I'm telling you that you cannot hold things back from me." He poured command into his voice. It was velvet soft, as was his wont. He rarely raised his voice. Right now, it was of the utmost importance that she understood him.

Ania raised her head slowly, her lashes lifting so that he was staring at those indigo eyes, eyes that had gone from the darkest blue to almost royal purple. "I suppose that you cannot hold things back from me when I ask you questions about your work." Sarcasm dripped from her voice.

"My work can get you killed."

She lifted her chin. "Perhaps I need to hold information back for the same reason. I told you, I'm not in a position to have a relationship with you. Especially since you're so bossy. I've never had anyone telling me what I can or can't do. My father wasn't like that."

"Perhaps, had I been around before your father was shot, it would never have happened. I take my job seri-ously. My number one job is to protect you. There is no doubt in my mind that you have come across their scents again. Not that night, but at some other time."

She remained silent. Glaring. Her lashes sweeping down and then back up. She had no intention of telling him anything.

Mitya shrugged his shoulders. "Locking you up seems to be the only avenue you are leaving to me, Ania. I don't want to start our relationship that way, but I will do anything necessary to keep you safe." He glanced at Sevastyan, who had slipped back into the room. "I believe my woman has some knowledge of who killed her family, but she refuses to say anything."

Sevastyan studied Ania's defiant face. "Vikenti found evidence of a sniper practicing on the property a great distance from here. He said without a doubt it was Ania."

Mitya looked from his woman back to his cousin. "You entertained the idea that she was out to kill me."

"It is possible."

"Why would I want to kill you?" Ania snapped, exasperated with them.

"My father wants all of us dead, I told you that," Mitya reminded.

"But it has nothing to do with me. I didn't even know you until my tire blew on the way home from that horrible date . . ." Her voice trailed off as she saw the look on Mitya's face and knew he realized what had happened that night.

"You were set up," Mitya said. "They're back to trying to kill you, and you know it."

"I don't *know*," she corrected. "I suspect. And no, Sevastyan, I don't want to hurt Mitya or you or anyone else you care about. I'm trying to get Mitya to back off and let me take care of my own problems."

Sevastyan shook his head. "I'm not certain women are worth all the trouble they put you through, Mitya. She's out to get someone, that's for certain."

"Who is it, Ania?" Mitya demanded. "Before you answer me, know that I'm moving into this house to aid your father. I'm also sending you back to mine with Sevastyan to lock you up and keep you alive until I have talked sense into you."

She paled visibly. "Mitya . . ."

"These things are nonnegotiable. If you don't cooperate, you give me no choice." He folded his arms across his chest and kept his eyes on her, willing her to comply. To come to the right decision.

"Is he always like this?" she demanded of Sevastyan.

"He gets worse." Sevastyan told the strict truth.

"Do you know how utterly unfair you're being right now?" She began to pace again. "I can't know your business, but you can know mine. You can make decisions that have nothing to do with you—"

He held up his hand, narrowing his eyes at her. "Let's be very clear on this, Ania. You're my business. From the moment I laid eyes on you, you became my business. You are claimed. No leopard would dare go against that claim. Our world is kill or be killed. You can tell yourself a million times that you aren't going to have a relationship with me, but we both know it's total bullshit. You are mine, and I will use any means at my disposal to keep you safe. Everything you do is my business."

She took a deep breath. "I ran across one of the men that was here that night. He was in the Bannaconni building. I had just come down in the elevator and he was standing beside it as if waiting for it. He was dressed in the same suits as the men Bannaconni has working for him. They're scattered around everywhere, looking like bodyguards. They're armed and without a doubt, they're leopard. This man was leopard. I didn't react, I just kept walking. I went to the parking garage as I always do, but this time, I got into a discussion with the parking attendant. The man came out and I watched to see what car he went to. He pretended to get something out of it and walked away.

"I attached a tracker to it as I walked by. My heel is a wonderful addition when I need to adjust my shoes. Men always buy it."

"Then you followed the tracker."

She nodded. "He went to Houston. But he also drove to Louisiana on the weekend, New Orleans to be precise. I have every place he stopped logged in my room."

"Do you know his name?"

She shook her head slowly. "I don't want to kill him until I'm certain of the others. And I'm not yet. I'm just confused."

Sevastyan gave his cousin a faint smile. "See what I mean, Mitya? More trouble than they're worth."

5

ANIA lay on her bed staring up at the ceiling. Night poured in through the window, and along with the darkness came the rain. She loved the way the drops sounded hitting the roof and windowpanes. She had a series of great arching windows that ran the length of her bedroom. She loved them, loved the way she always felt so free, bringing the beauty of the landscape right into her room. Or the storms. Or stars. It didn't matter; she had them all and never covered the windows so she wouldn't miss a thing.

She had the entire second floor to herself. Her parents had never invaded her space unless she'd invited them, which was often to show them some new thing she'd changed. She often painted or added little treasures she found in the way of furniture. She liked to find old solid pieces and restore them. Her covered balcony ran the entire length of the second floor on the side facing the rolling hills with all the trees and bushes. She would put the piece of furniture she was working on there in order to keep the smells of paint and thinner out of her rooms.

Her bed frame was one of the restored pieces. It was solid wood and very heavy. Four thick posters rose at the corners, and across the headboard were framed spindles, each two inches thick. Along the bottom of the bed was a series of drawers, just under the mattress springs. The drawers were heavy and intricately carved. Her grandfather had found the bed for her, and they'd had such an adventure together that day, she'd never forget it.

"You're crying." Mitya's voice came out of the darkness, just a distance away.

She closed her eyes tightly. She was. The tears kept running down her face in spite of the fact that she didn't want to be emotional. The entire evening had been emotional. "You're not supposed to know." She'd been very quiet, hadn't made a single sound, yet he'd known.

"I'll always know when you're distressed, *kotyonok*. I would comfort you, but right now I am the last person you want near you."

Was that the truth? She didn't think so. She didn't have anyone else. She'd understood what Mitya had been trying to convey to her long before he'd laid down the law. She could pretend she was angry with him only so long, but the truth was, he was right. And he was doing something she couldn't do. Her father was suffering. Sooner or later he would lose the struggle to contain his leopard and the cat would emerge, half-crazed, with no direction. Was she going to shoot it, knowing she would kill her father?

She flung her arm over her eyes. "None of this is your fault, Mitya. You were standing in front of me, telling me the truth, giving me no other choice but to face reality. That made you a convenient target. I'm sorry I got so angry with you. I don't even know what I said to you."

Her head hurt beyond imagining. She rolled over, facing toward the windows, watching the drops of rain run down the glass like tears. She was losing everything that mattered to her. Her life was gone. Her house had once been filled with laughter and love. Now there was only sorrow and fear. She couldn't blame Mitya for that, although he had broad shoulders and he was willing to take the responsibility if that made her feel better.

The bed moved slightly as weight settled beside her. Mitya. She knew he was close without looking. She would know his scent anywhere. She found just the smell of him comforting. He seemed invincible. Larger than life. She'd been taking care of everything—the business, her father, the household and tracking his killers—for so long, she almost didn't know how to just lay it all down and let him take over. She wanted him to, and yet she didn't. She was afraid of the consequences of allowing him to take over. He would do what he believed was right. Sadly, when it came to the decision about her father, he was right. She just didn't like the end results, no matter how necessary they were.

His hands settled on her shoulders, his fingers beginning a massage to ease the tension out of her. "Nothing you said was unwarranted, Ania. I am well aware you said things out of fear of losing your father."

"I feel lost. It's like I woke up one morning and instead of my familiar home, I'm in a labyrinth I can't find my way out of and nothing makes sense."

"You're not alone anymore. Between us, we'll sort everything out. I know Bannaconni, and I have friends in New Orleans. We'll find the truth."

She liked that he included her. He was a man to take over. He could be both ruthless and merciless, two traits she would need to rely on to get her through her father's passing and finding his killers, but those were the very things she was most afraid of in him. What would it be like belonging to a man who wouldn't listen to her when she needed him to?

"You scare me, Mitya." She decided the truth was best.

"I'm aware of that, but there is no need to be afraid. I would never hurt you."

Not physically, but she already felt bruised and battered, worn down by coming up against him. She was going to rely on his strength, but it was that strength that scared her the most when it came to living with him.

His hands were gentle, and that surprised her. He was incredibly strong, a big man, and yet when he touched her like this, he turned her inside out.

"I don't think I thanked you for dinner. It was really delicious."

"I didn't cook it."

There was a moment of silence. Her lashes fluttered, and she turned her head slightly to look at him there in the darkness. Amusement crept through her, a slow sensation that pitched her stomach into a curling roller coaster. After the terrible evening, she didn't think anything could make her want to smile again.

"Do you cook at all?"

"No. Never learned," Mitya admitted. "You?"

"No. Sadly. I'd like to say I'm great in the kitchen the way my grandmother and mother were, but I got more of my father's genes than my mother's. I like fast cars."

"You have your father's eyes. The color is unique. Very beautiful. Even on your father the color, shape and lashes are very feminine."

She did smile. She couldn't help it. "Mom teased him all the time about his 'girly' lashes. She said she was so jealous, but she had beautiful eyes as well."

"Does Annalise cook?"

"No. What about Sevastyan?"

"He might burn down a house if he tried. I don't think he's ever in the kitchen unless someone is baking. He has a fondness for sweets. It's always his idea to go to Evangeline's bakery. Well," he hedged. "Not recently. When I told you I was there often, I wanted to go every day after that."

"But you didn't." She closed her eyes and let his hands soothe her. "You stayed away. I think that means you have more discipline than I do. I almost stopped going there after I met Ashe and Evangeline. I really like both of them, and I was a little afraid whoever wanted me dead might follow me into the shop and try to shoot me there."

His hands stilled and then he pushed her thick hair to one side. She felt the touch of his mouth on the nape of her neck. Her sex clenched. Her pulse jumped. Blood pounded through her clit. Even her breasts ached. All from that one touch. His mouth on her bare skin.

"I don't like the idea of anyone shooting you, Ania."

His mouth wandered lower, following her spine. His lips whispered over her, barely there, but she felt that touch through skin and bone straight to her heart. She didn't want to love him. She didn't want her heart involved at all. She was leopard. She knew what his leopard claiming hers meant. Still, he would rule her if she loved him.

She knew herself. She wanted a family like her own. She wanted to have a relationship like her parents', all-encompassing. They would have been happy regardless of where they were or if they had money, even if there were no children. Their lives had been rich and fulfilled, extremely happy because they had each other. She would want to give that to Mitya, especially because he'd never had it.

"I don't particularly like it either, Mitya," she admitted, trying not to move under his ministrations.

His hands moved on her, stroking caresses over her bare skin. Where was her racerback tee? She'd deliberately worn her least sexy pajamas. She was one of those women who loved lingerie. She liked to sleep in silk or stretchy soft fabric that was sexy as hell. She didn't have much in the way of plain.

The tee was around her neck, pushed completely out of the way, and his hands stroked along her sides so that her breasts felt inflamed with his touch. He caught her around the waist and simply rolled her over, into him. Before she could protest, his mouth was on hers. Fire reigned. Hot flames that consumed her poured down her throat and invaded her insides. Flames rolled through her stomach and settled in her groin. Deep. Hot. Pooling there like a bubbling lake of pure magma. Heat rushed through her veins, fiery arteries branching in every direction to carry need through her to every cell.

His kisses were pure fire. His taste pure addiction. Each time he lifted his mouth just an inch from hers, she chased after him, needing more. He took her somewhere else. Somewhere perfect, a blazing paradise she wanted to spend her life in. He drove every thought from her head, leaving her with nothing but feeling. Nothing but cleansing fire.

His hands went to her breasts, stroking more heat. His thumbs brushed her nipples, and she cried out as the heat burst through her. There seemed to be a straight line from her nipples to her clit, and arrows of fire pierced low and wicked. He trailed kisses over her chin and throat to the curve of her breasts.

His mouth was hot, a cavern of blazing heat as he suckled strongly, his tongue flicking and flattening her left nipple alternately. All the while he tugged and rolled her right one so that her hips were bucking, and the thin pair of pajama bottoms felt like a terrible weight on her skin.

She didn't have a single thought to make him stop. Not one. She could only think of him. His hands, his mouth. His teeth. She hadn't known the scrape of teeth against her skin could feel so good. His hands slid down her rib cage and over her hips. Lower, taking the material with them, so the cool air fanned her heated skin.

He spent time on her breasts, sucking, using his tongue

and teeth, drawing her deep into his mouth and then stroking with his broad tongue. He was by turns gentle, almost tender, and then rough as hell, bordering on pain—but an exquisite pain, one that just balanced her right on an edge she had never been on and wanted more of.

His mouth traveled lower, his tongue tracing her ribs and then swirling around her belly button. She was sensitive there, and he took full advantage, tugging on her nipple and then kissing and tasting her skin around her belly button. His hand slid lower still, over her dark curls where she was already damp, showing her need of him.

He moved then, pulling her thighs apart to accommodate his body. He was a big man and needed a lot of room. For the first time she felt vulnerable, especially when she hesitated and his hands simply wrapped around her thighs and forced her legs wider.

"Mitya." His name came out a gasping plea instead of the *no* she thought she might say to him.

He looked up at her, his body stretched out between her legs. His hands were already stroking her inner thighs, fingers dancing so close to her heat she could barely keep from pushing down to try to fill herself with him.

His eyes glittered, and she knew the man was as fierce as his cat. Nothing would keep him from her. Nothing. That knowledge was both thrilling and frightening. Then his mouth was between her legs and she cried out, fire shooting through her, dozens of arrows hitting everywhere while electricity seemed to snap and leap off her skin in tiny sparks of red.

He knew exactly what he was doing, driving her up fast, holding her right at the threshold, keeping her there for long, excruciating minutes when she thought she might die if he didn't follow through while tension gathered and coiled. She felt the wave building like a wildfire out of control. She even heard the roaring in her ears.

His mouth needed to be insured. She had no idea

anything could feel that way, or make her burn the way he did. Her head thrashed on the pillow. Her fingers curled in his hair. Holding him to her. Pushing him away. Using him as an anchor. All three. She was out of control and it didn't matter. All that mattered was the feeling building. Growing in her. Rolling like dark clouds. Spinning like a ferocious tornado.

He knelt between her legs and freed his cock. He was fully clothed, the material rubbing along the insides of her legs, adding to the fierce sensations fueling her desperation. His cock was large and for a moment her heart slammed hard in her chest, but she was slick with need and frantic for him to give her everything. She needed him.

The broad head lodged in her entrance, feeling both velvet soft and firm, flaring so wide she wasn't certain she could take him. He pressed into her, guiding his thick cock deeper. The burn was back, this time spreading through her, impossible to tell if it was ecstasy or agony. Her breath caught in her lungs. Her gaze found his face. His eyes were almost feral, the blue so dark and wild she gasped, finally getting air, but now she couldn't look away.

He would own her. It was there, stamped into every line of his face. He would rule her with this, sex beyond her wildest dreams. No one else would ever satisfy her. She would be forever obsessed with him. Worse, she would crave him night and day. She knew she would give him whatever he wanted when he wanted it, because she would always need this.

There was one fleeting thought to try to stop him, but the craving was already too strong. She wanted more of that long, thick shaft. She wanted him buried in her. Moving in her. She couldn't stop the way her body reacted with more liquid heat surrounding him. Her tight muscles reluctantly opened for him, pulling him deeper, grasping at him greedily.

He was raw sex. Rough sex. Dirty sex. His hands moved over the cheeks of her butt possessively. He squeezed and massaged. He lifted her hips to him. Held her perfectly still while he buried himself deep. His eyes went to her breasts as each hard jolt sent them swaying.

"Fucking you is pure paradise." He nearly snarled it. "I'm looking at your mouth and I wish I had another cock to bury down your throat until you're nearly choking on me. Stretch your lips around me until you can't open any wider. The minute I saw you, I knew you'd be like this. Pure fuckin' fire."

His fantasies should have given her pause, but instead, the heat turned up another notch. She wanted those things too. She wanted everything he could give her. His thumb was moving along her cheeks, finding the seam and stroking her liquid between the firm globes. Then he pushed into her, almost to his knuckle, and the sensation was overwhelming. Her body clamped down on his and she was spiraling out into another realm.

She heard her choking cries of pure elation, but he kept moving through her orgasm, unrelenting, stroking deep like a piston. Harder. Faster. Then he was pounding into her, lifting her hips to meet his every demand until she was in a frenzy of need again. His eyes glittered at her. His hands were tight, strong, possessive. He changed angles slightly and the burn was back. Growing. Scorching. Spreading like a wildfire out of control.

Then his cock seemed to double in size, pushing at her tender sheath. Insisting she belong to him. A volcano, so hot it needed to explode. Her body clamped down on his like a vise. He swore between clenched teeth. The hot splash of his seed coated the walls of her channel, triggering the wild flames sweeping through her body in rolling waves of orange and red. She felt every jerk and throb of his cock as he emptied himself into her. Every splash pure fire so that aftershocks rocked her.

Mitya collapsed over top of her, giving her the complete weight of his broad, muscular body. He had the build of a leopard—dense, with roped muscles—and he was heavy. He trapped her beneath him and buried his face between her neck and shoulder. Then his teeth were in her. Pain flashed through her, but strangely, her body reacted with more liquid heat and several aftershocks. The bite felt more erotic than violent. He licked at the small wound, and that felt erotic as well. Everything he did was sexy. Everything he said was sexy. She was so lost she was terrified. Somehow, he had welded them together.

She didn't want him to move, although he was pressing her deep into the mattress and she had to breathe shallowly. He was buried in her and she could feel his heart beating right through his cock. She felt as if she truly belonged to him. For this time, when they both lay quietly together, she felt as if he cared for her. It wasn't about their leopards. They didn't have to be together. It was about them—two people. She wanted, even needed, to feel that, if only for a moment.

He shifted his weight far too soon, sliding out of her, sending delicious little shivers through her body as his cock withdrew. He kissed her breasts and then her throat before going up to her chin and finding her mouth. She tasted herself on his tongue and it added an extra layer of wickedness to the fiery kiss.

"Give me a minute and I'll get a washcloth," he said as he turned over to lie on his back beside her.

She lay very still, her heart beating far too fast. She'd just given herself to him. Wholly. No going back. She had no idea how he actually felt about her, and yet she'd locked herself into a relationship. "Mitya?" She had to ask. "We're exclusive, right? For as long as this lasts, we're exclusive."

He sighed. She closed her eyes against the sound. She should have asked questions before she'd had sex with him, not after.

"We're getting married, Ania. You're going to be my wife. Your female is my male's mate. You want another man, you'd better know that I'll fuckin' kill him with my bare hands. There aren't going to be other men in your life. No one else touches you. They don't kiss you. They don't put their hands on you, or their mouths. They don't fuck you. You're mine. You. Your heart. Your body. Your soul. That's all mine. There's no going back. There's no divorce. You have a problem with something I've done, you come talk to me about it."

She lay for a long time in silence, and then, just as he rolled to get up to get the washcloth, she sighed. He turned his head to look down at her. One hand slid possessively from her belly to her breasts.

"What is it?"

"That's all about what you're going to do if I take another man as a lover, or some such weird thing. At no time did I hear what you intend to do with other women."

"Baby, you've been outside for what? The last three years? Training to be a sniper? You think I'm stupid enough to let another woman touch me when you're that kind of woman? I'm not. I'm also not a man who would ever disrespect my wife, my woman, by cheating on her. I don't want another woman when I have you. You light up for me like no one else ever could. I intend to get every damn thing I've ever wanted or fantasized about from you. I don't like the word *no*, and don't expect to hear it from you in the bedroom. In any case, if I tried to fuck another woman, not only would you be after me, but my leopard would kill her."

She bit her lip, her gaze on his face. "You don't like the word *no*? What does that even mean? I imagine you're going to hear that quite often from me because you think you can rule the world."

"I rule *your* world, *kotyonok*, and that's all that should matter to you." He got up to go into the bathroom. He left the door open and she could hear the water running as he washed himself.

Ania stared after him, not quite sure whether he was teasing her. "You're not ruling my world. I've gone my own way for a very long time. I don't think Evangeline's or Ashe's husbands rule their worlds."

"Maybe not, but I'm not married to either of them. Don't worry, baby, I intend to rock your world as well as rule it." There was a trace of amusement in his voice. "Spread your legs for me."

She felt the blush start and was very glad it was dark. "I can do it, Mitya." She held out her hand for the washcloth.

"Not a good start, woman. You don't want to argue with me over something so ridiculous. Save your energy for battles that truly matter to you. I like cleaning you up. It feels like taking care of you, so spread your fucking legs and let me do it."

"Nice." She cooperated, but only because he was making her laugh and she needed to. Everything had been so intense, from the discussions about her father to the way he'd taken her body.

He was so gentle she had to blink back tears, proving she was far too emotional. He sat on the end of the bed while he slipped the warm washcloth down her thighs. "Ania, I intend to make your life a very happy one. I'm not going to be with another woman. I've spent years without any hope of finding you, and you all but dropped into my lap. You're beautiful. You like my rather rough style of sex. I need certain things from you in the bedroom, and it's clear you're not only willing to give them to me, but you get off on them too. I look at you and can barely breathe sometimes. Stop fighting me on this and try."

"You have all the control."

"Is that so bad? I'm a male leopard. A shifter. We aren't

human, and the rules for our society aren't the same. Put yourself in my hands and see what happens."

"If I don't, you're going to take control, aren't you?"

He nodded. His hand was once more cupping her breast, his thumb sliding gently over her nipple. "That's who I am, Ania. It will always be who I am. Just now you gave up all control to me and look what happened."

Her body was still singing. She'd even had a few aftershocks when he'd used the washcloth on her. She couldn't deny the sex had been amazing. Terrifying, it was so intense, but beyond amazing.

She moistened her lips. Could she? Could she give him control outside the bedroom as well? She wasn't certain she was capable of that. Or if she trusted him that much to put her interests before his own.

"Do I seem like a submissive yes-woman to you?"

"Why would you think I would want you to change? I like who you are. I don't want submission from you. I want your trust, yes, but I intend to prove to you that you can trust me. Because I'm willing to lock you up to keep you safe, does that make you think I want submission? You can fight me all you want. It isn't logical, and I think you know that."

She sat up slowly and scooted to the headboard. Mitya immediately tucked pillows behind her back. She caught the sheet to cover herself, but he tugged it down.

"I love looking at you. I think I could spend years just staring at your body."

That made her smile. "I would hope you'd want to do more than just look."

His eyes took on that feral, intense glitter that sent a shiver down her spine. "I could devour you, *kotyonok*." He leaned down and bit her inner thigh. It wasn't just a nip and yet instantly she was damp again. Her nipples peaked. He smiled at her. "See, Ania. Your body knows me. It loves whatever I do to you."

"That's because you totally short-circuited my brain," she admitted with a smile. That much was true. He had. The way he was looking at her made her want to experience his particular brand of sex all over again.

"Ania, can you at least concede that I'm right about your father? It is a debt of honor I must fulfill. When he can no longer stop his leopard, I have to be the one to handle it."

She bit down hard on her lip and felt the sting immediately, knowing she'd drawn blood. It wasn't fair to Mitya. She'd already accused him of being a murderer if he did what he said and allowed his leopard to kill her father's. But what did she want him to do? He was right.

"I hate that you're right. I hate that I'm not strong enough to do what needs to be done. I've known all along that I would have to find the courage and strength to go into his room with a gun, but I couldn't make myself do it. I kept hoping for a miracle." She took a breath. Let it out. Kept her eyes on his because it had to be said. She owed him that much. "Maybe you're the miracle for both my father and me."

He leaned forward and framed her face with his hands. "Thank you for that, Ania. I would never allow him to suffer."

She nodded, because she was certain that was the truth. "Thank you for having one of your men relieve Annalise. She wants to stay with him. She's been in our family since I was born, but she's terrified of his 'fits.' I'm terrified his leopard will emerge and harm her before she can get out of the room."

"Is she a shifter?"

"Yes, but her leopard never emerged. At least that was what my mother told me. She has no family other than me. I have always planned on taking care of her."

"Perhaps she will want to help us with our babies."

She blinked. "I haven't thought in terms of babies. Not once."

"You don't want children?"

She could tell he did. That it was important to him. For a moment, just because she tended to panic a little at the thought of actually living with him, she considered lying. But what was the use? He would hear the lie.

"Three years earlier, when it became apparent that my grandparents and mother were murdered, and then the try was made for my father, I accepted the fact that I wasn't going to live once I exacted my revenge. I was going to find who was responsible as well as those who carried out the actual attack. My future ended then."

His face darkened. He leaned in and kissed her. This time, his kiss was gentle, and her heart turned over. Her stomach tumbled, a long, slow drop.

"You have a future with me. I want babies. In the plural. As many as you'll let me make with you. Annalise can be a part of our family until the day she passes. She'll have quite a few men to boss around."

She found herself smiling at him. "She'll like that."

"I heard you were planning on selling. Let's keep both properties for now. The leopards will have more room to run."

"It will be more difficult and take more manpower to guard both places," Ania pointed out. She knew because she didn't have a lot of help and she'd been a little paranoid since the attempted break-ins.

"My woman. Thinking like a general."

He looked so pleased she felt her heart melt.

"I told you we would be perfect together. You have a good point, but I still think it will be better for the leopards. I can hire a few more men. Drake Donovan can find us shifters that need work."

She liked that he listened to her. She didn't want to sell the property, but she had thought it better not to have any ties where her enemies could trace her. "All right, then. I won't put the property up for sale."

"What about the family business? Do you want to keep that as well?"

She could have kissed him. "No, I think I'm done with all that. It was a relief to me when I made the decision to sell. I didn't tell my father, mostly because he thought I loved it. I love driving, but I don't love dealing with customers." She flashed a small smile. "I don't have the right personality."

"You don't like being told what to do." He stroked his chin as if he had a beard. "That's too bad. I was just about to give you a few commands."

His hand dropped to his lap and her breath caught in her throat. He was fully erect. Thick. Pulsing. Already leaking precious fluid.

"So soon?"

"I told you, *kotyonok*, I have my fantasies. Just thinking about what we can do together makes me hard as a fuckin' rock."

She licked her lips, her eyes on his cock and the hand loosely circling his shaft. "I suppose I should practice taking orders, just to be a little better at following them. In case of an emergency or something."

He leaned in to her to flick her nipple. Heat burst through her. "I think practicing is a good idea, Ania. I like your carpet. Nice and thick and warm. Slide off the bed and kneel right there." He pointed to a spot between his legs.

Her heart started pounding. Hard. Blood rushed to pool low. Her sex clenched. Nipples peaked. His voice had changed to the one that stroked velvet all over her body. The one that gave commands, and she wanted to give him everything. She crawled over to the edge of the bed and slipped off, obediently crawling between his legs to kneel between his thighs.

His hands cupped her breasts, thumbs strumming her nipples. "I love how responsive you are." He tugged and rolled, even pinched and flicked until her breath was coming in ragged pants and she was so damp she was slick.

"Kneel up, Ania."

She did as he said, and it put her exactly the height she needed to be when he stood.

"I want you to give my balls a lot of attention. Make them ache for you."

He was close. So close she couldn't resist bending a little lower, tilting her head up and running her tongue over his heavy sac. Between. Around. She stroked caresses with her tongue. Cupping him gently in her palms, she squeezed and massaged, all the while using her mouth to suck, kiss and lick until she heard his breathing change and his fist tightened around his shaft.

"Now my cock, baby. Lots of attention. Make me think you worship it."

Maybe she did, after what he'd done to her with it. She could see herself in love with that part of him when maybe his bossy ways weren't nearly as hot. Although there was something very hot about him giving her orders in the bedroom.

She licked up the shaft and all around the rim. Her hand went to replace his at the base, but he shook his head. "I don't want your hands on my cock." His gaze burned into hers and, once again, his eyes glittered with that feral, wild look that was terrifying and sexy at the same time.

She used her tongue to get him very wet and then she took the crown in her mouth, her tongue dancing over it, under it, stabbing, flicking and then stroking. She took him deeper, only an inch, but he stretched her lips just as he'd predicted and there was just a little moment of panic at the thought that he controlled how much of him was going into her mouth. At the thought, more liquid spilled between her legs, making her slicker. Needier. More wanton.

She sucked hard, switched to licks going up his shaft

and teasing his velvet crown before once more taking him into the heat of her mouth. Even to herself, it was hot. He caught her hair in one hand and held her head still while he pushed himself deeper. Her gaze shot to his. He didn't look away, but he held himself there and she began to suck.

At first, she was tentative, but then the feel of him in her mouth, the sexy way she knelt between his legs and his sac brushing against her chin got to her. Ania loved the way the hair on his thighs teased her breasts. He began to move his hips, pulling back to give her a breath and then sliding in.

"You look so fucking sexy, Ania," he whispered. "I love the way your lips look around my cock. It's so hot. Your mouth surrounding me with all that scorching heat. Can you taste me? I want to come down your throat, but you're not ready for that."

She would have taken him that way or tried to. The way he was looking at her gave her everything she needed and more to do whatever he asked, but she concentrated on hollowing her cheeks and sucking him when he pushed deeper and dancing her tongue up his shaft when he was giving her a breath.

Twice her hands flew up to his cock when he pressed deeper and she was alarmed. He shook his head. "Put your hands on your breasts. I want you rolling your nipples. When I'm in your mouth, baby, you think only about my cock. Nothing else. Just that. If I push deep, swallow. Breathe through your nose. Suck hard, but don't pull away and don't try to control what's happening. When your mouth is on me, it's all about you giving me everything."

She understood, and she forced her body to relax. He'd given her nirvana. She wanted to do the same for him. She began to think about his shape. His size. The things that made his body shake and his breathing change. She wanted to memorize every inch of him. Stroke her tongue along that prominent vein and dance over the vee under the crown.

She didn't realize at first that she was taking him deeper until she felt his entire body shudder, and her lashes lifted so she was looking into his eyes. He forced his cock from her mouth with a hiss of need escaping. His hands were already pulling her up.

"On the bed, Ania, hands and knees. Face away from me."

She crawled back onto the bed and did as he asked, her entire body already so slick, so sensitive, crying out for him. Her legs were trembling. Fingers of desire dancing up and down her thighs. Darts of fire ran from breast to clit, and deep inside her sheath spasmed in anticipation.

He caught her hips, pressed that broad crown to her entrance and plunged deep. Hard. Slammed inside her. It was so rough she nearly tumbled forward, but his hands were on her hips, dragging her back to him. He began to move, pistoning into her. She felt every stroke, so deep she was afraid he would come out her throat.

Her breath came in hard little sobs. Pleas. More. More. She needed more. He gave it to her, swearing in his language. Yanking her head back so she arched her back. Moving over top of her to change the angle. All the while his hips continued to drive into her, the rhythm fast and steady.

Then he was swatting her, smacking her cheeks with his hand, each slap spreading heat across her bottom until the nerve endings sang, adding to the vicious need growing out of control inside her. She felt him swell, push at the tender tissue. She cried out, and then her sheath clamped down hard on him, gripping like a vise and then squeezing and milking, desperate for every drop of seed he had in him.

She felt the hot splash of every rope of scorching seed he rocketed to the walls of her sheath, triggering a series of orgasms. His body flung her into that place only he could take her and she collapsed, falling forward, her heart beating too hard, her breath ragged, and her body still pulsing, alive and singing.

Mitya went with her, coming down over top of her, pinning her to the mattress, his head on her butt. He turned his head and sank his teeth into the middle of his handprint, triggering another aftershock. A huge one.

She closed her eyes and hugged the sheets. Outside the rain poured down onto the roof. Inside, Mitya rubbed her red cheeks and then down her thighs and up her back until his breath slowed and he rolled over.

She turned her head to look at him. "That was incredible. I never thought I could ever do that. I enjoyed having you in my mouth. Not just enjoyed it. I loved it." She had.

She had never liked it before, but she'd done it. She was generous to a partner, but having sex had never been close to what it was with him. Definitely, she wanted to try again, to see what else she could do. "You did that for me, Mitya. I was a little afraid, but somehow you gave me confidence."

"All you, baby." He rolled off the bed and went to the bathroom, cleaning himself and then returning with a washcloth. "It's only going to get better. All of it, Ania. Give us a chance."

She already knew she was going to try.

6

ANIA inhaled, taking in the wonderful aroma of the bakery. She hadn't been out of her house for the last week. She hadn't realized, until she entered the bakery, how isolated and lonely she had become never leaving her home. Watching Evangeline and Ashe serve their customers—their movements synchronized, as if they'd practiced them, never running into each other, like a wonderful ballet—made Ania smile. She'd been smiling quite often lately.

Every morning she'd visited with her father. Just having Mitya there had seemed to breathe new life into him. Mitya never allowed her to enter her father's room unless he or Sevastyan was with her. She didn't mind the decree because anytime she wanted to go in, Mitya always stopped what he was doing and immediately accommodated her.

She knew it was silly to hope. Antosha was dying and she had to keep that in her mind, but he'd seemed to rally these past few days. He couldn't talk very well, but each morning, he smiled at her, definitely recognized her and held her hand when she chattered away with him. Sometimes his adoring gaze went from her face to rest on Mitya. At once his expression would change, and her heart would nearly seize at the look that would pass between them. She went into her father's room often throughout the day, Mitya at her side. Mostly, Antosha slept, but always in the morning he was more alert.

Ania inhaled her latte and cinnamon-apple muffin. Evangeline looked up from serving a customer and smiled at her, a blaze of joy coming off her to welcome Ania as if they were old friends. She hadn't been open to meeting or making friends until she'd met Mitya. He'd changed her life in so many ways. He made her feel as if he couldn't do without her. He had no compunction about slamming her up against a wall and having wild, hot, crazy sex the moment they were alone together. It never seemed to matter to him where they were, he could suddenly bend her over a chair or take her on the floor in front of the fireplace. Sex was often, and it was always wild.

She was sore, a delicious, secret soreness that made her feel as if she really belonged to Mitya. He'd given her hope when she'd had none. They hadn't talked about the men who might have killed her family. He'd cautioned her to take one step at a time. He was reaching out to his contacts to find out who the man was that had come to her home with others to finish the job they'd started.

"Hey, girl. You haven't been in lately," Evangeline greeted, flinging herself into the chair opposite Ania. "We were hoping you'd come back."

"Mitya is keeping her prisoner," Ashe said, sliding onto the chair to the right of Evangeline.

"Ashe, need coffee," one of the bodyguards called.

"You know where the coffeepot is, Jeremiah," Ashe

returned, sounding snippy. "I'm not getting up when I just sat down. You waited on purpose."

Judging by the smirk on Jeremiah's face, Ania was fairly certain Ashe was correct.

"I see Evangeline is keeping you out of the kitchen," Jeremiah said as he rounded the counter to reach the glass coffeepot with the hot brew kept ready for customers.

Ashe gave him a rude finger gesture and turned back to Ania. "Ignore him. It's the only sane thing to do."

"Is he your brother?" Ania asked.

Jeremiah was clearly younger than the other bodyguards and he didn't have the rough, scary features or hard edge the others had. The way Ashe and Jeremiah interacted, as if they were affectionately annoyed with each other, made her think they had some close association.

Ashe flashed another grin at Jeremiah. "People think you're my baby brother," she announced with obvious glee.

Jeremiah returned the rude gesture. Even some of the bodyguards sitting at their tables pretending to read smiled.

"Jeremiah and Ashe are good friends," Evangeline said firmly. "We're more interested in you and Mitya. Fyodor and Timur are Mitya's cousins. Mitya was shot protecting Fyodor and me right here in the bakery."

Ania's heart clenched hard at the thought of Mitya being shot. She saw his body often. She knew every scar he had. She'd traced them with her fingers, with her lips and tongue. She saw how often he had to ease his body into a different position in order to stop pain he still experienced. "I knew they were close."

"Fyodor tells me Mitya is staying at your home with you."

Ania found herself smiling as she lifted the latte and took a drink. She wanted to moan it was so good, but she figured that would be considered inappropriate. "I think these men gossip more than women do. Yes, Mitya is staying with me at my house. My father is very ill and he's staying close to him."

"To him?" Ashe teased. "I'll bet he's not nearly as close to your father as he is to you."

Ania blushed. She had never been given to blushing, but the mischievous note in Ashe's voice, all-knowing, conjured up images of Mitya striding into her dining room and laying her across the table. He'd spent an inappropriate amount of time devouring her, because he said they were in the dining room and that made him hungry.

"You're turning red," Ashe added. "Lobster red." She nudged Evangeline. "You know what that means, don't you?"

"Stop teasing her," Evangeline said, laughing. "You're being awful." She sent Ania a reassuring smile. "I'd like to tell you she gets better with time, but it isn't true. She's a bit of a handful according to Timur."

A derisive snort came from somewhere across the room, from Jeremiah's direction. Ashe glared threateningly, causing Ania to burst into laughter. They made her feel part of their circle, and she needed that. She missed her family, the laughter and comradery. She hadn't had anything close to it for three years. Mitya had given her this.

"Tell us about you and Mitya," Evangeline encouraged, giving Ashe a warning look.

Ania rubbed her finger along the inside of the mug handle. "He was very unexpected."

Evangeline leaned closer. She knew that their bodyguards were leopard. All had excellent hearing. She lowered her voice even more. "Is something worrying you?"

Of course, she was worried. They couldn't live on sex. The sex was beyond anything she'd experienced. If they came together just for sex and lived separate lives, they would do fine. Mitya wasn't having any of that. She chose not to tell them how afraid she was that Mitya was taking over her life and she was just letting him. Instead, she gave them her other concern.

"My leopard has retreated. She was close to her heat and then she withdrew. I can barely feel her unless Mitya is close. She rises to reach for his leopard, but then she subsides, as if she is just going to sleep. She was so close. I know she was." Ania couldn't keep the worry out of her voice.

Mitya reassured her often that she was his for himself. He wanted her. But she knew without his leopard claiming her female, Mitya wouldn't be with her. He could tell her the same thing over and over, but she knew the truth. Her leopard soothed his. Her leopard had been the real reason Mitya had continued to seek her out. When he was close to Ania, his leopard was at peace.

"You said your father is ill, Ania," Evangeline pointed out. "Sometimes, when there is trauma in our lives, that can delay ovulation. The emergence is all about ovulation. Being fertile. You and the leopard having the same cycle."

"My nanny is leopard. Her leopard never emerged. She says she's too old now and will never experience her leopard being free. I don't want that for mine." She didn't want Mitya to leave her either. She feared if her leopard didn't rise she'd lose him.

"I think you're worrying for nothing," Evangeline said. "It's very clear that your leopard and Mitya's are a mated pair. She will rise when it's safe for her to do so. Leopards protect their human counterpart. She may be protecting you. You can only handle so much, Ania. Don't expect so much of yourself. You're taking care of your family business as well as your father. Right now, that's enough. Let your leopard take care of you."

Ania hadn't thought of it that way. It was possible she was so worried about her father that she couldn't deal with what would happen once her leopard emerged. She hadn't thought that far ahead.

"It's possible you're right," she admitted. "I hope you are."

"What's Mitya like?" Ashe asked. "He's always been a closed book. He looks scary. Is he?"

Was he? Absolutely. Ania was nodding before she could stop herself. "He expects obedience from everyone. The slightest thing he says," she admitted. "That can be . . ."

"Annoying," Ashe supplied.

"Terrifying," Ania qualified before she could stop herself. It was the first time she'd admitted that to herself. Coming up against Mitya would be frightening, and she knew it would happen sooner or later. Right now, she wasn't doing anything he didn't like or approve of, but she really wasn't a woman who relied on someone else to think for her. Was that what he wanted? She still didn't know, and they talked all the time. Or she did. Mitya listened.

"He wants to be involved in every aspect of my life."

"Most husbands do," Evangeline pointed out gently. "Certainly, Fyodor insists on it."

Ashe nodded. "Timur too. He drives me right up the wall."

"And do you give in and tell them everything?" Ania asked. "Every single thing you're doing and where you're going? Answering to them like you're a teenager?"

Evangeline shared a look with Ashe. Ashe wrinkled her nose. Jeremiah snorted, as if he'd taken a swallow of coffee and coughed it all over the table.

Ania rubbed her temples. "Normal people don't live like that, do they? Just because they're in a relationship? My parents were crazy in love, but I never noticed that my mother had to ask my father's permission to go into town and shop whenever she wanted. Or visit a neighbor. She just did it."

Evangeline very gently laid her hand over Ania's. "Has Mitya told you anything about his past?"

Ania drew back, nodding. She hadn't allowed herself to think too much about the things Mitya had disclosed to her. She couldn't imagine what kind of childhood he'd had—or what his psychotic father had shaped him into.

"It's different for all of us," Ashe said. "Do we like it? No. At least I don't. But they have very powerful enemies, and that means there is always danger. To them. To us. To any children we might have."

"I'm pregnant," Evangeline said softly. "As soon as I realized I was carrying a child, Fyodor's silly rule of taking bodyguards and letting him know my plans became entirely different for me. I realized why he felt he needed to know where I was and what I was doing. I wanted our babies protected."

"Mitya seems just a little obsessed with knowing where I am," Ania admitted. Her hand went to her throat and she stroked her fingers down it, just the way he often did. "He doesn't just ask something. He makes demands. Everyone immediately complies with whatever he's commanding. It isn't good."

"Is he unreasonable?" Evangeline asked.

Fortunately, a group of customers came in, their chatter sounding happy. Each time the door opened, a small bell announced more clients. This time a small cluster of five came into the shop, very clearly coming from an office close by, and behind them was a group of four men, all in suits, as well as two in jeans and tees. They'd dressed up their look with sports jackets, making them look as if they too had come from one of the many office buildings.

Evangeline and Ashe rose without a word and hurried to take their places behind the counter. Ania noticed the bodyguards blended into the room, reading from their devices, sipping at hot coffee or lattes, occasionally eating one of the pastries, but all were alert. They were spread throughout the room. Two were guards watching over Evangeline; two others kept Ashe in sight. Mitya had sent Vikenti and his brother Zinoviy. She always called Vikenti *Vik* and Zinoviy *Zen*. She didn't really think he was Zen, but it made her want to laugh when she referred to him that way.

She sipped at her latte and wondered why neither Ashe nor Evangeline seemed resentful of their partners insisting on knowing where they were at all times. She felt like an errant child, asking permission to go to work or to the bakery. What of her street racing? Sometimes she was just so restless she needed an outlet. Racing had always been that for her. It also kept her reflexes sharp.

Ania found it strange that Mitya seemed to know when she was right at the point that she needed to grab the keys and go find a race. He appeared out of nowhere, and wherever they were, right then and there, he was wild and crazy. The sex was always unbelievable. He wrung so many orgasms out of her that sometimes she couldn't even stand upright and would lie on the carpet naked, her breathing ragged, shocked at the way he could make her body feel. The need to race faded far into the background until she could barely remember she'd been thinking about it.

Did he know? Could he read her that easily? A suspicion came to her and she found herself frowning. Her female occasionally reached out to her, but rarely. She'd told Ania that her name was Jewel. When Ania was upset after seeing her father in the evenings, mostly because he was unresponsive then, she would murmur to her softly to comfort her. Often, Ania couldn't even understand what the cat was conveying. She communicated in images rather than words.

Do you talk to Dymka? She knew Mitya's leopard's name meant "smoke" or "haze." He'd been named that because he could move unseen among enemies. He was that stealthy.

At first, she was certain the female wasn't going to answer. She seemed lazy, wanting to retreat back to the safety of their body. Ania didn't think that was very fair since the leopard had gotten her noticed by Mitya in the first place.

Yes. He likes to talk to me.

A purring accompanied the images, as if Jewel was so

enamored with the male leopard, she couldn't think of him without a sensuous shiver.

It was all Ania could do not to roll her eyes, but at the same time, she understood. Mitya made her want to purr every time he touched her. *Do you tell him when I'm restless? Or upset?*

I do not like to see you upset.

That wasn't an answer, and yet it was. Mitya's leopard warned him when Ania was thinking of racing. Or maybe he didn't know what she wanted to do, but he could guess. Was he using sex to manipulate her into doing the things he wanted her to do? She groaned and put her head down on the table.

"Ania?"

The voice was deep. Strong. Very familiar. She raised her head to find herself staring into Alessandro Caruso's dark eyes. He was the oldest of the four Caruso brothers. She'd met him, over the years, quite a few times, but to her knowledge, she'd never noticed how good-looking he was. Her leopard, Jewel, was looking at him as well, making Ania's heart kick into overdrive. If Jewel was interested, it meant she was looking at Alessandro because he was a shifter.

"How is your father, *cara*?" He asked, toeing around the chair Ashe had vacated and sitting down without an invitation.

Vik moved closer, and his phone was in his hand. She tried a slight shake of her head, to stop him, but she knew, no matter what, Mitya was being informed. For some reason, that set her teeth on edge. She didn't need babysitters.

"He's in hospice," she admitted. "Thanks for asking. Most people have forgotten that he was hurt so badly there was no recovery." But the Carusos always remembered. What did that mean? Did they have a stake in finding out if her father died? She needed to know.

"I'm sorry, Ania. I know you were very close to your parents. This has to be hard on you. My father informed us you were selling your business."

She nodded. "It's a lot of work for one person. Even with employees, overseeing to make certain every job is done to our standards is difficult." She rubbed her temples without thinking. She had that headache again. Her skull felt a little too tight. Her skin hurt.

"My younger brother is very interested in cars. He's more of a hands-on person, and driving is his passion. The moment we heard, Donato was extremely interested. That's one of the reasons we came to San Antonio. I had a meeting with Jake Bannaconni and had hoped to get a meeting with you, but your lawyer said that wasn't possible."

"She was right. I rarely come into town because I don't like being away from my father, but I hadn't been out in a week and I just needed to breathe a little."

"I understand, Ania. I'm really sorry. Is there anything our family can do to help?"

His eyes slid over her, and to her horror, there was speculation there. For a moment, his gaze drifted over her body and then back up to her face.

She shook her head and sipped at her cooling latte. She glanced up to see Vikenti and Zinoviy both looking grim. A burst of laughter came from a large table of customers who had just come in. Apparently they were celebrating a victory of some sort, and according to them, it was impossible to do without Evangeline's chai cupcakes and Ashe's amazing blended drinks.

Ania could hear so clearly. The rain outside. The conversations. Breathing even. The three men who had accompanied Alessandro into the bakery were seated at a table close by. Vikenti was between them and Ania on one side and Zinoviy was on the other. She knew by the way Alessandro was looking at her that he was interested.

Twice, his dark eyes had changed to a very intense amber. At first there were golden flecks through the dark brown and then she was staring at something much more predatory.

She'd never been in this situation before and didn't know how to handle it. She wanted information from Alessandro, as much as she could get, but she wasn't very good at deceit.

"Do you do quite a lot of business with Jake?" Deliberately she used his first name, as if she saw the billionaire every single day and they were good friends. She'd met him twice. She worked out of his building. She didn't run in his circles, but maybe the Carusos did.

"No, this will be my first time meeting with him. A mutual friend arranged it. Drake Donovan. He's been a good friend to us for several years. He owns an international security company and is a close friend of Bannaconni. I had some business I wanted to discuss with him, but even our name didn't buy us an instant meeting."

He didn't sound in the least bit annoyed over that, which surprised her. The Caruso family was a powerful one. Most people gave them whatever they wanted. She would expect that Alessandro and his brothers might be spoiled.

"Donovan's did?"

He nodded. "Immediately. I didn't have the same pull with your lawyer, though." He laughed softly at his own joke but all the while his eyes were on her. Watching. Alert.

She really wasn't feeling good. Her body felt hot. Her breasts ached. Every time she moved, her nipples rubbed in the lace of her bra, inflaming them. She held herself very still, but anxiety was taking hold. That and the persistent headache that only seemed to be getting worse because her skull was too tight. Her skin felt too sensitive. Between her legs, fire danced.

She couldn't seem to breathe without breathing in Alessandro. She glanced up and suddenly the room felt like it was filled with too many men, all looking at her with lust in their eyes. She couldn't stop what was happening to her body. In another minute she was going to have to rip off her clothes before her skin was rubbed raw.

The bell over the door rang and a chill went down her spine. Before she looked up, she knew exactly who was walking through the door. Deep inside, her female leopard jumped, as if she were trying for freedom. Ania lifted her lashes and her gaze instantly collided with Mitya's. There was no expression on his face. None at all. But he looked ruthless. Dangerous. Exactly what he was. He didn't try to hide the killer in him. His eyes were dark blue. Flat. Cold. The eyes of a predator. His gaze moved from her to Alessandro.

Automatically she followed his gaze. Alessandro had gone on alert immediately. His breath hissed out and his face was a mask as well. She could see the golden flecks moving through the dark brown in his eyes, his cat close.

Her breath hitched in her lungs. She had no idea what to do. Bodyguards spread out. Mitya strode straight to her table, not even acknowledging Evangeline's greeting. He used long, purposeful strides. Ania attempted a smile, but her heart was beating like crazy and she could barely breathe.

He held out his hand to her, still looking at Alessandro. "You'll have to excuse my fiancée."

She rose. Alessandro did as well. "Mitya, this is Alessandro Caruso. Alessandro, Mitya Amurov."

Alessandro recognized the name. She could tell it meant something to him. His gaze had followed Mitya's hand as his fingers wrapped around Ania's arm and pulled her around the table to him.

The moment Mitya touched her, his eyes went that fierce glittery arctic blue she came to recognize as his leopard being close. She knew he was all predator, a savage fighting machine, both cat and man. He dragged her close, tipped up her chin, and his mouth came down on hers.

She could taste his anger. Not anger. Rage. She tasted possession. Lust. It rose in him sharp and terrible, and with his raw hunger came hers. She couldn't stop it, no matter how much she reminded herself they weren't at home. Her entire body ached for him. She went damp. Then slick. Then burning out of control. He was rough. Wild. Everything she'd come to expect, everything that made her addicted.

She kissed him back, her arms sliding around his neck, her body melting into his. She didn't hold anything back. She never did. It was always impossible. His hand slid into her hair and his kiss gentled. He lifted his head, his eyes burning into hers. "Are you all right, *kotyonok*?"

She shook her head, honest with him. Her body hurt so badly she wanted to scream. Her head was coming apart. Exploding. She could barely stand her clothes, and between her legs, she was on fire.

"It is good to meet you," Mitya said. "I wish I had more time, but we're in a hurry." He sent Alessandro a smile that was even more predatory than when he'd walked in.

Sweeping his arm around Ania, he walked her right through the astonished customers and out the front door to the waiting car. It was a town car with dark windows. Sevastyan opened the back door for them.

"You drive," Mitya ordered abruptly. "Only you in the car. Put the privacy screen up."

Sevastyan took one look at Ania and nodded. He waved Miron to the car behind them with two other bodyguards, Kiriil and Matvei. Vikenti and Zinoviy took the lead car. Sevastyan slid behind the wheel and pressed a button for the screen to rise between the seats.

The moment Mitya had the door closed, he caught at Ania's shoes, pulling them from her feet and tossing them to the floor. "If you like that blouse, take it off." His hands were already stripping her jeans and panties from her. She wasn't fast enough, and he caught the front of her blouse, shredding the material and releasing her breasts from her bra, almost in the same motion. The way he did that, ripping her clothes from her as if he couldn't get to her fast enough, always gave her a crazy thrill and yet some trepidation simultaneously.

Her clothes had been hurting her skin, but now the cool air seemed to inflame her even more. She writhed on the seat, edging on panic. His gaze was savage, the lines in his face carved deep with lust. He looked like the epitome of carnal sin. He caught her thighs, jerked her legs apart and lifted her hips to his mouth.

His tongue felt rough. It felt like velvet. It was pure flame burning through her as he licked and then sucked. He used the edge of his teeth. He was ruthless, implacable, devouring her as she screamed and thrashed, out of control, tears leaking out of her eyes, her body bursting into a thousand blazes, a conflagration that just seemed to grow hotter and hotter until she was almost convulsing.

Ania tried to push his head away, pleading, sobbing, but then realized she was begging him for more. She wasn't pushing; she was yanking on his hair. She was more out of control than he was. He flicked her swollen clit with his fingers, a hard tap that sent more flames bouncing through her, driving her up over and over until she really thought she might go insane.

"Stop." She whispered it, even as she pressed her body deeper into his mouth, needing more, desperate for more. "You have to stop." But he couldn't. If he did, she might die.

"I say when we stop," he snapped, his jaw slick with her cream, his eyes blazing at her, almost demonic, a wanton, carnal animal, savage and fierce.

His mouth was on her again, his fingers stroking through all that liquid spreading everywhere while he consumed her. He claimed every inch of her, with hands, mouth, teeth, fingers. Then he shoved down his trousers and dragged her down the seat so he was over her. There was no preliminary; he simply slammed into her, a hard claiming, driving through her swollen, inflamed folds.

She heard herself scream again. She dug her nails into his shoulders, desperate for an anchor. He surged into her again and again, so hard she felt the car shake on the road, but it wasn't enough. Deep inside, that coiling began, a fire so hot it grew and grew. There was no stopping it. The roaring in her ears became the sound of the inferno building in her.

He never stopped. Not when she writhed. Not when she struggled. Not when she thrashed. His hard features were merciless. She needed that, but it terrified her. Absolutely terrified her. Did anyone die from the heat of a leopard? She might be the first. He had to stop. He couldn't stop.

Then it was coming, that terrible, ferocious firestorm, racing through her, consuming her from the inside out. Burning both of them. It burst over her, a tidal wave of pure heat, the flames reducing her to nothing but ashes, flinging her out of her body so she was somewhere else. She felt him, the hard, uncontrolled jerking of his cock as he emptied himself in her. So hot. Her sheath painted with him. Burning his name in her for all time.

Mitya collapsed over top of her and she took his weight. Her body was shaking, and she realized she couldn't stop weeping. She flung her arms around his neck and breathed shallowly, trying to stop the flood of tears.

"Shh, baby, I've got you," he whispered against her ear. "I came as soon as I knew you were in trouble."

"I didn't know what to do." She hated admitting it to him. She hadn't realized her female was rising. She'd initiated the conversation about Dymka and maybe that was the reason her leopard again rose to the surface.

"It could have been so bad. He's one. A shifter. Alessandro. I had no idea she was going to rise like that. He recognized me and came over to the table to talk and then suddenly I was all over the place." She could barely get it out, hiccups interfering with every other word.

"Vikenti and Zinoviy immediately texted me when they suspected."

Mitya turned his head to catch her earlobe between his teeth, biting down hard enough to make her yelp. At once scorching-hot liquid surrounded his cock, burning her sheath. She felt the ripple of an aftershock.

"You should have texted that you needed me, Ania. The next time it happens, at the very first sign of her, you have to text me. I'll drop everything and come. If I'm too far out, I'll call in the helicopter."

"I didn't know." She was ashamed that she hadn't recognized the signs. "What if . . ."

"You were protected. You had Vikenti and Zinoviy. Evangeline and Ashe would have helped as well, the moment they realized you were in trouble."

He caught up her shredded shirt and eased out of her, his cock scraping along the tight walls of her sheath. She felt that dragging friction and sharp pain that triggered another aftershock. He cleaned his face and then his cock with the shirt before very gently wiping between her legs and thighs. He added water from a bottle and cleaned her a second time before helping her pull on her panties and jeans.

Both hands went around her waist to help her into a sitting position. "Babe, you have to stop crying."

His voice was so tender it turned her heart over. He'd never used that particular tone on her. She touched her face, and sure enough, tears still dripped down her cheeks. "I've never been so emotional in my life. I'm really sorry, Mitya."

"Don't be. You have every reason to be. I believe between you and your leopard you're leaking hormones all over the place." He buckled her seat belt as she leaned back against the leather.

That allowed her to give him a watery smile. "You looked so scary when you came into the bakery, I thought you were mad at me."

"You didn't do anything wrong, *kotyonok*. I knew the moment I stepped into the bakery and smelled him that Alessandro was leopard and he was close to you when you were going into a heat. Did you tell him you were engaged to me?"

"We hadn't gotten that far in the conversation. I was trying to find out if his family had been the ones to put a hit out on my family. He asked after my father, which he would either way. We worked for them, maintaining their cars. As I said, my father and grandfather drove for them sometimes, and that last drive each one made was for their family and the Anwar family."

He turned in his seat, his hand cradling her throat, his thumb tipping up her chin so her eyes were forced to meet his. "Ania, I warned you to leave it alone."

His voice had gone scary low. His eyes glittered at her, that dark menace that warned her he had gone from being sweet to suddenly dangerous.

"I know. I hadn't planned to do it, Mitya. He was there. He was asking questions. I just tried to lead him a little, but honestly, I couldn't tell anything, and then I was all over the place emotionally and physically. I couldn't hear myself think."

He bent his head and brushed a kiss against her lips. Then her chin. His hands dropped to her rib cage, nearly surrounding her. He kissed her throat and then his mouth was on her left breast, drawing the soft mound deep inside.

It felt decadent. Hot. Erotic. She sat pinned by her seat belt, naked from the waist up, with Mitya using his tongue, teeth and mouth on her breast. Each hard flick of his tongue on her nipple sent blood rushing through her veins. His tongue stroked rough caresses and then his teeth tugged hard. Bit down gently. Her blood went hot. She tipped her head back and arched, giving him full access.

Then his mouth was on her right breast, and his hand was at her left, kneading and massaging, fingers pinching down on her nipple until she wanted to scream. Then, when he let up, the blood rushed straight to her clit and pounded through her sex. He covered both breasts, with his hands and mouth, until the fire was back, a fevered pitch.

How could he do that when he wasn't touching her anywhere else? She'd never felt so beautiful, or so wanton. His hair brushed her skin, adding to the fire sweeping through her. He lifted his head, looking into her eyes.

"I want to fuck you until neither of us can breathe. You do that to me, Ania. Your leopard has subsided. So has mine, and I still want you. My fuckin' cock feels like it's going to shatter."

She circled his neck with her arms. "I'll take care of that when we get home." She knew they were on the road that swept up to the hills, getting close to home. Her heart pounded, and she ached for him.

"You'll take care of it now."

"Now?" Her hand dropped down to the front of his trousers. Her heart went crazy. Her mouth actually watered, and her breasts throbbed. She loved his voice when he went all commander on her. She didn't understand the difference when that same tone annoyed her outside of any sexual activity.

"Yes, now."

She rubbed her hand over the very expensive material. "I don't know, honey. Are you certain?"

His eyes blazed fire at her and he reached out, unsnapped her seat belt and yanked her down so she was lying across the leather seat. He stripped off her panties and jeans so fast she hardly realized he'd done it. She tried her best not to smile when his hands conveyed impatience and his eyes had gone feral. He opened his trousers, somehow managed to turn on the seat, and then his mouth was between her legs as he straddled her.

Hot. Wild. Insane. She caught his hips, but there was no stopping the press of his cock into her mouth. He might have been intimidating, as she had very little control. The leather of the seat was at her back and he rode her mouth, pumping in and out in a slow glide. She used her tongue and alternated licking and sucking, doing her best when he was controlling the action.

It was difficult to think when his mouth was attacking her, driving her up so fast while his cock burned her lips into a wide stretch and slid over her tongue, a scorching-hot treat. She dug her fingers into his hips, pulling him closer, her own hips bucking a frantic rhythm against his mouth.

Twice he went so deep that she nearly panicked, unable to breathe, but when she began to fight, he lifted his mouth from between her legs. "Stop. You're fine. I wouldn't let anything happen to you." He waited until she stilled before pulling his cock from her, so she could get air.

Already she was chasing after him, eager to get the pulsing promise as his cock swelled and she could feel his heart beating right through his shaft. He began that easy glide again, his mouth once more driving her wild, and then it happened a second time, his cock sliding deep, pushing her boundaries, her comfort zone, holding her helpless there. She tried to be still, but panic rose and once again she found herself fighting him.

"Ania." His voice was very calm. Just as before, he didn't move. "Learn to trust me. You're my world. I wouldn't harm you."

Again, it took a tremendous effort on her part to be still and allow him to cut off her air. The moment she stopped struggling, he pulled back, let her take a breath and then began that exquisite pumping again. His cock swelled, pushing at the silken mouth. She rubbed over him with her tongue. All the while her body coiled tighter and tighter until she couldn't hold back the waves burning through her.

His cock grew thicker, and then it was jerking hard, and she was forced to swallow the hot liquid pouring down her throat. There was something exciting, even thrilling, about lying on a back seat with his cock in her mouth, his mouth between her legs, orgasms rolling through both of them.

It took a moment to realize the car had ceased moving. A hand hit the top of the vehicle. "Get the hell out, Mitya," Sevastyan's voice was tight. "I'm heading for the bar and I'm done for the night."

Mitya moved, pulling his spent cock free of her mouth as he sat up. He gave a soft groan. His cousin was a shifter. A leopard. He had heard every sound coming from the back seat. Smelled every scent. Heard her screams. He had to be desperate for a woman. He cursed himself.

"Go ahead, Sevastyan." Mitya's hands on Ania's shoulders helped her into a sitting position.

"The others will be here if you need them."

Mitya heard the strain in Sevastyan's voice. "I'm sorry. I couldn't stop myself. She needed . . . care."

Ania wrapped her arms around her middle and rocked herself. Her body was still on fire, but now she was embarrassed. Mitya put his arm around her.

"Is that what you call it? I'm gone," Sevastyan snapped.

7

THE rain had finally stopped, although the windows were
covered with drops. Beside Mitya, Ania was asleep, worn
out by the nearly violent sex they'd shared in the car. He
kept his body tight against hers, his arm circling her waist,
hand cupping her breast. He inhaled her scent. She'd taken
a long bath as soon as they'd gotten home, hurrying into
the house and upstairs, his jacket covering her.

He found he could barely keep his hands off her. He
loved that he could touch her when he wanted. That he
could take her anytime, night or day. He'd gone so many
years without a woman's touch, without her hands or mouth
on him, because he feared when he achieved his release and
he was vulnerable, his leopard would strike at the woman.
Now, he had a woman he had come to almost revere, and
she wanted him every bit as much as he wanted her.

He knew Ania was still unsure of him. She believed he
was with her solely because his leopard had claimed her

leopard. She didn't realize Mitya had claimed Ania. She was his. He liked her. More, that affection was growing into something else. The way she cared for her father. The way she worried about Annalise's future. She was even paying for an apartment for Annalise, so she wouldn't have to see the terrible end to her father's life. The fact that she had begun her own investigation and was shaping herself into a sniper. He loved all of that in her.

He rubbed his thumb back and forth over the soft swell of her breast. Everything about her appealed to him, even that little streak of defiance she had. He knew she thought she could get away if she wanted. He also knew she couldn't. There was no going back for either of them. He pressed a kiss into the nape of her neck. He knew how lucky he was. The odds of finding his mate were a million to one, and yet she was there in bed with him.

He savored the sight of her, lying there curled up in that way she had. She was naked because he liked her that way. She complied with his wishes when it came to anything in the bedroom. Never once had she said no to him, not that he would have accepted that. The only reason his woman might say no was if she was afraid, and he didn't want her to ever be afraid of anything they did. If that happened, he'd back off and introduce her much more gently to whatever it was she feared.

He lifted his head again to look down at her face, the long sweep of her lashes and her full lips. He had never thought he was capable of love. He didn't count his cousins, because he didn't think in terms of love with them. He didn't identify emotion. But Ania . . . She was different. She was getting into him. Deep. He thought of her continuously. He didn't like her to be upset. He wanted her trust above all else.

Mitya considered what he was asking of her. She had to accept him, believing he was a criminal. Not just any criminal, but a very high-ranking one. He was asking her to do that. No, he was demanding it of her. He wanted her trust on every level, yet he had no intention of allowing her into his business. It was too dangerous, and he wasn't taking chances with her life.

In a very short time, he knew he had grown to need her. Not just the sex, although he was totally addicted, but the promise of her. The brightness of her. The beauty that was far more than skin-deep. He wanted her loyalty. Her faithfulness. Her love. That was the bottom line. He wanted Ania to fall so deeply in love with him, she would never consider leaving him.

"I'll never leave you," he whispered aloud. "We'll make this work, *kotyonok*."

Although Mitya spoke softly, barely allowing a thread of sound into the room, she stirred, her lashes fluttering. "Mitya? Are you all right?" She turned over, her body sliding against his. Her arms circled his neck and she laid her head on his chest. "I'm right here. Tell me what you need."

His heart did a slow somersault. His gut tightened into a thousand knots. That was why. Right there. How could he not fall in love? He hadn't intended to. This was about her loving him, not the other way around, but she was tearing him up inside. What did he need? Was he all right? That was Ania. Thinking only of him.

She kissed his chest. His throat. Up to his jaw. Little kisses. Nothing sexual about them, but they struck at him with far more intimacy than he could stand. He was afraid to love her. Afraid once he admitted it, even to himself, Lazar would strike. She would always be his greatest weakness. Lazar would hate that Mitya had found happiness. Found a woman who would lavish him with love. Ania was that kind of woman.

If he let himself love her, if he gave her that, she would give him everything in return. A house full of laughter. Her complete trust. Her body. Her heart. Her soul. That was Ania. She didn't do anything by half measures. He knew that by the way she cared for her father, by the way she practiced with a sniper rifle. She was thorough, seeing to every detail, and she'd be that way with him.

"Things are just a little too close tonight," he admitted because he had to give her something.

She blinked, and he felt the long sweep of her lashes against his skin. "Can I take it all away for you?"

He closed his eyes and nearly groaned. His body stirred; he felt the heat moving through him, pooling in his groin, but he didn't want her to do anything but sleep. He'd been rough. She didn't realize it, but her female leopard had made a big appearance. She was declaring to them she was definitely going to emerge. It would be rougher than ever, far more so, and Ania needed to be rested. Her body needed time to heal.

"I need to hold you close, baby," he admitted. It was easier to think he just needed sex. He was a very sexual being. Oral as well, as most shifters were, maybe even more so than most. He liked leaving his mark on her. His leopard was oral, and he knew her female would take the cat's teeth often, just like Ania took his. He wanted his relationship with her to be sexual, but it was more than that. It was this—the intimacy of holding her close. Talking to her in the night. Needing that as much as he needed her body.

He kissed the top of her head just as a prickle of unease slid through him. He turned his head toward the window. They were on the second floor and had the entire upper story to themselves. Her father had the master bedroom and his men stayed in the various guest rooms, by shifts, until their time to patrol the grounds. Annalise had moved to an apartment in the city.

The unease became more, spreading through him like a cancer. Dymka leapt at him, pushing at his skin, demanding to be allowed freedom. He ran the cat every night. He'd learned to let the leopard out to keep him

healthy. Sevastyan and some of his other cousins allowed
the leopards to carry out battles as long as they stayed in
control. It kept them fit and helped to get some of their
energy out, making them a little less of a constant handful.

With Ania and her female in such close proximity,
Dymka had settled and Mitya had been at peace. Now the
leopard was fighting for control. In a rage. Furious.

"Ania, get dressed, baby." He shifted her out of his
arms and was out of the bed instantly, pulling on clothes
he could get off fast if needed.

She rolled over, frowning, looking at him.

"Don't ask questions, just do it."

She muttered something under her breath that sounded
suspiciously like "bossy, much," but she threw back the
covers and was up, dressing hurriedly. He signaled to her
to stay quiet and behind him as he began sliding weapons
into various loops in his clothing. Texting Sevastyan and
his men, he warned them that someone was close to the
house. Each of the guards was expected to text a single
letter of the alphabet in response to let the others know
they were alive, well and alert. All but one texted back.

Mitya swore under his breath. The silent guard, Amory
Binder, was one of the leopards Drake Donovan had recruited from Borneo. He was younger than Mitya liked, in
his early twenties, and not as experienced as the rest of
them. Mitya needed men to guard against Lazar and what
he believed would be an army when his father made his
move, so he'd taken the kid on.

He texted the others to check on the absent guard. Sevastyan sent several private messages to him telling him
to take Ania and get to safety. He didn't bother replying.
Ania pulled a gun out of a small box she had under the
bed. He watched her load it. She should have had it already loaded, but he wasn't about to take up that argument
with her.

He went out of the room first, letting Dymka take over

all his senses. At once, he knew the house had been breached. He smelled . . . leopard. Dymka went insane at the idea that other male leopards were near his female. She hadn't yet emerged, and the bond wasn't complete. It took a moment to fight for control. He hissed his impatience at his cat.

"Stay close, Ania. They're in the house."

She nodded. She moved almost in unison with him as they made their way down the stairs. The open floor plan on the first floor allowed Mitya to see into the great room, foyer, formal dining room and part of the kitchen. A shadowy figure, all in black, made his way down the hall toward Antosha's room.

Ania started to move, to push past him, but he gripped her arm hard and shook his head. He put one hand on the railing and leapt over it, landing silently in a crouch, almost directly behind the intruder. The man spun, his leopard clearly warning him, shifting as he did so. Mitya was fast, his speed blurring. He'd had to learn to rid himself of clothes and shift in a heartbeat, to keep his father from breaking his bones.

Dymka met the large golden leopard in the air. The two heavy cats crashed together, ripping at each other's belly and genitals, teeth trying to sink into throats. Loose skin helped to save both animals as they hit the floor and rolled over and over.

Ania rushed down the stairs and took a two-handed stance with her weapon, trying for a shot at the golden leopard. It was easy to tell which of the leopards was Mitya. Dymka's coat was very distinctive. Mitya had named him Smoke because of his coloring and the fact that he could vanish into haze or fog easily.

It was impossible to get a shot off with the two leopards snarling and ripping at each other, rolling over and raking sides and bellies. Ania tried to ease around them to go down the hall to check on her father. The golden cat tried to break free and rush her. Dymka buried both front claws deep into the hindquarters of the golden leopard and pulled it back and away from Ania.

Mitya's heart, inside his leopard, nearly seized. The intruder was so close to Ania, she had to feel its hot breath on her face. She didn't freeze as he expected her to do. She put the gun almost right between the eyes of the leopard and pulled the trigger several times. The large cat sagged to the hall floor, the dead weight sprawling out along with pools of blood.

Ania leapt over the leopard's body and ran down to her father's room, Dymka right behind her. She grabbed the doorknob and yanked it open just as Dymka threw his weight against her. She went down almost completely under the big cat as several shots rang out.

"Dad," she whispered, horrified that anyone had managed to breach security.

There was the sound of breaking glass, and then Dymka was up and rushing into the master bedroom, Ania right behind him. The room was a mess, drawers pulled out, overturned and broken. The pillows were pulled out from under Antosha and ripped to shreds. The two vases had been destroyed. How the intruder had managed to rip everything apart so silently was anyone's guess. The intruder had gone out his window, breaking the glass to get out.

Ania ran to her father and checked his pulse. There was a gash over his left eye where someone had struck him with a pistol. She tried to wake him, but Mitya stopped her. He was back to his human form, naked, his roped muscles rippling as he took the gun from her, laid it on the bed and gripped her upper arms.

"What the fuck is wrong with you? Didn't I tell you to stay behind me at all times? Had you run into this room, he would have killed you. Damn it, Ania, what do you want me to do? Lock you up until this is over and have you hate me for keeping you safe? When I tell you to do something, you fucking do it." He punctuated each sentence with a small shake.

Dymka was still in a rage, a ferocious, vicious leopard needing a target. His mate had been in danger. She hadn't done as she was told. A leopard—no, two—had come onto their property and into their home. He hadn't been allowed to go after the second one. He remained close to the surface, driving his human counterpart's fury.

Ania had risked them all with her impulsive behavior. Dymka wanted her punished, and he raked and clawed at Mitya, determined to make her understand she had a responsibility to all of them, Mitya, Dymka and Jewel. She would have thrown them away to get to her dying father. It didn't make sense, and she had to learn.

Mitya breathed deeply, trying to force the adrenaline out of his system. The roaring in his ears and the blood running hotly in his veins didn't do anyone any good. He fought for control when Dymka tried to take over. Fortunately, Ania realized the male leopard was fighting for supremacy and she didn't struggle or try to defend her actions. She was trembling, but she remained very still.

Mitya looked down at Ania. His fingers were so tight around her arms that the skin had turned white. He slowly, one by one, forced his fingers away from her body and stepped back. "It's impossible to get in here. The alarm didn't go off. How the fuck did they get in?"

Sevastyan came striding in. He looked every bit as angry as Mitya. He didn't even blink at finding his cousin naked. "The alarm wasn't tampered with, Mitya. Someone turned it off. The only person we have missing is the kid."

Mitya gestured toward Antosha. "I'll need a washcloth and first aid kit. I take it the guards are securing the grounds and they've looked for Amory?"

"He's nowhere, Mitya, and if he were dead, his body would be out there. They didn't have time to carry it off and had no reason to." Sevastyan's voice was grim. He went striding from the room again, presumably to get the first aid kit and washcloth.

Mitya stared down at Ania. She had one hand on her father's chest, but she was looking at him. He expected anger. Tears. Something. Bruises were coming up on her arms from where he'd grabbed her. She might think he was angry, but Dymka had been the furious one. He'd felt fear. No, worse. Terror. He'd hit her with the heavier body of the cat, driving her away from the door and down to the floor. The bullets had hit right where she'd been standing.

"I'm sorry, Mitya," she said in a small voice. "I wasn't thinking. Jewel could have been killed. You and Dymka could have been killed trying to save me. It isn't even logical that I put everyone in danger when I know my father is already dying. He would be furious at me as well if he knew what I'd done. I really am sorry."

He stared down into her upturned face for several heartbeats. She didn't mess around and try to shift blame; she simply admitted her fuckup and apologized. She took his breath away.

"I have to admit, you scared the holy hell out of me, woman. Dymka too."

She gave him a faint smile. "I think had Dymka been in control, and not you, I might not have fared so well."

He touched the smudges on her arm. "I did this."

"I think your leopard helped," she said, and turned away from him to examine her father. "They didn't kill him, Mitya. Why? They could have so easily. Why wouldn't they?"

He looked at her father lying there, his color gray. His eyes sunken with dark circles around them. He looked thin and wasted. He looked ravaged, as if he'd been suffering for a very long time. Any shifter would know the struggle he waged every day with his leopard. They hadn't killed him because they wanted him to suffer. There was a good chance he would lose his battle with his leopard and the cat would kill Ania.

Mitya didn't share his conclusions with Ania. He couldn't. She looked fragile, as if one more blow would be the final straw. He circled her shoulders with his arm and drew her against him. At once she leaned against his strength.

"They were looking for something." He needed to distract her.

Sevastyan returned, handing his cousin a pair of jeans. Mitya immediately pulled them on and then, barefoot, went to Antosha's side. His breathing was shallow. He glanced up and met his cousin's eyes. Sevastyan knew as well as he did that the blow to Antosha's head and the trauma of the break-in were too much for the man to handle.

Ania went around to the other side of the bed and took her father's hand, stroking little caresses over the back of it with her fingers. Mitya cleaned the blood from Antosha's face very gently. The antibiotic cream was smeared over the entire cut and then he bandaged it. Antosha stirred. Moaned.

"I think he's full of pain," Ania said immediately. "I have pain medication the doctors said I could give him if he needed it." But she knew. She totally knew. Her beloved father. She'd taken care of him for the last three years and she would have gladly given him another thirty or forty of care. He was the last of her family. He was the man who had taught her everything and brought laughter and dance into their home.

"Come on, Daddy," she whispered. "Don't do this. You can get stronger. You just need to fight. I'm not ready." She was pleading with her father. He always heard her. "I can't lose any more family. We talked about this."

Her throat closed, felt raw and burned, or maybe that was her heart. She couldn't lose him, her last living relative. "I won't have anyone at all to love me, Dad. You said you wouldn't leave me. You *promised*." Her voice changed, came out a whisper. "You promised me."

Antosha's eyelids fluttered and then suddenly flew open, as if he heard her, but his head was turned toward Mitya. Whatever Mitya saw, he ordered very low and calm, but it was an absolute command: "Ania, leave the room now."

Ania shook her head, holding on to her father's hand, desperate to hold him to her. Her heart hurt, and her stomach knotted. Her lungs were raw from trying to catch her breath. She blinked. Looked up at Mitya, but her mind refused to comprehend what he was saying to her. She shook her head slightly. "Daddy"—her voice was soft, coaxing—"you have to fight back to the surface. Don't let your leopard control you."

"Ania. Leave this room." Mitya was implacable. "I won't tell you again."

"I'm not ready. He isn't done yet, Mitya." There was panic in her voice. "He's just confused after all the commotion. Anyone would be."

Antosha's face contorted. Beneath his skin something alive, something vicious, began to push to break free. The hand Ania was holding suddenly turned in hers, and razor-sharp claws struck at her before Sevastyan could yank her away from the bed. A red streak appeared along her arm, but she didn't cry out. The rake was deep and went from wrist to above the elbow. Blood dripped steadily onto the bed.

"Dad," she whispered. "Please don't do this."

"Get her the fuck out of here now, Sevastyan," Mitya snarled. His voice had gone low, an animalistic growl more than a human voice.

Her pleading gaze clung to Mitya's as Sevastyan circled her waist with one arm and lifted her off her feet. Mitya's eyes had gone fully leopard and he was already ripping off his jeans.

She exploded into fury, angry at everything. At everyone. Mostly at whatever would take her beloved father when he was all she had. She was leopard and her female was strong. She punched Sevastyan and tried to kick him as he dragged her to the door, knowing if she left that room, there would be no chance. No saving her father. No saving herself. She would be forever damned. Forever alone. She fought Sevastyan all the harder, punching, kicking, trying to bite him.

Her father began contorting, writhing on the bed, shoving off covers.

"Get her out of here!" Mitya snapped. "I don't care what you have to do." The words were barely discernible.

Antosha's jaw elongated, teeth filling it. Fur burst through thin skin. Those eyes fixed on Mitya and then shifted to Sevastyan and Ania. Mitya roared a challenge, staring into the crazed leopard's eyes, wanting the animal to feel the threat to him. Clearly, he wasn't taking a chance that the cat would leap toward his cousin and Ania.

The golden cat fought off the covers and leapt from the bed straight at Mitya. Ania screamed. "Dad! No!"

Sevastyan yanked Ania like a rag doll, turning her away as Mitya's powerful leopard met the smaller cat in the air, roaring back his own challenge. Sevastyan was enormously strong, and he wrapped Ania up with his arms, locking down her own arms, holding her in a way to render her feet useless when she tried to kick him. He managed to get her out of the room and kick the door closed behind them.

"Stop it, Ania. You can't save him, and he wouldn't want to harm you." He punctuated each word with a shake of her body as he half dragged, half carried her farther away from her father's room.

She fought harder as a crash signaled the two leopards hitting the floor and rolling around, claws scrambling for domination.

Sevastyan didn't make the mistake of letting her go. He carried her down the hall, stepping over the dead leopard lying in the way, continuing as if the carcass wasn't even there. Behind them, the roar of a leopard nearly shook the house. Immediately a second leopard, its voice a powerful saw, answered the challenge.

"Ania, stop fighting me. Stop fighting the inevitable. You knew your father was going to lose his fight and his leopard would break free. Be thankful Mitya is a strong enough man to face this for you. He gave his word to your father, and he's a man of honor. No matter the cost, he'll carry it out."

Once inside the great room, he set her on her feet. "I'm sorry about your father. I really am, but you've had plenty of time for good-byes. For last words. For all of it. When Mitya comes out of that room, he's going to think you won't even look at him because he did what your father asked."

She pushed off his chest and stumbled away from him to the fireplace. Resting one hand on the mantel, she put her head down and drew in great gulps of air, fighting for control. Deep inside, Jewel stretched. Became aware of her raging anguish, the sorrow so deep she couldn't breathe. At once, because Ania was so distraught, she pushed for the surface to protect her. Rising, she pressed outward, needing to shift in order to protect Ania.

Sevastyan could see fur moving beneath the surface of the skin, forcing it to rise in waves going through Ania's body. He stepped back, his hands going to his shirt. Mitya would kill him if Ania's leopard emerged, especially if she was in any way amorous, which she would be if she managed to rise to the surface and take control of Ania's form.

"Fight her off, Ania," he snapped. "Don't make this harder for Mitya."

She lifted her head to stare at him. He could see the eyes of her leopard staring back at him. She had peculiarly colored eyes, almost a deep, vibrant violet. He'd never seen a leopard with eyes that color. Blood dripped steadily from her arm, running down her wrist and hand to fall on the floor. Both could hear the drops, like the ominous ticks of a clock.

The sound of the leopards fighting in the other room became louder. There was a roar, abruptly cut off, and then complete silence. It settled over the house like a shroud. Ania screamed out a violent protest, the sound so raw, bursting from her soul, tearing through her throat, shredding her.

She turned and with one swipe took everything from the mantel, every picture of her family that she'd so lovingly placed in crystal frames. They fell to the floor and shattered, the way her entire family had been destroyed in just three short years. A lifetime of dreams, of hard work, of love and laughter, gone.

"Ania," Sevastyan said, his voice gentle. He reached a hand toward her.

He couldn't touch her. He couldn't say anything to her or she would shatter like the glass. Like her family. She ran up the stairs, breathing so hard her lungs burned. She had no idea if Sevastyan followed her or not, the roaring in her ears was too loud.

She slammed the door to her bedroom, turned the dead bolt and leaned her head down to keep from fainting. Heat banded across her eyes. A million memories flooded her of her father lifting her into the air, swinging her around. Her mother laughing and telling him to be careful while she shrieked for him to go higher and faster.

She ran across the room and ripped the covers from her bed in an effort to destroy the combined scents of Mitya and her. Her knuckles burned, a terrible ache, and then heavy claws ripped through blanket and sheets. She wanted to destroy his things, every bit of evidence that Mitya existed, the way he'd destroyed the last of her family.

She had nothing. *Nothing.* There was nothing left of the Dover family. And she'd been the one to bring about their final destruction. She ran into the bathroom, breathing hard, staring at herself in the mirror. "Traitor," she hissed.

She couldn't stand that woman, the one who had brought the Amurovs into their lives. For what? Not love. Not family. Sex. He wanted her for his leopard. She'd handed herself to him on a silver platter. It was possible the Amurov crime family had wanted her family dead. He'd admitted that once given sons, they killed their women. Still, what had she done?

"What did you do?" she shrieked at her image. "You stupid fucking bitch." She hurled bottles of makeup, cleanser, moisturizer, every beauty product she had at the mirror, shattering it. Destroying it.

This was her fault. She'd contributed by allowing anyone close to her. She'd sold her father and her family name for sex. "Whore." She threw everything she had, including drawers, at that image. She hurt so badly she couldn't think. Physically, mentally, emotionally, she was in agony. She had to destroy everything. It was the only way to stay on her feet, to keep fighting. Anguish was so strong, gripping her, crushing her until she was afraid there would be nothing left. She wanted nothing left. She couldn't face what she'd done.

She spun around when she heard the door rattle. Her lungs burned for air. She looked around frantically, knowing nothing could stop him. Nothing would stop him. Mitya Amurov was omnipotent. Invincible.

"*Kotyonok*, open the door."

There was no containing the anguish. No way to hold herself together. She ran from the master bath, across the carpeted bedroom, for the bank of windows. She went for the one on the left side of the balcony, throwing her arms up to protect herself at the last minute. She crashed through the glass just as the door burst open.

Ania didn't feel the cuts along her arms and hands because the terrible agony inside her refused to let up. They

were in pursuit of her now, the last of her family. The only
person left who could exact revenge. She *had* to get away.
Dimly she heard yelling. Orders. She couldn't make
out the words. She only knew she had to escape. Run. Run
so fast she wouldn't have to know what he was going to
tell her.

Her father was dead. Dead. Dead. She was alone in the
world and there was no one to blame but herself. She
screamed again, the sound bursting from inside her like a
terrible storm raging. She climbed onto the railing and
leapt, not even hesitating.

Jewel was close to the surface, pushing to take over,
trying desperately to help her, but the fury and distress in
the leopard only added to the chaos and agony in Ania's
mind. She'd never used her leopard before, not like this,
leaping from a second-story balcony. She landed on the
roof of the porch, slid, got her feet under her and ran to the
edge. No one was below her and she jumped a second
time, landing on the ground in a crouch.

A leopard called behind her. This was no challenge
but a command, and the adrenaline in her veins increased
tenfold. She ran. She had always been a fast runner, but
now she called up Jewel, and she ran like the wind. The
cool air slapped her face, but it couldn't remove the stain
of guilt. Or the rage. He hadn't let her try to stop her father
from shifting.

She screamed again, lifting her face to the dark, rolling
clouds, allowing Jewel to take charge while she cried.
While the tears blurred her vision. He'd always stopped
when she called to him. Always. She might have found the
right doctor to save him. She'd contacted so many. She
hadn't cared whether they were the doctors Antosha had
approved. He was all she had left. He'd fought to live. He
wanted to live. He'd told her so a million times.

She ran as if the devil was behind her, heading across

the rolling grades, away from the Amurov land. Her closest neighbor was miles away, but she knew her property.
She'd grown up there and she knew every acre. She knew
the trees and brush. She had a good chance of escaping.

As she ran, she tried to clear her head. She always had
a plan. She always thought clearly. She couldn't seem to
slow her brain. It was looping through her head, a white
noise that wouldn't stop. Just ahead of her, a man stepped
out of the brush. He wore only a loose pair of jeans. She
skidded to a halt, recognizing him instantly. Sevastyan.

He held up his hand. "Take a breath, Ania. Everything
is going to be all right." His tone was soothing. He was
deliberately trying to calm her.

"Stay away from me!" she cautioned, yelling. Her throat
hurt.

She turned away from him, ran a few feet and had to
stop as Vikenti stepped out of the tree line, still zipping
his jeans. There was sweat on his body. She felt drops running down her skin to pool in the valley between her
breasts. Her arms were wet. Slick. She glanced down at
her arms. In the dark of the night, with only a pale bit of
moon desperately trying to come out from behind the
clouds, her arms looked shiny, almost black.

Vikenti did the same thing Sevastyan had done. Holding his hand palm out, he stepped toward her, cutting her
off from that direction. "Sweetheart, you know me. Take
a breath. Your leopard is out of control and only you can
get her to stop."

Her vision was blurred, and she didn't know if it was
the weird way she was seeing, in bands of color that wa-
vered, or the liquid in her eyes she couldn't quite get rid
of. Her body hurt. Her lungs. Mostly her arms.

She shook her head and eyed the two men warily. Sevastyan was walking toward her with slow, unhurried steps.
Vikenti did the same.

"Don't come any closer. Stay away from me." She didn't recognize her own voice. It was low, husky. She wanted to rake at them, scream, strike back.

Ania whirled around and ran in the opposite direction, running toward the Amurov estate. It was the only way open to her if she wasn't going back to the house and disaster. She would have to face the truth, and she couldn't. Not when chaos, rage and guilt ruled her mind. She had no plan. No idea what she was doing. Nothing made sense.

"Ania, stop." Just ahead, Zinoviy was hopping around, dragging on his jeans for her modesty, and coming toward her. Slowly. He gave her a tentative smile. "Honey, I know you're upset. You have every right to be . . ."

"No." She shook her head violently. He couldn't say it out loud. He just couldn't. "Get away. All of you go away."

Kiriil and Matvei emerged from either side, each holding up a hand and trying to murmur soothing nonsense to her, but she couldn't hear what they were saying. The roaring in her ears was too loud.

"Ania." She heard that. So soft. How had she heard that low, caressing voice when she didn't hear anyone else? She closed her eyes. He was right behind her. They'd been distracting her all along, corralling her in while Mitya came up behind her.

She whirled to face him, almost choking. Her throat closed. Her skull was far too tight. Her teeth hurt and her clothes were so painful on her skin, she needed to pull them off. She whirled around to see Sevastyan close. Too close. Vikenti and Zinoviy were closing in on her on one side. Kiriil and Matvei on the other.

"Look at me, baby. Only at me," Mitya said softly.

She swung back to stare at him, but her vision was so messed up she couldn't see him. "I can't be here."

"I know. You don't have to be. Miron has the car waiting. We'll go home."

"I don't have a home. There's no one." She swung

around again. "I need you all to leave. Go away. I can figure this out." She was growing desperate. The only way out was to fight. She had to fight.

Jewel pushed close. She felt her rising. Felt her wanting to help. To take over.

"Mitya, she's going to shift," Sevastyan warned.

Mitya took her from behind, wrapping his arms tightly around her and lifting her off her feet. She exploded into action, throwing her head back, driving her heels into his shins.

"Get off me!" she yelled. "I mean it, get off me!"

"It's all right, Ania. You're safe. Just breathe with me."

"I want you to go. This is my property. Get off me now!" She fought with everything she had, punching at him, kicking, trying to turn so she could use her knee. She could hear someone screaming, and it was only the fact that her throat hurt that made her realize it was her.

Twice, Jewel attempted to shift, but Mitya refused to loosen his grip. The second time, there was the slide of fur and teeth sank into her shoulder in a holding bite. It hurt. Everything hurt. She still fought him, struggling so hard she nearly got loose. He caught her arm, but it was slick with blood and he slid off. She whipped around, raking across his chest.

Sevastyan came up behind her before she could do much damage, catching her around the waist and jerking her away from Mitya when she would have kicked him. Before she could do any damage to him, Mitya had her again, locking her to him.

"Ania, *kotyonok*, calm down. Breathe for me. Jewel's too close and she's scared. You have to take control."

"Fuck you, Mitya," she snarled. "She wouldn't be afraid if you weren't scaring her. Get away from me." Her voice came out more of a growl than human.

He caught both wrists, pinned them with one large hand and locked his arm around her back, forcing her tightly against him, trapping her arms and hands between them.

"Miron's almost here with the car," Sevastyan reported.

She could see lights through her blurred vision and they hurt her eyes. She forced air through her lungs. "I could have stopped him." She whispered it, her face pressed tightly against Mitya's chest, the fight draining out of her. "You should have given me the chance."

He stroked a caress down the back of her hair. "He was done, baby. He attacked you."

"He attacked me before and I was able to get him to stop."

"He was done."

She closed her eyes and let tears leak out. There was no way to stop them and she didn't try. She felt defeated. Jewel subsided, calming under the close proximity of someone in such control, the way Mitya was. He commanded everything around them, including her and her leopard. He made the decisions and she was expected to abide by them.

"Would you take me to a hotel, please?" She didn't open her eyes or look at his face. She couldn't. She could hardly bear that his skin was touching hers.

"I'm taking you home, baby," Mitya said. His voice said it all. Implacable. Commanding.

She was too tired to fight. She didn't care where he took her, because in the end, did it matter?

8

"YOU should have let me do the job," Sevastyan said. He paced across Mitya's great room. "She's had too many blows and that little leopard of hers has no idea what it's doing. Damn it, Mitya. This isn't over. I've got someone over at her estate waiting for the doc. We need a legit death certificate and he has to be cremated tonight."

Mitya sighed. "There's the matter of the leopard she killed in the hallway. Did we get an identity on him?"

Sevastyan shook his head. "No such luck. He was in leopard form. Looked as if he came from Panama. Hard to tell, Mitya. It just makes no sense. He definitely wasn't from around here. I took pictures and we can make inquiries, but he's not one of ours."

Mitya sat in front of the fireplace, not even bothering to clean the blood from his chest where Jewel had raked claws across him and torn his flesh. Ania was down the hall, in the master bedroom. She had steadfastly refused his help when he tried to take care of her arm. He'd done it anyway, because he was bigger and stronger, and in the end, brute force had won out, although he wasn't calling it a win.

He shoved both hands through his hair. "What about the other one, how did he get away?"

"We were thin. Very thin tonight. Kiriil and Matvei were sent to the other side of the house and the bastard had a clear path out of here. We all have his scent if we come across him."

"That hasn't been much of a help so far." Mitya was distracted and trying to keep his head in the game. Ania was all that seemed to matter to him at the moment. He wasn't certain how to repair the damage done. Her breakdown was harsh and real. He didn't know whether to give her the space she said she needed or force her to accept his comfort.

"Relationships are difficult, Sevastyan, when we have no idea how to have one."

"Are you absolutely certain she's Dymka's mate?" Sevastyan demanded. "Or yours? She doesn't seem in the least compatible. You're . . ." He trailed off, clearly searching for the right words. "There's no compromise in you. No give at all. You expect her to just follow your lead without explanation."

"That's called trust, Sevastyan." He answered his cousin absently, his mind already working the problem that he'd created by insisting he carry out his promise to her father. The man deserved to die with honor. He'd made certain there'd been as little pain as possible to the leopard when he'd delivered the killing bite. He wasn't sorry he'd done what he believed to be right. He was upset that he hadn't prepared Ania better for the outcome.

"Mitya." Sevastyan stood in front of him. "For once in your life, listen to what I have to say. Trust is something that is gained over time. Not because you take her to bed.

She's been living with a dark secret for a long time. She's angry and hurt and scared. This thing has now escalated way out of control."

Mitya shoved both hands through his hair again, making it wild and as out of control as he felt. He had his own blood on him. He had her blood on him. He had the blood of Antosha's leopard on him as well as Dymka's. He was a mess, and yet he couldn't move.

"What I did was right."

Sevastyan threw his hands into the air in surrender. "Yes, Mitya, what you did was the right thing. Absolutely. It was honorable. Sometimes, you can't do the right thing. For her, maybe it would have been better to turn that particular job over to me."

Mitya shook his head. "My father never chose the right way one single time. Not one, Sevastyan. I'm not ever going to be like him. We'll choose honor every time."

"At what cost? She's not going to accept you."

"That's impossible. We're a bonded pair. Dymka says Jewel is close. Just a little confused right now."

"What are you going to do when Jewel begins to emerge and your woman refuses you? What then, Mitya?"

"It won't happen."

"It's going to happen. You weren't looking at her face, I was. She's going to go the moment she thinks she can."

Mitya was done talking about it because the fact was, Ania was his mate. He knew she wanted him, she had just stepped off their path for a moment, and rightfully so. It all made perfect sense to him. Sevastyan could say they weren't compatible all he wanted, but he knew better. She just needed a little more time with him. Jewel had to have patience. A mating leopard would drive them beyond anything Ania could conceive. There was no way he was letting her out of his sight when she was so close to emerging.

"I've called for Drake to come. He and Joshua and a

couple of others will be flying out immediately. The memorial service has to be planned as well. The number one problem, aside from my beautiful Ania, is what happened tonight at her home. She should have been protected at all times." He couldn't imagine what would have happened had he not been there.

His eyes met his cousin's, and Sevastyan saw something there that made him wince. Mitya was a product of his father's twisted, maniacal upbringing. The man had wanted to bring the killer out in his son's leopard, teach him to rage and hate, to be cruel, so he would pass those traits on to his human counterpart. Lazar had managed to do that from the time Mitya was very young.

Mitya's leopard was a straight-up killer, and what did that make the man? It was there in his eyes. He couldn't altogether blame Ania for being leery of him. Or Jewel his leopard. Jewel even more than Ania had to be confused. She could read Dymka every time she rose, and she clearly read him correctly—and she feared him as much as she was enamored with him. At the moment that was what was driving Ania to leave him.

"Ania's father should have been protected in his own home. He might have been able to last a few more days, or weeks, long enough to see me put a ring on his daughter's finger, but instead, he had enemies come into his room and smash his things after bashing him with the butt of a gun. Tell me how that happened, Sevastyan."

"Drake sent us the man from Borneo. Amory Binder worked for him there, worked for his crew rescuing kidnap victims or delivering ransom. I liked the kid. In fact, I worried a little about him. I called for a check when I realized we'd been infiltrated, and he was the only one not to answer. I thought they'd killed him and fully expected to find a body. He knew the combination to shut down the alarm on the house. He had to have used it."

Mitya couldn't contain the adrenaline rushing through

his veins. He leapt up and began to pace, feeling his leopard close. The thought of a traitor that close to his woman and her father, without him knowing, was abhorrent to him. He needed action. He needed to find Amory Binder and challenge him. His leopard wanted out. Demanded to come out. He would hunt the bastard, track him and kill him. Mitya was inclined to let him.

"He let them in. I want to go back to the house, Sevastyan."

Sevastyan opened his mouth to protest, but then nodded. "They wanted something in that house. They assumed it was in Antosha's room, so they took the chance and looked for it there. By the look of it, it either wasn't there or we caught them too soon. In any case, we've vacated the house. We reset the alarm with a different code since Amory knew the old one."

Mitya was already stripping, his muscles rippling with power, with the need to hunt. He rolled his jeans, just as Sevastyan was doing. "Give the orders to surround this house. Keep her protected, Sevastyan."

"I'm going with you." When Mitya started to protest, Sevastyan shook his head and continued shoving his jeans into the small pack he secured around his neck. "Don't bother with the orders, fire me, I don't give a fuck, but I'm going with you."

Mitya didn't fire his cousin, what was the use? In any case, Sevastyan was a vicious fighter. He'd been raised much the same way as Mitya, and his leopard was experienced and brutal in a fight. "Give the order to protect her and let's go."

Sevastyan did as Mitya said but added his own orders. He was taking no chances with Mitya's protection. Vikenti and Zinoviy were already at the Dover estate cleaning up. They were from his lair, two men he counted on when he needed them. He trusted them with Mitya's life, and that was saying the most he could about them. He left orders for Kiriil and Matvei to handle Ania's security and then turned to Mitya, nodding that he was ready.

The two men went out the front door straight into the brush, shifting as they did so. It wasn't long before they were running full out toward the neighboring estate. They didn't want to take a car because the headlights might be seen. Their house was lit up, just as their yard was, but the Dover estate was dark and appeared deserted.

Ordinarily, leopards could run fast for short distances, but they were shifters, not wholly leopard or wholly human. They were conditioned to run for miles if necessary, and both men kept themselves in top shape. They were able to cut across the distance between the two estates, shortening the way considerably because the road had to curve around the properties. As they approached, they slowed and kept downwind, creeping up carefully onto the estate.

Vikenti and Zinoviy joined them just outside the house. "Thought we saw something out this way," Vikenti reported softly to Sevastyan. "We were just circling the house to look."

Both shifted back into their leopards and the four continued around from the southern side to the front. Mitya nudged Sevastyan and all four stopped as they came up on the landscaping around the front entrance. Two men were at the locked front door, one bending down as he worked on the lock. Amory and a stranger. Mitya's gut settled. He had him now.

Dymka lifted his head and sniffed the air, his whiskers warning him of everything and everyone close. Two more men were moving up on either side of the house. Another appeared to be around the back. Dymka turned his head, his eyes glowing in the dark, but it was Mitya giving the orders. He looked to Vikenti. Vikenti's leopard immediately responded, moving around the house to creep stealthily on the shifter assigned to guard the other side just in case. He dispatched the man before he even realized he wasn't alone and then made his way back around.

Sevastyan and Zinoviy took out the two guards on the sides of the house, almost right in plain sight of Amory and his partner. Amory suddenly lifted his head, looking right and left. He straightened slowly and said something to his partner, who whipped his head around and then called out to the men already dead in the yard.

Amory pulled a gun. "I know you're out there. Just back off and let us get what we need."

Dymka crawled forward, inch by slow inch, gaining ground, staying to cover. His hate-filled eyes remained on the traitor. This was the man who had all but killed Antosha and destroyed his relationship with Jewel and Ania. He crawled on his belly, using the freeze-frame stalk of the leopard, one that could be excruciatingly slow, but kept the animal, although he was large, from being seen.

"Mitya. Sevastyan. I know you're out there." Amory turned first right and then left, examining the flowers and leafy plants placed artistically around the front of the house. "Let's talk about this."

His partner had pulled his weapon as well and was doing the same as Amory. Once, he shifted just his upper body, utilizing his leopard to try to find where the enemy was. "They're out there, Amory," he declared, his voice tight.

"Settle down, Kris," Amory advised. "Just keep your back to the house and your weapon ready." He raised his voice. "The old man took something from us. Something important. We just want it back."

Mitya could care less what was taken. He wanted Amory dead. Dymka wanted to tear him and his leopard from limb to limb. Neither he nor Sevastyan made the mistake of answering. That would allow Amory to zero in on their positions immediately. Vikenti, however, moved back into deeper cover, and he had no problem centering attention on himself.

"Antosha assured us he didn't take anything." Vikenti had the ability to throw his voice from any direction and he did so, turning Amory and Kris toward the sound, which was quite a distance from where he actually was.

Kris lifted his weapon, but Amory calmly put his hand on it and lowered it. "The old man, Antosha's father, took it. We'll go in quietly and get it back. I'm sorry about Antosha. He was a decent sort, but he was dying anyway. No one wants to hurt Ania."

Mitya used Amory's inattention to creep within several feet of him. So close. Dymka had the traitor's smell in his nostrils. He pulled his lips back several times, exposing his teeth, his body nearly shaking with the need to kill.

"You killed Antosha, Amory." Vikenti made it a statement, careful to keep his voice a distance from where he was. "You're responsible for his death."

Kris had zeroed in on the exact bush where he thought Vikenti hid. He even took a step out from the safety of the long porch. Again, Amory restrained him with a hand to his arm and a shake of his head. Amory looked around carefully. The trouble was, he was focusing several feet out, expecting the main attack to come from that distance, not two feet in front of him.

"He should have been dead three years ago," Amory continued.

"You did that?"

"I was part of it. We needed to get into the house."

Dymka exploded into action, wholly fixated on Amory. Beside him, Sevastyan was on Kris, knocking the weapon from his hand, just as Mitya was doing with Amory. Dymka's teeth closed over Amory's arm and bit down. Amory screamed, but he was already shifting, fast, just as he'd been taught. The enemy had infiltrated Drake's organization and he'd been given the best training for his leopard, shifting under the worst circumstances.

He used his claws to rake Dymka's belly, desperate to get the big cat off him. The two tumbled over each other, rolling, the bites vicious, trying to find a way past the loose skin to get to vulnerable organs.

Sevastyan knew Mitya, and knew if he wanted answers, he would have to keep Kris alive if at all possible, because Dymka was going to kill Amory and his cat. Mitya didn't care one way or the other what the item was that was taken from Amory and whomever he worked with. He cared that this man had destroyed Ania's fragile faith in him. That this man had killed her father.

Dymka bit down hard on the front leg he'd already crunched nearly through the bone. This time, he heard a satisfactory snap and Amory's leopard screamed in pain. Dymka backed away. As the other leopard made a supreme effort to get to his three good legs, Dymka rushed him, going not for the throat but for the vulnerable other front leg. He came in from the side, raking with claws to open him up, but really to distract him from the true goal, that other leg.

At the last moment, Dymka looked as if he was sliding on past, but he rolled and came up under the other cat, fastening his teeth around the leg and biting down hard and then using his enormous strength as he rolled out from the cat, still holding its leg. The sound was audible as the leg broke, and Amory screamed.

Dymka came to his feet, circling the cat as it tried to spin to face him. Dymka rushed the leopard, over and over, slashing, tearing through the fur to reach skin and bone. Opening the belly. The heaving sides. Raking the throat. He came in from behind, attacking the back leg, devastating the leopard as he took out a third leg, breaking it the way he had the first two.

Amory shifted, desperate to spare his leopard. Better

to have Dymka kill him. The leopard rushed the man who lay on the ground with two broken arms and one broken leg, bleeding from numerous deep wounds. The leopard attacked his belly, ripping him open, mauling him, dragging him across the ground, but still not delivering the suffocating bite that would kill him.

Sevastyan had easily defeated Kris's leopard, the fight, in his opinion, so unfair he'd easily been able to control his leopard. The animal hadn't gone into a killing frenzy. He watched, as did Kris, as Dymka destroyed Amory.

"Why doesn't he finish him?" Kris asked, his voice twisted with emotion.

"Shut the fuck up," Sevastyan snapped. "You both caused this. You killed her family. Her entire family."

"The old man stole from us. *Stole*. We needed him to do a simple delivery, but instead, he kept it. He signed a contract. It was a business deal, pure and simple." Kris was breathing hard and the truth exploded out of him. In the short time his leopard had been fighting Sevastyan's he had sustained major injuries, and he'd surrendered immediately.

Mitya wasn't giving Amory the option of surrendering. Dymka kept at him, ripping through skin and bones, tearing at the body without killing him. Making him suffer.

"Mitya." Sevastyan kept his voice calm. Soothing. No judgment. "Pull back. You have to stop Dymka before it's too late."

Dymka raised his head and eyed Kris, as if he would change his direction of attack. Kris read the absolute hatred and cruelty in the cat's eyes. He shrank back, his arms going around his middle to protect that vulnerable part of him.

"Don't let him get me."

"You might want to tell us what the package was and why it was so damned important."

Kris went white. "I'm a dead man if I tell you."

Dymka abandoned Amory's dying body and turned completely toward Kris, focusing his entire attention on the man. He took three steps toward him and then whirled around and charged Amory again, roaring with rage, so loud the sound had to be heard all over the hills. Kris shuddered visibly as Dymka delivered the suffocating bite to Amory's throat, ripped at his belly with deadly claws and then once more turned slowly toward Kris.

"It's a book. Just a notebook. Evidence of our true enemies. That's all it is. A little notebook." The last was said with a whine.

"Who would our true enemies be, Kris?" Sevastyan asked softly.

"Donovan. Bannaconni," he burst out.

Sevastyan shook his head. "Everyone knows that."

"They have bosses on the inside working with them. The book has proof," Kris wailed. He wiped sweat from his face. "I'm telling the truth. That's all I know. Amory was put in place to get inside. To work with Donovan and get evidence at Bannaconni's. When the book was taken, we couldn't go in after it because Antosha was still alive and no one knew what condition he was in. It seemed business as usual."

Kris was giving up information he clearly didn't want to give, but he was terrified of Dymka. Shots rang out. Several bullets hit the side of the house. Three hit Kris, one between the eyes and two in the throat.

Dymka and Sevastyan both moved quickly, leaping away from the dead man and his partner. Sevastyan rolled as fast as he could toward the big leopard in hope of somehow protecting him. Mitya leapt toward Sevastyan, his large body covering his cousin's. Two more bullets hit Dymka as the leopard lay over Sevastyan.

Mitya immediately shifted, not wanting his leopard to suffer. The moment he did, he pushed the blazing heat of pain away, gripped his cousin and scuttled for the brush.

A bullet parted his hair and nearly sliced his head open. On the heels of that reverberation came another, this time the sound coming from a different direction, followed by something heavy falling from the branches of a tree. He could hear the cracking of small branches as it fell.

He lay there for a long moment and then rolled over to stare up at the dark sky. "Getting too old for this shit, Sevastyan," he announced.

"Who was on our side?" his cousin queried. "It couldn't have been Vikenti or Zinoviy."

Mitya turned his head to meet Sevastyan's eyes. "I have no fucking idea." He didn't.

"You hit?"

"Yeah, a couple of times. Not bad. Hurts like a bitch, though."

"Good. You deserve it. What the hell were you thinking? I'm head of security. If Vikenti and Zinoviy saw you protecting me, I'll be the laughingstock of my security team as well as everyone else's."

Mitya sent him a faint grin. "I told you not to take the position. Don't have too many people in this world that matter to me. You do."

Sevastyan shook his head and turned his face up to the sky in order to hide his expression. "Feel like moving?"

"Not on your life. Tell Vikenti to get the cleaners here again and get rid of this mess. Hope no one heard those shots and called the cops. Fortunately, we live far enough out that we don't have too many neighbors."

"They were looking for a fucking notebook."

"I heard."

"You think we're in that book?" Sevastyan turned his head back to look at his cousin.

"There's a good chance we all are. We're working for Donovan to clean this mess up. We have the cops after us, our women after us and now we're going to have every crime boss from here to hell and back after us," Mitya said. "I think staying right here on the ground is the best place for us. In fact, when the cleaners come, let's pretend to be dead and get a ride out of here."

Sevastyan laughed. "I do need some sleep. Every part of my body hurts like hell."

"Don't be a whiner. I'm shot, and you don't hear me whining."

"You losing a lot of blood?"

"How should I know?" Mitya tentatively brushed his hand down along his ribs and winced when he found the wound. His fingers found a sticky mess. "It isn't bad. Got two more, but they didn't really do more than sting me."

Sevastyan made a sound of disbelief. "We gotta get up, Mitya."

"You go right ahead," Mitya said. "Stand all you want."

The wind shifted just a bit and brought with it Vikenti's scent and something else, something more elusive but familiar. Mitya sat up fast, his eyes narrowing. "I thought you put the entire security team on Ania," he snapped. "Did you disobey a direct order?"

"Only the one where you didn't want me with you." Sevastyan sat up as well, looking around. "Is that her?"

"I'd know her scent anywhere." Mitya would. There was something beautiful about the way she smelled. Soft. Like the whisper of the wind touching his face. A natural scent. She didn't use fragrances, yet she smelled as if she did. "She's here, which means she slipped out right under the noses of your security people." It was an accusation.

"They'll hear about it," Sevastyan promised. "Do you think she plans on shooting us?"

"I wouldn't be surprised," Mitya answered. His woman. She probably had the fucking sniper rifle pointed at his heart that very moment. He softened his voice. "Think of the sex you'll be missing, *kotyonok*."

"That's it?" Sevastyan wasn't impressed. "That's all you've got? You didn't even say 'good sex,' or 'great sex.'

When you're negotiating for your life, you pull out all the stops."

"I'm shot, damn it. It isn't easy to think when you're in excruciating pain."

"Now it's excruciating." Sevastyan sounded sarcastic. "Which is it?"

"Would you mind getting dressed, Sevastyan?" Ania's voice came out of the darkness. "I'm not all that comfortable with staring at your naked body."

"Because I have a superior body," Sevastyan noted to his cousin. "She can't exactly stay true to you when she's always comparing your body to mine." He searched the brush, trees and landscaping for Ania but couldn't see her.

"She's extraordinary," Mitya said, meaning it. "Jewel hasn't emerged, but she still managed to slip past the guards and help out."

"I didn't just help out," Ania said. "I saved your asses." She strode out from behind them, the rifle pointed down, although she held it as if she knew what she was doing. She'd already demonstrated that she did know how to use it. Expertly.

"You want to tell us what you're doing here?" Mitya asked.

She tossed a first aid kit onto the ground beside him, laid the rifle close to his hand and crouched down to run her hands over his body. "I was listening to the two of you go at each other earlier and it occurred to me you weren't out to kill me, in spite of Jewel's worries. Your leopard is an asshole, Mitya. He should be reassuring her, not trying to dominate her."

A groan escaped when her hand slid over the gash in his side. She let up immediately and dug her flashlight into the ground beside him, spotlighting where the bullet had clipped him. He didn't bother to look. He'd experienced enough wounds to know it wasn't nearly as bad as it felt.

"Ania, you were safe with a security team around you. Why in the world would you come after us?"

"I'm not the stay-at-home type, Mitya. You may think we're compatible, but I wasn't raised to stay in the kitchen, and it isn't my dream. I heard what you both had to say and thought a lot about it. You took on a very difficult task when most wouldn't have."

She looked beautiful kneeling there in the dirt beside him, her gaze sliding away from his as she absolved him of guilt. His heart beat overtime. The knots in his gut began to unravel.

"Not that I believe Sevastyan when he says he wouldn't have done it. You have honor, and my father saw that in you and trusted you. I should have remembered that he was always a great judge of character. I'm very sorry for my outburst. I think I had a breakdown or something, but it wasn't right that I blamed either of you." Her gaze dropped from Mitya's to touch on Sevastyan. "I hope I didn't hurt you."

"No one is going to blame you for what you said or did when your father was attacked and then was dying," Mitya said immediately, sending his cousin a quick look.

He didn't need to. Sevastyan had his back to Ania, zipping up his jeans. "Little sister, I only wish I could have said or done something to help you. I'm not good yet with relationships, but I'm trying to learn."

Her hands were on Mitya, gentle as she cleaned his wounds, but she still wasn't really looking at him, and he needed her to. There was no doubt that she was emotionally fragile at the moment and, like Sevastyan, he didn't have a clue about real relationships, but he wanted to learn. For her.

He couldn't help putting his hand in her hair, tangling his fingers in the silky strands. "I'm so sorry, Ania. Your father was a good man."

She nodded. "Yes, he was." She didn't pull away from him, and he took that as another good sign. Just the fact that she'd saved them from the sniper and hadn't shot them herself, he figured they were lucky.

"Was it painless?"

There was a choking sound, and Mitya threw a helpless look at Sevastyan. He was leery of talking about Antosha's death when she'd just had a very emotional breakdown.

"Quick and painless, *kotyonok*. He deserved an honorable death and he got it. I made certain of that. His leopard was treated with all due respect."

"Thank you." She didn't look up but spent a lot of time washing the wound.

"How the hell did you follow us without us knowing?" Sevastyan demanded, changing the subject. "You didn't shift." He swung around to face her, his hands on his hips.

She shrugged. "I climbed down from the roof, stole a car—"

"Ania." Mitya's heart jumped. "You could have been taken or killed."

She rolled her eyes as she cleaned the wound and took a good look to make certain the bullet had just shaved off a great deal of skin and muscle but hit nothing vital. "Like anyone could keep up with me if they chased me. I took a little-known road that isn't paved and is barely there, that I've been using since I was a kid, and came around the back of the house."

"That was dangerous," Mitya said, still looking up at the sky. Little beads of sweat dotted his body, but he didn't move away from her hands as she worked, or make another sound of distress, although he wanted to, not because of the wound but because she terrified him with her courage.

"Not really. I knew you'd send someone to take out whoever was the guard in the back. Once I found him, I just went up to the roof and waited. If you didn't need me, I'd slip back into your house. My father taught me a lot about tactics and he said always have a backup. It just seemed like if they did that, and you were questioning a prisoner, they could have someone ready to kill them and you."

"I want to strangle you with my bare hands," Mitya announced.

"I want to kiss her," Sevastyan said. "Thanks, Ania, you did save our lives."

"She did," Mitya agreed, "but Vikenti or Zinoviy would have pulled the bastard out of the tree and killed him. Or they would have mistaken Ania for the shooter and killed her."

"I was never in danger," she corrected. "I was on the roof of the house shooting over you. He was in a tree facing the house, shooting at you. I think Vik and Zen are experienced enough not to make a mistake like that." She applied antibiotic ointment and then covered the area with gauze.

"You're going to be a major pain in my ass, Ania," Mitya said. Sevastyan had the right idea, keep the line of conversation away from all the emotion and back to something they were familiar with. She could just answer him without thinking, or even feeling if need be. "You have no idea what I want to do to you right now."

"I can guess." She shone her light over his body, inch by inch, searching for any other injuries. "Clearly you want to strangle me with your bare hands. Because you're such a kinky pervert, I imagine you'd like to put me over your knee and spank my booty."

"There's that," he agreed, "and since I can't strangle you . . ."

She gasped and leaned forward when she saw his leg. "You are a major pain in *my* ass. This is far worse than the one in your side and you knew it all along."

"Not yet I'm not a pain in your ass, but I'm going to

be," he promised. He closed his eyes. "Right now, I'm just going to rest a little bit."

"Sevastyan, have Vikenti bring the car. Call the doc, tell him to go to your place before here. Tell him Mitya is losing a lot of blood and might need a transfusion."

Mitya smiled at her bossy tone. His woman. She didn't think she was compatible, but she could take what they did. She'd been raised with one foot in their world. Her grandfather and father ran with the lions. They were certain to get muck all over them.

"Your grandfather kept a notebook that had information that could hurt a lot of good people," Mitya said.

"That would be the reason he didn't complete the drop. He wouldn't have wanted to be responsible for that. Especially if he knew or liked them."

She was probing the wound in his thigh. It had bled a lot, but he'd had bad, and this wasn't that bad. More like annoying. It hurt, but he'd had worse.

"It's still in there, Mitya," she said.

"Well, don't dig around for it," he advised. "Did you ever hear about a notebook?"

"No. If he told my father, the information was never passed down to me. My father would have told me. He probably would have told you. We need the car."

Mitya opened his eyes immediately. "*Kotyonok.*" He whispered the endearment. "I'm going to be fine. I'll live long enough to pull you over my lap and punish you for all your indiscretions."

He wanted to make her laugh, but she didn't. She looked scared. Her gaze shifted from him to Sevastyan, looking for reassurance.

"He's the devil," Sevastyan said. "You can't kill the devil, little sister."

"In the spirit of full disclosure, I feel I should state I have exceptional hearing. Lying up on the roof, the wind blowing toward me, I could hear every word you all said."

Mitya looked at his cousin and shook his head slightly. He didn't want Ania to know about their double life. They were already in danger from Lazar. That threat was a much bigger one, or at least it had been until Amory and Kris had come after a piece of evidence that could turn every crime lord against them. Ania might or might not have heard, but he didn't want her brought any further into danger. Hopefully everyone would think she was a beautiful piece of eye candy on his arm, one that didn't have a brain in her head. She'd run her father's business for the last three years, but she was selling it. Maybe . . .

"Mitya." Her voice was very soft.

He turned his head with a bit of an effort and looked right at her. Looking at her hurt, especially now that her eyes had gone a strange amethyst. Gorgeous. Such a deep purple, yet a hint of crystalline. He knew her leopard had to be beautiful. The little monster, wreaking havoc on all of them, but especially Ania.

"If I could get my hands all the way around your throat, I would strangle you with them. And if you fall asleep, I'm finding cuffs and you'll be immobile while I spank your booty and see how you like it."

Sevastyan turned away, coughing, as the car came up the drive.

She glared at him. "I have cameras everywhere and there's bound to be a video of Mitya covering your body with his, and just so you know, Mr. Security Expert, the next time I want to go somewhere and your hotshot boss says I can't go, I'll be playing that video unless you play ball with me."

"For God's sake, Mitya. Who is this woman?" Sevastyan wiped his face, smearing blood and dirt with his hand. "I think I was wrong about her not being compatible. She's the devil's bride."

Mitya shrugged his wide shoulders. Ania was leaning over him, wiping at the laceration bleeding profusely on his head, where a bullet had parted his hair. She smelled of gunpowder, the night, and that elusive fragrance that was all her. Her breasts were close to his face and all he had to do was turn his head slightly and nuzzle close. She wore a tank and little else. She must have gotten undressed to get in bed when she decided to eavesdrop. He would have to remember that she had excellent hearing and she wasn't ever going to be that woman relegated to the background.

He would have to find a good balance for them both. He wasn't going to have her carrying around a sniper's rifle or, worse, have Sevastyan put her on Mitya's security. He wouldn't put it past his cousin. He turned his head just as she shifted forward, cleaning the blood with her wipes. The action pressed her breasts against his cheek. He felt the soft curves and instantly his body reacted.

Hell. He was in pain. He'd been shot. He was lying on the ground stark naked and he was reacting to her. It wasn't her breasts. Well. Okay. It was and it wasn't. Her body would always give him an erection. That was just something they both were going to have to live with. He liked her sass. He liked her attitude. It was ridiculous when he needed her to do whatever the hell he told her to do, but still, that attitude gave him the hard-on from hell. His cock ached almost as badly as or worse than his body.

Ania sank back onto her heels and wiped the sweat from her forehead with her arm. "It's been a long night."

"I'm sorry about your father, baby," he said softly. "I swear, Ania, there was no turning back. He was too far gone, and he didn't try, not even when you called to him. He looked right at me, and I knew he trusted me to end his leopard as quickly and as painlessly as possible."

He had to tell her, even though he hated bringing it up again. He needed to tell her for both their sakes. Even though he wanted to do anything but talk about something that caused her pain and distress.

She brushed his bloody, matted hair from his forehead with gentle fingers. "I know, Mitya. Thank you. It couldn't have been easy on you. I don't know what to do about Jewel. She accepted your leopard, but now she is certain he will kill us both when she emerges. She's very afraid of him. What did he say or do to cause that?"

He didn't know, but he was sure as hell going to find out. The men were there, standing over him, ready to transport him to the car.

Sevastyan and Vikenti got their arms under him. "Are you ready?"

Mitya took a deep breath and steeled himself. Pain burst through him, radiating outward through his entire body, wrenching his gut. Sweat broke out. Air burst from his lungs, raw and burning.

Zinoviy had the door to the back seat open and they put him onto the leather seat. Sevastyan took the sniper rifle and put it in the trunk. Ania slipped in next to Mitya and Sevastyan got in close to her while Zinoviy took the front seat with Vikenti.

"I'll find out, baby." He had no idea. Dymka hadn't shared with him any conversations he'd had with the little female, but something had upset her. Whatever it was had nearly cost him Ania. The leopard had helped to drive that emotional storm, feeding Ania's painful sorrow rather than soothing and consoling her.

"Did you have a plan to leave me?"

He tipped sideways until his head was in her lap. She stroked caresses through his hair, uncaring of the blood she was getting on her or the seat.

"Of course I do. It's a good one too. I don't do too many things without a plan. Running wasn't going to work. You obviously would have come after me. I knew at the memorial quite a few people would come, including Drake Donovan. He specializes in protection. I was going to ask him to help me."

Mitya went still. Sevastyan did as well. Vikenti and Zinoviy glanced back at her.

"Ania, Drake is leopard. He has to abide by the laws of the leopard world. We're a bonded pair. Jewel accepted Dymka as her mate. He can't interfere."

"Not as a leopard, but he runs a protection agency, and by all accounts, he stands for women. I would have approached him as a woman, not a leopard. I would have told him I was terrified and ask for his protection. What could he have done?"

"He would have been killed," Mitya explained quietly, his heart pounding all over again. "I would never have allowed him to take you from me. I would have challenged him to fight and he would have had no choice but to accept. I would have killed him."

She was silent, chewing on her lower lip, her brows drawn together in a little frown. "But that's the leopard world."

"It isn't separate, Ania. He has to abide by the laws." Mitya made every effort to keep his voice soft. He reached up to take her hand, pulling it from his forehead, although he hated to lose her stroking fingers. "I'll talk to you more about this later." Because truthfully, he was too damned tired to go into it.

"Lights on. Doc's car's in the driveway," Vikenti announced. "He was already on his way to Ania's estate, so he was close."

"Thank God," Sevastyan said. He glared at Kiriil and Matvei, who both looked guilty. They stood right out in front, ready to be harshly reprimanded for allowing Ania freedom.

9

THE memorial for Ania's father was held on the fourth day after his death. Mitya arranged everything. He stood tall and straight, looking so invincible, she knew no one would ever suspect that he was injured in any way. They held the short service at Mitya's estate rather than hers because they didn't want anyone wandering around.

The cleaners had come and had gone through the grounds as well as every room, mopping up every bit of evidence that anything violent had happened there. Her father had been cremated as all shifters were. No evidence of them could remain. Mitya and his staff had planned every detail, including adding more security. They did so in order to accommodate the various families attending the service.

Nearly every crime family was represented. Fyodor Amurov and his brother were there, along with Joshua Tregre, Elijah Lospostos, Emilio Bassini and Fredo Lombardi. The

Caruso family as well as the Anwar family showed up from Houston. Jake Bannaconni and Drake Donovan arrived with their wives as well. So many people came to pay their respects to her father.

Ania stayed very close to Mitya, feeling so sad she could barely breathe. Mitya seemed well tuned to her every emotion because he kept his arm around her, holding her beneath his shoulder, sometimes answering for her when she couldn't summon up any kind of pleasantry.

She liked having Evangeline and Ashe there. Although they mingled with the other women, they stayed very close to her and more than once diverted attention from her. Inevitably, Mitya had no choice but to let her go with the women while some of the men insisted on talking to him. He looked to Evangeline and Ashe as usual, and they came up on either side of her to shield her from the crowds.

"Let's get you something to drink and maybe a pastry," Evangeline said. "I'm sure we can find somewhere quiet to sit."

The moment she was outside of Mitya's protection, Alessandro Caruso came over to her with his father, Marzio. Ania would have avoided Alessandro if possible but knew it would be terribly rude to do so with his father. She let him take her hand and lean over it as if he might kiss her knuckles with old-world charm.

"Ania. You remember me? You used to come with your grandfather or father and sit on the floor playing while we talked. My beautiful Ann would sneak you treats your father said you couldn't have."

She managed a wan smile. "I do remember those times. They were wonderful."

"Your father was my friend for many years. I should have visited him more often, but these last few years have been tough on my Ann, and I left most of the business to my boys and just stayed in with her. I regret that."

"My father loved Ann. He wouldn't have wanted you to do anything else."

Marzio Caruso looked around the room and then caught her wrist very gently. His sons were suddenly there, all four of them, making a pathway for their father to the little room off the great room, the one few people had entered. She saw immediately that it was held by the Caruso security force.

"I would like to speak to you alone, Ania, and the matter is extremely private," Marzio said.

She gripped Evangeline's hand, her lifeline, and looked at Ashe, hoping both would stay close. "I'm not certain it's a good idea right now," Ania replied, keeping her voice steady. "I've been upset over my father's death. I have no other family, and losing him has been a terrible blow."

"I know how close the two of you were," Marzio said. "But surely so many years of friendship warrants me a little bit of your time."

She didn't know how to graciously refuse him. She nodded to Evangeline and reluctantly let her allies go. Evangeline and Ashe moved just a little distance away.

The moment the two women put distance between them, Kiriil and Matvei moved close. "Ania," Kiriil said gently. "Mitya gave specific instructions."

Ania lifted her chin at Marzio, grateful beyond anything that Mitya, even out of her sight, was looking after her. "If you wish to speak to me, my bodyguards have to be with us."

Marzio frowned. "They will report every word to Mitya."

"There is no choice in this matter." She was already on emotional overload and she was fearful of anything Marzio said to her. She was okay with not having the conversation, and the head of the Caruso family could clearly see that. He nodded abruptly.

Ania entered the room with both Kiriil and Matvei,

who immediately took up the two best positions in the room. Once the Caruso family entered, everyone else left, leaving her alone with Marzio's sons and their personal bodyguards. She was extremely grateful again for her two bodyguards, something she hadn't thought possible.

Ania decided she had to come out of the fog she was in and take charge. She indicated the two armchairs. "Would you care for something to drink?"

"No, no, *cara*, I know you have spoken to Alessandro and he has indicated to you that Donato would like to purchase your business. That is for another discussion. This one is one I don't wish to have because I fear it will ruin our friendship, and that is very valuable to me."

She tried to keep her frown from showing. She didn't have Mitya's expressionless mask. "Please continue, signor Caruso."

"Marzio, Ania. We won't be formal. It is your alliance with Mitya Amurov that is distressing me. This man is not a good man. His father is one of the worst of the *bratya*. Everyone fears him. There are rumors of this man coming here to either kill his son or do business with him. In any case, you cannot win with a man such as Amurov. They are violent and have no problem killing women and children. They deal in things we would never think to deal with. They kill rather than keep their word. These are not good men."

He patted her hand. "I don't say these things to you lightly or to upset you. I weighed whether or not to approach you but could not neglect my duty to Antosha's beloved child."

"I appreciate that you care enough to talk to me," she said, uncertain how to reassure him. Now she knew why he didn't want a witness. She didn't dare look at her bodyguards, and knew Mitya was going to know everything said, probably before she had a chance to tell him. It was obvious that Marzio was sincere. "But you do business with Mitya. All of you do."

"Business is one thing, allowing a man like this to have a treasure is something else. Alessandro tells me your female is close to the Han Vol Dan."

She glanced at his son. The brothers were across the room, giving their father privacy, but she knew they could hear every word. She inclined her head slowly.

"I have four sons, all good men. All willing to marry you and treat you with the respect you deserve. Alessandro in particular would very much like to have a chance with you."

She leaned toward the patriarch of the Caruso family. So far, everything Marzio had said was the strict truth. She could hear the ring of sincerity in his voice. "My leopard has accepted Mitya's leopard's claim. They are bonded together. You know that's sacred. Once done, the law of our people is strictly on his side."

Ania was extremely glad that Mitya had touched on that very thing a few days earlier. She wouldn't have known what to say.

"Your female isn't as certain of the bond as you appear to think," the older man said, his voice gentler than ever.

Ania cursed her wayward leopard. She was new at this, bonding with her female, happy she had her, but not knowing what to do when Jewel was so afraid of Dymka. She had to get Evangeline or Ashe alone for a talk.

"They're bonded," she repeated. "My female is nervous, yes, but she accepted the pairing."

"It has to be her first cycle, and she can make a mistake."

This was worse than it would have been had Marzio been talking to her about her father's death. She feared that subject was coming next. She glanced toward the door. One of Marzio's sons, Benedetto, leaned against it.

He was a good-looking man and very serious. There was no laughter in his eyes, just that focused stare that told her his leopard was very close. She sent up a silent prayer that Jewel didn't suddenly decide to rise.

"Marzio, it is too late to have this conversation, although I appreciate your concern."

"He can be challenged."

Her gaze jumped across the room to Alessandro. At the same time her heart accelerated, and every leopard in the room heard. She shook her head. "Don't let any of your sons try that, Marzio, please. First, I know I am his mate. I *know* it. I can't say in all honesty that I'm not nervous sometimes, but I can say I know I'm supposed to be with him. You can't defeat him in a fight. None of you can."

The moment the words were out of her mouth, she wished she could take them back. These men, his sons, were strong, healthy and full of pride. She had just as much as told them she didn't think they were nearly up to challenging Mitya or his leopard—which she didn't, but she should have been far more careful.

"You know a little of his past, Marzio. I know quite a bit more. His leopard is a fighting machine. In any case . . ." She made a move to stand. "Mitya is my choice."

Marzio laid a gentle hand on her knee to keep her from moving. "If this is your choice and I can't persuade you to listen to reason, I will have to accept it. Just be aware you have allies in the Caruso family. Your father was a friend I cared about. Do you know who was behind the supposed robbery? He spoke to me a few times right after the shooting occurred and he indicated at that time that he believed his family had been targeted."

She lifted her gaze to Marzio's. He was telling the truth as far as she could tell. He probably had discussed the subject with her father. They had been close friends prior to the shooting. She couldn't tell by looking into his eyes whether or not he was her greatest enemy. A betrayal from him would have been devastating to her father. Would Antosha have told her if he suspected Marzio had betrayed him?

It was difficult to resist looking at Kiriil or Matvei, but it wouldn't have done her any good. They would be wearing expressionless masks and looking right through her, pretending they didn't hear a word.

"My father discussed this with me a few times, but he was as clueless as I am. I believe, as you do, that someone targeted my family. They made a couple of attempts on me as well."

The moment she admitted that the room went electric. Marzio suddenly looked different. Healthy. Younger. In much better shape. He also looked furious. "What did you say?" It came out a whisper, but at the same time it was loud, the sound carrying through the room with a dark menace.

Ania realized she didn't really know this man any more than she knew Mitya, although she'd been raised from her childhood in and out of the Caruso household. Like Mitya, none of the brothers had shown interest in her until her leopard began to emerge. Was there anything such as love in a leopard relationship anymore? She knew Marzio loved Ann. Her father had loved her mother. Her grandparents always showed love for each other. But Mitya? His cousins? Maybe they weren't capable of real love. Their fathers had tried to beat it out of them. Had they succeeded?

She feared she could fall hard for Mitya, really love him. He needed someone to love him, to show him a gentler way, but if he didn't return her affections, their relationship ultimately wouldn't work. She would need to know she wasn't second to her leopard. She wanted to be loved the way her father had loved her mother. Still, she had made the commitment, promised herself—and him— she would try.

"Ania? Someone tried to kill you?"

She nodded slowly. "Actually, one of the times was that day you called to have me look at the two cars that were vandalized."

"A setup, using our family," Marzio hissed. "And more than once. Tell me what happened."

He sounded like her father. "I was nearly home, and they used the same setup as they did with my grandparents. I was raised around cars and driving. I could see it was a trap. There were two cars, one chasing and one waiting. I was able to get away."

"This makes no sense, to go after you. Why was your entire family targeted?"

"I have no idea. My father and I discussed it, but he didn't know either."

"Would your father have told you?" Marzio asked. "Pardon me, Ania, but you are young and a female. This is not done, talking business like this."

"My father had one child, a girl, and he treated me as he would a son. I grew up learning every aspect of the business, learning to fix cars and driving. He drilled it into me that our word was our bond and it was to never be broken. He often discussed things with me I knew my mother or grandmother didn't know, and I knew not to bring the subject matter up with them. He would have told me if he knew why, simply because I was in danger."

Marzio leaned back against the high-backed leather chair. "This is not good. I had hoped you at least had a suspect or knew the reason your family was targeted."

She shook her head. "I don't."

"You know your father took packages and delivered them for various families, including mine?"

Alessandro and Benedetto both straightened from where they were leaning on the wall and door. Even Cristo and Donato, the younger sons, came to attention. Clearly, they didn't want their father bringing that subject up. It was the same in every leopard family. Women weren't allowed. She'd made a commitment to Mitya by saving his life when he was being shot at, but that had been made under the emotional toll of the day. Now, she was doubting her own sanity.

"Yes, of course. My father and grandfather both drove. I was being trained so I would be able to do the same. In fact, after my father was shot, there were four contracts left unfulfilled. I carried them out." She had to work at keeping her voice very even, not at all defiant. She wanted to appear matter-of-fact, as if women were included in the business world of these men every single day.

"Ania, I want to take you home with me and keep you safe," Marzio said. "Instead, I must let this Russian, this man with a past that raises too many questions, protect you." He sent one contemptuous look at her bodyguards, as if they were totally inferior to his. "He is not a good man. I have lived around many dangerous men, but this one, this man you choose, he is the most dangerous of any of them."

She didn't need him to tell her that. Jewel knew and had pulled back, trying to be cautious. Ania seemed to be running toward Mitya again. She feared the physical chemistry between the two of them was so explosive she wasn't seeing straight. It took discipline to keep her hands folded neatly in her lap. She wanted to rub her temples. They were pounding, the headache probably from all the tears she'd shed the last few days.

A polite knock at the door indicated they weren't going to have any more time alone together and Ania was grateful when Benedetto moved, opening the door to allow Evangeline to stick her head in, with her usual smile. Ania could see that she was worried and gave her a look that said to come all the way in, which, thankfully, she did.

Marzio rose at once. "I'm taking far too much of your time when you have others who would like to pay their respects."

Ania rose with him and gave him a kiss on either cheek. His sons, to her astonishment, kissed her on either cheek, Alessandro holding her hands tightly for a moment.

"If you change your mind, call me, Ania. If this is your leopard's first cycle, she will accept another male if the one she first chose isn't right."

Ania didn't know what else to do, so she nodded. "Thank you, Alessandro. I really appreciate your interest in her."

"In *you*," he corrected.

She flashed him an uncertain smile and then watched as the family left, Benedetto closing the door behind them, leaving Evangeline and Ania alone with the Amurov bodyguards.

"Are you all right?" Evangeline asked. "I stood outside the door, so I could hear some of it, but the gist seemed to be they want you to leave Mitya and take one of them for a mate. Ashe texted Mitya, but told him your bodyguards were with you. He sent back a text that they had already informed him." She sent Kiriil and Matvei a smile. "I'm baking something special for them."

"I would have wanted you to bake them something special had they not informed Mitya. When this is all over, I'm hiring my own bodyguards loyal to me." She glared at the two men.

Kiriil smirked. Matvei covered a grin.

Ania ignored them and threw herself back into the chair. "Sometimes I think I'm going crazy. Jewel seems to be a very popular leopard, and she hasn't even emerged." She tried not to sound bitter or resentful, but she couldn't help it. She took the opportunity to rub her pounding temples.

"Honey, talk to me. What's wrong?" Evangeline took

the chair Marzio had vacated. "I know we haven't known each other that long, but I genuinely want to help."

"You know Mitya far better than I do. He seems so all-powerful. He wants instant obedience without question. He's scary, Evangeline, but his leopard is worse. I'm supposed to just trust everything he says and does. I'm my own person. I'm not in the least bit a 'yes' kind of woman. How can this be right if we're not what the other needs? Is the relationship only about the leopard?"

"I'm very much in love with Fyodor, and he is with me." She rubbed her hand over her pregnant belly. "I can barely stand being away from him, and luckily enough, he's like that about me."

"And that could be all it is—pure luck. Fyodor fell in love with you because you're you, Evangeline. You're sweet and accommodating. You don't question every little thing. I do." She did because someone was out to kill her family. She did because Mitya had admitted that the men in his family had always killed the women they chose to have their sons. A little shudder went through her.

Evangeline leaned forward. "Honey, why would you think Mitya doesn't love you?"

"It would be impossible in such a short amount of time. Love doesn't happen that way."

"Love can happen in all sorts of ways. In any case, how do you feel about him?"

"I don't know." Ania tried to be honest with herself. "I think of him all the time. I worry that he does dangerous things. He told me about his father, and that's just plain scary. But there's this terrible fear that just won't go away."

"Fear of what?"

"I don't know. I can't tell if it's me or Jewel. I only know when I think too much, I can't breathe." She forced herself to be honest. "I know myself, Evangeline. I won't stay if I don't feel he loves me. It won't be enough that our leopards are bonded. I'm trying to convince myself that it will be good, but only the sex feels good between us."

"You need to sit that man down and tell him your fears, Ania."

"I don't want him to say the things he thinks I want to hear."

"He isn't a mind reader. None of them are. Mitya, Fyodor, Timur, Sevastyan and Gorya, actually all of them, lived extremely difficult lives as children. They don't know the first thing about a relationship. I didn't either, but Fyodor and I have sort of figured it out. We talk a lot. If you're going to be with a man like these men, you have to communicate with them. They want a home and a family, but they don't know how to get those things. They're looking to you to show them the way."

Ania sat back, stretching her legs out in front of her. She was so tired. Death was exhausting. Just thinking about her father and the loss of every family member was so emotionally draining that she couldn't breathe. Her lungs felt raw and were burning. Her throat felt the same. Her eyes burned from shed and unshed tears.

"Mitya has been wonderful throughout all of this," she admitted. He wasn't in the best of shape, and neither was she, so they hadn't had their crazy, wild sex. She had to admit, she needed that affirmation that he still wanted her, even though she appreciated him giving her space. "He took care of all the details."

"As he should," Evangeline said. "Talk to him, Ania. Tell him your fears. If you do, the two of you can figure out why Jewel is so frightened. Turning to another man won't help you. That, for certain, will only scare you more. Mitya is committed to you. I know he is because Fyodor asked him straight out. He would never let another claim on you go unchallenged."

"You mean another claim on my leopard," Ania corrected. "How can you tell Fyodor loves you for you?"

Evangeline frowned. "I feel it every time he touches me. When he looks at me. It's there in the things he does for me."

Ania couldn't help thinking that Mitya had been shot several times, and yet he'd planned her father's service and stood at her side the entire time, not letting on in the least that he was hurt in any way. He stayed close to her, shielding her from scrutiny, from too many people crowding close when she could barely stand straight. He gave her strength through the entire service. Was that a show of love? Maybe his actions spoke when he couldn't with words.

"I don't know why I'm so afraid to talk to him about this. I think it's because if he doesn't react well, he'd crush me."

"When a problem crops up, does he crush you?"

She couldn't say he did. In fact, when she'd been in trouble at Evangeline's bakery, Jewel acting up in front of Alessandro, essentially teasing and flirting with his leopard, Mitya had been wonderful to her. He hadn't blamed her in the least. More than once, he'd reacted very differently than she'd expected him to.

"No, he's been sweet to me, but he's horribly bossy."

Evangeline flashed her a smug little grin. "They all are. We mostly ignore that, unless we can see it really matters to them. If it matters to me, I let Fyodor know. He finds a way to deal with my 'mutiny,' as he calls it." She laughed softly. "I really love that man."

"I guess I'm ready to face the masses. Is it thinning out at all?"

"Not really, but Mitya and Sevastyan are taking care of making certain every family is thanked for coming. They've made the rounds quite a few times. So have Fyodor, Gorya and Timur. You're family now, so we're closing ranks around you."

That made Ania feel better. Much better. She hadn't thought that when she was married to Mitya, all of the others would be related to her. She liked the idea of having them all for family, especially Evangeline and Ashe.

Another knock at the door and Ashe was there, framed in the doorway, looking gorgeous as usual. "There's a gentleman here who would very much like to pay his condolences in person, Ania, and have a few words with you if you're up for it."

She stepped aside to allow Ania to see the man behind her. Bartolo Anwar was head of one of the two major crime families in Houston. There was the Caruso family and the Anwar family. Bartolo's family had been in Houston for generations. The Carusos had migrated there from Florida and taken over the ports.

"Of course." Ania stood and went to the older man, both hands out.

Bartolo took them and pressed kisses to her knuckles. "I am so sorry this happened to your *padre*, Ania. He was a good man."

For some reason, the sincerity in his voice caused tears to well up. "Thank you, signor Anwar. You were always a good friend to him."

Behind him, the two bodyguards that he never seemed to be without entered the room, glancing at Kiriil and Matvei, but then taking up positions against the wall. Bartolo had lost his wife in childbirth many years earlier. He had two sons, Enrico and Samuele, as well as a daughter, Giacinta. The daughter was very sickly, much like her mother, and she didn't seem to leave the house ever. Bartolo and her brothers seemed very protective of her.

"Please come in and sit down," Ania invited, waving toward the chairs. They were the most comfortable in the room, although Ania hadn't found a single sofa or chair that wasn't one she could sit in for long periods of time. Whoever had purchased the furniture for Mitya's home—and she was certain it wasn't him—had done a very good job.

Bartolo had entered without hesitation. His bodyguards had split up, moving to either side of the wall and positioning themselves so they could easily see the door and anyone who might try to enter. They were also opposite Kiriil and Matvei. For some reason, that made Ania feel a little uneasy.

Evangeline was pregnant, and Ania wanted her out of the room. It wasn't like there was any kind of threat to either of the women. Bartolo had been very sincere in his condolences.

"Evangeline, honey, would you mind scaring up some coffee for me? I think I need caffeine." She hoped that Evangeline got the hint.

Evangeline nodded. "No worries. I'll make a new pot. Would you care for a cup of coffee?" she asked Bartolo.

He shook his head. "No, thank you. I've been eating and drinking your delicious food since I got here. I'd heard of your bakery but didn't believe anything could be as good as everyone was saying. I was wrong."

Evangeline beamed. Ania decided Bartolo could be a threat to any woman, he was so charming. As Evangeline slipped out the door, Bartolo's two sons entered.

Ania sent up a silent prayer that they weren't there for the same reason Marzio had seemed to be. She forced a smile as she looked up at the two men. She didn't know them as well as she did the Caruso brothers. The Anwars were a little older and always working.

"It has been far too long, Ania," Enrico, the oldest, said. Like his father, he took her hand and pressed his lips to her knuckles with that same charm his father had.

"It has," she agreed and then sent a smile to Samuele, hoping there was no more kissing of any part of her. Mitya and his raging leopard were going to be smelling men all over her. She glanced nervously at her bodyguards, but they appeared to be part of the wall, not human or shifter—and no help.

"Ania," Samuele greeted. "I'm so sorry about Antosha. He was a good man."

She nodded, because what could she say, her father was a good man. Still, he had his feet in a world of criminals. He had been much more immersed than she'd first thought.

"I'm sorry to bother you with this. I know it isn't a good time," Bartolo said. "But your man guards you like a treasure." He glanced at her bodyguards. "He is a jealous man." He laughed as if in approval. His sons smiled a little. Smirked maybe.

A small chill went down her spine. Was she being fanciful? This was the family her grandfather had been taking the package to three days before his death. Her grandfather had been very good friends with Bartolo's father and had watched Bartolo and then his sons grow up. She had considered, of course, that they were the ones to put out a hit on her family, but it hadn't felt right. Now, sitting with them, she just didn't know. Her body was reacting as if she were in danger, yet no one had made one threatening move toward her.

"I suppose he can be," Ania conceded, unsure where the conversation was going.

"We need a driver. You are that driver, Ania. There is no one else as good as your grandfather or father. The package is small and must get through to New Orleans, to some friends of ours there."

She stared at Bartolo, a little shocked. It was the last thing she expected to hear. "I don't drive for anyone, not anymore." That was the truth. She wanted to, she missed the adrenaline rush. "I'm selling my business. Donato Caruso is buying it. You might talk to him."

Bartolo shook his head. "It has to be you, Ania."

"You know Mitya would never allow such a thing," she said softly, admitting it aloud. She wasn't happy to say it. It made her sound like a "yes" woman, but it was also the best excuse in the world and one a man like Bartolo would understand. She even lowered her lashes and looked as submissive as possible. She should have gone into acting.

"We will double the money."

The fee had always been a small fortune. To double it was ridiculous, and that only made her all the more suspicious. She shook her head. "You can talk to Mitya. If he agrees, then I'll drive for you, but, signor Anwar, there are several good drivers. Even if you think someone will try to intercept, there are dozens of decent drivers."

"Not like you."

She'd done some street racing. Make that a lot of street racing. That had been one way to hone her driving skills and get the adrenaline rush she craved. But she hadn't done any driving where others could see her. She'd pinned up her hair and used a street name, mostly so her father and grandfather wouldn't find out she was sneaking out to race. She'd been doing that since she was sixteen.

There was such conviction in Bartolo's voice, as if he knew about her driving skills. How? As far as she was concerned, it was impossible for them to know, so why keep pushing for her?

"Perhaps, but I'm getting married to Mitya, and he has very strong ideas on what his wife should or shouldn't do. I don't think taking jobs racing across the country comes under the heading of what he'd prefer. Like I said, you can have a word with him about this. I'm not entirely opposed to driving for you." She flashed her sweetest smile. Her words were sincere enough, not lies, because she *loved* driving.

Fortunately, even though Mitya didn't want her involved in any way, she was certain Sevastyan would give in and include her—privately of course—in Mitya's security team. Sevastyan had questioned her twice about her abilities with weapons, but he'd been most interested in her driving skills.

Bartolo sighed. "Your man is difficult, Ania. He comes

from Russia. His father is a great *vor* there and controls most of the ports. He rules with an iron fist, very bloody, and he wipes out his enemies the moment they show themselves. Mitya is a product of this man. Some say he is even more ruthless. If that is so, I don't want to get on his bad side by suggesting his wife drive for us."

Ania leaned toward him and lowered her voice as if they were co-conspirators. "I don't want to get on his bad side either." She flashed a small smile, almost teasing him.

Bartolo shook his head. "Girl, you're wasted on that Russian. He might be the best at business, but he won't ever know what he's got in you."

"I'm really sorry I can't drive for you." On one level that was the strict truth, but on another, she worried that the Anwar family might know more than they were saying about her family's deaths. "Signor Anwar, Joshua Tregre is here. He's from New Orleans. Is it possible he might be able to help? I've never met him, but I know Mitya and Sevastyan both know him. Fyodor's wife, Evangeline, is his cousin."

Bartolo stood up, shaking his head, indicating their private meeting was over. "No, no, don't worry your head. We'll find a solution." He walked to the door, waiting for his bodyguards to go out first. He hung back, turning to her. "Do you know why your family was targeted, Ania?"

She shook her head. Tears burned close all over again. She had to stop being a faucet at the mention of her family. "No. I talked several times with my father about it, but he didn't seem to know either. He was very . . . upset. He counted everyone he worked for as his friend. He thought work had to be involved, but there was no reason that he knew of that would make a friend become his enemy."

"He had no territory for power-hungry families to want to grab." Bartolo sounded as if he was musing aloud. "He carried packages for others as well as my family. Could he have seen something others wanted him dead over?"

"If he had, he certainly didn't tell me. And then did my mother and grandmother see it? Did my grandfather? I know I didn't, and they still came after me."

Bartolo had one foot out the door when she told him. He stopped dead in his tracks. Frozen there. Very slowly he turned back to her, as did his sons. "Ania, are you saying someone has tried to kill you?"

She nodded. "Yes, more than once."

Bartolo looked at his sons. "Find out who did this thing. She's protected. Spread the word. If someone has a hit out on her, they had better retract it or we will be merciless coming after them. Our families go back a long way, Ania. A long way. You are one of us, and there are few shifters left. We need every woman. I see why Mitya would guard you so carefully. I was upset that you were with him before, but now I'm glad."

He leaned down and brushed both her cheeks with his dry lips. "If you need me, you call. Call one of the boys. It doesn't matter what time, day or night, Ania, you call, we'll come."

That choked her up. "Thanks, signor Anwar. That means so much to me." He sounded so sincere and almost angry. No, he was angry. The looks he was giving his sons made her think he wanted to start a war.

Both Enrico and Samuele hugged her and followed their father into the great room, where many of the guests were still gathered. Mitya and the others emerged from the den. She could see Mitya looking around for her. He spotted her almost immediately, as if he had radar. He murmured something to the men and came across the room toward her.

The crowd parted for him. Mitya was just that way. He started walking, easy, panther-like strides, confident and a little on the lethal side. She made herself really look at him. He was a big man, a good six four or more, his shoulders wide and his chest broad. He had the roped muscles of the leopard, and when he moved, he had that same easy, almost lazy stride that could turn into a blur of motion that fast.

His face was rugged male. A strong jaw with that perpetual five-o'clock shadow. Those piercing, focused eyes that could melt her when he fastened his gaze on her. His nose was very aristocratic, or it would have been had it not been broken at one time. That, along with several scars on his face, particularly around his left eye, only served to make him look even more gorgeous to her.

Mitya came right up to her, his hand cupping her face, thumb sliding over her skin. He inhaled sharply. "Why is it, *kotyonok*, that you are always surrounded by men?"

"I don't know. It just happens." She tried a tentative smile because he wasn't smiling. Not at all.

"And why is it that I get that information from your bodyguards and not you?" His tone was mild, and his thumb continued to caress her cheek.

She leaned into his hand. "Probably because I left my cell upstairs in the bedroom, but I was very grateful to have Kiriil and Matvei looking after me while you looked after our guests."

He bent his head to brush her lips gently. "You look tired, baby. I'll get these people to go. Drake is staying with his wife at the Bannaconni ranch. Elijah and Eli are staying at a hotel near the bakery. I think Joshua is staying at Fyodor's. In any case, tomorrow is another day. They'll be coming back tomorrow, and you can visit with the women while I have a meeting with the men."

They were definitely going to have to have a talk, but not now, not with so many guests still there. They'd come to honor her father, and she loved that, but she wanted them all to go home. Mitya swept his arm around her.

"After everyone is gone, Sevastyan will do a sweep to make certain there are no listening devices anywhere or cameras left behind." Mitya gestured toward the stairs.

"We know no one has gotten upstairs. I had men stationed on the stairs to prevent that."

"Did anyone try?"

He smiled, looking a little bit like a pleased wolf. "Several, but they were stopped and noted. Go on up, and I'll join you in about a half an hour. It won't take longer than that to get everyone moving."

A bath would be just the thing to get all the kinks out. She still found it astounding that grief could cause the body to hurt every bit as badly as it did the soul.

Ania looked up at his face and she couldn't help framing it with both hands. "Thank you for taking care of all this for me. For taking care of me. You were the one shot several times only four days ago, but you still did all this for me. I really appreciate it."

"I'll always take care of you, Ania."

She looked into his eyes for a long time, searching for something that was just out of reach. She couldn't find it. She didn't even know what it was. At that moment, Jewel was very quiet. There was no terrible fear welling up to tell her to run. There was only this man who had done for her what was unexpected and wonderful. She went up on her toes and brushed her own kiss across his lips.

"A bath sounds perfect. If you would say my good-byes to everyone, I would greatly appreciate it. Especially Evangeline. She looks tired, and she really helped me out this evening, running interference."

"I'm sorry I had to slip away for a few minutes. I had to warn Bannaconni and Drake that something wasn't right. Amory worked for Drake, and he'd been in Bannaconni's home. Emma, his wife, often cooked for the men working for them. They ate in the house, family style." His voice turned hard. "I don't like to think that Amory sat at their table with Emma and the children, eating the food she prepared for them, and then betrayed them."

"I don't like it either, Mitya. Of course you had to warn

them. There could be listening devices in their homes." She
put her hand on the banister, suddenly needing to go somewhere quiet. She'd been born into the world of criminals,
but she'd always lived on the fringe. She looked around at
the men and women in Mitya's home. Almost every single
one was involved in some way or another in crime. Shaking
her head, she turned and walked up the stairs.

10

MITYA reached down to lift his woman out of the cold bath. She was sound asleep, curled up like a little drowned kitten. Her hair floated around her like a mermaid's might. Long and thick, she had hair most shifters had. When he looked very closely, he could see the various colors streaked through the dark strands. Her lashes were thick and long, like her dark hair, and there was the faintest scattering of freckles across her elegant nose.

He loved her mouth. Her lips were full and formed a perfect bow. When she smiled, she had straight, white teeth, although on the bottom, there was one tooth that was just a little crooked. He was particularly fond of that tooth.

Water poured off Ania's body as he cradled her against his chest. Immediately she turned in to him, seeking warmth. His body was always hot, and she used him like her personal furnace. One-handed, he wrapped a towel around her, trying to soak up the water dripping from her hair. Lashes fluttered and then lifted. She smiled at him, and immediately his heart ached.

"Hi."

"You stayed in the bath too long. You're shivering."

"Your fault," she declared, burrowing closer as if she could get inside him.

She didn't have far to go; she was already inside, wrapping herself around his heart, and he wasn't certain how it had happened. He kept drying her off, using just one hand as he seated himself on the edge of the bed. He held her against him with the other, although she didn't try to pull away. She felt elusive to him, as if any moment she might make a run for it.

He bent his head and inhaled her fragrance. He loved the way she smelled. He had to face it, even if it was only privately, he loved everything about her. "Why did I smell all those men on you?"

She sent him another smile, this one a little mischievous. "You leave me alone too long and they just flock around me like I'm a magnet."

He knew she was teasing him, but it was the truth. She just wasn't aware it was the truth. "I recognized Marzio Caruso's scent." It had to be said, and he knew it would come out gruff. He felt murderous every time Alessandro Caruso got near Ania. "His sons were close to you as well."

"Marzio had a lot to say. I was nervous at first, talking to him, afraid he might be the one responsible for the death of my family. I didn't want it to be the Carusos. My father was friends with them. Good friends. I knew it would have broken his heart if he found out Marzio had ordered a hit on him. On all of us."

"You don't believe it was the Carusos?" He wrapped her hair with the towel, soaking up the water even as he held her close to him. She wasn't wearing a stitch and her skin gleamed a soft peach from the light shining through the bank of windows along the west side of the bedroom and the glass roof overhead. The roof had a seal that covered the glass most of the time, but when he wanted, he could open the double doors and let the moonlight into the room. He had them open now.

"I honestly don't know, Mitya, but it didn't feel as if Marzio was involved. He mostly was there to tell me you were a man to do business with but not a man to marry. He was worried about me."

"I see. And did he have a solution for this?"

"He thought I should marry one of his sons. If not, I could seek asylum in his home."

Mitya did his best to remain relaxed. His woman was lying in his arms, naked, drowsy, sexy as hell and totally relaxed. She hadn't left with Marzio, not that she would have gotten out the door. He did need to know whether or not he had to make a visit to Houston. If he didn't like what he heard, Marzio and his sons were going to have very short lives.

"You're still here," Mitya pointed out.

She let her lashes drift down again. "Better the devil you know and all that." Her voice was teasing. Her lashes lifted again and her eyes blazed a vivid indigo, a deep purple that always took his breath.

"Mitya, I don't want Alessandro Caruso. I'm not attracted to him. I seem to be rather attracted to you. So much so, every other man pales in comparison."

His heart pounded. She was amazing. He knew she had reservations. He also knew she was a little afraid of him. Okay, being truthful, quite afraid of him, yet she had the courage to tell him how she felt.

"That's a good thing, Ania. I don't want to have to fight for you, but if that's what it takes, I certainly would. You're more than worth it."

"I need to go to bed. I'm really, really exhausted."

He had already pulled back the sheets and blankets, so

it was easy enough to round the bed, put a knee into the middle of it and gently deposit her onto the mattress. She rolled over, curling like she did when she wanted to sleep. Knees to chest, hands tucked under her pillow. He used the towel to wring the rest of the water from her hair. Somewhere, he knew there was a hair dryer. If he didn't use it, that much hair would get a good portion of their bed wet.

"Mitya?"

He had hurried to the bathroom to start rummaging through the drawers. He half turned. "Yeah, baby?"

"I really don't want anyone else. It's Jewel. Something's really wrong there. How do we figure it out? I don't know what to do."

Unlike Mitya, Ania hadn't known her leopard. Jewel hadn't made an appearance until she was actually in the throes of the Han Vol Dan. Now, she was emerging, pushing her way to the surface, demanding to be allowed out. They hadn't completely formed their bond of trust with each other. She was learning to talk to her leopard, but it took time. He, on the other hand, was very familiar with Dymka and his vicious, terrifying ways.

He found the appliance he wanted and brought it back to the bedroom to plug in. "I'll talk to Dymka and find out the problem." He turned on the dryer and sat on the edge of the bed, directing the heat through the mass of damp strands.

"Please do it now, Mitya. She affects my ability to think straight. When she's very close to the surface, I can't tell if she's the one afraid or if I am."

Another straight admittance. He really liked that trait in her. That *please* twisted at him. One part of him liked to hear her say it, the other part was a churning mass of upset stomach. He hadn't heard the word often. That wasn't exactly the truth. He had heard it when he was extracting information for his father, or deliberately going after someone his father said was a traitor or hadn't paid the money owed. When he'd been his father's enforcer, he'd heard that word too many times.

She started to turn toward him, but he had her hair in a fist and she couldn't move.

"Just lie there, *kotyonok*."

"What's wrong?"

She was too connected to him. He cursed under his breath. "I'm going to talk to him now. Just give me a minute or two. He can be difficult." He hesitated, and then made his confession. She was going to find out anyway. "That was an understatement. Dymka is moody, edgy, merciless and ruthless."

"Like you?"

There was no accusation or judgment. There was no humor either. He had to own that one. "Like me," he admitted. "Ania, I would never hurt you."

"Talk to your leopard before you tell me that. I have the feeling he threatened Jewel." There was the tiniest bit of denunciation in her tone now.

Dymka. He wasn't going to waste any time. *Why is Jewel so afraid of you?*

His query was met with silence. Mitya's anger instantly began to stir. *Fucking answer me right now. You said something or did something that has her retreating. Worse, she's willing to forgo her bond with you and find another mate.*

An explosion of rage greeted that statement. *That will never happen. I will kill any leopard that tries to take her from me.*

Mitya was certain Dymka would do just that. His leopard was bigger and stronger than most others. He was far more experienced. He had been a fighter since Mitya was a toddler and had honed his skills over the years, fighting time and again with more experienced leopards until he was so proficient others avoided him.

What did you do? She is so frightened. Ania is having a difficult time as well.

There was a short silence. *She rose in the bakery.* Rather than actual words, the image of the bakery and the men in it was shown to him. *The leopards wanted her. All of them. I could smell it on them. And one reached for her. She is so young she didn't realize what she was doing, and then she liked it. She liked having rivals surrounding her.* Again, there was an explosion of rage.

Dymka had a short fuse and wouldn't tolerate much from his wayward mate. Mitya sighed. In some ways, he was the same. He wasn't giving Ania room to wiggle around. He wanted her where he could see her every minute, and after the display of stealthy disobedience, of independence, slipping through his security guards to follow them, he had to plan for other ways to keep her safe.

Mitya also knew, every time Alessandro Caruso got close to Ania, Mitya turned as murderous and as vicious as his leopard.

If this is her first life cycle, Dymka, she is afraid and doesn't know what to do.

Then she should rely on her mate.

Mitya nearly groaned aloud. That sounded just like him. He wanted Ania to rely solely on him and, in fact, he demanded her trust. He hadn't given her reason to trust him, built that connection between them over time. No, he'd demanded it.

Who was the driver? Mitya? Or Dymka? Was each making the other worse? Mitya made every effort to be very relaxed and calm in the hopes that his moody leopard would listen to him. *Jewel is so afraid of you that she is desperate to escape. Did you threaten her?*

There was another short silence and Mitya's heart sank. That answer had to be yes. The male had said or done something to spook Ania's little female.

I knew you would be angry with me, Dymka formed

visual images in Mitya's mind. *I know I shouldn't have. She is very afraid as it is. I told her I would give her the beating of a lifetime if she ever flirted with any other males or, worse, allowed them to touch her.*

Mitya drew in a deep breath. He knew his leopard, and there was more to it than what he had admitted to Mitya. *What else? I want all of it right now, Dymka.* He rarely used that tone with his leopard. Dymka had saved his life so many times. More, he'd taken countless beatings when Mitya was a child to save him.

I told her Ania would suffer even more, that you would beat her as well to pay for the things Jewel did. The admission came out in a rush, as if the leopard wanted to get it over with.

The images of Mitya standing over Ania, his fists poised and fury on his face, Ania on the ground, sickened him. He couldn't imagine how young Jewel felt. No wonder she was desperate to protect her human counterpart. Fury burst through him to rival the rage of his cat.

I would never hit her. Or harm her in any way. I would remove any threat to my bonding with her, but no matter what she did, I wouldn't hurt Ania. After living with Lazar, do you believe threats like that work?

They worked for Lazar.

Mitya forced calm. He shut off the blow-dryer, unplugged it and took it into the master bath, needing to move. Dymka had a point. Threats had worked for his father. He frequently beat his wife as well as his children. He tortured men into submission. Everyone fell in line with him because if they didn't, it was worse for them.

Is that the kind of relationship you want with Jewel? For her to be afraid of you? He was cautious in his question, choosing his images carefully. Was his leopard that fucked-up? If he was, what kind of hope did he have for his own relationship with Ania? His leopard's mood definitely affected him.

I want her to be mine.

For the first time, Mitya felt the desperation in the leopard. He took another calming breath, trying to understand what was going on in the cat's mind. *Explain.*

I am angry all the time and I make you that way. You are happy with Ania. I feel it. I am at peace when Jewel is close. No anger. It is the first time I can remember I don't want to kill. It is the first time I can remember you don't want to hurt someone. Jewel and Ania make us better. But Jewel rose with other males close and she invited them even closer.

Anger and rage were back instantly at the memory. The leopard wanted to pace and Mitya gave him that, pacing the length of the master bedroom and back, over and over like a caged animal.

She risked what we had. She risked your happiness. Our peace.

How did one explain to an animal? As intelligent as Dymka was, the traits of the leopard were ingrained in Jewel. Nature drove her during a heat. He had to try to make the cat understand.

Jewel has never been through a heat at the same time as Ania. The drive is tremendous. All females can be very amorous and flirtatious during that time. She will draw you close and then rebuff you. That is their way. She had no idea those males were going to be in the bakery. She has no control over when she rises. Dymka, what you did, threatening her, was wrong. It only drove her away from you.

There was a long silence. He felt Dymka's need to emerge stronger than ever, but knowing he had threatened Ania, even through Mitya, didn't make him feel she was safe.

I would never hurt Ania.

She is fragile compared to you. One bite, one swipe of your paw, and you could kill her. If you kill her, you kill

Jewel and you kill us. Mitya made that clear. *If I lose Ania, I will not continue.* He wanted that clear as well. If his leopard needed firm guidelines and boundaries, he was going to give them to the cat.

I am aware. The tone was conciliatory.

Jewel may well try to repress her heat to prevent the mating ritual, Dymka. That was no threat but a very real possibility.

Again, there was a long silence. *I want Ania to bring Jewel close. I will talk to her.*

Mitya wasn't positive that was such a good idea. Ania was exhausted, but she was also still very wary of Mitya. She may have committed to him and was certain she would follow through with that commitment, but he knew if her leopard pushed her to run, she would do so. He didn't want that threat hanging over his head. Not when he knew what was coming. Or who.

Drake Donovan had brought the news that Sasha Bogomolov in Florida had sent him word that there were rumblings in the Russian communities that Lazar had been making inquiries. Joshua had told him that Lazar himself had reached out to him, asking questions about Mitya, Fyodor, Sevastyan and Gorya. He wanted locations and how many guards. He was offering big money for information.

Mitya didn't want to share that news with Ania until he had cemented their relationship. She thought him bossy. He wanted her to know there was a reason he needed to be bossy. Her safety was paramount. To complicate matters, there was the very real threat to her. If her grandfather had taken a notebook Amory had filled with damning information about Jake Bannaconni and Drake Donovan, who had asked for the information? Who had hired Amory in the first place, and why? The notebook had been sent from New Orleans to the Anwars in Houston, but it had never arrived. Her grandfather had been the driver.

What kind of coincidence was it that at the same time, her father had made a delivery to the Caruso family from New Orleans? Had he bothered to look at the notebook? He knew it was simply a small book being sent. Would that have aroused his suspicion? Had one been sent to both families?

Where was the notebook now? Where would her grand-father hide it? Had the Anwar family become suspicious of Drake Donovan and Jake Bannaconni? It wasn't as if most criminal elements knew Donovan was no one to mess around with. And Bannaconni was notorious for bringing down businesses. He'd hit a few mob-owned businesses, but the majority he took apart were legitimate. That left the question, what else was in that notebook?

Was there evidence against Fyodor? Or Mitya? Joshua? Even Elijah? All of them had banded together to take down the worst of the crime families. In a way, for Mitya, it was to try to make up for some of the horrendous crimes he'd committed working for his father. He knew it was the same for Fyodor.

Mitya was very aware he was born to be a *vor*. He'd been raised to be the kingpin. To rule a lair. He knew no other life, nor was he suited to any other. He had tried to be a bodyguard. He didn't want the temptation or corrup-tion power could bring. He saw what it had done to the leaders of the lairs in his world back home. He saw evi-dence of it here in his new home as well. Friends turning on friends.

"Mitya." Ania sat up slowly, pushing back her heavy hair, the action lifting her breasts as she scooted to put her back to the headboard. "What's wrong? What did Dymka tell you?"

"He wants to make things right with her."

"You're very agitated."

It was merely an observation, not an accusation, but for some reason, his temper flared. Instantly, he realized

Dymka was ashamed and didn't want his woman to know what had been said between the two of them.

If you want her to understand and allow you close to Jewel, I have to make her understand.

Mitya continued to pace, trying not to look at Ania. The covers were pooled around her waist, but she'd lifted her hands to her hair, trying to tame the mass. He couldn't help but stare. He liked her breasts. He liked how perfect they were. The soft mounds, the tight little buds that grew even tighter for him when his mouth was on her. Her legs shifted under the blankets, drawing his attention there. His body responded in spite of the fact that he was every bit as agitated as she'd observed.

Tell her. She will despise me.

That is your judgment on yourself, not hers on you. Mitya hoped he told the truth.

He returned to the bed, standing close to her, his hands on his belt buckle. He slowly stripped off his trousers, thankful he'd removed his shoes earlier. "He was jealous when the other leopards were surrounding you in the bakery. And furious with Jewel when she rose. He didn't understand that she had no control over the timing. He also didn't understand that a female—"

He broke off realizing he was getting into murky waters. His shirt floated to the floor. "A female leopard," he corrected, "can be very flirtatious during a heat. They are vocal and very amorous. They will call a male to them and then rebuff them quite viciously. Two minutes later they will crouch down and call to the male again."

She began to braid her hair, her eyes on first his face, but sliding down to his cock and then back up again. Biting her lip, she nodded. "I looked it up once. There isn't anything on shifters, but there is plenty on leopards."

"Then you know. Dymka was angry with her. He didn't realize she was behaving naturally."

"Like a wild, out-of-control sex maniac." She blushed.

"Like I get with you." Once again, her gaze dropped to his cock.

His erection was thick and very prominent. He liked that she looked, and she obviously liked what she saw.

"I believe it is mutual, Ania. And I like it. I knew what to expect, so I have an advantage you, your leopard and mine don't have. In any case, he was so angry, he threatened her with a beating. Leopards can be extremely rough with one another, so that wasn't the worst he could have said. Jewel didn't like it, but I expect she would have been okay had he stopped there. He threatened you with *me* beating you."

Her hands stilled in her hair. He thought she went a little pale.

He reached down and caught at the blankets. "Do you think I would hit you? Ever?"

She hesitated before answering. When she drew in a breath, her breasts rose and fell. She dropped her arms. "I think Dymka drives you, and if he was raging . . ." She didn't finish but looked a little anguished, as if she was terrified he'd be angry with her for even considering it, yet she couldn't help herself.

"There is always that fear, but as I grew older, I became stronger. Very strong. I had to be in order to resist my father. In doing so, I found I had much more control over my leopard and his mood swings. I learned to handle him and the various negative emotions he brings to me. I know absolutely, without a doubt, I would never hit you in anger or rage. I despised my father for hitting my mother, and I would never want to be that man."

Relief crept into her eyes. He went to the bottom of the bed, reached out and caught her ankles, yanking them apart. Her gaze jumped to his face. Wild. Purple. Instantly sensual. So much heat.

"I know you're tired, *kotyonok*, so you aren't required

to do anything but sit there and rest. I want to indulge myself."

His fingers surrounded her ankles and slid up her calves. He loved the feel of the silk of her skin. "In any case, the minute Jewel heard Dymka had threatened you, she wanted no part of me for you, or Dymka for her."

"That makes sense."

He could tell her breath had caught in her throat. She sounded as if she strained for air. He continued to stroke her legs, stretching them wider apart, his hands massaging her knees and then just above them. He liked looking at her welcoming liquid glistening between her lips for him. So beautiful. Telling him she liked his particular brand of lovemaking.

"I explained to him that we are not Lazar. We do not rule by fear, particularly our women. He understood. He already knew it was wrong but didn't know how to make things right. He wants to talk to her. I told him he would have to wait. I want my time with you. I've missed you." He'd been very careful with her since her father died.

He leaned down and nibbled his way up the inner thigh of her left leg, followed that up by licking up the same path and then using his teeth, scraping back and forth as he tracked that same trail. Her entire body shuddered, and she would have shifted her legs, but he held on to them, his body between them. He kept her spread wide open for him.

He looked up at her. "Baby, what did I say? I'm in the mood to indulge myself. That means you don't move. You stay where I put you."

He bit down on her soft, sensitive inner thigh, up high, close to her entrance. He made it count, wanting her to see he could reprimand her in a sensuous, erotic way. His tongue immediately stroked a soothing rasp over the sting.

"Ow!" She glared at him, but she didn't pull her leg away.

More fresh honey spilled from her body. He swiped his finger over it and drew it into his mouth before switching his attention to her right thigh. He repeated the same action on that side, nibbling, licking and then scraping with his teeth gently. Because he'd nipped her on her left, it was only fair to repeat the same action on the right.

"Ow!" she snapped again and caught his hair in her fist.

She didn't try to pull his head away, which was a good thing. Mitya smiled against her leg. "You look a little like a prune," he lied, rubbing at the inside of her thigh. Up high. Close to where she wanted him to touch. But he didn't touch.

Ania tried to stay still for him, but she squirmed just a little. He lifted his head. "Woman. You are not listening."

"You're making the rules impossible on purpose."

"So I can indulge my need to punish you." He bent his head and lapped at her clit. Her entire body shuddered with pleasure and her fist tightened in his hair. He lifted his head again.

"You have a need to punish me?" Her eyebrows went up, but there was color sweeping up her breasts and into her neck and face. Her nipples were hard little peaks.

"I like seeing your very pretty ass cheeks with my handprints all over them. I like biting your ass too," he admitted. "And then rubbing all that heat in so it spreads through your pretty little pussy and I get the benefits."

Ania nearly choked. "I see."

"If you don't want me to indulge that side of me, you had better stay very still." He lifted his head and suddenly jerked her body down, using her thighs, so she slid along the mattress until she was lying flat.

She let out a small cry and then stifled a laugh. "You're so crazy, Mitya."

"I'm so hungry, Ania," he countered, and cupped her bottom with both hands to lift her hips from the bed. He blew warm air over her, half expecting steam to rise. He could feel the heat pour off her. "If I could, I'd eat you a hundred times a day," he said, meaning it. "I love the way you taste."

"How do I taste?"

"Like you're mine." He bent his head to her and settled his mouth over that slit dripping with his own particular aphrodisiac. For him, her taste had that exquisite taste of wild honeycomb, fragrant with citrus or sometimes lavender, like now. She tended to linger on his tongue, reminding him often how different she was. He savored every bite, lick, his mouth, tongue and teeth moving over and in her. He suckled her clit, savoring that exotic flavor.

Her breath hitched and then exploded outward. Became ragged. Labored. Raw. She panted his name. Sobbed it. She didn't move, holding herself still for the longest time. Then it was impossible, just as he knew it would be. He used his fingers, his thumb, drawing out liquid and spreading it over her. When he buried a finger in her and then used his thumb between her cheeks, her hips bucked.

Smirking, he lifted his head, waited until her eyes were open and then he moved up over her, blanketing her body, so her breasts pressed into his chest and she could barely breathe. "Bad, bad girl," he whispered, framing her face with both hands. "You weren't supposed to move." He took her mouth, kissing her with her honey on his tongue. She didn't pull away from him.

"My face is a mess, baby. Lick it clean for me."

She didn't hesitate. Her tongue lapped at him, removing the sticky honey from his left side. Then she was kissing him, sharing every drop with him before doing the same on his right.

His cock jerked and pulsed. Nearly exploded. She was sexy beyond his wildest imaginations. The moment she was finished, and he could see she was really struggling to breathe with his weight smashing her into the mattress, he was suddenly on his knees, and he rolled her over, trapping her hands under her. Before she could move, he was between her legs again.

"I do love this ass of yours, Ania," he shared, rubbing the firm, tight globes. He ran his finger between her cheeks. Teased her. "Someday, baby, I'm going to introduce you to all kinds of very delicious, dirty things. Right now, I'm indulging myself."

He didn't wait. His hand was big and each swat was hard, leaving her cheeks red. He varied the pattern of hard and gentle, not wanting a rhythm she might catch. He stopped abruptly and began to massage, spreading the heat, just as he'd said he would. His fingers dipped into her pussy, finding her slicker and hotter. He grinned.

"I love how you love the things I do to you."

She pushed back with her hips and he immediately removed his fingers and began all over again, swatting her cheeks. Just before he was certain she would protest, he began massaging, rubbing, kneading. He spread kisses and then bit down in the middle of his handprint.

Her breath hissed out of her, but she pushed back into him. Mitya immediately repeated the action on the other side in order to be fair. He caught her hips and yanked her to her knees, already on his. His cock in hand, he slammed home, nearly driving her back to the mattress. She cried out. Chanted his name. Pressed back into him with his every surge forward.

Fire raced up his spine, roared through his cock. Her tight muscles were so scorching hot he felt the burn right through his entire groin. He felt her heartbeat through her sheath and knew she felt his through his cock. His fingers swept back and forth along the crack of her cheeks. She was slick with honey and he pushed his finger into her, deeper than he'd ever gone, so he could feel his cock working her.

She sobbed his name and pushed back into him as the bundle of nerve endings heightened her pleasure even more. He couldn't slow down, his hips driving deep over and over. He was so addicted to the sizzling flames he never wanted to leave her. He broke out in a fine sheen of sweat, and still he didn't stop. He worked her body hard, and when the first orgasm hit her it was like a tidal wave, impossible to stop. It was all he could do to maintain as it engulfed him, her body clamping down, threatening to take him with her. She cried out but he kept pistoning into her right through it, so the friction was incredible.

Ania collapsed onto her elbows but now he held her hips with both hands, helping her to drive back into him every bit as hard as he was surging into her. His breath was sawing in and out of his lungs, so labored he wasn't certain he would survive, but it didn't matter. Nothing mattered but the time he spent in her body, in that tight, scorching-hot place of pure pleasure. He kept driving.

Her body tightened around his. Clamped down like a vise. For a moment it was as if everything stopped. Held his breath. Then it came, a tsunami beyond anything he'd experienced. Her muscles felt like a million hot tongues of silk, working him, sucking him dry, milking and pumping, squeezing and burning until the hot splash of seed coated her walls over and over again.

He collapsed over top of her, driving her to the mattress. Both lay panting, desperate for air. He couldn't move, his heart pounding and his cock pulsing. Every ripple of her body squeezed his sensitive and very spent cock, but he didn't have the strength to pull out of her. They lay together for a long time, just feeling their bodies and the way they burned together.

Eventually, Mitya forced himself to roll off of her so she didn't die from lack of air. He swept his hand down her back to her bottom, gently massaging her cheeks. He loved her skin. He loved the feel of her. He loved the fact that no matter what he did, she was on board all the way. She never protested when he collapsed over her, even though he mashed her into the mattress.

Her face was turned away from him, so he took advantage. "I know you think I'm with you for my leopard. I'm not, Ania. I'm with you for me. You've given me more than I ever expected to have for myself. I never thought any woman would ever be able to live with me. Or put up with the things I want in a partner. I thought it was impossible for any woman to love me . . ."

The moment he said that, her head whipped around, her eyes on his face. "Why in the world would you ever think that?" she demanded. "Mitya, you're a wonderful man." A faint grin crept over her mouth, turning up her lips and lighting her eyes. "Without your exceedingly and annoyingly bossy ways, you're really quite wonderful."

He leaned in to her and kissed her nose. "You like my exceedingly bossy ways."

She made a show of rolling her eyes. "I like you, that's for sure."

He sobered instantly. "Do you think you could love me, Ania? Given time? Is that even a possibility? I'd rather know now than wait to see . . ."

"You're such a goof. Do you really think I'd be here because you threatened to come after me if I ran? I would go to Drake, or to one of the other families. I'm here with you because I've already found I can't be without you. I may be scared out of my mind, and I don't know if that's because Jewel is, or I at least have some common sense, or it's a combination, but I went out of the house that night because the thought of losing you was too much for me."

"I can tell you without reservation, Ania, and I don't know the first thing about love, so I'm not certain this is the greatest declaration, but I can't do without you. If there is a person on this earth, other than my ridiculous cousins who got me into a mess, I can say you are the person I love. And since they got me into the mess, you're far up the line in front of them."

Ania started laughing. She rolled onto her back and

stared at the ceiling, her arms crossed over her stomach, laughter spilling out of her like a golden symphony. "You're so crazy. Your ridiculous cousins got you into a mess? And I'm in front of them because of it? That's your declaration of love?"

Her eyes met his and she suddenly rolled over again, this time flinging her body over his, sprawling over top of him, the laughter fading from her gorgeous eyes. "That's the best declaration of love I've ever heard, and I'm going to cherish it. I honestly thought I didn't matter to you, Mitya, other than as someone who held Jewel."

His teeth scraped gently down her ear. "It's the other way around. Dymka is very lucky that Jewel does it for him."

"He'd better be good to her."

"I think he's learned his lesson. Let me clean up and get a washcloth for you. Then we'll let the leopards talk and see if they can clear things up between them."

"Jewel's very sulky."

"She's going to rise very soon, especially if we get any wilder. Leopard sex is rough and often, Ania. When I take you, I mean to be gentler, but it isn't working. I think Jewel is close to rising whether or not she wants to."

"Are you saying when Jewel and I are no longer fertile at the same time, you and I aren't going to have our crazy, wild sex together? Because I won't be happy about that."

He grinned at her as he shifted off the bed. "No, babe, I'm not saying that. I'm just saying that leopard of yours is in for a shock if she refuses to speak to him. We aren't going to take chances that she rises without me being around. From now on, wherever I go, so do you."

She didn't protest, although he thought she might. Instead, she smirked a little, which gave him pause as he washed himself and then got a warm washcloth for her.

"Are you up to something?"

"Why would you think that?"

She was more relaxed with his ministrations now. She

just widened her legs and let him wash her. He enjoyed taking care of her. He still thought she might be up to something.

"Ania," he cautioned.

She smiled and shook her head. "I don't want her emerging without you being around. Remember how awful it was for me in the bakery without you? If you don't remember, I certainly do."

He couldn't argue with that, although he regarded her suspiciously.

11

"I DON'T know why men think women are the gossips," Evangeline said, sliding into the chair across from Ania. "They're all in the back where my husband has his office, if you can call it that—mostly he eats my pastries—and they're talking about things I'm not supposed to overhear."

Ania couldn't help smiling. "Do you want to know what they're saying?"

"Absolutely not. I like baking my pastries and selling them to happy customers. The bakery is really popular, I think thanks to the fact that I'm married to Fyodor. This is the cops' favorite place, and there seem to be a lot of cops around."

"I think it's more likely your bakery is popular because your pastries are the absolute best." Ania leaned her chin into the heel of her hand. "How's the work coming on the coffee shop? I know the wall was torn down and building had started, but I don't hear any hammers."

"It's so frustrating," Evangeline said, wiping her hand across her forehead. "Not that I want anyone to come to work sick, but the actual work was only supposed to take a few weeks. I think it's more like a few months. Everyone seems to have gotten the flu. The foreman said he was going to hire a few new workers. Timur wasn't thrilled with the idea, and they went round and round."

"Timur is like Sevastyan, isn't he?" Ania observed. "I'm getting to know everyone a little bit better." She frowned as she watched Evangeline press her hand to her mouth. Her hand was trembling. "Are you still sick? I thought that went away after the first few weeks."

"I think it usually does," Evangeline conceded. "Unfortunately, remember I told you I have hyperemesis gravidarum? It just means I get very sick and sometimes need fluids. Mine doesn't seem to be going away. The worst is, it can reoccur with other pregnancies, which doesn't have me looking forward to more children."

"That's terrible, Evangeline," Ania sympathized. "I'd hate that." She looked around the beautiful bakery. Clearly, Evangeline had put her heart and soul into her business. "You love this place, don't you?"

While she carried on the conversation, she practiced watching people on the sidewalk passing by. What were they wearing? What did they look like? Height. Weight. Hair color. Could she identify them again? Sevastyan talked a lot about gait. How someone walked. They might disguise appearance, but few changed the way they walked. Cars on the street. Packages. Really pay attention to packages. Anyone walking close to the bakery. Anyone coming into the bakery. Did they have a package? When they walked out, were they still carrying the package?

She needed a lot of work on observation. On the other hand, no one could match her driving skills. No one could match going over a car looking for bombs or anything at all out of the ordinary. Cars were her thing. She could name every make, model, color, engine; she could practically tell Sevastyan what kind of wipers were on a car.

She hadn't said a word to Mitya that she was trying to worm her way into his security unit. He'd lose his mind. He was so protective of her she could barely go to the women's room without five men following her in. Still, she wasn't giving up. Sevastyan didn't want her as a bodyguard, but he did want her to drive. They'd even discussed ways to get Mitya to agree to her driving him around.

There was only one small problem in the way. Sex. Mitya liked her in the back seat with him for a reason. The moment the car was in motion and the privacy screen was up, he wanted her mouth on him, or he wanted his cock in her. He sipped drinks off her skin, pouring them over her breasts and into her belly button. Once he shook up champagne and sprayed a small amount of it inside her, and then spent nearly the entire drive home sucking out every drop he could find. He *loved* sex in the car.

Okay. He loved sex everywhere. Sometimes he took her on the balcony at their home. Outside in the flower gardens. Once it was on the rooftop when he'd had her go up to see the stars. It didn't matter where they were, he was more than willing to be inventive. She doubted if he'd give up sex in the car just so she could drive. In all honesty, she wasn't certain she would give up sex in the car with him just to drive. She loved it every bit as much as he did.

She sighed and kept watching those passing by. According to Sevastyan, the foot traffic had increased by quite a bit in the last few weeks. That was good for Evangeline's business, but not so good for those on security.

"Fyodor wanted to expand this room as well," Evangeline said. "But after seeing how long it's taking for Ashe's coffee shop to be built, I said no. I don't want my customers to listen to the hammers going all day. In fact, I was going to see if Fyodor could find a way for them to work in the evenings after I'm closed. I know that's an inconvenience, but maybe if we pay more, it would be worth it to the crew."

"That's a good idea. Timur would like that as well."

Evangeline made a face. "He wouldn't. He likes being able to watch them like hawks. If he wasn't down here, what if they snuck something into my kitchen? That's how he thinks. Timur would prefer me to give up the bakery and stay at home. He thinks once I have the twins that's what I'll do."

"You won't?"

Evangeline shook her head. "I'm already working on a nursery here at the shop. I've been drawing it out, just the way I did this shop and Ashe's coffee shop. Fyodor and Timur own all the buildings. The one beside the coffee shop is going to be empty in two months. I asked them if I could have that shop as well." She flashed a small grin. "They think I really want to expand. I want to make a really nice nursery and playroom for the twins. That way I can have them down here when I'm working."

Ania laughed softly. "I think you are amazing, Evangeline. How do you do it? I think I'm tough and then Mitya starts handing out decrees and I just seem to fall in line. You don't argue, you just kind of do what you want."

Evangeline shrugged. "You have to pick your battles with men like Fyodor and Mitya. All the cousins. They have certain things that really matter. Safety is huge to them. Huge. I watch Mitya's face when he's around you. He thinks the sun, moon and stars revolve around you. That's dangerous, because his protection factor is already enormous. Couple that with the way he loves you and you don't stand much of a chance of winning an argument when it comes to matters of safety. It just isn't going to happen. You have to resign yourself to that."

Ania shook her head. "I already have felt that edge with

him a few times. Still, I love driving fast. It was always my outlet. I have this need sometimes for the big adrenaline rush, and I'd sneak out and street race. I've considered doing it a time or two. But then we have wild sex and the urge passes." She laughed at herself but at the same time she felt a little guilty that Mitya could get around her so easily.

"Do you feel like racing is a big dream of yours? Because if it is, you need to talk to him about it."

Ania knew it wasn't. "No. Sometimes I just want that rush. Sex with Mitya is better."

"Honey, if you really love him, you have to give him the things he needs. Do you really need street racing? No, probably not. You like it. You get a rush from it, but it isn't something you need or crave with every fiber of your being. So concede there, jump him and get your rush."

She looked around her and then gestured. "This shop represents my independence. My ability to rise above my childhood. I need it. I might not forever, but I do now. I had to sit my man down and let him know exactly what the bakery meant to me."

"And he got it?"

"With some talking. The thing is, when they love you, when you're their world, they will listen because they want you happy. Timur doesn't care so much about my happiness as he does about my safety. He curses a lot, but he accommodates what I need. Now, Ashe. If she says she wants the shop and it's important, that man will do handstands to give it to her. Still, she stays within the parameters he gives her for her safety."

Evangeline leaned toward her. "But you deserve to have your dream, Ania, whatever it is. You sold your family business, so there must be something else you've always secretly desired."

Ania looked into her latte as if that would give her answers. "I always thought I would have to take over the family business. I'm not very girly, but . . ." She hesitated and looked around again. "If I wasn't driving, which I would love to do for Sevastyan, then I wouldn't mind trying my hand at designing cars."

"Why shouldn't you do that?"

"It isn't hands-on. My father wasn't that thrilled when I talked to him about it." A flush of heat slid over Ania and her breasts suddenly felt swollen and achy. Her nipples pushed against her lacy bra, rubbing, hurting, yet at the same time, a flame of desire. She touched her tongue to her upper lip. "Excuse me, Evangeline, I think I need to go to the ladies' room."

Ania got to her feet and started to turn just as the little bell over the door sounded. She glanced over and her heart dropped as Alessandro Caruso strode through the door.

You horrible little hussy, she hissed at Jewel. *You wouldn't even talk to Dymka, but the moment he shows up, you're rolling over and trying to get laid.*

She didn't so much as wave before practically running to the restroom. Little beads of sweat trickled between her breasts. Her clit pulsed and throbbed like a living flame. She burned between her legs. Staring into the mirror, she could see that her eyes looked dilated, a dark purple that resembled two drenched pansies pressed into her face. She gripped the sink as another wave of heat rushed through her. Her sex clenched emptily. She could barely breathe.

Jewel, what are you doing? I can't betray Mitya. I won't. I'll live in this restroom before I do that.

Jewel seemed to be in a state of complete chaos. Fear, need, hunger and desperation were all mixed together in one terrible churning storm. *I'm sorry.*

The moment the female leopard apologized, Ania realized both of them couldn't be out of control. The leopard had no idea what was happening to her. She was still very much afraid of Dymka. She'd stayed as still as possible, huddled in a miserable little ball while the hunger and need continued to wash over her. She'd delayed her rising. Prolonged the agony. All to save Ania from Mitya and his fists.

Ania took several deep breaths to try to get past the rising need. It came in waves. She was on fire. Every part of her body burned until she wanted to scream. She couldn't imagine what poor little Jewel was experiencing, and yet the cat hid, refusing to allow her mate access to her so that Ania would be safe.

We can handle this, sweetheart, Ania crooned. She kept breathing deeply, putting her head down as if to stop a faint. *Give me a minute and I'll get us out of here.*

She should have gone to the back, where the kitchen was. Where Mitya was in another seemingly endless meeting with Fyodor. The cousins liked to get together and talk. It couldn't all be business, but they pretended it was.

"Ania? *Kotyonok?*"

She closed her eyes, savoring the sound of his voice. Her savior. He was always there. Always ready to do whatever was necessary. She knew he was very aware of the condition she was in. The moment he opened the door to the ladies' room, he would smell her raging hormones. Every male in the shop was most likely aware.

"Tell me what to do, Mitya." Her voice wasn't her own. It was sultry. Sinful. Temptation itself. Lower than her own pitch, mixed with the chuffing sweetness of a leopard. "She's so scared and so am I. She's fighting it and I don't know how to help her."

"Can you make it to the car?"

Ania swallowed hard. It seemed a very long way to go, yet if she and Mitya went crazy in Evangeline's restroom, she'd never be able to face anyone again. "I have to make it," she decreed, not at all certain she could.

Her skin felt too tight for her body and she itched

everywhere. Wave after wave of something moved just under her skin, adding to the discomfort. Her clothes felt like a terrible weight on her, and the fabric added to the irritation until she wanted to rip it off of her and shred it so it could never touch her again.

"Come here." Mitya held out his arm. He had his coat off. He almost always wore that long trench coat. Long, *heavy* trench coat. All the cousins did.

She went to him on feet that were locked into shoes that felt too small. Every step hurt. She kept breathing, concentrating on her little leopard, trying to make the cat feel as if Ania knew what she was doing and was confident and in control. When she reached Mitya, she raised desperate eyes to him.

"We've got this, baby," he crooned gently.

He swung the coat around her shoulders, enveloping her in his warmth. In his scent. In him. Her heart turned over and then pounded. Everything he did felt caring. His arm followed the coat, sweeping her under his shoulder, next to his side. Tucking her in tight, her front to his ribs, so he sheltered her completely.

"We have to hurry," she whispered.

Mitya's answer was to shove open the restroom door and step out with bold confidence. Sevastyan, Vikenti and Zinoviy were waiting, the two brothers stepping to either side of them, Sevastyan leading the way and Miron bringing up the rear. They went out of the bakery as a group, Ania keeping her head down. She knew normal patrons would never have a clue anything was wrong, but every shifter would know she was in heat—including Alessandro.

The car was right in front of the building, double-parked, forcing traffic to go around it. Sevastyan yanked open the back door on the passenger side and Ania slid in. As she did so, Mitya pulled back his trench coat and slid in as well. The privacy screen was already up. That didn't matter. Nothing mattered but getting to Mitya's body. To have room. She needed room. She was almost sobbing and had to force air into her lungs and calm into her mind.

"Where can we go, Mitya? I don't think I can wait. She's hurting, and I have to get her to the surface. She needs him. She's terrified but she needs him." Even as she explained, she was dragging off clothes, uncaring that the car hadn't moved because Miron wasn't in the driver's seat yet. She just had to get the offending fabric off her skin.

"Sevastyan will get us to the hill country. I've phoned ahead and if they drop us near the Bannaconni ranch or Perez's, the leopards can run there. They'll have plenty of space. It will take them most of the night to make their way home."

The confidence in his voice steadied her. The fact that he'd already thought how best to provide for Dymka and Jewel amazed her. She didn't have the clarity needed to think that far ahead. The best she could do was not lose her mind right there and let her little female down.

Mitya also was shedding his clothes, but not nearly fast enough to suit her. She threw her shirt and bra down on the floor and went to her knees between his legs. Her mouth found his cock and immediately her world centered there. He was hot. Hard. The shape and feel of him amazed her. His girth stretched her lips, but it was such an amazing feeling to have him in her mouth. On her tongue. She lapped at him. Got him wet and slick. Fed off the droplets leaking from the broad crown. The taste of him made her squirm with need.

His hands went to her breasts, kneading the soft curves. Each flick of his fingers and brush of his thumbs over her nipples left her feeling as if a flame had touched her over and over. She arched into his hands even as she took him deeper into her mouth. She wanted to swallow him whole. She wanted the taste of him to stay with her always. Her hands went to his heavy sac, gently squeezing and massaging, not nearly as rough as he was getting with her breasts. She needed him to be rougher. She needed him so much she knew tears leaked from her eyes and her body had gone nearly bright red her temperature had soared so high.

"Ania, I love every time you suck my cock. Nothing is sexier, but right now, I need to be inside you. Get on the seat, on your hands and knees."

Mitya used his commanding voice, the one that was rough velvet, the one that no one, least of all her, dared refuse. She reluctantly allowed his cock to slide off her tongue and immediately faced away from him, looking out the window as she climbed onto the seat.

Mitya's hands slid over her body possessively and then he was at her entrance, finding her slick welcome. Without any preamble, he slammed into her. Hard. She cried out as the fire engulfed her, moving through her body from her sex to her belly and breasts and then right up into her brain. The flames seemed to roar over her and she pushed back into him, needing him to do something. Anything to make that terrible burning stop.

He wrapped his arm around her waist and surged into her again and again. It wasn't enough, and she couldn't stop sobbing. Begging. His body hammered hard into hers, driving her forward on the seat until her breasts were plastered against the window. The coolness of the glass felt good against her red-hot skin. But it wasn't enough. Nothing seemed to put out the fire that burned out of control through her body.

"Mitya." She wailed his name. He had to save her. Save Jewel.

"We'll be out of here in a minute or two, baby," he assured softly.

The confines of the car were killing her. She needed space. She needed to move. She needed him to pound harder. To do things, all sorts of things, to put out the terrible fire raging through her.

Mitya's calm saved her sanity. She clung to that as his body continued to piston into hers. He gripped her hips hard as he surged into her, dragging her back into him. Each time his cock drove through her tight, reluctant folds, the friction sent waves of scorching heat and savage pleasure rushing through her. It was violent, it was brutal, it was the most amazing sex she'd ever experienced, but it wasn't enough.

She was going to die if the flames didn't stop. They were consuming her. Eating her alive from the inside out. She had no idea how long Mitya's body pounded into hers, but suddenly the car stopped, and pulled to the side of the road. Mitya withdrew, his hands biting into her hard.

"What are you doing?" she wailed. "You can't stop. You can't."

"Trust me, baby. This will be so much better."

He opened the door and dragged her out into the fading light of the day. The other cars were out of sight. The car had been left on the side of the road, the fencing telling her they were near Bannaconni's ranch. They were out on a private road, but still in plain sight of anyone passing by. It didn't matter. Nothing mattered but making the fire stop. Miron had gone from driving their car to hopping into one of the others and disappearing down the road to leave them in privacy. She had no idea where Sevastyan was.

"Mitya." Her voice was filled with urgency.

The breeze felt cool on her skin. There were droplets of water in the air, a very fine mist or a promise of rain—it didn't matter, her hot skin soaked it up.

Mitya caught her in hard hands, spun her around and lifted her up onto the hood of the car. He yanked her thighs apart and she fell back, throwing her arms out to keep herself from slipping. Then she screamed, uncaring if the entire valley heard her. His mouth was there, hotter than hell, devouring her. Eating her alive, his tongue flicking hard at her inflamed clit. His teeth found her and tugged, biting down just hard enough that he triggered an explosion. The waves rolled through her entire body like flames.

He took his time eating her, his fingers working her, front and back, driving deep and then shallow. By turns gently and then rough. His mouth never stopped moving, tongue stabbing deep, then licking, his teeth biting down until she screamed with need, pain and pleasure mixing together to add to the wild, hot ride. It wasn't enough. The burn just got hotter until she was writhing, out of control, begging him for something she didn't understand.

He dragged her from the hood, spun her around again and shoved her over it, bending her at the waist, kicking her legs apart. Then his hand was there, turning her red cheeks to a brilliant crimson, sending those flames unfurling throughout her entire body. Each stroke was a blaze of fire and it radiated outward, stroking scorching heat deep inside so that flames rushed up her spine and down her legs, licking up her thighs, until she was an inferno.

Mitya took her savagely, half-mad himself with the drive of his leopard and his woman completely in the throes of her heat. Her body was his and he used it, riding her hard, stroking, petting, swatting and biting when the need drove him. His cock felt like a red-hot steel spike, so hard he might shatter. She was so tight and scorching hot, he thought he might burn up while inside her, and yet nothing could stop him from taking her. Nothing. No one.

He knew he was acting like a man possessed, but it didn't matter. He wanted to crawl inside her, stay in that paradise that was more hell than heaven or more heaven than hell, the madness claiming both of them. Her screams drove him on. The way she pushed her sweet ass back into him, desperate for his cock, seeking his hand. The way she reacted when he buried his finger and then two between her cheeks as he fucked her harder and harder. All of it came together into a whirling vortex of complete pleasure.

Both of them had spiraled out of control. They moved together in a savage dance, while heat and flames burned them alive. He felt his body grow hotter and harder. Hers coiled tighter and tighter. Then she screamed again, a long, low sound somewhere between ecstasy and torment. Her body clamped down on his and he felt that same ecstasy and torment. The vise was vicious but felt so damn good he couldn't think straight. His cock jerked hard, while her silken muscles milked him like tight, skilled fingers. Jet after jet of hot semen rocketed out of him, splashing the walls of her sheath, coating them with him. Branding her his.

Her breath was coming in a singsong cry, soft, almost heartbreaking music. He pulled out of her, turned her into his arms and took her mouth. Her kisses were like those flames crawling through his body, stirring his senses, driving him mad.

"She needs to come out, baby," he whispered, resting his forehead on hers. She had her eyes closed and he waited, feeling the shivers moving through her as her female fought the natural emergence. He waited until he was looking into her eyes. Those dark purple eyes, dripping with fear, ringed with a dark ferocity that told him Jewel was very, very close. "You have to help her, Ania."

"Tell me how."

He barely recognized her voice. Her leopard was so close she was affecting Ania's speech patterns. He felt the ripples under her skin. The pushing of the leopard in her body.

"Talk to her. Reassure her. Coax her. Tell her how she'll run free and her mate will find her every bit as alluring as I find you."

Ania's gaze clung to his for a long moment and he knew she needed almost as much reassurance as her leopard. Her body was still on fire. Inflamed. Her hips pushed hard against his, rubbing. She found his thigh, straddled it and rubbed, the sexiest thing possible, and just that fast his cock was as hard as a diamond.

"Can't you be in me? I want to ride you, Mitya. Let me have your cock."

He knew he shouldn't. Hell. Who was he kidding? There was no way to stop himself. He lifted her into his arms and waited for her to wrap her legs around him. He buried himself in an inferno, taking his breath, robbing him completely of all good sense. The moment she sheathed him, the familiar fire was there instantly. He laid her on the hood of the car again, dragging just her bottom off, so he could drive into her as he gave her instructions. It wasn't easy to think, but it was necessary.

"Try to connect now, while we're fucking. This is mating, this is what she needs. The feel of her mate's cock driving into her, putting out that fire for her. Share it, Ania. Share how this feels with her. The beauty. The savagery. The balance between brutal and bliss. Lure her to the surface."

"I can't think."

His hands went to her breasts so only the strength of his body kept her in position. Each time she slipped toward him, he slammed his body into her, driving her back onto the hood. His fingers were rough, tugging. Rolling. Pinching. "Do it, damn it."

Ania nodded, her gaze clinging to Mitya's. He was so strong. His face was carved into a mask of sheer sensuality. Lust was there in every line. In his eyes. Flames seemed to burn in his eyes, turning them that deep arctic blue. His hands were nearly as hard as his cock, but she wanted harder. She wanted to feel his teeth. She wanted her mouth on him. She wanted . . . just wanted. Her mind was so chaotic, but her body was in a frenzy of need.

There was no disobeying Mitya when he used that tone, and she had to get past the fires roaring through her and reach her leopard. It was the only way for this to stop. If it didn't stop, she feared she'd go insane. The hard drive of his body sent her back skidding along the hood of the car. She could still feel the way his hands had smacked her bottom, and between her legs she was so slick and hot she thought she would implode. Or just burn up.

"Damn it, Ania. Do what I tell you or I stop."

He couldn't stop. There was no stopping. She stared up at the sky. The sun was setting, so that streaks of gray slid through the fire of orange trying to peek through the clouds rolling across the sky. Every stroke sent matching flames streaking through her body. She reached deep.

Jewel. Baby, I'll help you. I'll be with you every step of the way.

What if he hurts me?

She felt the leopard tremble. Both knew she was so close there was no turning back. She had no choice. She had risen, and the raging hormones were doing the rest. Taking them both over. Giving neither a choice.

He'll only do it once and then we're gone. I swear to you, if Dymka hurts you, Jewel, I'll take us far away from here where they'll never find us. It would kill her to leave Mitya, but if he couldn't control his leopard, then she had no business being with him.

She knew the moment Jewel accepted her fate. Mitya seemed to know it as well. Most likely, Dymka was very close to the surface and was telling his companion exactly how close Jewel was. He would sense her. He would know her scent and just how ready she was.

Mitya increased his speed and changed the angle, jerking her legs up so he could hit that place inside her that sent her careening over the edge. She was engulfed fast, her entire body, taking Mitya with her, so that it seemed the world retreated, throwing the two of them together into a fiery realm of sheer pleasure. She heard herself keening his name. Sobbing it. Chanting it. When she could breathe, open her eyes, the aftershocks still shaking her, he was dropping her legs from around him and lifting her off the hood.

"Call to her, Ania. She's so ready. Call to her." His voice was hoarse, almost a sawing.

Looking into his eyes, she could see the leopard. Unlike Jewel, unlike Ania, he was calm. Those usually malevolent eyes were steady, amber rather than yellow, wholly focused on her. Watching. Waiting.

Ania took a breath. *Now, Jewel. You can run free. Tease him. Entice him. Play.*

Jewel had obviously made up her mind because the next thing Ania knew, she was on the ground, on all fours, her skin feeling as if it was shredding, too small to accommodate the bones, so much denser than her own. Her jaw hurt, stretched, elongated, teeth filling her mouth so fast she was terrified, her heart beating out of control.

Mitya's hand stroked over her head, calming her. "Breathe, *kotyonok*, you're doing great. She's almost out. Relax and let her take over. You'll still be right there. You'll feel the freedom as well. I'll be with you the entire time."

His voice was steady. Mitya was the man who could always be counted on. His voice held that rough velvet tone that meant he was in command and needed to be obeyed. She forced her shivering body to relax and allow the shifting to happen. It was both exhilarating and terrifying. Her body felt like it was coming apart. It hurt. Every joint. Every bone. Her teeth. That hurt the worst. Or maybe it was her skull. The itch was horrendous.

The actual change felt slow and unsteady, as if Jewel pushed, retreated and then pushed again. Like Ania, she had no idea what she was doing. The female was definitely in her first life cycle with Mitya. She had no past experience to draw on.

Then suddenly there was fur covering her body, beautiful, astonishing fur. It was thick and long, the undercoat a gorgeous white. Not golden brown, but pure white with thick black rosettes. They were widely spaced, each almost a perfect circle of dense black. The coat was impressive and different, but definitely Amur, a winter snow coat that was so beautiful and different, she would have been hunted relentlessly in the wild for that alone.

Mitya stroked a hand down her fur, murmuring his approval. Jewel was on the smaller side, weighing not more than sixty pounds, but she was compact and sleek, with roped muscles moving beneath her thick fur. Mitya shifted easily, his experience showing. The transformation was done in close to a second, maybe three at most, his large body suddenly completely different, one moment standing on two legs, the next, Dymka was there, those intimidating eyes completely focused on his mate.

Dymka was large for an Amur leopard. Most large males weighed around a hundred and six or seven pounds. Dymka, clearly, was closer to two hundred pounds of sheer fighting muscle. His body dwarfed Jewel's, towering over her as he stood beside her, his chin sliding over her back possessively.

She trembled for a moment and then looked into his eyes. Ania felt the impact. Dymka was conveying something important to the female. Ania tried to adjust her imaging to what the male used. *You are safe with me. She is safe with me. I will guard you both with my life. Mitya will do the same.*

The reassurance was done by shoving images into Jewel's mind, just as Ania did when she talked to her female. Dymka was much better at it. He had a lot of practice communicating with Mitya.

Jewel tossed her head up, gave Dymka a flirty look and then leapt away from him, heading toward the field where the heavy brush seemed a gateway to the trees just on the other side. The moment she began to run, pain burst along her hip, on her right leg, as if something had shaved through her fur, right along her hip, and stung a long line there. Dymka hit her hard in the side, driving her off her feet so she rolled over and over, his bigger body pushing hers. They ended up in a tangle of limbs just past the first line of brush.

Dymka nudged her to her feet, his body between hers and the road. She realized she'd narrowly escaped being shot. The male was already protecting her. He wanted her to run toward the trees, keeping to the brush. She took off, Dymka prowling after her, shielding her from the road as she made a dash for the trees, her heart in her throat.

The sound of a rifle firing and the ugly splat of a bullet sending leaves and vines whirling in the air before they settled to the ground urged her to greater speeds. She managed to make it unscathed to the trees and ran just beyond them before stumbling to a halt, her heart pounding so hard she could barely breathe. Dymka came to a stop as well, standing close to her, protectively, using his rough tongue to gently lap at the stinging right hip. Then a deeper sound announced a second weapon into the mix.

Sevastyan, Mitya said with confidence. *He'll take out the shooter.*

Ania wanted to ask all sorts of questions. She wasn't certain how to get her body back in order to ask them, or whether if she pushed images into Jewel's mind, Dymka could read them. She tried.

Do you think Alessandro followed us? She used the image of the oldest Caruso brother and an image of him trailing after them.

We'll know soon enough. He'll be dead. Vikenti, Zinoviy, Miron and Sevastyan will hunt down whoever did this if they haven't already killed him. There was a grimness to the images he was conveying, so she knew it was Mitya providing the information. He sounded like he would personally hunt down anyone who had shot at them.

You have to shift. I need to check the wound.

Jewel needed Dymka desperately. There was nothing to be done about the shooter now. Sevastyan would take care of that. She knew Mitya's cousin enough to know no one would escape him once he set on their path. Her female deserved her time. She was burning up, almost as if she was running a fever, and that fire had started, the one only her mate could put out.

Jewel is fine. It is a surface scratch only. Fortunately, she had just leapt away from Dymka and the bullet just grazed her. She wants her time with her mate. I say give her this night. You can look at it in the morning.

Ania found herself waiting for the verdict. They all did. Jewel. Dymka. Her. That told her, more than anything else ever could have, that it was Mitya in command of them all. He had the control. She hoped he would always use it wisely, because she wouldn't always blindly follow him. She wasn't built that way.

I don't like not taking care of my woman, but I trust that you would say so if either of you was hurt badly.

There was both reluctance and warning in his tone. Triumph burst through her. He had listened to her. More and more she was beginning to believe he would do that, listen carefully and take into consideration what she said.

You know the way home, little Jewel, she whispered to her female. *Take your time with Dymka. Don't let him push you into anything until you're ready.*

Jewel gave a little sniff. The sniper had thrown her for a moment, but now that she was assured by Ania and Mitya that it was being taken care of, she was back to her most alluring. She had her mate close and her body was driving her, needing his attention—just not yet. It couldn't be *that* easy for him. She wanted him to earn it. He was a big cat, and sadly, there weren't challenges to him. She would have liked that. Male cats vying for her attention.

You little hussy.

It is good that he knows others want me. I am more valuable to him.

I think you're valuable enough.

Jewel began to move away from Dymka, throwing him coquettish looks and rubbing along the tree trunks to spread her alluring scent. She became quite vocal, calling out as she wandered through the trees, rolling on the ground to spread her pheromones everywhere. She rubbed along the trees and rocks and called out continually.

Dymka paced along behind her, showing patience Ania hadn't thought he was capable of. He didn't try to approach Jewel until she began to run, playfully throwing up pawfuls of leaves and swiping her claws along thin tree trunks. Every few yards she slowed to allow Dymka to circle her, coming close when she crouched. If he got too close, she rebuffed him with a swipe of her paw. He leapt away, far too fast to get caught.

Jewel liked the attention, and not quite ready for the male, she took advantage, leading him across two streams, playing in the water, throwing the liquid into the air and dancing around for a few minutes before running again toward Mitya's estate. It was several miles away. They had to cut across Eli Perez's property. It bordered the enormous Bannaconni estate.

The two leopards had gotten deep into the Perez property, heading toward a grove of trees, Jewel vocalizing repeatedly, her call becoming more amorous and urgent with each passing mile. It had grown very dark and more than once she had rested, Dymka guarding her, careful to stay a small distance away. She continued to rebuff his advances, but he was persistent, staying just close enough to let her know he wasn't going anywhere.

Jewel sent out another call. To Ania's horror, three males roared in answer. Jewel shivered when Dymka came to life. His answer was more than a challenge. There was a hunger for battle, a need as deep as the one driving him to mate. He welcomed the challenge and told the other males to bring it on.

12

DEEP in Jewel's body, Ania was concerned that they had crossed private land, land owned by shifters. Shifters who worked for Bannaconni and Perez. It was possible, even probable, that the males had heard the young female calling for a mate. It would be natural for the males to answer the call of a female in heat.

Mitya. We can't let the males fight one another.

Jewel gave a little sniff. She might be timid, but having males fight over her was a good thing, not a bad one. Ania ignored her. She reached out again to Mitya. Instead of the usual calm, steady man, in his place she found a being eager to accept the challenge the three newcomers had roared.

Mitya. Someone had to be the voice of reason. *Let's make a run for it.*

There was the briefest of hesitations, and a chill went down her spine. Jewel felt it as well as she went still. Waiting.

For some reason, Ania felt as if there was an axe poised just over her neck. *What is it? Just tell me.*

Those leopards are not local, kotyonok. They are men from my father's lair. I recognize the voices of their leopards. In the old days, they would turn their leopards loose on Dymka to hunt him.

Ania found herself shivering violently, even buried deep inside Jewel. She knew some of Mitya's history, because he'd shared it, but she also knew he'd whitewashed it—that it had been far worse than he'd ever portrayed.

Can we run?

I have no intention of wasting my strength on running. Dymka will defeat them. While two come at him, the third will go after Jewel.

Ania cursed herself for being so far into the frenzied heat that she hadn't thought to put a pack containing weapons around her neck. *How did they get this close without our side being tipped off?*

She had to work to suppress the desire to urge Jewel to turn and run. Even if she did, with three big males coming to fight Dymka, one would easily come after her. Jewel had no experience in battle. None. She was on fire, desperate now for her mate, but the other three males would be on them in minutes.

We'll find out. Clearly there are traitors. Jewel will have to be protected, Ania. These males are fighting machines. Killers. They will tear her apart.

Even though she's in heat?

Dymka roared a fierce rejection of any of the three getting close to Jewel. *They would kill her. These leopards are conditioned to crave blood and fighting.*

Ania knew that was true. Still, Jewel was on her first life cycle. She could be anyone's chosen mate. That could give the three males reason to pause before they decided to kill her.

Do you have any weapons in your pack, Mitya? Because,

naturally, he hadn't been so far gone that he hadn't come without a small pack around his neck. Not the way she'd been.

A knife.

Give it to me. She poured confidence into her voice, both for herself and for Mitya.

They didn't have a lot of time to argue and Mitya didn't ask what she was doing, so she took control of her form, taking it back from Jewel, so that she was once again Ania. She had to get to her feet, shaky from that transformation, her body feeling as if it hadn't quite caught up with itself. She took just enough time to note that Dymka was a huge leopard, one of the biggest she'd ever seen. That shouldn't have surprised her, because he was a big man, but she still hadn't expected such an intimidating animal when she was regarding him through human eyes.

The leopard was worked up, pacing back and forth, roaring out his challenge, emitting a sawing, violent call that reverberated through the valley. Ania wasn't quite certain how close they were to the border of Eli Perez's property, but they had to be closer to Mitya's estate than Bannaconni's. Night carried sound, and hopefully, because it was such a still night, the sound of the leopards challenging Dymka for Jewel carried to Bannaconni and Perez.

"Hey, Dymka," she crooned softly. "I need the knife out of the pack around your neck." She tried not to be afraid of the raging cat, but he was extremely intimidating up close.

Dymka turned his head and regarded her with red flames in his eyes. Her heart accelerated until she thought she might faint from sheer terror. She didn't have a stitch on. Clothes, no matter how flimsy, felt like armor when facing a feral, savage leopard. She tried to walk toward the pacing cat with confidence. That failed when he swiped the dirt, sending up a cloud of leaves, twigs and clumps of debris. Still, she forced herself to put one foot in front of the other until she was right in front of him.

Up close, he dwarfed her even though he was on four feet and she was on two. He was a big cat, and yet could move fast. She'd seen his blurring speed. That gave her confidence. Dymka and Mitya both exuded confidence. She knew they were worried about the third cat, the one that would go after Jewel. She had to find a way to handle that one. The cat would be experienced; Jewel wasn't.

She dropped her hand in Dymka's fur because it was impossible to resist feeling that luxurious coat. He was beautiful. Beneath that fur, she felt his roped muscles moving, rippling, sliding under his skin. Deftly, she unzipped the pack, took out the knife and impulsively dropped a kiss onto the top of the leopard's head.

"Good luck, Dymka. You keep Mitya safe and I'll keep Jewel safe." She made the pact with him, needing him to make certain her chosen man didn't get captured, hurt or die.

The large leopard licked up her face, his rough tongue rasping over her skin. Cats could remove skin from bone with their tongues, yet his was gentle, a gesture of comradery. She whirled around and ran to the one spot she felt Jewel could at least stay protected for a short period of time.

She hurried over to the tree where she felt Jewel had the best chance to hold off the male who would be coming for her. They were getting closer, their sawing challenges ripping through the night, setting the adrenaline flooding her body.

Your plan? Mitya hissed it. He was already moving toward the tree she'd selected to use. It was tall, but the trunk wasn't particularly hardy, and the branches quickly became thin and straggly.

Years ago, when I was barely ten or eleven, my grandfather took me out fishing. We talked at great length about all sorts of things and he ended up showing me how to make spears and traps.

As she talked, she began sharpening as many small but thick sticks as she could. She pointed to the ground beneath the tree. Because it had recently rained, the ground was soft. As soon as she finished one small spike, she began sharpening another. It had been a particularly fun day with her grandfather, and she cherished those memories.

I practiced making the spear and the other traps he showed me. She was the type of dedicated person to keep working at it until she was extremely proficient, just as she had with her shooting and driving.

Mitya emerged the moment he understood her plan and he quickly began to shove the spikes into the ground. They were no more than about nine inches and it was easy to push them into the soft dirt. In a matter of minutes, they had a lethal section under the tree. She quickly went up the tree, laying the makeshift spear into some flimsy branches.

"Jewel's small," she said. "Those branches can take her weight, but not a male's. If I can get him to climb up after me and then fall onto those spikes, she has a chance."

"Those spikes aren't going to kill a leopard, Ania."

"I don't have to kill him. Only delay him. I hope to hurt him badly enough that you won't have to fight so hard to kill him."

Mitya slung his arm around her neck. He smelled wild. Feral. Even his skin felt different, as if his leopard was so close fur might break through any moment.

"I'm crazy about you, woman," he whispered.

He kissed her, and she couldn't think straight for a moment. They broke apart, Mitya shifting in that split second, moving away from her fast. Dymka would have to fight two very experienced leopards and he couldn't be distracted. He had to keep attention centered on him.

Ania knew her plan was a good one. She was very for-
tunate that Jewel was so small, and her weight would be
an advantage in the tree. Quickly, she gathered a few
rocks and took them up the tree to place in various
crotches of limbs, and then, after finding a good branch
that would hold Jewel's weight, she once again hurried
down the tree and called on the female to retake the form.

It was so much easier the second time. Ania had been
a little afraid of shifting without Mitya right there, but she
let go of herself faster and it didn't hurt quite as much now
that she knew what was going to happen. Jewel wasn't as
afraid of emerging as she had been before.

We can do this, Jewel, Ania reassured with as much
confidence as she could muster. *Dymka is unstoppable.
They cannot defeat him. He will fight to the death for you.*

The female was desperate, in the throes of her heat,
and she couldn't stop rubbing her enticing pheromones
everywhere, on every tree trunk, the brush, along fallen
logs. She spread her alluring scent across the ground leading to the small tree Ania had selected in order for her to
be safe.

Jewel didn't want to be safe. She wanted the males to
fight over her. Dymka needed to prove he was the stron-
gest, the fiercest, the male who deserved her. On the other
hand, if he wasn't going to hurt her and his human counterpart wasn't going to harm Ania, then he would be her
choice. He should just have to prove she was right in her
selection of him.

She made certain the ground, fallen tree trunks and
every bush were filled with her tempting, enthralling
scent. That was exactly what Ania wanted her to do. Lure
the third cat away from Dymka.

A roar from the male cat had Jewel's head snapping up,
and she turned to face the meadow that separated where
she was from the other tree line. Three cats burst from the
brush and Ania's heart nearly stopped. They weren't as big

as Dymka, but that just meant they were a little more compact. Their fur, even from a distance, looked as if it was tattered and ripped, old scars on other scars preventing the fur from growing in places.

They looked far more experienced at fighting than she had counted on. *Jewel, get to the tree, now.*

Jewel had it in her mind to show the three intruders what they would be fighting for, but once she saw the shockingly fierce faces of the cats, their malevolent yellow eyes ringed with red, noses wrinkled into snarls and stained teeth, she wanted nothing to do with them. She almost stumbled over her own paws getting to the tree.

Ania forced her to stop right at the base on the far side from where they had placed the stakes. *Cover them with leaves, Jewel,* she chided. *We have to get the cat to come at us from the other side and then, when he climbs, come around to this side. He can't suspect the spikes are there.*

She tried not to be annoyed with her female. Like Ania, she had no real idea of what she was doing. *I know that you're afraid and you're also in heat, but you have to trust me to guide us in this situation. If you refuse to listen to me, we have no chance at all. Those cats are here to kill us, not become your mate. Even if they mate with you, they will kill you after.*

Jewel hadn't wanted to believe it but now, seeing them tearing across the meadow, eyes burning, not looking like cats in the throes of a frenzied mating call, she had no choice but to understand. Every instinct was warning her that if she didn't listen to Ania, they were going to die. She tossed up leaves with her paws and then went around the tree doing the same before rubbing over the trunk right where she planned to go up it.

Now, Jewel. We'll see better. They're almost on Dymka.

Ania couldn't imagine that every property owner in the rolling hills couldn't hear the terrible roaring challenges from the four males. There was satisfaction in that. Bannaconni and Perez would know there was trouble. Sevastyan was never far from his cousin. He would come as well. They just had to hold out.

Jewel went up the tree, using her claws to climb. Ania directed her to climb up the side they needed the unsuspecting male to climb, but in order to get to the higher branches, he would have to circle around to the other side. The higher branches were noticeably weaker and creaked ominously while taking Jewel's weight.

Ania's heart pounded, hoping she hadn't misjudged. Another roar nearly stopped her heart. They were on Dymka, leaping at him ferociously, all three of them, hoping to bring him down fast. She didn't realize she was nearly taking back the form, forcing Jewel to turn in the direction she wanted so she could watch the terrible fight happening a short distance from the relative safety of the tree.

One cat, a particularly motley one with dark-tipped fur, leapt on Dymka's back, hoping to break the spine. Another hooked claws into his hindquarters, trying to drag him backward while the third went for his throat. Jewel's claw gripped the tree trunk hard while Ania debated. Maybe she should have tried to help Mitya instead of taking to the tree like a coward.

As she took that first tentative step, pulling her claws from the trunk, Dymka threw off the dark-tipped leopard, hurling him into the one clawing at his hindquarters so that the two cats came together in a tangle of legs and claws. Dymka rose onto his back legs, standing tall, ripping and slicing with lethal claws at the third cat, opening his belly, going for genitals with blurring speed.

The third cat fell backward and Dymka was on him, going for the kill, a suffocating bite to the throat. His mouth closed over the fallen cat, but the leopard was already twisting, coming back to its feet, so Dymka got a mouthful of fur. The dark-tipped cat rushed him again, while the last cat, the one with a particularly long scar where no hair grew, circled around and came at Dymka's head.

Ania could see the leopards had fought together before. Their movements were coordinated. Deliberately, she urged Jewel to call out, a mating call, a female in need, calling for mates. Jewel did so immediately, her call genuine and a little desperate.

Nature was nature no matter how their human counterparts tried to stamp it out of them. The males all turned their heads toward that call. Dymka took full advantage, raking over the eyes of the scarred one, gouging with razor-sharp claws so that the animal shrieked in pain and tried to leap away, blood pouring from his eyes. Dymka followed the bloody cat, unwilling to let go of an advantage, while the dark-tipped one leapt to bring him down.

Ania, inside Jewel's body, cried out, which made Jewel do the same. The female's voice sang through the night, a symphony of need, calling to her mate. Both Ania and Jewel watched in horror as the dark-tipped leopard landed hard on Dymka's back, his claws digging deep, his teeth viciously going for the back of the neck. Dymka rolled at the last possible second, twisting his flexible spine so that he appeared almost folded in half. Most of his body weight was sheer muscle, thick ropes and bands all over his body. As the big male rolled under the dark-tipped cat, he used his claws and teeth to rake at the leopard's belly, opening more lacerations.

The third cat, his coat redder than the others, looked away from the fighting, sniffed the air several times, suddenly whirled around and began running toward Jewel's tree. Ania couldn't quiet her heartbeat for a few seconds. Both Ania and Jewel nearly fell from the tree in terror. The cat looked invincible as it ran toward them.

The wind had picked up and blew at them, carrying

small droplets of water with it. Fingers of mist began to creep across the valley into the hills, moving slowly, looking like a giant hand waiting to enclose them. Jewel turned her head to look from the oncoming red cat to Dymka. The cat with the bloody eyes was running in circles, indicating, she was certain, that he had lost his eyesight. It was the dark-tipped cat that was fighting with Dymka now, and he was clearly good at battles. The two cats came together in what was clearly a fight to the death. The two combatants slashed at each other, looking for an opening.

Dymka circled, keeping his movements tight, making certain he wasn't giving the other cat any openings, nor was he going to allow himself to be pushed back toward the bloody, sightless leopard he couldn't forget for a moment was still dangerous.

He recognized all three cats. The one he'd blinded was a man called Taras, a lieutenant of his father. He was a particularly mean man, very ugly in both his looks and his actions. He liked hurting others, and often had his cat chase, kill and eat young children. Taras's cat had chased him repeatedly, once leaping from a building out of hiding, slamming into Mitya's back, driving him to the ground. Mitya still bore the scars on his back from the leopard raking his skin open, almost to the bone. As a child, he'd lived in fear of Taras, as did most of the children in the lair. Lazar had allowed his behavior to go unchecked.

The reddish-colored leopard was a man everyone despised, including Lazar, but the *vor* kept him around because his reputation with women terrorized the lair and amused him. He was named Albert, and no female, whatever the age, was safe from him. He didn't care where he was, or where the woman or child was, he would do whatever he wanted with them. Sometimes he simply raped them, but more often than not, he tortured them sexually first. No one dared interfere with him. He liked to hurt others, and small females were his first choice of target.

The dark-tipped leopard was one of Lazar's most trusted men. Kronya had often "disciplined" Mitya, beating him and then having his leopard rip Dymka to pieces at Lazar's whim. Kronya was used to leaping on the younger males at Lazar's direction and beating them. The trouble was, as he enjoyed his role just a little too much and too often, the boy was so damaged after the beating that Lazar would simply indicate to his right-hand man to finish it with a kill, or they left the child there, dying slowly, his insides crushed by the vicious pressure. Often Mitya had been on the receiving end of Kronya's punishments. The man had taken great pleasure in hurting him, taking it that little bit too far on accident, so that Mitya had been one of those children lying broken and bloody on the floor.

Kronya reached out to him now. *Mitya. Your father isn't here to save you this time.*

Mitya didn't answer. His father wouldn't have saved him if he was there. Most likely he'd been the one to order the three men to kill him. And he didn't feel there was anything to say to this cruel coward of a man.

Dymka went inside Kronya's protected shoulder, raking his teeth down neck, shoulder and side, so that streaks of red dripped from the fur. He leapt back as Kronya attempted retaliation, whirling around and striking out with his front legs. Dymka seemed to hesitate and Kronya turned his injured side away from the large cat.

Dymka attacked, using his weight and the dense muscles to drive him forward. He used his legs to propel him with blurring speed, a battering ram, slamming into Kronya's side, knocking him off his feet, sending him sliding across the dirt so that leaves and dirt geysered into the air to mix with the mist and fog.

Dymka followed the leopard, his teeth closing around the throat with a vicious snap, driving for the suffocating bite that would end the life of one of his father's most trusted men. As he bit down with great satisfaction, Taras, guided by the sounds of the battle and half-mad with rage and pain, tore at Dymka's hindquarters.

ANIA watched the reddish-colored leopard race toward them, only stopping to sniff Jewel's alluring aroma. He sprayed over the bushes and trees as he went from place to place, claiming Jewel for his own. He roared at her to come to him. Jewel made herself smaller, trying once to shift out from under Ania.

We've got this, baby, Ania cooed. *He's too big to get to you. The branches can't handle his weight. Dymka will come when we need him.*

She couldn't see the leopards as well through the rapidly thickening mist. It was just as well. She needed to keep her wits about her. This leopard was scaring the hell out of Jewel—and her, if she was truthful. She had to believe Dymka would come if she needed him.

Jewel was becoming desperate, needing a mate. That fire burning so hot had transferred to Ania as well. Every part of her ached and burned as she felt Jewel's frantic need. The male was close now, coming around to the correct side of the tree where Jewel's scent was the most potent. He stared up at her with those gleaming, malignant eyes.

He looked evil. Wholly evil, as if he'd been consumed by a demon. There was no trick of the light, not with the fog and night falling fast. Whatever was inside that leopard was wholly corrupted.

Ania shivered and took a better grip on Jewel. She had to be in control at all times, so her leopard wouldn't accidentally shift when she was needed the most to keep the other leopard's main focus and attention on her.

The creature roared a command. It was clear he was telling Jewel she had to get out of the tree. Jewel cringed, but she didn't move. She remained very still, looking down a little defiantly at the male. Ania was proud of her. She knew the female was hurting, was desperate for a mate, yet she didn't give in to nature. She followed Ania's lead and remained in place.

The male slammed his retractable claws into the tree trunk. Those claws could be used for cutting, holding, killing, fighting or climbing. A ligament was attached from the thick, hooked claw to the bone at the tip of each toe. Muscles, tendons and ligaments allowed the front claws to be used like switchblades. They were lethal weapons when needed, and right now, the male ripped at the bark, sharpening them with deadly intent.

Keeping his eyes on Jewel, holding her terrified gaze captive with his malicious one, the male began to climb. Ania waited until the cat was closest to the spot where he would have to circle around the tree to the other side in order to climb up farther.

His head appeared between the branches, and she shifted just one of Jewel's legs, or tried to. It wasn't nearly as easy as she thought it might be. The upper half of her body shifted, leaving her head, torso and arms exposed. The yellow eyes flared. The nose crinkled into a snarl as he drew back lips to expose his stained teeth.

Ania flung a rock into his face. She snapped it, very hard, using her leopard's strength. The rock hit him right on his nose and the animal slipped backward. He howled in rage as he dug his claws into the trunk to keep from falling.

Ania wanted to move, to follow his descent with more rocks, but she held steady to her place. He could possibly get to her if she went to the lower branches. They were stronger and would hold his weight. Not their combined weights, but definitely his if he stood on them and reached for her.

He climbed again, his eyes twin pinpoints of hatred in the sea of spots. The wind blew, and she caught his foul scent. The breeze felt good on her hot body, but it brought with it the promise of more mist. She wanted to see clearly. She *needed* to see clearly. More than anything else, she had to stall, to keep Jewel and herself alive until Dymka could get to them. The rock was in her fist, up by the tree trunk. Her eyes met the horrid leopard's and then she saw the man staring at her. He was just as evil as his leopard; more so, because he was the one driving the animal.

She didn't wait for his reaction. She sent the rock pelting into his face, smashing into his open mouth with enough force she hoped to break teeth. Her second throw hit his left eye dead center and the animal slid a second time, barely catching himself, hooking his claws in the tree trunk to keep himself from falling to the ground.

Enraged, the animal roared over and over, calling out his hatred and need for revenge. For retaliation. The sound rolled out over the hills, the wind building to take it out even further. Ania, shivering in cold and fear, shifted so that Jewel faced the maddened male. When he looked up again, he saw only the face of the female.

She let out another call, the need in her voice very real. The wind caught her scent and scattered it through the trees, carrying it far. For a moment the male seemed disoriented, as if he didn't know exactly what he was doing. He hesitated and then began to climb toward the female again.

Ania wasn't certain what his human counterpart thought he was going to do. Reach for Jewel and yank her out of the tree? Climb up with her? Was there a plan? She waited, counting the seconds, watching for an opening. Jewel stayed very still, the bait to lure in a dangerous predator.

A gust of wind caught the tree and sent it swaying. Jewel had to dig her claws into the branch and hold on until the wind subsided. Another gust nearly sent the upper canopy of the tree into another one. She hadn't counted on the weather turning against her. The red leopard was in a much better position. His part of the tree was solid. Stable. Not swaying the way the top of the tree was. It was as if the tree were trying to throw Jewel out of it.

STILETTO claws pierced Dymka's hindquarters and yanked at him, dragging him backward off Kronya. As Taras hauled him off the other leopard, Kronya leapt to his feet and sprang at Dymka in a clearly coordinated move he had used numerous times with the other leopard. Dymka did the unexpected. Rather than face Kronya, he leapt into the air and, using his flexible spine, twisted in midflight to land on Taras's back with his full weight.

He slammed into Taras so hard he drove the other leopard to the ground. All four legs sprawled out sideways. There was an audible snap and the leopard screamed and screamed. He tried to rise repeatedly but was unable to move. He even tried crawling, using his legs to pull him forward, but it was impossible.

Knowing the cat couldn't help Kronya, Dymka backed away, circled the fallen cat and, all the while watching the dark-tipped leopard, darted in to deliver the suffocating bite to Taras. Immediately, just as Dymka knew he would, Kronya attacked. Dymka whirled around to catch the underbelly of the cat as Kronya hurdled over the top of him. He eviscerated the cat, hooking the deadly claws into his belly using the leopard's momentum and his own immense strength to help shred the skin and fur.

Dymka spun around, rolling away from both cats. He glanced toward the tree Ania had chosen to make their stand in. He couldn't see Jewel through the thick mist. He caught glimpses of Albert as his cat tried to claw his way up the tree to get to Jewel. Dymka was relatively unscathed. The three cats had underestimated him. They were used to going after a leopard together, the victim fearing them and barely able to fight back.

Mitya had learned to fight them. He had studied each cat's weakness over the years. He had watched how they fought their victims. Even how they chose them. He was in his prime and he knew, when they came, they would underestimate him, just as his father would. The one thing that could defeat him was treed and alone, fending off a killer who enjoyed preying on females.

Dymka turned his attention back to Kronya. The cat too was looking toward the tree Albert had climbed. A crafty look came over its face and immediately a chill went down Mitya's spine. Kronya roared to Albert, clearly conveying to the other leopard to kill Jewel. Dymka leapt on Kronya where he lay panting through the pain, knowing if he moved, he would leave behind his intestines. Dymka landed hard on the leopard's back, digging his claws into the shoulders while he delivered the suffocating bite, cutting off the sawing roars abruptly.

A strange silence settled over the hillside and meadow, like a dark shroud of death. Kronya didn't struggle. He knew he was dead already. He didn't even try to delay the inevitable, not even to buy more time for Albert. He just let Dymka kill him.

HE'S coming and he's so mad, Jewel whispered to Ania.

This is what we've been waiting for, Ania assured, doing her best to pour confidence in her voice.

Both of them were burning up. Ania was so uncomfortable she wanted to scream. And hot. It didn't matter that the mist was cool and the breeze had grown into an actual wind, her body temperature was soaring. Jewel was in even worse condition, panting, sides heaving, her body crouching there in the crotch of the straggly limb she was perched in.

Ania did her best to caution the leopard repeatedly not to move. The branch was no bigger around than a quarter and it bent and bounced up and down with every ragged, panting breath Jewel drew.

The reddish coat on the male had taken on a sinister look. It was wet with the mist now, and looked almost as if blood tinged the undercoat. It was a grisly, bizarre image Ania couldn't get out of her head. Those eyes staring up through the spots on his face had gone from a sickening yellow to an eviler red. They glowed like a demon's eyes fixed on Jewel—focused completely. Unblinking, a predator whose entire being was concentrated on killing prey.

Let him come, Ania whispered. It was all she could do not to tremble, but Jewel was so frightened, she had to show courage.

The cat clawed his way closer until Jewel was staring directly into his triumphant eyes and he reached his front leg the remaining distance in an effort to hook his claw into the smaller cat to drag her off the branch.

Ania shifted as fast as she could, uncaring how much she managed to shift. It was only her arm and hand that mattered. She had gone over the moves hundreds of times in her head and she caught up the spear smoothly and slammed it into the cat's throat. Blood erupted, a great river of it. Jewel tried to back away. Ania held her ruthlessly in place.

The reddish-furred cat fell backward out of the tree and landed on his side as he tried to turn in midair and failed. He landed hard, driving the spikes deep into his side. He screamed horribly, gurgling between each shriek of pain. He thrashed around, trying to unstick himself from the spikes buried in the ground.

She hadn't had the time to set up too many of them and

the ground was very soft, so the leopard was able to roll to his feet. The wound in his throat was deep and he coughed, spraying out more blood. He looked up at the tree and his eyes met Ania's. Her heart nearly stopped. He was coming back, and he was really, really angry.

Mitya. She said his name softly, a chill going down her spine.

The leopard jumped for the tree trunk and just hung there for a moment, his eyes glaring up at her and blood running down his chest. He clawed at the bark, digging in deep, so he could move up the trunk inch by inch. Foot by foot. Gaining ground as he climbed higher.

He would be waiting for her to stab at him with the spear, Ania knew. She had to believe he was like Mitya, able to shift with blurring speed. If he yanked the spear out of her hands, he could attack Jewel with it, drive her out of the tree so she would fall to the ground below. Even if she missed the spikes and the dirt was really too soft to kill her, she could still be dazed, or break a leg. Ania couldn't let that happen.

Could Jewel outrun the male? He was badly injured. Blood poured from his throat and dotted his coat on his left side. Still, it was a terrible chance to take. As long as Jewel remained on the branch, she had a better chance of remaining out of the male's reach.

Ania didn't take her eyes from the cat clawing his way up the tree trunk. The wind blasted her face and she stayed very still, even though the droplets of water in the air were very cold on her skin. She didn't care that the horrible man driving his leopard to such depravity could see her upper body. If anything, his gaze continued to drop from her eyes to her breasts. Let him be distracted. She had only to wait for Mitya. He would come. She knew he would.

The cat managed to make his way to just below the branch Jewel stood on. Ania calculated her weight. If she shifted entirely, she could climb to the next branch and she doubted if, even in human form, the male could get to her. If she tried stomping on his paw or hand, he could just grab her.

Every possibility slipped through her mind. She stayed very still, her hand gripping the spear. She let him see it. Let him see she was afraid and agitated. He would expect that. He wouldn't think she would be using her brain. Plotting. Planning. He reached up toward her with a slow, stealthy paw, those hooked claws inching toward Jewel's leg.

She moved her arm and his gaze flashed to the spear. He wanted her to try it. She saw he was ready, and she pulled her arm back as if she was about to thrust it toward his face again. Instead, she shifted entirely and kicked him as hard as she could in the throat. He went sailing backward off the tree and landed almost on top of Dymka.

The large male cat had crept up, ready to drag Albert from the tree, but Ania had gotten in a very hard, very well-placed kick. Her foot throbbed and hurt, feeling as if she might have broken every bone in it, but she knew it was only a momentary pain. She hated the sight of blood on her foot, so she shifted back to her leopard form and told Jewel to start the descent from the tree.

Below them, Dymka administered the suffocating bite to the reddish-coated leopard and then instantly roared out a challenge to any other cat that dared to come near his female. Jewel clawed her way down to the ground and ran a short distance away from the tree and the dead leopard beneath it.

He rushed between the dead cats, immediately traveling back to the two he had dispatched first. He slapped the ground, sending leaves and twigs into the air as he attacked the dead leopards, roaring his hatred of them.

Then he was running back to the third cat, circling it, sending dirt and leaves over the remains in contemptuous swipes of his paw before turning to Jewel. She ran from him, heading toward the deeper trees where a stream moved through the acreage. She didn't get far before nature took over and she rolled, stood back on her feet and looked at her mate flirtatiously.

She hurried another five or ten feet and crouched. Before she could reprimand him or send him away, Dymka was on her, his heavier body blanketing hers, his teeth sinking into her neck, deep enough to draw blood, holding her in place while he mated with her.

For the rest of the night, as they made their way back to Mitya's estate, the two cats had rough sex every twenty or thirty minutes. It went on for hours. When they weren't having sex, Dymka stayed close to her, rubbing along her sides and nuzzling her neck. His tongue lapped at the bite marks on her neck and she tried to soothe his battle wounds.

By the time they made it to the house, Jewel was exhausted and stumbling with the effort to walk. If it wasn't for Dymka urging her forward, she would have just lain down and gone to sleep. As it was, when they got to the porch, she curled up into a little ball and put her head down on her paws.

Mitya shifted, his face grim, his mouth tight. "Ania, *kotyonok*, you need to shift for me."

Too tired.

"I know." He was patient. Already he was looking for Sevastyan. Furious that a shooter had nearly gotten to his woman and that three leopards his father had sent had attacked them. "You can't sleep there. Just shift and I'll take you inside to the bedroom."

Ania did so, although he could see it was an effort and she didn't do it well. She also, like him, needed a shower.

13

"WE'VE got two factions coming at us," Mitya explained. "There's no doubt about it, although it is possible they are now working together. Lazar is making his move. He wouldn't do it unless he was certain he had the upper hand. That means he has allies and he may have someone on the inside. We knew he was going to come after us sometime. That isn't news. We can get back to him in a bit and decide how we're going to handle it."

Mitya looked around the room. These were the men he was supposed to be able to trust with his life and the lives of those he loved. He didn't trust so easily. Fyodor, his cousin, had brought him back into the world he was most comfortable in. One of crime, deceit and treachery. Those in this room were supposed to be the ones that were solid, part of an alliance forged in hell and written in stone. Fyodor trusted each of them. Mitya . . . not so much.

Trust was earned, often through life-and-death situations. He had stepped between Fyodor, Evangeline and bullets. He'd nearly lost his life, but his cousin knew with absolute certainty that Mitya would never betray him, that he was willing to give his life for him and his family. That was trust. That was how it was earned.

Jake Bannaconni was a businessman. He owned a cattle ranch. He was considered a ruthless man, willing to take apart any company, and his enemies had to be careful because he found legitimate ways to destroy them. He was a man many feared, but there was never a whisper of him being anything but legitimate. There wasn't a shred of anything illegal attached to his name. Somehow, and Mitya didn't fully understand how, Bannaconni was part of their coalition. When one didn't have anything to lose—like their life—Mitya wasn't certain they would be as committed as they needed to be.

He paced across the room and turned back to look at Drake Donovan. "Amory Binder worked for you in Borneo. You vouched for him. Got the job for him with Bannaconni and then here, with me. You had Sevastyan hire him."

There was Donovan. The start of all the conspiracy, the gathering of shifters to get rid of the worst of the criminal element of shifters—men who had risen to the top to become crime lords and claim territories. Drake's vision was to remove them permanently and take over their territories, weeding out the worst of the crimes and keeping some level of sanity.

It wasn't a bad idea, it just put those doing the work in double jeopardy. They would be hunted constantly by the police. Their families would always carry the taint of criminals on them in regular society, and if it ever became known that they were double-crossing crime families, they would be hunted down and killed.

Drake nodded. "Yes. Amory came to my team in Borneo highly recommended. I was already here in the States working with Jake at the time. According to those on the team, and I spoke to every single one of them, Amory did his work in an exemplary fashion. When he asked for a job here in the States, I didn't hesitate. Many of the shifters want to come, even if it is just to experience work here. He went through additional training and was first put with Joshua."

Joshua Tregre was Evangeline's cousin. He was now related to Fyodor, which made him family. Mitya liked the man. He was very steady, very calm. But liking and trusting were two different things. In fact, he made certain to put Joshua in the one chair at the large round table that had the least protection.

Amory had returned to New Orleans. He'd evidently worked for Joshua, who held the New Orleans territory. Mitya didn't believe in coincidences. He remained silent, waiting for Joshua to speak. It took a few moments, which didn't surprise Mitya. Joshua was a thoughtful man and would weigh his words before speaking.

"Amory was a good worker. Evan was responsible for his training, and he's one of the best. He had no complaints and said Amory had amazing reflexes and would go far in the business of retrieving prisoners as well as being a bodyguard. I met him a few times, but for the most part, he didn't work closely with my crew. He was transferred within three months to help guard Jake's family right after his training. I believe he asked for that transfer, but I can check with Evan just to be certain. He's right outside the door."

Sevastyan, always quiet and rarely noticed when he was still, stirred from his position, where he could get to Mitya if needed. "Who were Amory's friends when he was with you?"

Joshua frowned and drummed his fingers on the table. "Amory hung out with two of the crew I didn't know very well at the time. I had just been named to take over the territory Rafe Cordeau held. I believe it was Eli Perez who killed Cordeau. Eli worked for the DEA, and they'd been after Rafe for some time. Rafe went after Eli's woman, Catarina. With Rafe dead, the territory was open and fair game to any of the crime families looking to expand, so I was put into that position. Being new, I had to go slow and figure out who I trusted and who I didn't."

"So there were several of Rafe's men who stayed with you?" Sevastyan persisted.

Joshua nodded. "Yes. Evan and the others, my people, watched them closely. I can't say they all integrated into my family, but they worked hard and didn't give me any trouble. The two men Amory became friends with are Colten Schultz and Fargo Day. Like I said, they do their jobs and appear to be good men to have, but they have never become close to any of my crew."

Drake frowned. "Do the men have access to your control room, Joshua? Everyone can be watched and recorded from that room."

Joshua shook his head. "Only my most trusted men are allowed in the control room. They aren't counted among them."

"Are any of the old crew allowed in there?" Sevastyan asked.

"Only one. A man by the name of Palmer Blanchard. He comes from an old and respected family of shifters in the bayou. He and his brother are the only ones left."

"Did Amory spend time with him? Or his brother? Presumably the brother works for you as well," Mitya said.

Joshua nodded. "He does. Palmer's brother, Louis, is especially good with the locals. They trust him, talk to him and inform him of anything out of the ordinary in our territory. I saw Amory with Louis a time or two, but not with Palmer. Again, that doesn't surprise me. Palmer is serious and quiet, Louis is outgoing and open."

"Did anyone other than Amory ask or volunteer to work for Jake?" Mitya persisted.

"Several of my men," Drake said. "They go there to work closely with Jake. He has death threats all the time and they come in from credible sources. It's a high-octane gig and therefore a popular place to work."

Fyodor sent Jake a grin. "Nice to know everyone wants you dead."

Jake smirked. "I'm very popular."

That surprised Mitya. The man didn't deal in crime, but he had credible death threats, enough to draw some of Drake's men.

"Trey Sinclair comes to mind," Drake said. "He worked with me in the rain forest for quite some time and then came to the States and requested working with Banna-conni. There are others." He looked at Jake.

Jake's face had settled into hard lines. "I can't imagine Trey would betray me or my family. He's with me most of the time as a private bodyguard. All the men working for me have done so for a while. Most guard my family. Trey and Jerico are my personal bodyguards and they come with me everywhere, including my office." There was an edge to his voice as if the idea that anyone would question those men irritated him.

Mitya knew Trey Sinclair and Jerico were in the next room with a few of the other bodyguards who hadn't been allowed into the meeting. Now Jake knew why. Mitya wasn't going to make any apologies no matter how upset Jake became. The guards might be innocent, but if they weren't, they had access to Jake and any information that passed through his hands.

"Ania's family was murdered. All of them. She's had attempts on her life prior to becoming my fiancée. Since then, we've had a few other tries. It appears that both her father and grandfather agreed to take packages to two different families in Houston. Her grandfather picked up a package in New Orleans and was taking it to the Anwar family in Houston. Her father picked up a package in New Orleans as well and took it to the Caruso family in Houston. The package that Ania's grandfather was taking never arrived in Houston. Supposedly he never delivered it."

There was a small silence. Mitya kept his gaze on Joshua. He held the New Orleans territory. It was Joshua who spoke first.

"The package didn't originate from me. As far as I know, no one came to the house to pick up anything for delivery elsewhere."

"Was there someone who was upset because you took over for Cordeau? Someone who wanted that territory?" Mitya asked.

Joshua shrugged. "I have no idea." He indicated those around the table. "I was asked to take the position and, like an idiot, I agreed. I had no idea I'd find Sonia and have to ask her to share this life with me. I do my job and I hold that territory, but I've never had an attack on me."

"I'm in New Orleans," Drake said. "My wife is from there and we continue to make our home there. The lair was really a mess and I took that over. There is crime there, and sometimes it feels as if we can never get a handle on it, but if there's a specific boss wanting to take over from Joshua, I have no idea who it could be."

Jake sat back in his chair, his shrewd eyes on Mitya. "What's in the package? I presume you know."

Mitya could see why he was considered a force to beware. Those eyes said a lot, and part of that was his burning, focused leopard close to the surface. He was waiting. He knew that package had something to do with him.

"I had a little time to interrogate another shifter working with Amory. We haven't found the package, but he was looking for it, as was Amory. He claimed there was dirt on Jake and Drake and a lot more. By dirt, I believe he meant proof that you two are working with us. Or more to the point, we're working with you. Information like that could get us all killed."

He had resumed his pacing, that nervous, pent-up energy, the kind that told him his cat was as needy as he was for his female, and as anxious about her safety as he was. "The question here that's important is, was anything written down that could possibly link us together? All of us sitting here at this table? And did they have proof?"

Technically he wasn't sitting there—and it was deliberate. The others would put it down to his leopard and his female's heat, but it was because he trusted his cousins—and no one else. He was the newest member to ascend to the throne of crime boss. He'd taken over Patrizio Amodeo's territory after Fyodor had killed the man for attacking Evangeline.

He was acutely aware of Ania upstairs in his bed. Alone. She was exhausted and hurting. She needed him and yet he had to be downstairs, conducting bullshit business with others he was uncertain of. In Russia, he might have killed them all and gone straight from a bloodbath to soothe his woman. Hopefully, he was long past that. Evolving. That's how he thought of himself, but he knew better. He was the killer his father had shaped him into. It took discipline to hold himself in check. He was determined that he would work on strengthening that discipline every single day, so he would never become what his father wanted him to be.

"Absolutely not," Jake said. "That would be madness. There is no trail leading from us to any of you other than our friendships. Men make alliances all the time. Drake has made it clear that he moves between both worlds because he needs the information and good graces of the various families. Those of you sitting at the table are not the only families he's friends with, and that's very deliberate. As for me, I'm known to be Drake's friend. I am known to associate with men who live and work in the shadows. No one has ever questioned who I become friends with."

"Someone appears to be questioning it," Fyodor said. "And they've clearly worked and lived around you. There must be damning evidence in that notebook for them to want it so badly."

Jake shook his head. "There's not anything concrete, that I can guarantee. They may have suspicions, but half the world is suspicious of what I do."

"Jake." Drake spoke quietly. "These people are willing to wipe out an entire family to retrieve that notebook. There has to be something in it. Why not make another copy and send that, or use an electronic version? The Dovers are well-known and off-limits. Whoever killed that family has made enemies if it ever comes out. And that's another thing. They have to be very powerful not to have a whisper of this on the streets. Your family could be in jeopardy. Mine. Joshua's. Certainly, Mitya's is. All of us in this room have a stake in this." He switched his gaze to Mitya. "Do you have the notebook? Does Ania?"

Mitya kept his face an expressionless mask and his body relaxed. Deep inside, knots twisted in his gut. "No. If I had the damn thing, I would know what the problem was and who was coming at us." He rubbed the annoying five-o'clock shadow he could get five minutes after shaving. "My best guess is someone became suspicious of Jake and for whatever reason began watching him. What is it that you've done that could make someone take a hard look at you?"

"I target companies that launder money," Jake said. "I buy them up and destroy them, which eventually strangles those needing to launder money." He shrugged. "I've been doing it for years. Drake just helped me focus more sharply on the companies that are suspect."

Joshua drummed his fingers on the table. "That's the

tie-in, Jake. Before Drake, you probably randomly chose companies to take apart. Now you specifically target mob companies."

"I don't make mistakes like that," Jake denied. "I make certain to do both."

"If one of your trusted guards is a traitor, could he have overheard a conversation between you and Drake? Something he could note down and show at a later date?" Joshua persisted.

"That's always a possibility," Jake admitted. "But that would be like you believing Evan betrayed you, or Sevastyan, Mitya. Would you believe Timur would betray Fyodor? You have to put things in perspective. I trust Trey and Jerico. They've been with me for some time now and worked with Drake before that."

"No one wants to believe someone they care about would betray them, but my own father and my uncles betrayed us. My father had Gorya's father killed. All for what? And then there's Joshua's father. In this room, all of us have seen betrayal by the people we love. It is a sad fact of life, especially in the life we've chosen," Mitya said. "We have a problem and we don't know how deep it's gone. If we can't find the notebook, we have no idea who our enemies are."

"The Anwar family is one of the oldest in Houston," Drake said. "They held that territory exclusively until the Caruso family moved from Florida to Houston and took over the port there. What kind of a deal was struck between the two families, no one knows, but they never went to war, and there wasn't a single killing over the takeover."

Fyodor looked up. "It is possible the notebook was being delivered to convince the Anwar family to side with whoever is behind this."

"That's a definite possibility," Elijah Lospostos said. "We've got Fyodor and Mitya and me, known in our world already as criminals. Drake, Eli and Jake are known as good guys, working with cops. Eli *was* a cop. We're all friends. That definitely would give someone pause if they were looking for reasons to doubt us."

"How do we find the notebook?" Eli asked. He was sprawled out, feet in front of him, chewing on a toothpick as if he didn't have a care in the world. He had been the one to help dispose of the bodies of the three shifters on his property.

"I don't know yet," Mitya admitted. "I'm hoping Ania will have some ideas. This isn't the best time for her right now." He glanced at the door again, knowing she would be burning up soon.

He'd had to call a meeting and try to ferret out who might be a traitor, but he heard the ring of truth in every word said. Several times he'd glanced at his cousins; all of them but Gorya was in the room. Fyodor, Sevastyan and Timur hadn't indicated that they heard a lie. Gorya was out with the bodyguards, hoping to discern if any of them was the enemy.

"There is also the possibility that my father, Lazar, has managed to slip into the country. His three lieutenants managed to do so without a single rumbling or whisper of a rumor. Any thoughts?" Mitya threw it out there, watching their faces carefully.

"If they came through Miami, we would have been informed immediately. Sasha Bogomolov runs Miami. He would have told us immediately. He knew Lazar and Rolan, your uncle, would eventually make a try for you. No one is going to get into Miami without his knowledge."

"Unless one of his men is working for the same people Amory was working for," Drake said. "The Caruso family run the port in Houston. They could have come in that way."

"Alessandro Caruso keeps hanging around Ania, although she admits, prior to all this, he was never that interested," Mitya said. "The old man wanted her to dump me and choose one of his sons. It's understandable, but the timing seems suspect given that none of them approached her after her father was shot."

"The bottom line, gentlemen," Drake said, "is we have to all be careful and watch one another's backs. Don't just trust blindly. Make certain you know who you're putting your faith in because you're putting your life in their hands as well as those of people you love." His gaze moved over Jake, but he didn't single him out.

"How soon will Lazar strike at you again, Mitya?" Joshua asked. "We can stick around for a while if it would help."

Mitya shook his head. "Whoever is out to get Jake and Drake is somewhere in or around New Orleans. The problem originates there, I'm sure of it. We need eyes and ears in that area. Watch the men you're uncertain of. See where they go, who they talk to. We have a mutual enemy and he's patient. He's so patient he put people in place to activate when needed. Drake seems to be the person they go to for training and also for validation. If he endorses them, no one ever questions it."

That much was true. Mitya was the only holdout because he didn't know Drake the way everyone else did. And he had Lazar for a father. That meant he had little trust or faith in anyone, least of all a stranger.

"I'll start going over everyone who might have applied for work around the same time Amory did. Also, I can match up various people Amory worked with. A pattern might emerge," Drake said.

"I think we're done here," Mitya said. "I appreciate everyone coming, especially to Antosha's service. It meant a lot to Ania. She needed to see that her father was well-respected. The last few years have been rough."

"What do you plan to do with her property?" Fyodor asked.

"She wants to keep it for now," Mitya said. He didn't look at Sevastyan. He hoped eventually his cousin would buy the property as his home.

"I can see that, no breaking ties. Evangeline still has her house as well," Fyodor said. "She has a difficult time whenever I bring up the subject of selling."

"You told us what Ania did in that tree," Elijah said. "She's tough, that one. Having neighbors who won't even acknowledge you or pretend to be your friend and then talk behind your back is extremely hard on women and children." He knew from experience. His family was generations in the crime business.

His Ania may have been tough, but it had taken a toll on her. Jabbing a blade into a man's throat wasn't as easy as it looked in a movie. She'd seen the results instantly. The horror of what she'd done had spread across his face. She'd been splattered with his blood. There were repercussions to being brave. He cursed that he needed to shore up their defenses instead of sharing the bed with her. She needed to be held. Or maybe he needed to hold her.

The others made noises about leaving, but it took close to an hour for Drake, Jake, Eli, Joshua and Elijah to actually leave. The moment they were gone, Mitya and his cousins made their way to the den, where the room was smaller and warmer. The fireplace was lit to combat the cold the dripping rain outside brought with it. As always, because he was rightfully paranoid, Sevastyan made certain there were no listening devices in the den. He'd already swept the meeting room and declared no listening or recording devices had been left behind.

"Jake has to have spies in his camp," Timur announced. "He doesn't want to think that he does, and I can't blame him."

"It's insane not to believe us," Mitya said.

"He believes us," Timur said. "He'll be careful. No, he'll try to set traps. He's a smart man and he won't tolerate a traitor near his family."

"He may have had a succession of them," Mitya warned. "It sounds like they trained with Drake to put all suspicion aside. From Drake they went to Jake. All of us have men that trained in the Donovan Security Company. His word has been gold. There aren't that many shifters, and they needed jobs that would allow their leopards to have some freedom. Drake provides that as well as a very real service to those families who need them. Not just bodyguards; kidnappings have become so prevalent that someone is needed to deliver money or take back the victim."

"For some of these men to have worked in Borneo for at least a year, this has gone back far before Jake and Drake got together with the idea to rid the crime world of shifters. That's too recent. Elijah was the first the idea was pitched to. So why were these men being sent through Donovan's training?" Fyodor asked.

"He is the best in the world," Timur said. "His reputation is impeccable."

"Do you suppose whoever is behind this began to get suspicious when Jake began taking apart companies that laundered money?" Sevastyan asked.

Mitya shrugged. "We can speculate forever, but the bottom line is, we have an enemy who is coming after us. We might not be the main target, but we're in their sights because we're seen as being friendly with Drake and Jake."

"We're leaving out Eli Perez," Timur said. "He was DEA. He had to have made enemies. He has an impressive arrest and conviction rate. I spent a good deal of time investigating him. He took down Rafe Cordeau, although he's not gotten credit for it, nor does he want it. He could have enemies."

"He came on the scene too late," Mitya pointed out. "At least for the start-up of this thing. To get sleepers in place, someone began orchestrating this a few years ago. Eli became part of it recently."

"We've got a big fat ugly spider sitting in his web somewhere, waiting for someone to step into it so he can devour them," Gorya said.

"I believe Lazar has stumbled across them once or twice but doesn't know the significance of them," Mitya said.

He knew his father. He made it his business to know him. Lazar believed he was far superior to any other man walking the earth. He thought himself stronger and more intelligent. The best at everything. He believed he had the right to do anything he wanted because he was that entitled. He would never think that anyone would be able to suppress an ego in order to further their agenda. Whoever this spider is, he doesn't need the spotlight, and that makes him doubly dangerous.

"Lazar coming at us at this time is nothing more than a coincidence?" Sevastyan asked, but there was the merest hint of disbelief in his voice. Like Mitya, he didn't believe in coincidences.

"I didn't say that," Mitya said. "I think this spider uses anything to his advantage. Lazar wasn't quiet about trying to find us. It wouldn't be that difficult to help Lazar find us and even offer to help him get into the country quietly. Lazar would think the spider was afraid of him and wanted favors owed. I think it doesn't matter to our spider what happens to Lazar or us. He wants his notebook."

There was silence. The cousins looked at one another for a long time. "We knew it was coming," Fyodor said with a sigh. "I'm sorry about Ania, Mitya. You need to be looking after her and her leopard, not worrying about your father trying to kill you."

Mitya nodded, because what was there to say? Ania was his first priority, but when someone was trying to kill them, he had no choice but to defend them.

"We'll get out of here, Mitya, but watch yourself and now your back."

"Fyodor, you have several of Drake's shifters working for you, just as I do. Just as Joshua does."

Mitya looked at Timur, wanting him to understand just what trouble they were all in. Lazar might pay a million dollars for someone to kill them. That was a straight up-and-up business deal. The spider might order someone to pull out a gun at the dinner table and kill the whole family. It was much more difficult when you didn't know who your enemy was.

"I understand," Timur said. "I'll be looking over every single one of the men we hired from Donovan's agency again. And I'll be watching them."

Gorya nodded. "We'll make certain Fyodor and Evangeline are safe. Evangeline can't move fast anymore. She's pretty sick. I wish she'd walk away from the bakery if only for the rest of her pregnancy."

Fyodor sighed. "I don't think that's going to happen, and I'll be there from here on out until the issue with Lazar is resolved and this spider shows himself."

"Timur, you and Gorya are at risk from both enemies as well," Mitya pointed out. "Just because you've chosen to be the head of security doesn't mean either of them will spare you. Just the opposite. You're between them and their prey."

Timur grinned at him. "Don't much like to be called that, Mitya. I always thought I was the predator." He stretched. "You need anything else from us?"

"No. All of you believe both Drake and Jake? They aren't a part of this in any way?" Mitya was compelled to ask. He didn't think so, but conspiracy had been his life when he'd lived with his father.

All of his cousins shook their heads. "Drake and Jake are on our side," Fyodor said. "I believe every man sitting at that table is one that can be trusted."

Mitya wished he felt the same. He was trying. He wanted to have that many friends in his life that he could count on—that his family could count on. He had been working toward that place when all this had happened, and he went right back to being the untrusting, careful man he'd always been. He didn't let others in. He watched over his cousins as best he could. They were his only family, and they were vulnerable. Fyodor had a woman he loved. Timur did as well. That made them targets for a man like Lazar.

Fyodor headed for the door, turned back and unexpectedly took Mitya's shoulders in a strong grip. "Be safe, Mitya. Watch your back at all times. We can't afford to lose you."

Mitya nodded, a hard lump unexpectedly blocking his throat. "Same goes for all of you."

Sevastyan walked them out while Mitya went on up the stairs, needing to be close to Ania. He entered the bedroom, inhaling deeply to take in her scent and judge how close she was to needing him again. Her scent was everywhere, an enticing fragrance that settled in his lungs and made him feel whole.

He took two steps closer to the bed and realized she wasn't in it. The blankets were piled up as if she were sleeping in the middle, but there was no Ania. His heart nearly stopped, and he fought the roar of rage. Quickly, he hurried to the master bath, but she wasn't there either. He turned slowly, staring at the bank of windows to the wide balcony. Had someone come in? Was it possible? Could she have been taken right under the nose of every single shifter who had been at the meeting?

He slid open the glass doors to the balcony and found himself closing his eyes in relief. Ania's scent was heavy outside. It was raining, but the roof overhead kept the furniture from getting soaked. A few feet from the door were two chairs and a small table. Ania was curled up in one of the deep cushioned chairs, staring out at the silvery rain, a blanket covering her. She turned her head and smiled up at him as he approached.

"Your meeting is over?"

She was so serene, when he'd been a bundle of nerves. He'd nearly lost his shit, turned into a raging leopard just because she wasn't in his bed and he'd been afraid. *Afraid*. That wasn't a word he associated with himself often.

"I thought someone had come up here and kidnapped you." He didn't mean to make it sound the way it came out. His voice was a growl of reprimand. An accusation.

"After what happened earlier, I can assure you, honey, that I wouldn't allow myself to be kidnapped. That would make me so angry I'd have to kill someone." She lifted the blanket and he saw the gun she held in her lap. Beside her chair was a rifle with a scope.

The relief that she had come out onto the balcony prepared was tremendous. On the other hand, he detested that she would have to consider taking weapons with her when she just wanted to sit outside on her balcony and watch the rain. He couldn't blame her for wanting to be outside. It was cool and beautiful with the silvery drops falling. The rain on the roof sounded like music.

Even though Mitya understood, he still wanted to shake her. She'd scared him. He didn't take well to that. Neither did his leopard. He forced himself to sit in the chair beside her. "The meeting didn't give us anything new, *kotyonok*." His voice was edged with disappointment. "I was hoping for something. Anything. I know Lazar is here. He had to have come in from Houston. I'm sure of it, but I don't know who helped him."

She closed her eyes. He could see the fan of her lashes against the single light from the bedroom. He didn't like that she was backlit. There were no houses or rooftops for a sniper to lie in wait, but there were hills. He got up, went into the bedroom and turned off the light. When he returned, there were tears on her face. The sight nearly broke him. Mitya reached down, gathered her up—blanket and all—and sat back down in her chair, holding her close.

"The Caruso family runs the docks in Houston," she whispered. "Alessandro came into the bakery just as Jewel was rising. He saw us leave."

He brushed a kiss along her temple. Gentle, because she needed gentle, even though at the mention of Alessandro, both Mitya and Dymka wanted to rip something—or someone—apart. "Is that why you're upset? You think that means Alessandro or his family betrayed your father and you?" He tried not to sound anything but calm.

She shook her head. "It's the blood. I showered and scrubbed my foot. I even took two baths, but I can't get his blood off me. I can feel it, Mitya. Hitting me. I fell asleep on the bed but it woke me up. When I kicked him, it splattered all over my foot and leg."

Mitya tightened his arms around her. "You know it isn't on your skin, baby. It feels like that when you take someone's life. It isn't meant to be easy." It was easy for him. Too easy, but he knew that wasn't right.

"That man, as bad as he was, was someone's child. Someone's sibling." There was a sob in her voice.

He didn't tell her that Albert had earned his place in Lazar's upper echelon by helping his father kill his own mother. She didn't need to hear that shit. "I don't know what makes a man turn bad, but he did. He hurt a lot of women. You stopped that. He'll never be able to hurt a child or woman again." She needed to hear that at least. He pressed her face into his shoulder and then stroked her hair gently, rocking her.

"I know I had to do it to save us, but I didn't know he would take a piece of me with him when he died."

He took a breath to keep from reacting. "Albert was the worst of my father's lieutenants. He was a very sick individual. He didn't care what age they were, old or very, very young, he liked hurting females. He liked humiliating them. That man doesn't get a piece of you dead or alive. His blood isn't on you, Ania."

He bunched her hair in his fist and pulled her head back, so he could look into her eyes. "He doesn't get one little part of you. I could tell you things he did, but those things are so vile you would never get them out of your head. All three of those men were cruel and they liked hurting others weaker than they were. My father is the worst of all of them."

Her eyes searched his and then she nodded, her lashes sweeping down. Mitya took her mouth. Those trembling lips. The knowledge of what he was saying was in her eyes, slowly sinking in, but he didn't want her thinking about Albert, or Taras or Kronya. He wanted her to forget they ever existed. He could take on the burden of those vile men, but he didn't want any part of them touching Ania.

The moment he kissed her, his lips moving over hers, he felt the familiar fire erupt deep inside him. She seemed to pour some accelerant down his throat so that it spread through his veins and arteries, moving into his belly to build into a conflagration so hot and wild that by the time it hit his groin, he was already going up in flames.

She always gave herself up to him completely. Ania never held back with him. She surrendered herself to him, gave herself into his keeping, and he loved that about her. His hands moved beneath the blanket and found her naked under a shirt far too big for her. Shaping her rib cage, he pulled back far enough to look down at her.

"You're wearing my shirt."

She pressed kisses to his throat and then gave him a look that told him she wasn't happy he'd interrupted their kisses with something so mundane.

"It isn't like I have any clothes here, Mitya. I thought about sneaking out and going to the house to get some, but I knew you wouldn't like it. And Sevastyan said if I did it again, he'd insist you punish me." She tossed her head, sending her hair flying, her eyes flashing fire, body posture stating "just try it."

Mitya couldn't help but laugh. Sevastyan might think he could intimidate Ania, but he didn't think anyone could—with the exception of him, and that wasn't going to last long.

"You're so right, I wouldn't have liked you sneaking off. Your skills are extraordinary, but the guards are all leopard."

"So were my grandparents and parents as well as Annalise," she said, smugness evident. "I had to learn to be even better at sneaking out than other children. It became sort of a game. They knew I was going to try, and they did what they could to prevent me going out on my own, mostly, by the way, to race cars. I love street racing. I could be anonymous. No one knew who I was. I loved it."

He tugged her hair. "I won't like it if you sneak out and try street racing. You're done with that."

She shrugged. "I did promise you, and I keep my word. But I am going to keep up my skills. That's important to me."

He began to undo the buttons on the shirt, unwrapping her like a gift. "Later, we'll get your clothes. I have plans for this morning." He looked at the sky, already becoming light with the dawn. "Dymka has them as well."

14

DYMKA was giving him hell. Every step Mitya took hurt like a son of a bitch. He couldn't stop thinking about sex. He couldn't stop the hot blood coursing through his veins. Ania was being driven just as hard, so that even though she was trying to get her things together, she rubbed her body along the bed seductively. Unknowingly. But Mitya saw every single detail and inhaled the pheromones she was throwing off with every breath he took.

Mitya stayed close to Ania as she moved around her bedroom, pulling clothes from her drawers and closet. She folded them meticulously, placing each item in the suitcase. She wandered around the room several times and then would go back to choosing various pieces of clothing to take. He knew the trip would be emotional and would take a toll on her. It didn't help that the leopard's heat was riding her so hard.

With every other article of clothing she chose, she would lift her arms and smooth back her hair, shake the long, thick mass out and then go back to folding her clothes. Each time she did it, his body felt like she was taking a flaming whip and lashing him, sending streaks of fire straight to his cock.

She wore only his shirt and nothing else. He liked it on her. She'd chosen one of his dress shirts, a light blue with long sleeves. She had them rolled up and the hem fell almost to her knees. The shirt was longer in the back and front, showing her thighs and sometimes, when she walked or picked something up, the creamy curve of her hips. He knew he shouldn't be thinking inappropriate thoughts when she was emotional. It was difficult to watch her as she chose each item, and he couldn't help but let his mind wander to other things, especially when her body language was blatantly seductive.

"Ania, we've got movers coming to pack everything. You only need a few clothes, just enough to get through the next couple of days." His voice was gruffer than he intended.

She looked up, frowning at him. "It's difficult to know what I'm going to need."

He didn't want to point out to her that she was wearing his shirt and as far as he was concerned, that was all she would ever need. He knew the moment he said something she would change immediately, so he kept his mouth shut.

When they'd woken, he'd made love to her slowly. Gently. He wanted her to feel what he was feeling when he looked at her or touched her. The leopards had taken over almost the moment they were finished, leaping out of the house, exploring the acreage and stopping every fifteen or twenty minutes to mate. Jewel's heat was driving them, and because they'd had so many interruptions, the heat seemed more intense. Mitya felt driven every time he saw or scented Ania. He could barely keep his hands to himself, and he knew she was suffering as well.

The constant burning had to be difficult to cope with, but Ania tried. He suggested they get some clothes for her and search her family home for anything that might point them in the direction of where her grandfather had stashed the package he'd kept. She complied without a protest, even though she only had his shirt to wear and the material rubbed on her nipples, making the burn even hotter.

Dymka was always rough when he took Jewel, but when he wasn't on her, he nuzzled and licked her, showing affection in the way he cared for her. He wasn't the type of cat to play, so running with her through creeks and leaping over logs, rolling together in leaves, was a huge expression of how the leopard felt about his partner. Still, that roughness transferred to Mitya.

He liked rough sex. He wasn't a man to play either, unless he was playing sexually with his partner. But he tried. For Ania, he tried. Dymka was a dangerous animal and always on edge. That meant Mitya was as well. Now that Dymka had a mate, he wanted her every moment, and Mitya was no different.

The leopards slept on and off in between mating sessions. Eventually, Mitya had directed Dymka to take Jewel back to the house. Once there, he had carried an extremely tired Ania upstairs, bathed her and then put her in bed, pulling the blackout, privacy screens to allow them to sleep, which they did, for most of the day.

The emergence, he realized, was extremely hard on the female. Ania had circles under her eyes and bruises on her body. She had teeth marks on her. With her pale skin, those dark smudges really showed. She looked tired but determined. With everything else going on as well, and the losses she'd suffered, Mitya couldn't blame her if she wanted to lock herself away from everyone, but Ania wasn't like that. She had good old-fashioned grit. She just kept picking herself up when life knocked her down.

"Would you mind if we went into your grandfather's apartment?"

She turned slowly from smoothing out a pair of jeans and sank onto the edge of the bed. He couldn't help but notice how the shirt rode up on her hips and she rubbed her thighs together to relieve the burning that just wouldn't quit for either of them.

"I don't mind, Mitya, but the apartment's been cleaned. After they died, Annalise went in and packed everything. She gave clothes and things like that to the thrift stores. There was nothing in the apartment that indicated a package taken from his job. He never said a word that there was a problem to any of us, including my father."

"Do you remember how he acted?"

She nodded. "He was different. All of us noticed it. Very withdrawn. When my grandmother tried to talk to him, he snapped at her, which, believe me, he never did. Looking back, I think he didn't know what to do, but he didn't want to involve anyone else in what he thought was a problem with one or more of the families."

She tapped her thigh, the only sign of nerves, and then closed the suitcase. "We can go down there now. You have to remember, at the time, none of us knew he had kept something he shouldn't have. Even after my father was shot, we didn't put it together right away. We knew they'd been run off the road, and that their deaths weren't really an accident, but we didn't know why. For all we knew, some crazy person had gone after them and they were randomly chosen."

"Where is Annalise?" He tried not to be suspicious of the woman. She was leopard, yet she had acted as if she hadn't known what had been happening when Antosha had struggled with his leopard to keep it from emerging. She had cleaned the apartment and would have found the book had Ania's grandfather hidden it there.

"Annalise has the apartment I found for her, you know that. I told her she could stay here, but she didn't want to stay alone. I can't blame her." She looked around the room and then sighed. "It doesn't feel like home anymore. Annalise feels like family to me, and I want to make certain she's always taken care of."

He had no problem with that. If Annalise was really what she seemed, then he hoped to offer her a position in his household. Once Ania started having his children, they would need a nanny. Annalise could be quite helpful.

"Baby, leave that," Mitya said when Ania began to go through her drawers again. "I've got movers coming to pack up your things."

"I don't like the idea of strangers touching my clothes." Ania ran her hands down her body, clearly unaware she was doing so. Twice she cupped her breasts and brushed her fingers over her nipples through the material of the shirt she wore. Both times she gasped and flushed.

His cock was so hard he thought he might not live if he took a step. It was difficult to think, but one of them had to remain sane. They just had to get this done and then he could figure out how to make love to his woman without bruising her. She needed care, not more rough sex, although watching her, he wasn't certain if that was true either. Trying to do the right thing wasn't easy.

Ania led the way back down the stairs, looking very comfortable in his shirt, as if she were wearing an elegant dress. He wondered if she wore panties under it. As they moved down the stairs, he let his hand slide down the curve of her back to the tail of the shirt, bunching it in his fist. His knuckles brushed bare skin. Heat spiraled down his spine.

"I love your ass, Ania." He wanted her to be distracted. He needed her to be. The house had become a memorial, a shrine to the dead. He wanted Ania to stay among the living. Her family were all gone and only ghosts remained behind.

He opened his hand to palm her left cheek as she walked, feeling the muscles bunch and give. His thumb slid over her soft, firm skin.

She glanced at him over her shoulder, and her eyes held a dark lust. "You like everything about my body."

"That's true. I wouldn't mind sitting you on the landing and taking time out to eat you. I'm feeling a little like the Big Bad Wolf."

Her laughter rewarded him, spilling over so the notes felt like gold to him. A little shiver went down her spine and she pushed back into his hand. "You're always feeling like the Big Bad Wolf. Don't try to pull the wool over my eyes and act innocent."

"That's bad," he said. "Really bad."

She went down the long hall, past her father's room, to a door that she unlocked with the keys she'd taken from her room. Once open, she stepped back to allow him through first. The room was immaculate, as if it had just been deep-cleaned. If Annalise had done this, she'd done it as a labor of love. No one kept empty rooms so pristine.

He looked around. There was very little furniture and nothing personal whatsoever. "Did Annalise find anything at all that he specifically left for your father or you?"

She started to shake her head and then frowned. "He had a journal and there were entries for my father. The journal should be in my father's desk in the den."

"Did you read it?"

"My father showed me a few entries, just because they were loving and sweet. Mostly about my grandmother and me. The rest, he kept to himself. But, Mitya, if there was anything about a package my grandfather had failed to deliver to the Anwar family, my father would have told me when I asked."

"Maybe, Ania. And maybe, like your grandfather, he wanted to keep you safe."

"I don't think I'm very safe, Mitya. If that was his purpose in not telling me, he didn't do a very good job of it."

She didn't sound bitter, although her words could have been taken that way. She sounded sad. He slung his arm around her neck and walked her out of her grandparents' apartment. It was cold and felt empty. Ania needed to feel warm and carefree. He had to give that to her. More than anything, Mitya wanted to make her happy.

As she led the way to the den, her body slid subtly along his. He felt every curve. Deep inside, his leopard raked him, every bit as aware of the pheromones she was throwing off as he was. Ania seemed to slide against every wall down the long hallway, so that her alluring fragrance filled the entire area, from floor to ceiling, so he breathed her in with every step he took.

Mitya felt a little as if he was going out of his mind. In his ears there was a roaring thunder. He felt edgy. Tense. There was a part of him that was there, taking care of business. Most of him was all about desire. Lust. Hunger. That kind of hunger cut through his soul, leaving him jagged and feeling like a jackhammer was ripping through his head.

It took tremendous discipline to stay on task. To keep his mind on the reason he was there in that house. She moved out from under his shoulder, which should have given him some relief, but then he was looking at her body as she moved so seductively through the den to the other side of the room.

Her father's desk was an old-fashioned rolltop, which surprised him. He would have thought Antosha would have had a much more modern glass one. Ania ran her hand over the wood and then pulled out another key. She unlocked the top drawer, reached in and hit something he couldn't see. Immediately a little hidden drawer sprang open from one of the two curved wooden pieces that formed the legs.

Mitya was more interested in the way she bent down to open the drawer, giving him flashes of her bottom. He really wanted to take a bite out of her. Instead, he waited while she crouched down, her legs slightly apart, just enough that he could see the honey glistening on the tight curls covering her mound.

He curved his palm over the hard length of his cock. She looked up and smiled at him. She knew exactly what she was doing to him. He wanted to catch all that wild hair in his hand and shove his cock down her throat. Sevastyan and the others were too close. He nearly groaned aloud as she shifted her legs, supposedly to get closer to the small secret drawer. He could barely breathe, but somehow her scent found its way into his lungs.

He wanted to roar. He wanted to lift her up and slam her down on that desktop. Take her right there. He could taste her in his mouth. Hot desire. Pure lust. It rushed over him like a tidal wave of madness.

Ania pulled out the journal and held it up. He took it with a cursory glance and then shoved it in his pocket.

She deliberately ran her tongue around her lips, wetting them. Looking up at him. His cock felt like a dagger. Diamond hard. Titanium. Her hand slipped to the front of his trousers.

"Too bad we're not alone. My mouth would feel so good sealed around your cock, wouldn't it?" she whispered. "But as usual, we're surrounded by all these guards. I'll bet you would like the things I could do to you. Or better yet—the things you could do to me."

"Stop teasing me, *kotyonok*," he warned. "I don't particularly give a fuck whether or not they're here. You keep it up and you'll be on your knees sucking me dry right in front of them."

She laughed because she knew it wasn't true. He would never tolerate his men watching her have sex with him. The leopards were one thing; her human counterpart was something altogether different. His threat was empty and they both knew it. Well, he thought he knew it but the strange roaring in his head and the jackhammers drilling into him told him otherwise. A few more minutes and she wouldn't be safe.

He called out gruffly to Sevastyan to make certain her suitcase was in the car and to bring it around. Backing Ania into the wall, he took her mouth while his hands went under her shirt, slid up her belly to her breasts and began to knead those soft, perfect mounds. The way they felt in his hands. So soft. Creamy. Perfect. He wanted to devour her. Maul her. Take everything she was for himself. He was rough, and she gasped, giving him even better access to her mouth.

His head began to buzz, and he was on a terrible high from just her kisses. He pinched and pulled her nipples. Hard. Equally as rough as his kisses so she was gasping and pushing her breasts into his hands. One of her legs slid around his so she was riding his thigh, trying to bring herself off.

"Not happening, babe," he whispered. "You know better than to tease a leopard." He refused to allow her relief.

The burn was there in her eyes. Almost as desperate as he was. He smiled wickedly and pressed his fingers deep, fucking her that way but stopping when her hips surged forward to meet his. Every now and then he flicked her clit so that she gasped and tried to ride his hand the way she had his thigh. His trousers had spots on them from her cream, and he felt as wild and feral as his leopard.

"We're ready for you," Sevastyan called, his voice tight.

"Leopards are driving us," Mitya said. "We'll need a little privacy."

"I see that," Sevastyan said. "Every leopard is very aware, Mitya."

There wasn't anything Mitya could do about that. Ania's body was throwing off the pheromones that would drive the male leopards mad, but Sevastyan insisted on bodyguards. They were under attack and needed their best men around them. The female leopard and her human counterpart were driving them all mad.

"Hurry, baby, let's get to the car." Mitya nearly dragged Ania out of the house, hand on the small of her back, pushing her down the walkway to the car. "Take us up the road until I say different," he ordered Miron and yanked open the back door.

Ania took her time climbing inside. Instead of just slipping onto the seat, she put her hands in first, bending, so the firm cheeks of her ass peeked out at him from under the shirt. She crawled in, her bottom swaying in invitation.

Heart pounding, he swatted her hard. His handprint came up immediately, a bright red beacon on her pale skin. The sound and the sight of that red handprint on her pale bottom sent a streak of lightning jolting through his cock. Sweat trickled down his body.

"Move it."

Her laughter taunted him, and she slowed her crawl, looking seductively up at him over her shoulder. He swatted her again and leaned in to bite her. She cried out in need and lowered her torso to the seat, rubbing her nipples over the leather through his shirt. Her bare bottom was in the air, an invitation he couldn't resist.

He heard his own roar, out of control. Lightning kept striking along with his hand. He heard the slaps, heard her moans; his cock fucking hurt so badly he thought he might go insane. He palmed her heated cheek and then slid his fingers into her welcoming opening, smearing her liquid over her lips and clit and then between her cheeks. Before he could push his finger into her tight little hole, she had scooted out of the way to allow him inside.

The moment the doors of the car closed, heedless of the men in the front seat, Mitya was on her, unbuttoning her shirt so the edges parted and her full, rounded breasts peeked out at him. His hands dropped to his belt buckle, hastily opening it and dragging his trousers from his hips, down his legs and off. He'd never needed clothes gone so much. Just having them touch his skin seemed an abomination. His cock raged at him to be free—a monster now, every bit as enraged and hungry as a feral leopard.

Sevastyan put up the privacy screen with an oath, reminding Mitya he was so far gone, he hadn't thought to do so himself. His frenzied hunger had taken him right over the edge. She'd driven him out of his mind with her teasing.

"Need your mouth, woman," he ordered, his voice hoarse. "Right now. I want to shove my cock down your throat, fill you up with me." He did. He didn't want to be gentle or accommodating. He didn't want to have to worry about anything but pleasure. His pleasure. Hot and bright and a miracle of pure sensation. She could do that with her mouth. Ania could do things with her mouth he hadn't thought possible. What she didn't know, he was teaching her, and every lesson was a hot, instructive exploration. His cock burned in that inferno, desperate for what only she could give him.

His cock was so hot he thought he might explode. She slipped to the floor at his feet as he widened his thighs to accommodate her. She looked perfect there, gazing up at him, her face almost demure as her hands stroked his inner thighs and then settled around his heavy sac. That wasn't where he wanted her mouth, but it felt amazing when her fingers caressed and gently kneaded and then her tongue began licking like that of the little kitten he called her. Her tongue covered every inch of his balls, traced the velvet sac, and then she was running the tip up and down between his balls and his backside.

He wanted to close his eyes and savor the feeling, but he couldn't. He had to stare into those eyes. See her breasts swaying with each movement she made. He couldn't resist pinching her nipples, watching the dark flush slide under her skin. He tugged, stretching them, her gasp telling him that he created two hot points of pain that spread flames from her breasts to her sex.

"We're changing position. You turn. Sit back, right there on the floor, press your back to the seat and then lay your head back on it."

Ania complied without asking any questions. The back of her head rested on the seat, stretching her throat. His heart pounded as he moved around in front of her. There was very little room, so he was bracing himself, straddling her body, his cock positioned right over her mouth.

She stared up at his cock and heavy sac, her eyes wide. He placed one hand on the back of the seat and the other around his cock.

"You can touch my thighs or balls, baby, but not my cock. I control this, not you."

He watched her throat as she swallowed, apprehension in her eyes. He didn't blame her. His cock looked and felt like a monster. He was nearly insane with wanting her. He felt as if every cell in his body was screaming for her body, for the things she could do to him. He wanted to roar with rage, with hunger, with need.

"Open your mouth."

She licked her lips and his gut tightened. He reached down and pinched her nipple hard. When she gasped, he caught the base of his cock and pushed half of it into her open mouth. Heat surrounded him. Swamped his every sense.

"That's it, baby, fucking take me down. Suck. Right now. Just suck." He couldn't close his eyes to savor the feeling of her wet, hot mouth surrounding him, because the sight of her lips stretching around his cock was the most erotic thing he'd ever seen. She didn't have a choice the way he'd positioned her. His cock pinned her there, along with the weight of his body. He controlled everything, and she knew it. She had to accept whatever he demanded.

She sucked hard, her cheeks hollowing and her tongue lashing him with pure fire. Lightning streaked up his spine. He threw back his head and roared as fiery pleasure washed through him.

"Harder," he admonished, pushing deeper.

She choked and tried to pull away from him but found it impossible. He waited until she settled, and then shook his head. "You can do this, *kotyonok*, you've taken me deeper. Think of my cock, how to worship it, how to make it feel better than you've ever made it feel." He gave her a breath of air and then pushed deep. "This is your cock, made for you, made to bring you pleasure. Think how it feels when it's between your legs. Suck hard. Make it feel so good. Only you can do that, Ania. Make it good for me."

She suckled harder, her eyes wide, liquid forming. She began to struggle a little for air again and reluctantly, he pulled back to let her take a breath. One. He pushed a little deeper than he'd gone the last time.

"You're going to take me all the way down this time," he said. "Harder, Ania. I want you to suck me dry."

She tried to comply, her mouth working, her tongue teasing. He let her breathe and then pushed deep until he felt that resistance. She didn't struggle, but he saw her fight it. He loved watching her fight for him. For his pleasure. His woman, giving him everything he asked for even when it wasn't easy.

"Relax for me."

The thought of her struggling for him, fighting off the need to breathe, controlling her gag reflex, her fear, all for him, was mind-blowing. The knowledge heightened his pleasure. Watching her lips stretch impossibly around his girth, seeing her throat as she tried to swallow him down, her nose fighting for air, eyes watery but filled with that dark lust, intensified, even amplified, the ecstasy of her hot, silken mouth.

"That's it, baby. All the way. Swallow me. Suck it out of me." His balls were drawn so tight.

Her hands came up under the velvet sac and she began to stroke caresses over them. Her fingers closed around them and he thought he might explode down her throat, but he fought it off. He didn't want this to end.

Her lips glistened and when he pulled back to allow her to breathe, his shaft was wet and hot. He pushed into her mouth and began to pump long strokes. He kept her head pinned on the seat as he filled her.

"Swallow, Ania. Swallow me," he said as he bridged her throat. "Use your fingers to get yourself off."

She struggled to obey him, and then tight muscles constricted and stimulated him even more. It was paradise, a place he didn't want to leave. Her fingers crept down her belly to disappear between her legs. The moment she started working herself, she relaxed even more. She had given herself completely over to him, and he took his time, feeling the stroking caresses on his inner thighs and sac as he thrust in and out of her mouth, and then down her throat.

He felt his balls tighten even more as the friction increased and grew so hot he knew he couldn't last. His cock grew, thickened, pushing her boundaries even more. "You almost there, baby? Hurry. Catch up."

Her fingers worked frantically as he pushed his cock

deep, his hips thrusting, his mind in a red haze. Thunder roared in his ears.

Her eyes went to his and even with her mouth full of him, she managed to nod her head to tell him she was there.

"Let go, baby, let yourself come. Swallow every drop, don't let one escape," he ordered, because just the idea of telling his woman what he needed, and her complying, was a further turn-on.

Her eyes went completely liquid as his cock swelled more and began to jerk and throb as his seed rocketed down her throat. Pulse after pulse. He watched her trying to take him down even as her own body erupted into a fiery orgasm.

When his cock stopped jerking and pulsing, Mitya slowly withdrew. Ania drew in air, her head still back, her eyes dazed and heated. She'd never looked more beautiful to him. He didn't move, balancing with the sway of the car, legs straddling her body, his semihard cock right over her.

"Make sure you get *every* drop, *kotyonok*." Beneath his skin he could feel the heat of his leopard, pushing to surface, needing his mate. The growl in his voice and the demands were all shifter, a dominant predator hungry for more.

Her tongue felt soothing, a velvet rasp as she cleaned him, the way every female in their species cleaned her mate. He savored that feeling, loved watching her, wished they could start all over again, but the chaos in his brain was receding enough for his brain to function properly. The leopards needed to run free, to mate again, to spend time together.

His men were leopard and could smell the pheromones Jewel and Ania were putting out as well as hear everything they said—and did—to each other. Mitya had no idea how to defuse the situation with his leopard's needs and Sevastyan's need to keep them safe.

He dropped his hand on Ania's head, rubbing his thumb over her cheekbone in a little caress. Very gently, when she was finished, he helped her to sit up and then loosened the cap on a water bottle to give to her. Ania drank gratefully.

Mitya continued to stroke caresses over her face and then her lips after she drank. He smeared the cool water around her lips, knowing they had to be sore. Everything on her was probably sore. He knew he needed the contact more than she did.

"Wish I could be gentle with you, baby," he said softly, meaning it. She deserved gentle. "Fucking leopard is pushing at me hard. I can't blame him. Every time he gets to be with his mate, something seems to happen. That makes him crazy. He wants to go hunting. Thinks that will stop it all."

"She's desperate to get out," Ania said. Her voice was strained. Hoarse.

He winced, and his hand went to her throat, fingers gently stroking. "Sorry, *kotyonok*, you're probably bruised."

That brought a brief smile. She looked up at him but made no move to get off the floor. She looked exhausted. "I'm bruised all over, one or two more isn't going to matter."

He hated that. He knew she was right, but he still hated it. Her body was covered in smudges, bruises, teeth marks and evidence of wild mating.

"Can you get up?"

She gave him another faint smile. "Probably, but I think I'll just stay here for a minute or two until I know I'm under control. She's getting crazy on me and it makes it very uncomfortable."

"He's the same way, Ania."

"They have to have time together, Mitya. Isn't there

somewhere we can go away from here where we can let them have a few days together without a threat?"

Mitya's first thought was no. How could they leave when she had some unknown faction trying to kill her, and his father was finally making his play to kill them all? He forced down that first negative reaction and considered her request.

"I don't know if we could get away with it, Ania. Sevastyan has everything in place to watch over us at the house."

She shrugged. "But our homes are so big, and it would probably be easier and take less effort to protect us somewhere smaller. More intimate. The leopards wouldn't have as much room to run, but they probably won't care as long as they aren't interrupted constantly."

Ania pressed the cool bottle of water to her forehead. "At least think about it, Mitya."

He wanted to give her the moon, but he knew wherever they went, they were going to take their problems with them. The leopards weren't going to run free without incident. In fact, each time they emerged, the risk was greater that they would be shot. A sniper was much more difficult to catch than one might think. It took one person with a rifle lying up on a hillside.

She leaned her head back and closed her eyes. "Do we even know what we're doing, Mitya? I feel like we're just running in circles. When we have two minutes together, we have wild, crazy sex and then something terrible happens. I don't know you at all, and you don't know me."

Mitya sank back onto the seat, his thigh beside her head. Sinking his fingers into her hair, he rubbed the silky strands together. "I know it feels that way right now, baby. Many leopard couples have already been through one or two life cycles together. They have old memories, even if they can't remember them exactly, and the draw between them is there so the Han Vol Dan goes much more smoothly. They feel as if they know each other already. We don't have that. We're building it. Jewel's heat won't last more than a week, and things will cool down enough to give us breathing room."

She rubbed her hand up and down his thigh, but she didn't respond. Mitya didn't like that she went silent on him. He tugged on her hair. "*Kotyonok*, you're exhausted. You lost your father. You have people trying to kill you for whatever reason. I think you have every right to question what's happening. I just want you to remember one thing. I'm that man that's going to stand for you. No matter what happens around us, I'm not going anywhere."

She took another long drink of water. "I know. I do. I'm just . . . tired."

"I'll have Sevastyan turn the car around and take us back to the house."

She pressed the bottle to her forehead again. "We still have to let them out. Jewel isn't going to let up until she's with Dymka."

Mitya didn't have the heart to tell her that wouldn't change anything. Dymka was even more upset and out of sorts than Jewel or Ania. It was all Mitya could do to control him. His own moods weren't much better. The entire situation was fucked.

"Let's just get home." He reached for his trousers.

"I don't think I can face any of them yet," Ania said softly. "I don't even know what I'm doing when it's on me like that. I can't think."

She was crying. He heard it in her voice. Tears. When he looked down, he could see wetness on the tips of her lashes and tears running down her face. His heart stuttered. Turned over. He reached down, caught her around the waist and lifted her easily onto his lap. He was grateful for the strength of his leopard, for the strength of his body. She was on the smaller side and picking her up was easy.

He cupped the side of her face, his thumb brushing at the tears. "I know this feels like it isn't ever going to end, but I promise you, it will. We'll sort through it together, Ania. I haven't shut you out of anything. I've been up front about the kind of man I am."

"I know," she whispered. "I'm sorry, I'm just feeling a little overwhelmed. Not everything feels like love, even when I'm trying to show you the way I'm coming to feel."

He'd been selfish. There was no question about that. He knew himself; he knew that when the leopard was driving him with his moods, he would be selfish again. "I suppose it didn't feel like love to you, and I know you need that. The way you gave yourself to me felt like it to me."

"Don't get me wrong." She still didn't look at him. "I loved it. I love when you're like that, the things you say are sexy and you feel powerful and all mine. I like taking care of you, but I don't always feel confident in us."

He forced her head around, so he could look into her eyes. "You don't feel confident in us?" he repeated, astonished. He frowned, not letting her look away. "Do you still think I'm with you because of my leopard?"

She shrugged. "No one even looked at me until she went into heat. Suddenly there are men coming around, you one of them, saying how beautiful I am. No one said that before."

"We didn't meet before, Ania. That night, when I saw you in the rain, I knew then that you were mine. I *knew* it. There wasn't one moment of doubt." He bent his head to brush a kiss across her lips. "I've fallen so deeply in love with you I don't even know what to do about it. I'm not a poet, baby, and I'm never going to be. I don't have pretty words. But when I touch you, even when I'm rough, especially when I'm rough, that's raw and honest. That's me feeling so intense I'm barely in control. For a man like me to lose control, Ania, it has to be love."

She tipped her head back, leaning against his shoulder

to look into his eyes. He saw her cat close, but he also saw her, those indigo eyes that could melt his heart every time. Her eyes searched his, as if looking for his soul. If that was what she needed to know she was loved by him, he'd find a way to give that to her.

"Let's go home, baby, and we'll let the cats have their time. We can talk this out in a private setting." His hand dropped to the nape of her neck in an effort to ease the tension out of her. "I never want you to feel as if you aren't loved for you. For me, what I feel is all about you. There isn't going to be another woman in my life. Not ever. And when I die, I'm going to die knowing I get to be with you in eight more life cycles."

She sent him a tentative smile. "You might regret that."

He shook his head. "That's the one thing I'm absolutely certain of, Ania. I have no doubts. I can see why you'd have them. I can be a selfish lover . . ."

"You can be a generous one as well. I meant what I said, I love the way you were with me. I just don't always feel confident."

"You should—"

The car pitched sideways. A shot rang out and then another. Something hit the glass on the driver's side. The car bounced and swayed sideways, nearly out of control. Mitya caught Ania by her shoulders, thrusting her toward the floor. Already her hands were on the buttons of the shirt, closing it as she turned toward the window to try to see out.

"Stay down," he hissed. "Sevastyan, lower the screen now."

In the darkness, they could see the other two cars giving them chase. Flashes lit up the darkness as more bullets spat at them. Spiderwebbing appeared on the windshield and the driver's side window. An SUV crashed into them, driving them sideways, pitching Ania off the seat. Mitya tried to catch her, but he was pulling up his trousers and missed.

The windshield shattered on the driver's side and Miron pitched to the side, slumping down in the seat. Sevastyan caught the steering wheel, but the weight of Miron's foot was on the gas pedal. The car fishtailed out of control, careening off the SUV.

15

ANIA practically leapt over the seat into the front, yelling at Sevastyan to drag Miron from behind the wheel. She was already sliding behind the wounded man, moving so fast Mitya didn't have a chance to yank her back to him.

"Seat belts," Ania yelled, her hands on the wheel, the car miraculously and impossibly sliding around the SUV as if they were in some movie scene.

Sevastyan used his leopard's strength to drag Miron over to the passenger side and away from Ania. She glanced in the rearview mirror, and to both sides, but how she could see anything with the car in a spin and everything happening so fast, Mitya didn't know. Like Sevastyan, he pulled weapons out of compartments and moved to the driver's side of the car to cover that side. It wasn't easy with the car in a spin, but he managed.

"Seat belts," Ania snapped a second time.

Clearly her mind should be on controlling the vehicle,

and not her passengers, but under the circumstances neither man mentioned it.

The car straightened out and shot away from the SUV and the other car pursuing them. Sevastyan had his phone out and was texting his men. "They're not that far out," he reported. "Can you handle this, Ania?"

"Don't insult me," Ania said. She glanced at Miron. "How bad is it?"

"He's holding," Sevastyan replied tersely.

The two cars were trying to sandwich them, coming up on either side. Mitya let off two rounds, hoping to keep the shooter from making a try at Ania. He detested her being exposed like that. The driver's side window was bulletproof. It shouldn't have shattered the way it did. Now she was the one the shooters were targeting, wanting to stop their vehicle.

She suddenly hit the brakes, and the moment both cars were a foot in front of her, she spun the heavy town car as if it were small and sporty. Mitya nearly ended up in the front seat with the others. The car flew back down the road, leading away from their residence and back toward the main highway.

Mitya glanced at the speedometer. She was still accelerating, and she showed no signs of letting off the gas. He noted she looked cool, hands steady on the wheel, eyes ahead, while his heart was pounding like a runaway freight train. He detested not being in control. She'd turned the town car into a road rocket. He had no idea one could get those kinds of speed out of it.

As they approached the on-ramp, a long winding curve that spilled out onto the main highway, a large Ram truck shot out of a side road, one unpaved and barely a trail. It should have plowed into the side of them, sending them careening into the boulders and hill on the other side of the road.

Somehow, and Mitya honestly didn't know how she did

it, Ania had spun their car once more, away from the new attack. The breath slammed out of his lungs as he looked back at the truck that had nearly taken them out. It had to stop before its momentum carried it into the very boulders it had planned to send the town car into.

"Fuck!" Mitya yelled at the top of his lungs. "Turn around, Ania. Fucking turn around."

She didn't hesitate, and she spun them back, taking them right to the bumper of the truck that had tried to assault them. She stopped like she did everything, fast and efficiently. Mitya didn't give a damn, he was already out of the car, going up on the driver's side, Sevastyan matching his long, angry strides on the passenger side. Both fired almost simultaneously, nearly emptying their weapons into the four men in the truck. Mitya went for head shots. He didn't recognize any of them, and he could have cared less who they were.

Ania laid on the horn, snapping him out of his fury. He glanced up to see two cars speeding toward them. He and Sevastyan ran for their vehicle and dove in as she once more headed for the highway.

"Feel better?" she asked.

Was there amusement in her voice? He met her eyes in the rearview mirror and glared. There was a hint of laughter in them. "Damn it, Ania, you could be killed."

"Not likely," she answered. Sassy.

He didn't know whether to kiss her or turn her over his knee—if they survived. She shouldn't be having so much fun. Miron was leaking blood all over the front seat. Sevastyan looked as if he might shoot both of them, and he wanted to kill every single fucker in the two remaining cars. He'd had enough. These men were not Lazar's. Not one of them he'd just shot. He knew the men from the lairs in his homeland, and none of them were recognizable. He wasn't even certain they were leopard.

He glanced at the head of his security. "You recognize any of them?"

The car was on the long circular ramp and about to be spit out onto the highway. Again, Ania was accelerating. Mitya found himself clutching at the seat, his teeth clenched as they burst into the lane almost on top of a little van going half their speed. Their town car was pulling away from it before the driver managed to find his horn.

"Tell me what you want me to do."

Ania was speaking to *Sevastyan*, not him. Mitya didn't know why that enraged him, but it did. "What I want you to do," he snapped, "Is lead these bastards right into *our* trap. Sevastyan, I want at least one of them alive. A couple would be better. Get on the fuckin' phone and make this happen." He poured command into his voice.

He'd been born to lead, and right then, he was leading his enemies into a trap. His woman was driving the car, but he had to accept that. He'd have a word or two with Sevastyan once this was over. Clearly, there had been some agreement between the two. "Let them catch up, Ania, but just give them glimpses until we've got everything set."

Ania nodded. "They're on the highway and threading through traffic."

"Hopefully we don't have cops out tonight," Mitya said. "But if we do, lose them."

"Of course." She sounded confident.

It was difficult not to have faith in her when she was so at ease with the high-speed maneuvers she'd pulled off.

Mitya texted one-handed, holding his weapon ready in the other. He needed to warn his cousin Fyodor. Telling him what was happening was imperative. He had to know that the enemy was persistent. Whoever had put together the package for the Anwar family was coming after them. He had no idea who or why, but he was determined that this trap that had been sprung on them was going to be turned around and they would benefit.

"Need a helicopter to transport Miron and a surgical team," Sevastyan said. "I called for that as well. They'll be waiting at our drop point. Ania, can you circle around and get us back to the road leading to home?"

"I was born and raised in the hills above San Antonio. I know every exit and every back road. That gives me a little bit of an advantage. It helps that I was taught to drive on these roads by both my grandfather and father. I know places those following don't have a prayer of knowing. That means yes."

She wove in and out of traffic, keeping her speed steady as she headed for the exit they needed. She wanted a quick turnaround, off the highway and then right back on.

"The boys will set up just before Bannaconni's ranch." Sevastyan sent Ania a quick glance. "Can you get us there before they catch up to us?"

Ania didn't deign to answer.

Mitya had time to take a breath and let himself admire her. The ride, now that they weren't spinning madly and being thrown all over the car, was smooth even though they traveled at a high rate of speed and had to make lane changes more than once. Ania was absolutely confident behind the wheel of the car. He was used to driving with Miron, who always clutched the wheel and spent half his time looking in the rearview mirror rather than concentrating on what was ahead of them.

As a bodyguard, Miron was one of the best—as a driver, not so much. He'd volunteered and sincerely tried to improve. Maybe it wasn't such a bad idea to allow his woman to drive—but he enjoyed their back-seat fucking. He wasn't about to give that up. He had never looked forward to driving around before; now he made excuses to go out.

"Have you been able to stop Miron's bleeding?" he

asked as he peered out the back window, watching the SUV gain a little ground on them. The Audi was caught behind a red Cadillac. When the driver realized there was someone on his bumper, he startled and hastily changed lanes without signaling, just as the Audi did the same. The Audi nearly rear-ended the Cadillac. Mitya smirked a little, certain Ania wouldn't have made that mistake.

Ania suddenly cut across traffic, shooting in and out of the cars, timing it perfectly so she hit the exit before the SUV could adjust and take it as well. He was all the way over in the fast lane before she made her move. Within seconds they were curving around and going under the pass in order to get back on the freeway heading in the direction Sevastyan wanted them to be going.

"Damn it, Ania, you lost them," Mitya snapped. "The plan was for them to follow us."

"They'll follow," she assured, easing off the gas as they came up on the other ramp. "If I hadn't pretended to try to shake them, they'd be suspicious and maybe wouldn't have followed."

"They aren't behind us." He pointed out the obvious. He wanted to explode at someone. He was that angry. He'd had enough of these men coming after them for some mythical reason no one knew about.

"The Audi's fast and will catch up, and the SUV will take the next exit just a mile or so up the road. No worries."

"We're not on a fuckin' picnic," he growled. He detested that she was anywhere in close proximity. He didn't want to take a chance she could be hurt. He also didn't want her anywhere around when he interrogated whatever prisoners they could take alive. He intended that their last hours on earth wouldn't be pleasant ones. God knew, she already had every reason to run. He didn't want her to see the real man and what he was capable of doing to another being—or how good he was at it.

Ania's eyes met his in the mirror. "I know, honey," she

298 Christine Feehan

replied softly. "I'm well aware these men mean business. I lost my family to them. I'm not about to lose you, or Sevastyan or Miron, to them as well."

There was determination in her voice. Heartache. Mitya wanted to kick himself. Dymka prowled just below the surface, an unrelenting, merciless drive to kill. The leopard wasn't alone in that need. Mitya had the same unforgiving, ruthless, implacable drive to kill, only he wanted to torture every single scrap of information he could from them first. Dymka backed off a little when he was certain Mitya was on the same page with him.

When the leopard stepped back, it allowed Mitya to better get a grip on his anger and dial down the ferocity level. Ania was already nervous about their relationship, and he could feel her pulling back. She'd all but told him she felt she didn't know him. Torturing and killing those men, even if they were enemies, might not be the best way to reassure her he was doing his best to turn his life around.

"Audi coming up behind us," she reported as she accelerated onto the highway, somehow finding a small space to squeeze through to the middle lane, and then they were in the fast lane threading through traffic.

She slowed once to a sedate speed and sent a smirk to the mirror as a cop slid silently up behind the Audi, trying to catch them.

Mitya caught a glimpse of the SUV making its way through traffic. There wasn't as much traffic heading in this direction, away from the city toward the hills and wine country. The SUV spotted the cop and was forced to slow as well. Ania's speed was just above the limit, and she added one and then two more miles per hour. They crept away from the two cars chasing them.

"Is everyone in place?" Mitya asked Sevastyan. He couldn't help the clipped voice.

"Yes."

"Just our people?"

"The ones we trust," Sevastyan said. "Fyodor and Timur brought the crew they trust as well. We didn't alert Bannaconni or Perez this time. We'll handle it. Fyodor has a place we can take any prisoners to."

Ania's gaze slid to his in the mirror and then her eyes were back on the road. Mitya ignored the uneasiness creeping into her gaze.

"How the fuck did the glass break on Miron's window? It's supposed to be bulletproof and new. That looks as if the sun degraded it."

"Had it outfitted a couple of weeks ago," Sevastyan said. "Replaced everything just to be safe. Jeremiah took the car in because Miron was busy." He didn't point out that they'd been trying to keep Mitya safe while his leopard went crazy over Ania's, but he did glance her way.

"Jeremiah? The kid? No way is that boy a traitor."

"You have to worry about him, Mitya," Sevastyan said. "He came from Borneo, same as Amory. Drake recommended him, same as Amory. They both worked for Jake Bannaconni at Drake's suggestion. He could be a plant."

"He's not a plant," Mitya said. "You know damn well he's not a plant. He's got ADHD or something, Sevastyan. No way would anyone recruit him for a long-term undercover operation. It isn't him. Where'd you take the car?"

There was a small silence. Ania glanced at Sevastyan. Mitya saw her hand tremble for the first time. Her unease had nothing to do with the fact that their exit was coming up fast. She began to make her way over to the slow lane.

"Took the car to Houston. The Anwar family outfits cars like ours," Sevastyan said.

Ania had known that. Of course, she knew. She grew up around all the families in San Antonio, Houston, probably other places as well. She knew the shops, anything at all that had to do with cars or a crime family. Her grandfather and father had groomed her to take over the business. They'd been friends with Bartolo Anwar, his two sons, Enrico and Samuele, and she'd probably met Barto-lo's daughter, Giacinta, as well.

"They're following," Ania announced. "No cops fol-lowing, they'll be coming at us aggressively."

Mitya glanced back. "Move it, Ania, keep us out in front of them."

She accelerated immediately, and used a road he'd never been on, a shortcut he presumed. The surface wasn't asphalt, but more gravel, stone and rock set with oil. She didn't slow down, even when she made the sharp turn onto the road. It was narrow with a deep drainage ditch on ei-ther side. Mitya and Sevastyan exchanged a long look, and Mitya shook his head. His woman was a little terrifying, and sexy as hell with her confidence and driving skills.

"Miron?"

"Hanging in there. I got the bleeding under control, but he needs a medic. They'll have one waiting," Sevastyan reiterated.

"They're on us," Mitya told Ania.

She didn't so much as glance at him but kept driving down the narrow road. There was water in the ditches and occasionally a very large culvert. She looked relaxed, as if she were driving leisurely on a country road, not hurtling along at a high rate of speed over what amounted to gravel.

He saw the passenger in the lead car stick his head out the window, gun in hand. Mitya threw himself to the pas-senger side and immediately had his window down. The driver accelerated. Ania suddenly hit the brakes. The Audi tried to do the same when it realized they were going to hit. The shooter caught at the door frame and Mitya shot him in the head. Ania hit the gas just as the other car hit their bumper. Had they not been moving forward so quickly, the car would have taken quite a jolt, but they barely felt it.

She shot the town car through the narrow lane and up around a curve to a dirt road that threw so much powdery dust into the air behind them, Mitya couldn't even see the other cars. Then she made another swift turn and they were on the main road leading to the high-end estates back in the hills.

"We're about to reach a half mile from Bannaconni's ranch. Tell me where you want to go," Ania ordered.

"Get us right past the cattle road there."

"Do you want them on our tail?"

"Absolutely. By a couple of car lengths. We're cutting them off, giving them nowhere to go."

"They're leopard," Mitya reminded. "They'll want to shift when they see they're caught in a squeeze."

"We're prepared," Sevastyan said.

"I'm letting Dymka loose," Mitya said. "He can mop up. Let Fyodor and the others know."

"Don't like that, Mitya," Sevastyan cautioned. "He's difficult to protect and so are you when you turn into a loose cannon."

"I want you with Ania," Mitya said. "I mean it, Sevastyan. I don't want a fuckin' scratch on her." He was already shedding clothes again, calling up his raging leopard, feeding the animal his own wrath. They'd come at him over and over. They'd killed Ania's family. He'd had enough.

"Mitya, it's my job to protect you."

"It's your job to do what I ask you to do. She's my world. You take care of her."

Ania opened her mouth once to object, but his eyes met hers in the mirror and she closed her mouth, seeing who he really was. He wasn't taking shit from anyone, not one objection. The car accelerated slightly as the two cars giving chase picked up speed to catch up.

"The minute they come in behind you with a barrier, you drive to the house," Mitya ordered Ania. "Straight to the house. I want her in the safe room, even if you have to carry her there yourself."

Ania drove past the cattle road and instantly accelerated to get out of the way. Behind them, a huge semi rolled
out straight across the road, hauling a cattle trailer filled
with hay. As it did, the first, then second car slammed into
it. Immediately the sound of gunfire filled the air as the
men concealed behind the hay opened fire on those in the
Audi and SUV.

"Stop." Mitya had the door open and was already shifting before Ania could stop the car.

The huge leopard leapt from the car and rushed toward
the two cars caught now between two cattle trucks. The
cars couldn't move forward or backward. Gunfire mowed
down two occupants, the driver and front passenger of the
Audi. The back doors popped open and a leopard rushed
out, running full out, zigzagging to take him into the
brush, using the cover of his friends as they returned fire.

Dymka immediately changed direction and went after
him. The leopard was big, nearly black with rosettes set
deep in his fur. Dymka increased his speed in order to cut
him off from escape. He hit the dark leopard in the side
hard, driving him off his feet, so that he rolled partially
down the small slope they were on. Dymka followed him,
roaring his challenge, daring the dark leopard to get to his
feet and fight.

The leopard rolled over once more and sprang up, using his flexible spine to spin his body toward Dymka, rising in the air on his hind legs to meet Mitya's cat as he
came in, all teeth and stiletto claws. They crashed together, slicing at each other, trying to tear open bellies and
rip at genitals. They hit the ground at the same time, slashing at muzzles and trying to get an advantage so they
could get to the neck and deliver a suffocating bite.

Loose skin and roped muscles prevented either leopard
from immediately and effectively ending the fight. They
broke apart and circled each other. Mitya felt the fierce joy

in his leopard as if it were his own. The leopard reveled in the challenge of the fight, and this leopard was worthy of his attention.

The dark leopard feigned an attack, coming in toward his neck and then suddenly whipping around to go at Dymka's hindquarters. He tried to grab with both front paws, looking to hook deep and drag his opponent back and then throw him down. Dymka had seen it all and he was ready, using incredible speed and power to nearly fold his body in half as he spun around to face the other leopard and drive forward, coming under the head straight at the neck. He caught the cat in his jaws, teeth biting deep.

The dark leopard fought valiantly, ripping at him with his front claws, but Dymka was big and strong. He shook his opponent hard, throwing him off his feet and then, taking a firmer grip on the throat, held him pinned to the ground. They stared at each other, eye to eye. Mitya had hoped he could spare this one to interrogate later, but he could see the leopard was not going to submit. The hatred and resolution were there, regarding Dymka, even knowing that submission might save his life.

Dymka held him there while he struggled and then grew still, until the life faded from his eyes, leaving a magnificent leopard dead. Mitya cursed as Dymka stepped back from the body, roaring his victory. He paced away, slapping dirt and grass with his paw and then raced back to the leopard and swiped at him. It took several minutes for Mitya to get his leopard to control his nature and look toward the battle.

The sound of gunfire had faded. He saw Fyodor and Timur standing beside the two cars. There were bodies on the ground. Fyodor signaled to him, pointing toward the hillside across from them. Dymka turned his head and then, leaving the others to clean up and hopefully take any live prisoners back to the house, he sprinted up the hill, looking for the lone escapee Fyodor had indicated had come this way.

It only took a few minutes before he caught the leopard's stench. He pulled his lips back in a silent snarl and wrinkled his nose in a warning display. The leopard had made it into a grove of trees on Bannaconni's extensive property. Dymka followed him unerringly, catching a glimpse of his passing, a partial track mark, bruised leaves on a bush and the unmistakable stench of his spray proclaiming the territory belonged to him.

Without warning, a bullet skimmed Dymka's shoulder, so that a bright hot flame of pain burst through him. The big leopard dodged and rolled, coming to his feet on the other side of the bush his opponent had marked. He crawled back toward the trees and deeper cover on his belly, careful not to move any branches and give his position away. That didn't stop the man from firing his weapon over and over into the brush where Dymka had disappeared.

The shifter had had the good sense to take a pack with him, something Mitya hadn't done. He'd been so eager to fight, to challenge other leopards and give his cat a workout when he was so moody and dangerous. He also hoped to be able to interrogate one of the men trying to kill him. Kill him? Or Ania?

They had found her grandfather's journal. He should have read all the passages leading up to his death, maybe that would have given him a clue as to who was behind this plot to start a war.

Dymka continued his forward momentum. The shooter had moved after he'd fired the first shot and then followed that with a volley, but Dymka knew all about that ploy. The cat had sprayed his offending odor everywhere, hoping Dymka wouldn't be able to track him. Hoping he'd be intimidated by the leopard claiming the territory as his own. Dymka raged to get at the enemy, but he was an experienced fighter and he didn't make the mistake of just rushing after the man with the gun. Mitya was certain their enemy had deliberately used the weapon in the hopes that Dymka would come after him.

Leopards were notorious for turning back on their enemies and hunting them. Dymka was no exception, but he'd also been learning lessons on fighting technique since he was a very small cub and Mitya's father had his lieutenants turn their leopards on him. Sometimes Lazar's leopard joined in the frenzy of ripping the young cub apart. He'd learned patience in a very hard world.

Dymka circled around to get behind the man. He had him spotted now. The man was up in a tree, naked, ready to shift when needed, but he was swiveling from one side to the other, trying to spot his enemy. Dymka inched forward, using the freeze-frame stalk of his kind. He couldn't rush the man as long as he was in the tree, so he stayed very still, not moving a single blade of grass.

Time passed. Gunfire had long since ceased. The sound of trucks starting up could be heard in the distance. Dymka didn't so much as twitch his tail. His hot gaze never left his prey. The man took his time, studying the terrain around him, looking with more than human senses, relying on his leopard to find any enemy close.

Dymka was downwind and never moved a muscle. He just waited with the patience taught to him by the lessons those terrible leopards had given him as he'd grown up.

Eventually the man began to climb down from the tree. Mitya studied him, trying to place him, but he could swear he'd never seen the man before. He had darker skin, as if he spent time in the sun. He looked weathered, although he was on the younger side, perhaps in his late twenties. This was not a man he had any kind of feud with. He wasn't Russian. He slipped once, scraping his backside on the bark and swearing in a language often spoken in Bolivia— Aymara. That shocked him.

Drake Donovan definitely had ties in Bolivia and

throughout all of South and Central America. He had ties practically all over the world. Was the vendetta against Drake? If it was, it didn't explain why after Ania's grandfather was killed, her father was shot and she was targeted.

Dymka didn't move as the man jumped the last few feet, landing in a crouch and going still, looking all around him. Dymka lay about ten feet from him, concealed by taller grass, blending in with his surroundings.

Other than the pack he wore around his neck, the man was naked, and he didn't seem in a hurry to dress. Clearly, he intended to shift and travel as a leopard across the Bannaconni ranch. He took a cautionary step in Dymka's direction, still grasping the gun.

Dymka kept his eyes on the weapon. The man took another step, still looking around him, the gun dropping almost to his side. The big leopard charged, exploding from the grass, crossing the short distance in half a second, swiping one paw at the gun, nearly severing the arm as he sent the weapon flying.

Immediately, the man tried to shift, his body contorting fast, jaw elongating, fur beginning to burst through skin. Dymka took him all the way over, his heavy body pinning his enemy, teeth closing on the throat.

Mitya tried to back him off. He needed a prisoner to question, but there was no stopping Dymka once he went for the kill, not when he was so enraged and frustrated in the midst of the Han Vol Dan. He killed the man and then dragged his body over the hillside, back to the group of men waiting for him.

Mitya waited until Dymka released the body, dropping it almost at his cousin's feet, and then he shifted. "Prisoners?" It was the first word out of his mouth. He *needed* a prisoner. Just one. Two would be better, but one would do. He needed to get to the bottom of this mess.

Fyodor shook his head. "Sorry, Mitya. They're all dead."

Mitya caught the jeans Timur tossed to him and stepped into them with the ease of long practice. "What the hell, Fyodor? Not one alive? That's bullshit."

Fyodor shrugged. "There were two left alive. No one shot them. One surrendered. He put his hands into the air and we all ceased fire. The other one shot his friend in the back of the head and then shot himself. There wasn't a whole hell of a lot we could do."

"We'll need their identities. Someone has to know them."

"They're definitely from out of the country," Fyodor said. "South America, I'd guess. None of them have identification on them. Their clothes are new. None of them had anything on them that would give their identities away." As he spoke, he was eyeing his cousin's shoulder, where blood leaked down his arm in a steady stream. "You might want to take care of that."

Mitya glanced down at his shoulder, a little surprised to see the blood. The pain had faded as he'd fought the second leopard, and he had regarded the slice through his skin as nothing more than a nuisance.

"You look like hell, Mitya," Timur said as he tossed a towel to his cousin. "Sevastyan is royally pissed. I don't think your woman was very cooperative either, so that made him really angry."

That sobered Mitya immediately. Sevastyan wasn't a man who got angry often, but when he did, no one was safe. "Not cooperative?" he echoed.

"She fights dirty," Timur continued. "And she's apparently skilled."

Mitya closed his eyes for a moment and sent a few curses out into the universe. Ania was going to be equally as pissed as Sevastyan. "Maybe I'll wait before I head home. See if Jake's wife can do something with this shoulder."

"Coward," Fyodor said. He signaled for the men to back the cattle cars off the road and out of sight. They'd piled the bodies onto the trailers in the hay. They would be gone over with a fine-tooth comb, subjected to fingerprinting, photographs, facial recognition, every kind of way to identify the men who had tried to kill them.

"Couple of things bother me," Timur said as he walked with Mitya toward the car waiting for them. "These men had nothing whatsoever on them to identify who they were, yet in the lead car, there was a matchbook from the port in Houston. None of them smoked, or if they did, they didn't carry cigarettes on them, but conveniently, there is a matchbook identifying the port and, specifically, the Caruso restaurant."

Mitya didn't like that either. He slid into the back seat and moved to make room for Fyodor. Timur took the front passenger seat. Their men would continue with cleanup. They'd contacted Bannaconni to let him know of the ambush and what had happened, so he wouldn't be blindsided. His security had to have heard the shots, and they didn't want law enforcement called until all evidence was gone. Every leopard body had to be properly disposed of. That meant burning them was necessary, but Mitya wanted to identify the men and where they came from. Burning them immediately might keep that from ever happening.

"We found an advertisement for the company that does bulletproof glass, the Anwar company, but in the SUV," Timur continued. "That isn't all, Mitya."

By the tone of his voice, Mitya knew he wasn't going to like what was said next. He wrapped his arm with the towel and leaned forward to get the water bottles out of the ice. He handed one to each of his cousins. "Just tell me."

"There was evidence pointing to you, as if you had something to do with killing Ania's family. I've got all of it and was careful not to touch it so we can lift prints off it, but—"

"What kind of evidence?"

"I imagine it's the gun that was used to shoot Antosha Dover. It was in a bag and has your fingerprint on it. Fyodor could see there was a print and he lifted it and tested it, using the fingerprint scanner. We're all in the FBI database. Your name popped up instantly, Mitya."

Mitya was silent, frowning. The car was already in motion, carrying him back to his house—to Ania and Sevastyan. "This doesn't make a lot of sense unless someone wants to start a war between all the families."

"A war?" Gorya echoed. He was driving, and he glanced over his shoulder at his cousin. "Why would someone want to start a war? That doesn't even make sense. No one wins."

"What other explanation is there? Why else would they be planning on planting evidence against both of the Houston families and against me? They probably have other items they can scatter around to indicate some of the other families," Mitya said.

"If that's true," Fyodor replied, "then that little notebook that was on its way to the Anwar family has to contain incriminating evidence, manufactured or not, against Drake Donovan and Jake Bannaconni. We're all being played."

There was a small silence. Mitya drank half the bottle of ice-cold water. He put his head back and closed his eyes. If that gun had been found by the police, he could have been arrested for Antosha's murder. Would Ania believe him to be innocent? They had a very delicate balance going.

Jewel had been very suspicious of him, believing he might harm Ania. The two leopards had a rocky start and still weren't fully bonded. He certainly hadn't convinced Ania that she was his world. He hadn't had that chance. Neither had Dymka. Each time they tried, something catastrophic seemed to happen to prevent that final sealing.

That lack of bonding was slowly driving Dymka insane with jealousy, rage and sexual frustration. In turn, those black moods were on Mitya. That didn't make it easy to show love and be gentle with his woman. He wanted to hit something. He thought Dymka challenging and fighting the two big leopards would take the edge off his dark moods, but if he was anything to go by, it hadn't helped.

Mitya was restless and edgy, feeling as though he had to find a way to bind Ania to him so permanently she would never think of leaving him. If he didn't, outsiders could tear them apart. He wouldn't survive that. He'd survived many things, but he'd had the taste of something good, something miraculous, and he couldn't go back to that empty void he'd lived in for so long. He had to find a way to make Ania realize she was at the very center of his world.

"Is Lazar orchestrating this?" Fyodor asked. "You know him better than anyone, Mitya. Is he behind this?"

Mitya thought about his father. He was a cold, cruel man who would love nothing better than to start wars between crime families in another country and then sit back to watch the fun. He'd take credit, because his ego was so large he needed others to know and acknowledge how superior he was. He was also an instant gratification kind of man. He'd had his way for so long in everything within the lair, and the surrounding territories, that he had become so entitled, he never waited for anything.

He would have come after Mitya the moment he found out where he was and, in fact, had put into motion his plans to punish and kill him almost immediately when Fyodor had openly begun using the name Amurov.

"No. This doesn't feel like him at all. Don't get me wrong, he's here. He's close. He got in through the Houston port, I'm certain of that. I don't know if the Caruso family helped him—my guess is they did, not realizing they were bringing in the enemy—but in any case, he's here and he wouldn't be if he didn't think he had an advantage in some way."

Fyodor sighed. Again, there was silence as the cousins contemplated Mitya's assessment. It was Gorya who raised the question they all had on their minds.

"If not Lazar, who? And is he targeting us? Or are we just part of the larger picture?"

"Damn it," Mitya said. "If one more thing happens, I'm going to lose Ania. Our relationship is so precarious right now. And she doesn't know anything about what we're doing. That's going to add more pressure." He shoved a hand through his hair and winced when his shoulder protested. "I need a fuckin' break. Just a small one."

"Bring her to dinner tomorrow night," Fyodor suggested. "She likes Ashe and Evangeline. The more we encourage her to be around them, the better the chance you have that she wants to stick around. She'll realize she isn't alone. The women will help her whenever she needs someone to talk to."

Mitya was selfish enough to want his woman to do her talking to him. Still, he couldn't say it was a bad idea. He found himself nodding. "Thanks, Fyodor. She'll like that. And it would be nice to just have a dinner without drama."

Fyodor laughed softly. "I didn't promise you there wouldn't be any drama. It's my experience that when women get together, drama follows. It's some kind of natural phenomenon."

"How is Evangeline? Is she up for company?" Mitya asked.

There was a small silence again. Gorya glanced in the rearview mirror, and Timur turned to look fully at his brother.

Fyodor sighed. "She's pretty sick. She can't keep food down as a rule. It can get pretty bad. We've got a nurse in the home now. She's staying with us and gives Evangeline regular fluids. I've actually set up a small area at the bakery in the back room where Vera can give her fluids if she needs them. I also put a cot in the back for her."

Timur made a noise in his throat that came off like an angry growl. "She shouldn't be working. You have to stop giving her every little thing she wants and think about her health, Fyodor. You'll be kicking yourself if she loses the twins."

"I want Evangeline happy. So far, the babies haven't shown signs of distress. Evangeline wants children, and the last thing she'll do is risk losing them. She'll stop when she feels she has to or if the doctor tells her she needs to. You don't understand the importance of that bakery to her, Timur."

"If it ever gets to be too much and you can see she's risking her life to keep going, what then, Fyodor?" Timur demanded. "Because that's a very real possibility."

"Then I'd burn it to the ground without her knowledge. Promise her a new one and take my time getting it done. I can delay the hell out of any building project. I do it all the time. In the meantime, though, Timur, if she needs this bakery to fulfill something in her, I'm giving it to her."

Mitya admired Fyodor. He did. He loved the man, but he didn't agree with him. Timur didn't either. Mitya would have burned the bakery down a long time ago if he thought it could get his woman killed. That was part of the problem. Ania was an intelligent woman. She read people. That was part of her gift. She read him, and she knew he was dangerous. Her leopard knew. He was ruthless when he felt it was necessary. Each time she was determined to commit to him, something happened, and she came up against his personality. That hadn't helped his cause one bit.

He wasn't looking forward to facing her after his decree that Sevastyan do whatever it took to get her in the

safe room. Sevastyan was every bit as ruthless as Mitya.
Although he appeared a little more charming, he was a
man who would do whatever it took to get the job done.
He thought like Mitya. Stop it before it had a chance to
happen. He would burn down the bakery as well.

16

ANIA glared at Mitya from the bed where Sevastyan had secured her. She was lying on her back, her hands in cuffs—and they weren't the soft play ones either. They hurt her wrists. If she was honest, they probably wouldn't hurt if she hadn't gone crazy and fought. She knew better. She couldn't break out of steel, but she'd tried.

It hadn't helped that Sevastyan had watched her with that dispassionate look on his face, the one that infuriated her, his arms folded across his chest. He hadn't said anything at all, just stared at her with that unnerving, unblinking way he had.

She'd kicked him several times before he'd gotten the cuffs on her. She'd scored two great shots to his gut, driving the ball of her foot deep, eliciting a very satisfying grunt from him. Then she'd scored another great shot to his thigh. She was positive she'd given him dead leg, but he was Sevastyan and he hadn't given her the satisfaction of letting her know if she had or hadn't.

He'd waited until she kicked again, caught her ankle in the vise from hell and snapped a cuff on her and then secured that to the bed. He hadn't even smirked, just given her that blank stare. She'd been cautious then. She only had one weapon left. She wasn't going to give him her other leg, not if she could help it.

He'd walked around the bed, cuffs dangling from his hands, and she'd eyed him warily. Where had he gotten all those handcuffs anyway? Were they already in the safe room, and if so, did they belong to Mitya? She doubted it. He would have padded cuffs, not ones that dug into skin and left bruises.

Sevastyan had moved with sudden blurring speed, catching her ankle, snapping the cuff around it with practiced ease and then securing the other end to the bedpost, almost all in one movement. He'd looked her over carefully and then turned and left her alone, sauntering out the door as if he hadn't had a care in the world.

He didn't know it, but she believed in revenge. She'd had plenty of time to give it a lot of thought, just how she would make his life miserable. But then time passed, and she got angry with Mitya. After all, this was his fault. He gave orders in that low voice, smoldering with rage but as cold as ice, and he expected everyone to obey him. Clearly, Sevastyan was unhappy with the orders, the same as she was. No, this was Mitya's fault.

She glared at him when he stepped into the room and then she noticed the bloody towel he had wrapped around his bicep and shoulder. "What happened?"

Mitya glanced down at his shoulder as if just noticing it. He shrugged. He was wearing only a pair of light blue denim jeans. They rode low on his hips and he was barefoot. He looked amazing, but then he always did.

"Just a graze. He wasn't the best shot. I hear you gave Sevastyan some trouble."

"He's a complete bastard even if he is your cousin."

"He was following orders."

His blue eyes slid over her. The way his gaze drifted over her and the tone of his voice sent a little shiver creeping down her spine.

"Uncuff me, Mitya."

His eyebrow shot up. "I don't think you're in a position to give me orders, *kotyonok*. In fact, if I were you, I might try being nice. You're in a little bit of trouble."

She scowled at him. "Why would I be in trouble?" she demanded. "I wasn't the one bossing everyone around, deciding who went where and letting their total bastard of a cousin shove me into this room and then *cuff* me to the bed." She yanked on the cuffs. "Take them off."

Again, those blue eyes moved over her and this time he didn't bother to try to hide the flames flickering there. He managed to look like sin incarnate. Her breasts instantly ached, nipples pushing hard against the shirt she wore. She still had no clothes other than Mitya's too-big shirt. Sevastyan had dragged her into the safe room, and then, when she'd fought him, he'd very coolly handcuffed her to the bed.

She was suddenly aware that her legs were spread wide and the shirt had only two buttons closed. His gaze had dropped to the junction between her legs. She wanted to squirm under his gaze and close her legs. Instead, she felt the slick heat begin to dampen her bare lips.

"I need a shower." Mitya turned away from her and headed to the bathroom built into the safe room, which was really more like a small but very luxurious apartment.

"Mitya." She hissed his name, but he paid no attention, not even turning around.

Ania bit her lower lip and studied the post her right

hand was attached to. Was it possible to slide the cuff up the post and off? Sevastyan had attached the cuff around one of the smaller places between large wooden bulbs that made up the ornate post. There was no way she could get the cuff over those spheres that climbed up the post.

She took a deep breath and listened to the water running in the shower. He was definitely in a mood. He didn't look at all happy with her, although he had a rather impressive bulge in his jeans, not that it was anything new; Mitya was often hard or semihard, which she had always thought was a plus. She wasn't so certain now. Not that she minded playing bondage. That could be fun, but not when he was in whatever mood he was in now.

She tried to ignore the fact that the longer she lay there, spread out like a starfish on top of the bed, the more the fire between her legs grew. There was nothing she could do about it either. She couldn't relieve the burn with her fingers, or even rub her thighs together. Her heart accelerated and even her stomach did a slow roll in anticipation.

It felt like forever before Mitya came strolling out of the bathroom, toweling off his wet hair, another towel wrapped loosely around his waist. He didn't look at her but rather went to the light panel, and immediately the room was plunged into darkness. He fiddled with something, and dim lights in the ceiling above the bed came on, pouring down on her, spotlighting her body.

Her breath caught in her throat. She hadn't expected that, and it made her feel very vulnerable, far more so than the cuffs. The cuffs were for playing. Something fun they could laugh about together. But the lights shining on her body made her feel exposed. It was strange that the handcuffs made her feel like his sexy plaything. She liked playing the part of his plaything. But those lights . . .

He opened drawers and pulled things out, walking back over to place a few items on a small end table. She turned her head to try to see what he'd placed there, but she couldn't. She moistened her lips and looked up at him and instantly swallowed anything she planned to say. He had that look again.

"Do you remember when we talked, and I made it very clear that when I told you to do something necessary for safety, I expected you to do it?"

She tried to outstare him, but he just stood there, never blinking, just looking down at her without moving or speaking. She had the feeling he could do that all night. She nodded.

"I want you to answer me, Ania."

"I remember," she said. "But—"

"There are no 'buts.' We had an agreement."

"Mitya," she protested, her heart accelerating. Why did she have to love the combined trepidation and exhilaration he always caused in her when he used that tone? When he had that look? Her blood felt so hot rushing through her veins she was afraid she might burn from the inside out.

"You agreed, Ania," he said softly. "You gave me your word."

She wasn't certain she'd given her *word*. A promise. She shook her head but wasn't certain what to say to get her out of the trouble she was certain she was in.

He still towered over her, slowly moving the towel through his hair. He looked gigantic. She'd known he was a big man, but lying on the bed, lights playing over her body like a marquee, she felt small and a little helpless.

"Are you angry with me?" She didn't like that her voice sounded hesitant.

He continued to look at her with that focused, intense stare. Her nipples felt diamond hard, and she was very glad that at least the shirt covered them. He could see the dampness glistening on her bare lips and there was nothing she could do about that. Once she realized the shirt was working its way up her thighs and hips with all her squirming and fighting, she tried to lie very still.

Mitya gave a slow nod. "I believe I am. You don't get to treat my men the way you did Sevastyan when they are simply following my orders. They have no choice but to follow my orders. You're making them miserable for no reason other than you felt like throwing a tantrum and you knew they couldn't retaliate."

She blinked. Shocked. "A tantrum?" she echoed.

He tossed the towel to one side and caught her foot in his hand, the one she'd been wiggling over and over. He began a slow massage, his gaze still on her face. "What would you call it when Sevastyan is putting you in a safe room, following my instructions, and you kick him repeatedly?"

Put like that, maybe it did sound like a tantrum. She was thoroughly angry that Sevastyan was forcing her to be locked in a room without even knowing if Mitya was alive or dead. But Mitya was right, Sevastyan was following his orders.

"I didn't like being forced into a safe room while you were in danger," she murmured, lowering her lashes. She detested that she had to concede the point.

"That isn't an excuse, Ania. You know it isn't." His voice was the same, very low but compelling, holding that note of censure and that little bit of anger she wasn't used to.

His hand slid up her calf and then higher to stroke her thigh. He kept looking at her, not taking his eyes from her face to look at her body. Somehow that made her all the hotter.

"I don't like you abusing my men. It isn't right just because you know they can't retaliate," he reiterated.

She thought Sevastyan had made his point with the cuffs, but she kept her mouth shut. In any case, he was right. She'd kicked Sevastyan, and the worst he'd done was force her to stop by using the cuffs. It was humiliating at the time. Now she was embarrassed by her behavior.

"We're getting married immediately and you're going to fully commit to me. There will be no divorce. Not ever. We're shifters and we're going to live by shifter rules. You don't have to always like it. In fact, just like today, there will be times when you don't like it at all. But you don't walk away. We work things out."

"And if we can't agree?" she said quietly, her heart beating too fast.

"Then we do things my way. You will learn, over time, to trust me. I love you. You're always going to be the center of my world. The business I'm in is dangerous, and I'm not about to let it overflow to you or our children. When I say you're to be tucked away someplace I know you'll be safe, you go without question or argument."

"Mitya." She shook her head.

He leaned over her, caught the shirt and yanked, popping the two buttons holding the two halves of the material together. He was casual about the sudden violence, so much so that it set her heart hammering in her chest and blood pounding through her clit. He reached out to the end table and removed a pair of scissors. He cut the shirt into strips, so he could pull it off her without removing the cuffs. Now the lights played over her bare skin, creating shadows and hollows almost lovingly.

"Yes, Ania, that's the way it's going to be. You love me. I know that you do." His hand slid between her legs, two fingers plunging deep, making her cry out. He lifted them into that light right in front of her eyes. "You want me just like this. You tied down, waiting for me to do anything to you. It makes you hot as hell, doesn't it?"

She considered lying, but one couldn't lie to one's mate and get away with it. Besides, the evidence was gleaming on his fingers right in front of her eyes. She nodded slowly. He pressed his fingers to her lips, forcing her mouth open so he could push his fingers inside. "Suck them clean the way you sucked my cock this afternoon."

Her clit pulsed at the raw sexiness of his demand. Her sheath clenched. What about him made her feel so helplessly compelled to do anything he told her? And why did she love it so much? And him? Why did she love him so much? She sucked on his fingers, tasting herself, tasting her need of him. Her hunger for him.

"I'm through with your indecision, *kotyonok*, and I'm not a man to tolerate something when I'm through. I didn't like your behavior today and you're never going to act like that again. You will apologize to my cousin."

That would be a bitter pill. He might deserve an apology, but he was *such* a jerk sometimes. She knew Mitya saw it on her face that the last thing she wanted to do was tell his cousin she was sorry for anything.

The look on Mitya's face scared her as he stood up. He caught the towel he had around his waist with one hand, pulled it off and tossed it aside. His cock was standing straight up. Thick. Feral. Long. Her gaze went to his erection and got caught there. He was amazing. Just looking at him put the wild taste of him in her mouth. She licked her lips.

What they'd done earlier had been unexpected and even a little difficult, but she'd loved it and she wanted to do it again. She loved the feel and shape of him, the heat and silk over steel of him. He was beautiful, and he could make her feel so good.

He put one knee on the bed beside her hip and bent his head to her breast. He sucked her left mound into the hot cavern of his mouth. His tongue was wicked, flicking and slapping at her nipple and then pressing the tight bud to the roof of his mouth. His teeth scraped back and forth, alternately gentle and then hard so that she wasn't certain what she was feeling. Each time his teeth bit down, lightning shot from her nipples to her clit.

He tugged and rolled her nipple and then lavished more attention on it, sucking and teasing with his tongue and teeth. Her breath came in ragged sobs by the time he lifted his head, his hands busy, sliding a small ring over the bud and then tightening it. She gasped and looked down to see him twisting a clamp.

"What are you doing?" Fire spread. Kept spreading. The heat didn't stay on her nipple but spread through her body, until she felt like she might come apart. She couldn't tell if she was feeling pleasure or pain, only that her sheath was pulsing, every nerve ending alive from her breasts to her sex.

Mitya didn't answer her. He bent his head to her right breast and began all over. She was helpless to do anything but watch the lights play in his damp hair. He used his mouth ruthlessly, expertly. His tongue was a weapon of pleasure, his teeth moving between pain and pleasure until her head was spinning and she was crying out with need. Her hips wouldn't stop moving, no matter how hard she tried to keep them still. Once more, his fingers were tugging and rolling and pinching, pulling her nipple into that tight bead that he pushed the ring over. Fire came. Hot. Wild. Out of control. Spreading through her until she wanted to beg him for release.

He sat back and regarded her with that same intense, focused look. "I've told you the rules, Ania, and what I expect of you, but you don't seem to think I'm serious. I am. I'm not letting you go. I'll make you happy every damn day of your life, but you will follow the few rules I have laid out for you."

She shook her head, trying to form a coherent thought when her body was so close to crashing over the edge. "They aren't a few rules, Mitya, it's a dictatorship. I knew you'd be like this. I was hesitant for a reason."

Almost idly he reached down and flicked the three little bells that fell from her nipple onto the side of her breast. They sounded a little muffled and he picked them up and tugged. She gasped and tried to sit up more to keep the fire from bursting through her nipple.

"I suppose you could call it a dictatorship, if that's what you'd like. You want me. You want us." He tugged again, his gaze on her face as her breath burst out of her in a rush. "You want this, don't you? Who else knows what you need, *kotyonok*?"

She couldn't look away and that light was on her face, showing him everything. Revealing exactly what her needs were. There was no way to hide from that light. She loved what he was doing and at the same time she was afraid. That thrill of the unknown added to the intensity, that and the way he didn't change expression. He simply looked at her as if she belonged to him. As if her body belonged to him and he could play to his heart's content.

She loved that look on his face. She loved him. How had that even happened? She was caught up in something she didn't fully understand, but she knew he was the man for her. "Yes," she admitted in a low tone.

He leaned down and brushed a kiss across her mouth. "Just a reminder so you don't forget, *kotyonok*, I'm madly in love with you. I know you have a difficult time even thinking about sharing your feelings for me, but you have them. I can see it in your eyes. I have no problem telling you, although sooner or later you're going to figure out that you have me wrapped around your finger."

He flicked the little string of bells again, sending fire streaking through her body. He glanced at her foot, the one she couldn't stop wiggling, and then he stood up and very gently took it in his hand. His hand moved up to her ankle and rubbed around the shackle.

"Does this hurt?"

"I'm trying to be still, so it doesn't rub, but it rubs anyway."

The key, evidently, was on the small table where he'd

laid several items out. He opened the cuff and rubbed her foot very gently around her ankle and then spent another couple of minutes examining her skin. His hands were gentle and stroked caresses. She felt every one of his touches like fingers of desire dancing up her leg to settle deep in her burning sheath.

He rubbed a soothing cream on her ankle, wrapped it in something soft and furry and then, to her consternation, snapped the cuff back on.

"Mitya." She moved, and her breasts suddenly became twin points of fire. A storm of flames flickered over her skin and settled in her nipples. The streaks radiated outward, shooting like lightning down to her already inflamed clit.

He smiled at her as he removed the cuff on her other leg. He took his time rubbing her foot and then her ankle before applying the cream, then the soft fur before replacing the cuff. He didn't speak as he came around the bed and opened the handcuff, releasing her right arm. She pulled it down immediately, or tried to. Mitya had already taken possession and massaged her from shoulder to hand. It felt like heaven.

"I have decided this one time, you will not have to apologize to my cretin cousin. He's living in the dark ages. He doesn't mind his women feeling a bit of not-so-erotic pain. That is not for you, no matter how much I love seeing you like this, on my bed, waiting for me to do anything I like. No apology, and I will speak to him about using something else to restrain you."

"Restrain me?" She wanted to be outraged, but her body was in overdrive. What she needed was release. The tension coiling tighter and tighter was killing her. She needed . . .

"A bite of pain here and there enhances, not takes away from, the experience. Unless I'm punishing you. That's different."

Her entire body seemed to clench with sexual need. He was driving her insane with the way he massaged and rubbed her arm, hand and even individual fingers. "Punish me?" She nearly squeaked it.

He applied the lotion to her wrist and then wrapped it before once more cuffing her. "Yes, *kotyonok*, punish you. I can't let you get away with what you did tonight. You need to learn that lesson."

"I'm not five."

"If you were five, you wouldn't be in the position you are in right now, Ania." He flicked the bells with his fingers and then rounded the bed to get to the other side. The fire that was only a breath away flashed through her body as the bells jingled.

She gasped, her body going liquid. Her gaze kept straying to his cock. He looked unbelievably hard. He liked what he was doing to her, that was evident. As he took her other hand and began to massage it, she licked her lips and tried to map him out in her mind. The weight of his cock was unexpectedly heavy. She liked the shape and thickness. The flared head was broad and smooth like silk. The shaft was thick, hot to the touch and felt heavy on her tongue. When she took him in her mouth without him being in control, she had to work to get him more than halfway in, but she was determined that eventually it would be easy, although she enjoyed having to work to please him.

"You aren't paying attention."

Her guilty gaze jumped to his face. "I'm paying attention," she lied. She was, just not to whatever he was saying.

"I think we're going to reposition you."

"If you take the cuffs off, I'll get into any position you want me in," she offered.

He unlocked all four cuffs on the posters. "Turn over. Lie on your belly."

She did so reluctantly, eyeing him warily. The little

bells jingled and swung wildly, sending all kinds of sensations crashing through her. The moment she lay on her hard nipples she cried out, the fire burning on the tips and sending those flames licking at her clit.

He stretched her arms out and locked them into position before shoving quite a few pillows under her belly, raising her bottom into the air. He didn't stretch her legs out, but rather forced her to her knees and locked the ankles to the sides of the bed frame. She was helpless again and feeling more vulnerable than ever.

The bed dipped, and her breath caught in her throat. His hands went to her hips. Big hands. He smoothed his palms over the round cheeks of her bottom. And then his mouth was there. Right there. Feasting. Devouring her. Driving her insane so fast she saw colors streaking across her vision. It was hot. Scorching. That tongue of his, a wicked weapon he wielded like magic, giving him power. So much. It didn't matter as long as he never stopped. She was close, so close, her body gathering itself, desperate for release.

Mitya lifted his head and wiped his jaw on her buttocks, his shadow rasping over her sensitive skin.

"What are you doing? Don't stop," Ania wailed.

"I'm sorry," he said. "Did I forget to tell you this isn't for your pleasure? This is for mine alone. You don't deserve to feel pleasure."

His hands kneaded her cheeks, his thumb sliding in between her bare lips to collect the slick liquid that spilled from her body. He rubbed it along the seam of her buttocks over and over. Each time he pressed deeper into the small star, her heart pounded. There was no way to stop the liquid heat from telling Mitya she was turned on by everything he was doing to her.

Without warning, he smacked her left cheek hard enough to make her jump. Fire spread through every nerve ending. More liquid leaked. He collected it and used it to press between her cheeks. This time, he pushed a finger deep into her sheath so that her muscles clamped down to hold him prisoner in a fiery silken vise. His thumb stroked that slick little star and then pushed inside.

Her breath caught in her throat. Her entire body cried out for his. Every nerve ending was alive and inflamed. He began to pump his finger and thumb in and out of her. Fighting for breath, she began to ride his hand, pushing to get him deeper, desperate for release. So close. She was so close.

His other hand came down hard, smacking her right cheek again and again. All the while those clever fingers pushed deep into her, curling to find that one spot that could send her off, rubbing for just a moment. He was alternating cheeks, turning them bright red while her body shuddered and begged for release. She was always right on the edge. The need drove her mad. She heard her own voice pleading as she rocked back into him.

His free hand began smoothing over the red handprints, spreading fire over and into her skin, so that it raced along every nerve ending and built into a firestorm of flames burning through her sex.

"Mitya." Ania nearly sobbed his name.

"What is it, *kotyonok*? Is there something you need? Don't you like this?" He knelt up on the bed, his body between her legs, his hand on her back, pinning her there while he pressed the broad head of his cock against her slick, hot opening.

"I need you." She found herself rocking back and forth. Each time she did, the little bells pulled against the sheet and tugged at her nipples, sending those lightning strikes straight to her inflamed clit until it pulsed and throbbed and felt as if it was bursting with need.

"I'm right here."

"Your cock," she qualified. "I need it in me."

He leaned over her, the broad head of his cock sliding

over her bare lips, teasing her, tempting her, driving her mad. "I love seeing you need me. I love hearing you beg me for my cock. I especially love when you worship it with your mouth. What I don't love, baby, is you putting yourself in harm's way just to prove you're my equal and you can do anything you damn well want."

"Mitya." Her breath came in little sobbing pants. She couldn't move her body to get relief, she could only wait and pray he gave it to her.

"Yes, baby. That's my name. I'm your man. I'll give you the fuckin' world, any damn thing you want, but you have to know you're living with a dictator and you have to be okay with that." His hand came down on her right cheek, and then he rubbed at the flames, spreading them. "When I say go to the safe room, you fuckin' go."

She closed her eyes, unable to stop rocking, unable to stop seeking all of his cock. That beautiful instrument that would assuage the burn. Her breasts ached; every vein in her body pulsed with the hot blood rushing through them.

"That requires a statement from you, Ania."

"Yes. I'll go." She heard the sob in her voice. The plea.

His cock slammed home, and the fire engulfed her. Her muscles clamped down on him like a vise, locking him to her. He stilled, the head of his cock pushing into her cervix, just holding there. She felt his heart beat right through that thick shaft. She felt the vein throbbing, pulsing with power.

"You never put my men in the position you put Sevastyan. If you hit them or kicked them and they retaliated, know that I would kill them." He bent over her, his mouth against her ear. "I am not just saying that. It is not an empty threat. If a man hit you, I would kill him. If Sevastyan had lost his temper and hit you, I would have killed him. My cousin. A man I love and respect. A man only doing what I asked him to do. Do you understand what I'm saying, Ania? You never put them, or me, in that situation."

She nodded her head as his teeth closed over her ear and he moved his hips, sending a charge of electricity zinging through her body.

"I understand," she whispered. She did, but she couldn't think. Her body was on fire, every sense overloaded. Thunder rolled through her mind. Chaos reigned in her brain. There was only one thought. Mitya's cock. His beautiful, perfect cock. She needed it desperately.

He knelt back up, caught her hair in his fist and yanked her head back. His hips began to move, a hard plunge that had her crying out. There was no stopping being vocal. She didn't care who heard. He moved in her with absolute confidence, the way he did everything. He knew exactly what he was doing, and he gave it all to her. Hammering deep. Again and again. Changing his rhythm. Switching from rough to gentle. Excruciatingly slow, but so hot she could barely breathe. Pistoning like a machine, a jackhammer, a swift brutal invasion that had her sobbing for more.

She couldn't move. He had her effectively pinned. She could only take what he gave her, all that delicious heat. The fire. The lightning. Every brutal plunge sent her breasts rubbing along the mattress so that the bells jingled and pulled, stretching her nipples and breasts, shooting lightning strike after strike straight to her clit.

It seemed to go on forever, that wild wave building and building, growing so large it threatened to take away her sanity. She couldn't find air, the dizzy feeling heightening the euphoric high that came with the friction as her muscles coiled tighter around his cock. She didn't want it to end, but she needed the release.

She felt his cock grow thicker, pushing against the tender tissue, the small desperate muscles that tried to stretch even wider to allow him to stake his claim on her insides. Then his cock was jerking hard, and the hot splash of his seed coating her sheath triggered the tsunami. It rolled over her, crashing through so that her insides tumbled and rolled, and she was flung far out of her body, someplace else where she floated in absolute ecstasy.

Her body throbbed and burned, pulsed with those lightning streaks, and lights burst behind her eyes. She heard his voice soothing her. His hands stroked over her skin. He eased her down and immediately released her ankles. She just stretched her legs out and let the after-shocks consume her.

Nothing had prepared her for that. No orgasm she'd ever had came close. She heard her heart thundering in her ears as he released her hands next. She pulled her arms back to her and tucked them close to her head, drawing her knees up until she was in the fetal position. Just that action sent another orgasm rolling through her.

"I need you on your back, *kotyonok*," Mitya insisted, his hands moving her into the position he wanted.

She felt his fingers at her breast. "The blood is going to come back fast, baby, and you're going to feel it."

Before she could respond, he slipped the clamp off. Every nerve ending burst with the stimulation as the blood immediately rushed back to her super-sensitive nipple. She opened her mouth to scream, but no sound emerged. His eyes locked with hers, Mitya bent his head and sucked her nipple into the soothing heat of his mouth.

She didn't know if it was the stimulation of the blood coming back or his mouth triggering more quakes, but her body seemed bent on doing her in with orgasms.

He lifted his head, looking wicked. "There's still an-other clamp to remove, *kotyonok*."

She shook her head. It had been painful. It didn't mat-ter that the pain had turned to pleasure. Her mind rejected the idea of that clamp coming off.

"It can't stay on, Ania," Mitya said in a reasonable voice, that voice he used when he told her she wasn't to *ever* put his men in the position she'd put his cousin. There was reason—and the tiniest edge. "You shouldn't wear clamps for more than fifteen minutes at most. And you're not used to them. You're going to be very sensitive for the next few days. It has to come off now."

His fingers touched the bells and then caught the little chain, tugged idly, watching her face, watching the sensual burn climb into her eyes. It was easy to see the rippling across her belly as another wave hit her.

"I like that you'll be sensitive. You're both in heat and you'll need us. Over and over." He flicked the bells and watched them swing out. Pull. Tug. Torture with streaks of fire. His fingers went to the clamp, moving with excruciating slowness.

She held her breath, her heart beating too fast. It was going to hurt when the clamp came off and the blood rushed back. Her gaze clung to his. She felt each turn of that screw. The sudden freedom. That pause and then a wave of pain that ripped through her body, burning through veins to her core.

She reached for Mitya, caught him by the nape of his neck and dragged his head toward her chest. He didn't make it easy, and his gaze never left hers. "Please," she whispered.

He licked her nipple and then drew her breast into his magic mouth. Within seconds, the pain had turned into something else, that amazing sensation that sent another orgasm crashing through her, equally as strong as the last one. She panted through it, feeling every stroke of his tongue, the flicks and licks, the suckling that allowed her body to come down gently.

He wiped her face and then bent his head to lick at the tears. "You're all right, baby. It was just intense. Maybe overwhelming, but I had you the entire time. I wouldn't let anything happen to you."

She knew that. Deep down, in her very soul, she knew Mitya wouldn't let anything happen to her. He was right, she'd never felt anything like that before, and it was intense and overwhelming. She wouldn't want it every day, but she knew someday, she'd be willing to go there again with him.

He kissed her eyes and brushed kisses over her wet cheeks. "I'm right here, Ania, and I'm not going anywhere." He sat up and pulled her into his arms, rocking her gently. He tugged one of her hands to him, turning it over to inspect the faint bruise coming up under her skin. "I might really have to beat the shit out of Sevastyan."

She pressed her face into his chest. "Where in the world did he get those cuffs?"

Mitya shrugged, his broad shoulders rolling expressively. "My cousin is very dark. One doesn't want to know where he gets this shit or why. At least I knew there were optional liners."

Her head went up and she glared at him. "How did you know? Have you ever been in this room with someone like that before?" She couldn't help holding her breath. She knew she certainly wasn't his first woman. She might not be the first he'd played with like that. Judging from his experience, probably not even close. But she didn't want to know someone had shared that bed with him.

"Not a chance, Ania. The only people who ever know about our safe room are family. You're my family. We're getting the license and getting married. I don't care about the ceremony as long as there is one and we do it fast."

"Small," she said immediately.

He nodded. "And quickly, as soon as the paperwork is done. We'll go to the Bexlar County Clerk's office in the morning and get the license. There's a seventy-two-hour waiting period that can be waived. We're going to take advantage of that."

The way he stated it, she knew he thought she'd argue. She didn't want to argue, she wanted to go to sleep with Mitya wrapped around her. She had a million questions to ask him about what had transpired and whether or not he'd found out anything of importance, but she couldn't bring herself to ask. She already felt Jewel pressing on her, desperate to be free with her mate.

"Sounds good," she agreed. "Do you think if we didn't have so much crazy sex, the leopards wouldn't be in such a frenzy to be together?" There was a wistful note in her voice, she couldn't help it. She loved sex with Mitya. Any kind of sex. But she was so exhausted she wasn't certain she could walk straight, let alone think straight.

His hand slipped to the nape of her neck, his fingers massaging, trying to ease her tense muscles. "I know it's hard on you, Ania. I should be more careful of you. I'd like to tell you it's just Dymka driving me, but it's not. I'm not a gentle man and I'll never be."

She turned her face up into his throat, nuzzling him. "I like you just the way you are. I'm just not getting enough sleep and my muscles are sore after Jewel goes out for the night with Dymka. They go at it every fifteen minutes."

His soft laughter was music to her.

"I envy those cats their stamina. Come on, *kotyonok*, let's get you in the bathtub for a few minutes before we let the cats run."

He lifted her into his arms and carried her to the master bath, sitting on the edge of the tub while he filled it. "You saved our lives today. Miron, Sevastyan, you and me. Scared the hell out of me, but you were in complete control at all times."

She didn't open her eyes, but she felt more pleased than she had a right to be. It was because the praise came from him. Mitya. She had thought he might not want to talk about it, let alone give her a compliment.

"Seriously, Ania, I've never seen anyone drive like that. You were more than impressive. I was proud of you."

She smiled and turned her face against his chest. "I'm really good at driving, and I love it."

"Now I have a major dilemma. Give up sex in the

back seat or have the best driver in all the States driving for me."

Her heart nearly burst. Her eyes flew open. She had to see his expression, see if he meant it. He was looking at her with such tenderness and pride, she wanted to weep. "Maybe we can have both. I'll drive some of the time, and we'll let Miron have his job back part of the time." She planned to ask Sevastyan to schedule her to drive when there was a possibility of danger to Mitya. She was going to have to get back into his good graces.

Mitya brushed a kiss across her lips and then gently lowered her into the blissfully hot water. Life had gone from scary awful to good.

17

MITYA stood over the bed looking down at Ania's face. Two days had slipped by without answers, but they'd been busy. They had the license for their marriage, and that had been the most important thing to him. The leopards had had two full nights to be with each other, which was why Ania was sound asleep even though it was well beyond morning. He'd closed the privacy screens in order to darken the room, wanting her to sleep as long as possible. Even Sevastyan had mentioned she was looking fragile.

Love welled up. The emotion came out of nowhere, overwhelming him. There was no way to describe to Sevastyan how he felt about Ania, but he'd tried. Sevastyan could be very disconnected, and that worried Mitya. He knew what it was like to have to sleep with bars on windows and heavy locks on doors because his leopard might slip out.

With a small sigh, Mitya turned resolutely away from the bed and made his way downstairs, where he knew the others waited for him. His cousins—Fyodor, Timur and Gorya—played pool, patiently waiting. Fyodor and Timur had wives, women they loved and held close to them. They understood that some things, like making certain she was asleep, mattered. Gorya showed no signs of annoyance, but then he wouldn't. He wasn't that kind of man.

Sevastyan was making his rounds, probably for the hundredth time. The man never seemed to sleep, and he prowled around, suspicious of everyone. He didn't like the fact that Fyodor had brought along his wife's cousin, Joshua, from the New Orleans territory. They needed allies, and Fyodor trusted Joshua. Sevastyan didn't trust anyone, and Mitya couldn't blame him. He didn't trust easily, and he didn't really know Joshua. What he did know could give Sevastyan pause.

Joshua was born into a shifter family in the swamps outside New Orleans. His grandfather was a criminal who believed he had the right to any woman he wanted—including daughters-in-law or granddaughters. Joshua's father tried to get his wife and child out of that environment, but they were betrayed, and his father lost his life. His mother took him to the rain forest in Borneo, where they met Drake Donovan. Joshua was given the territory in New Orleans vacated when the crime boss Rafe Cordeau had been killed.

The bottom line was that Joshua had strong ties in New Orleans. He ran the territory where Amory had worked and had been friends with a couple of the shifters who'd stayed to work for Joshua. Joshua also had strong ties to Drake Donovan. Very strong ties.

Who could they trust? Any one of the shifters Donovan had sent to them could be out to kill them. Was that how Ania had felt? All alone in her home, her father dying?

She didn't know it, but he had someone watching Anna-lise as well. He hoped she hadn't been bought off by who-ever was out to get them, but she'd tried to contact Ania several times and each time, she'd had barely a decent reason.

Mitya pressed his fingers to his eyes. His woman couldn't take much more. Having thought it, he knew it wasn't the truth. He didn't want her to have to endure any more, but she could take it. She was strong. She'd come out of this even stronger.

He went to the window and stood in front of it, hands in his pockets, something that made Sevastyan crazy. He was fully aware he presented a good target. He often stood in front of the window in a kind of defiance of his father. Lazar was getting closer. He didn't know how, but he felt him. It had been many years since he'd woken from a sound sleep to find his father standing over him, looking as if he might kill his son. Usually, he'd gotten off with a beating for not being aware of danger close. Those inci-dents had honed his survival skills. Now, he knew Lazar was not only in the country but somewhere close. He stood at the window, looking out toward the hills, wondering if someone was up there with a sniper rifle.

"Mitya, get the fuck away from the window," Se-vastyan snapped, entering the room through a side door. "Vikenti and Zinoviy found some tracks up in the hills just about three miles from the house. We backtracked them to the road. Someone is nosing around."

"Who?" Mitya asked, turning toward his cousin. Se-vastyan was a master at reading tracks. If someone from his father's lair in Russia had left those tracks, he would recognize them.

"Get away from the fuckin' window and I'll tell you." Sevastyan turned his back on Mitya and walked across the room. The pool players put down their cues and suddenly were paying close attention, watching the drama unfold between the cousins.

Mitya scowled at his head of security. "Are you going to ever get over it?"

"Probably not. Next time, I'll cut out your fuckin' heart and be done with it," Sevastyan snapped. "I decide where our people go, not you, otherwise this is a waste of my time." He stalked over to the other side of the room, picked up a bottle of bourbon, poured a small amount in a glass and tossed it back.

Mitya had never seen Sevastyan do that. Not ever. He kept his shit tight at all times. He really had angered his cousin, and for the last couple of days, Sevastyan had been curt to the point of rudeness. And he was right. Sevastyan was head of security. He was responsible for Mitya's safety and now Ania's. He would be responsible for the safety of their children when they had them. He hadn't been fair to his cousin.

He walked away from the window and sat at the table they'd set up in order to have a meeting. "You're right, Sevastyan. I was wrong." That was difficult to admit aloud, especially in front of his other cousins, their body-guards and Joshua with his, but Sevastyan deserved it. He was dedicated and thorough. He risked his life over and over in order to keep Mitya safe. "It won't happen again."

Sevastyan wasn't a man to make another grovel. He merely nodded and then dimmed the lights in the room. He had already sent instructions to his men to be vigilant, keep in constant contact and add extra patrols along the hills where a sniper could sit with a rifle and maybe get a decent shot at them.

The others gathered around the table. Joshua didn't ask questions, he just waited to see what the summons was all about.

"Aside from the fact that Lazar is definitely in the country and close by, we have a new enemy," Mitya began.

"One we have no idea of. He appears to be working in the background, close to or using Drake Donovan to plant his people in every one of our territories—more specifically, right with our security. We all use shifters to guard our families. There aren't that many, and few are trained in the way Donovan trains them. Every one of us takes his recommendations."

Mitya reached for the pitcher of ice water. "I wish I could tell you I know a lot more about this enemy, but I don't. Only that they're powerful enough that rather than be taken prisoner, they will suicide."

His cousins had been as shocked at that as he had. Shifters didn't take their own lives, not when that meant killing their leopard as well. It wasn't done. He recapped to bring Joshua up to speed. "I was attacked, although Ania was with me so she may have been the target. They came at us in cars. It was a very coordinated attack." He glanced at Sevastyan.

His cousin didn't like the spotlight. He had been groomed to take over his father's lair when Rolan died, but he hadn't wanted the cruelty of the lair any more than Mitya had wanted any part of his father's lair. Sevastyan didn't look uneasy. He never did. He looked almost bored, but Mitya knew he was alert and clocking every detail, every expression.

"They knew where we were going to be and approximately the time we'd be there," Mitya continued. "We managed to turn the tables on them and set up our own trap, but in the end, they were all dead. That includes the one who shot his friend and then killed himself."

Joshua spread his hands out as if studying his palms would give him answers. He looked around the table at the others. "You all think that we have enemies in our camps?"

"What other explanation is there, Joshua?" Fyodor asked. "Amory, and you met him on more than one occasion, clearly worked for this unknown enemy. He came from the Donovan Security Company with the highest recommendations."

Joshua sat up straight, his blue-green eyes going as hard as diamonds. "There is no way in hell Drake is dirty. No possible way. I've known him for years. If someone is recruiting his employees, he'll find them, but he is not behind this or in any way a party to it."

"You'd stake your life on that?" Mitya demanded.

"Absolutely. Drake Donovan is not dirty," Joshua said. He raked a hand through his blond hair and then shook his head. "I can understand why you'd think it. I can."

He looked around the table at the Russian cousins. Two of them had taken over territories vacated by men like Rafe Cordeau, men willing to commit any kind of crime for money and power. The Russians had been born into the life, although theirs had been an upbringing of unbelievable cruelty. Tension stretched to a screaming point. Trust was fragile.

"Drake is absolutely innocent. He would be the first to conduct a purge if he was presented with evidence that his business was being used by an unknown enemy. I know, because the moment you informed us after Antosha's death, he's been conducting interviews with each of his employees. He'd done it in the past, so there's no way he'll tip the enemy, but he's already looking."

"Joshua"—Fyodor leaned toward him—"if he is innocent, as you believe, no doubt he has several of our enemy's sleeper agents in his employ. He didn't find them before when he conducted interviews, and they were allowed to slip through the cracks to work for us. You, for certain, have one or more in your employ. That means, at any time, someone close to you, someone you trust, can take out a gun, put it to your woman's head and pull the trigger."

He paused to let that sink in. Sonia, Joshua's woman, was his life. The idea of a trusted bodyguard suddenly turning on them was abhorrent.

"I believe that all of us have at least one or more of these plants in our ranks," Mitya said. "They all have a common denominator. That would be Drake Donovan. We have to decide how much we actually trust any of the others in the coalition enough to keep them in the loop one hundred percent. We may never get any other information than we have right now."

Mitya switched his attention to Joshua. Fyodor trusted him, or he wouldn't have brought him to the meeting. They'd all agreed that Joshua was the first. He knew the others, and he would be the one, along with Fyodor, to decide if they could expand their circle. There was risk. The more they brought in, the better the chances that one of their enemies had slipped in a plant as well.

Someone was trying to start a war, and they were doing it by sowing seeds of mistrust and doubt throughout the crime families. They had to know, without a shadow of a doubt, who their friends were. They couldn't reveal too much and chance information getting back to an enemy.

Fyodor knew Elijah Lospostos was one of the first to form the coalition with Drake. The Lospostoses were known internationally as a ruthless crime family that ruled with an iron fist. They tended to take over, swallowing smaller territories to add to their own. Elijah, like the Russians, had been born into the life and had wanted out—at least that was his claim. What better way to take over then to turn everyone against one another?

"We've got to go carefully," Mitya said. "I know that I have to deal with Lazar, but at least I know who my enemy is and how he's going to come at me. Even the why of it. With this one, he's entirely unknown, and we aren't the only targets. Joshua, they had several items they planned on using to incriminate various families, both with the police and to turn the families against one another."

Joshua let his breath out. "You're saying whoever this

person is, he wants to start a war between all of us. Every one of the families."

Mitya nodded slowly. "That is my conclusion. I have no idea why, but since I have no clue who this could be, and I just took over, I have to assume I am not the real target. I somehow stumbled into the line of fire."

"Ania's family got their attention," Sevastyan said, his contribution unexpected. "That's how you came to their attention. Through her." He looked up alertly and held up his hand to indicate silence.

The door to the study opened and Ania wandered into the room, looking as if she'd just stepped out of the shower. Her hair was damp and pulled back in a long, thick braid. Her face was scrubbed clean of all makeup, not that she used much, but she looked like a young teen, not the accomplished woman he knew. Her slim jeans hugged her body, clinging to her curves. The top she wore covered her and yet showed off the allure of her breasts. She made Mitya's entire body come alive just looking at her.

He smiled at her and held out his arm. "You're awake."

"Yes. And you're having a meeting." There was the slightest hint of accusation in her voice. She looked up and smiled at the others. "Hello, everyone. I didn't know you were coming. I would have made certain you had dessert and coffee at least."

"We won't be long," Mitya assured.

"I suppose that's the cue for me to leave, especially when you seemed to be talking about my family." She kept her tone mild, but he heard the bite in her voice. He couldn't blame her. Had he overheard someone talking about his family, he would want to know what they were saying.

"Yes, *kotyonok*," he said as gently as he could, "that is the hint for you to leave. When we're done, I'll come to you and—" He broke off, seeing the hurt on her face. He detested that he put that there.

Ania shrugged. She couldn't entirely blame Mitya. Okay, she couldn't blame him at all. This was squarely on her shoulders. She wanted things to work out with him. She loved everything about him, but not his life. Not when a good portion of who and what he was couldn't be shared. She'd never really have him. The in-between, no matter how good, couldn't make up for her lack of closeness with a man she loved. One moment everything was wonderful and then the bottom seemed to drop out just as fast, as if she were on a roller coaster. She thought they'd made a breakthrough, but looking at him, she knew it wasn't so.

It hurt to know that he would discuss her family with others and not with her. She had known that going in to the relationship. She'd grown up on the fringe of crime families. They'd all been decent to her, more than decent. They'd been friendly and nice. She hadn't known for years that they were involved in anything shady and she'd been shocked when she'd found out.

She ignored Mitya's outstretched arm. She wasn't about to play that game in front of his friends. He would pull her to him, give her that smile of his that always melted her insides, kiss her, take her breath away, rob her of her heart, and then dismiss her because she was little more than an ornament on his arm, or a toy in his bed, one he was extremely good at controlling with sex.

Ania turned her back on the men sitting around the table and went out the door, her back ramrod stiff, her shoulders straight. She half expected to hear laughter following her, but instead there was silence. She kept walking.

The house had a similar floor plan to the one she'd grown up in. Mitya's house was a little more ornate. It also didn't look lived in. When she'd first moved in, she'd been excited to realize the house needed work to turn it into a home. She liked changing things around in order to warm rooms and make a home look inviting. Her mother had been an interior designer, and she'd grown up watching and helping her transform homes. Now, when she looked around, all the excitement was gone.

She'd done this to herself. She hadn't listened to reason. Her leopard's heat was pushing her, and if she was telling herself the truth, she loved sex with Mitya. It didn't matter how he touched her, she craved it. She'd gone so far as to let him dictate to her that they were getting married immediately. Mitya was a smart man, he knew sooner or later she would wake up from her dream state and realize what they had together would never be enough for her.

"Ania?"

She nearly jumped out of her skin at Sevastyan's soft voice directly behind her. She turned, shocked to see that he was so close. Jewel hadn't warned her, which meant he was that stealthy.

"You scared me. Jewel didn't warn me." She might as well admit her leopard's flaws. She didn't mind, only in the sense that she felt safe in the house, but it was difficult to tell Sevastyan the truth. "She seems to sleep a lot in between coming out to run with Dymka."

His expression became even more difficult to read as his gaze moved over her speculatively. "Mitya will talk to you about everything as soon as the others are gone. He doesn't like exposing you to anyone, especially when we know there are enemies in our midst."

She was shocked beyond comprehension. Why in the world would Sevastyan try to smooth things over between Mitya and her? She took a couple of steps back to put space between them.

"I owe you an apology. I shouldn't have taken it out on you that I was upset with Mitya relegating me to a safe room. I'm used to making my own decisions and being part of my family's lives. My grandfather and father raised me to take over their business. They trusted me with family secrets. My mother and grandmother did the same. I'm not used to being shut out just because I'm a woman."

"I can understand that you would feel that way."

She attempted a little smile, which was genuinely difficult when her world was crumbling and she knew there was nothing she could do about it. "It is what it is."

"You know better than that," Sevastyan said gently.

She hadn't known there was any gentleness in him at all, and for some reason his tone made her eyes start to burn.

"Some women are very content to be an ornament for their husbands, Sevastyan. There's nothing wrong with that if that makes both parties happy. I'm not that kind of woman. I'll take the blame for letting it get this far. I love him. I do. I feel it deep down. Everywhere. It's deep and true and protective. I even understand what drives him to shove me in a safe room or act like I don't have a brain in my head and pretend I have no idea what he's doing. But it isn't something I can live with forever. I'd never be happy."

"You need to tell him these things."

"He knows."

"Tell him, Ania," Sevastyan urged. "He might know, but he doesn't want to. He wants you safe. That's his number one priority. I know what that feels like, that deep sense of urgency. I can barely function when he doesn't do the things necessary for his protection. And now I have you. Both of you are stubborn and throw yourselves straight into the line of fire."

Ania knew what he said was true. Mitya did that, and so did she. She could see how that wouldn't be fair to a man dedicated to protecting the two of them.

"You have no need to apologize to me. I was happy to put the cuffs on you and tie you to that bed. I'd do it again without hesitation. I'd do it to Mitya too if I didn't think he'd pull out a gun and blow my head off the instant he was free."

In spite of the knots in her belly and the lump in her throat, Ania found herself wanting to laugh at the idea of cuffing Mitya to a bed.

"I have to agree, he would most definitely be in a killing mood if you did that to him. It doesn't matter that you didn't mind putting me in cuffs, it matters that I disrespected your job and you when it was a difficult time for you. I really am sorry, and I hope you can accept my apology."

He studied her face. "Little cousin, I don't like you hurting this way."

She stepped back again, not wanting to face what had to be looked at. The mess she'd created. "I'm heading upstairs to the balcony. The night air soothes me."

Sevastyan sighed. "I don't like you exposed that way. I think we've got a couple of snipers prowling around. I'd much rather you use the back patio. It's completely protected. Fenced in, no one will know you're out there."

He'd couched his preference in terms that would allow her to argue if she chose, but she knew, in the end, like Mitya, Sevastyan would get his way. She nodded and flashed a fake smile. "No problem." She switched direction.

"Give him the chance to explain things to you."

She just shrugged, lifted a hand as if to wave and started across the room to get to the patio, which was outside the kitchen.

"Ania." He waited until she turned back to him, one eyebrow raised. "He'll never let you go. You made the commitment. You need to find a way to make it work. He isn't easy, but he's worth it."

Before she could reply, Sevastyan had turned away to stride back in the direction of the den. She shook her head and wrapped her arms around her waist. She didn't like the feeling of being shut out. It hurt. Her family had been so close and loving. She couldn't settle for less than what she'd grown up with.

She detoured long enough to pull her grandfather's

journal out of the drawer where they kept it. They'd both read through it and couldn't find anything out of the ordinary, but it was the only thing they had that might tell them what her grandfather had kept.

Her grandfather, by turns, could be short and to the point, or poetic or detailing some place he'd seen that he thought they all had to go because it was so cool. Like Ania, he liked to doodle. Each entry had a drawing beside or around it. He actually was quite good at drawing cartoon characters and animals, but frankly sucked at any human or plants or trees. They often laughed together over his progressively worse drawings.

She remembered sitting with him for hours as a child, paper on the floor, brushes and paints scattered between the two of them, checking each other's artwork and giving advice. He always listened to her as if every word she spoke was gold. Out of politeness, she'd done the same for him, although his suggestions were outrageous and made her giggle.

Tears burned again. She missed her grandparents and parents. She missed that close connection she'd had with them. She felt lonely and sad.

She caught up a blanket and headed toward the kitchen. Two shifters were there. She recognized Vikenti and smiled at him. He was always nice to her. The other one was named Josue. She'd met him only once, but had seen him a couple of times outside with the others patrolling and once in the house drinking coffee. She sent him a tentative smile as well.

Both men rose when she walked in. She wiggled her fingers indicating for them to sit. "Just heading outside to sit under the stars, Vikenti," she said. "I need the fresh air."

"Did you pass it with Sevastyan?"

She nodded, trying not to be resentful. Evangeline never seemed upset by the bodyguards accompanying her everywhere. Ashe, who was definitely independent, had

them as well, and she tended to ignore the entire situation.
Why couldn't she be more like them? She already knew
that answer. She went to the back door and yanked it open,
needing to be alone.

Evangeline and Ashe knew without a doubt that they
were loved by their partners. Timur and Ashe worked as a
team. Fyodor definitely led the way, but Ania was certain
that when Evangeline asked a question, her man answered.
She knew what was going on in his life. She wasn't shut out.

Forcing her mind away from Mitya, Ania pulled two
chairs together and got comfortable with her feet up. She
wrapped a blanket around her because the wind had a
definite bite to it. The outside temperature had dropped,
and adding in the wind only made the temperature all the
colder.

Vikenti stuck his head out of the kitchen. "You want
something hot? Coffee? Hot chocolate? Anything at all?"

She dug her fingers into the journal. That was something her grandfather always did if she got in trouble. He'd
sneak her hot chocolate with whipped cream. Her parents
always pretended not to notice.

"Hot chocolate would be lovely, thank you," she agreed.

"Coming right up," he said and winked before closing
the door.

She liked him. She liked Zinoviy. There were a couple
of others she was getting to know. Kiriil and Matvei.
Miron. They seemed part of Mitya's family. Now she
didn't know what she was going to do. If she decided she
had to leave, it would break her heart, but if she stayed,
she knew she would grow resentful and angry. She
wouldn't do well in the environment Mitya wanted her to
live in.

What did she want out of their relationship? Respect.
She wanted him to respect the fact that she had certain
skills. She wasn't a shrinking violet. She also was intelligent. She would go to a safe room if there was immediate

need; otherwise, she wanted to be able to help as much as possible. She was an excellent shot. She could drive better than any of them. Mitya had at least acknowledged that, but she was no longer certain he'd meant what he'd said about her being able to drive for him.

Very slowly she opened her grandfather's journal, almost reverently. She had things her family members had left to her, but it was the little things she found she treasured. Everything in the journal was in her grandfather's handwriting. Every drawing, every cartoon and doodle was done by him. He had entries that went back years. Loving things to her grandmother. Memories of her mother. He'd written specific passages to Ania. She treasured her memories of her father sharing those entries with her.

She ran her finger down the last page, where her grandfather had several entries. Each one was sloppier than the one before it. That was one unusual thing. Her grandfather never hurried, and he was proud of his handwriting, and most of the notes were written with a flourish. The last three appeared to have been scribbled. At first she entertained the idea that someone else had written the last few logs, but she knew every swirl of her grandfather's writing, and these had all been written by him.

He'd been agitated, or his writing wouldn't be such a mess. She put her head back to look at the stars. They were desperately trying to peek out through the swirling clouds. "Think, Ania. Put the pieces together. Who called to hire a driver?"

She tapped the pages in the journal while she considered. Ordinarily, whoever had the package called and paid to have it delivered. She sat up straight. Her grandfather had come into the kitchen to taste the spaghetti sauce his wife was making. She had laughed and playfully slapped at his fingers. He'd told them—her mother, grandmother and her—how Bartolo Anwar had asked him to go pick up a package in New Orleans for him. He hadn't wanted to go because he was getting older and he didn't like the distance he would have to drive. Bartolo had promised him double his normal fee. That wasn't unusual, but the fact that the caller sending out the package hadn't been the one to ask for a driver was.

For the first time a little frisson of excitement slid down her spine. Bartolo had to have had a name and address where her grandfather would go to pick up the package. Someone had to have that information. Her grandfather couldn't have stood on a street corner and called out that he was there to drive for someone. She could ask Bartolo.

She pulled out her phone and hit the light to better see the entries in her grandfather's journal, specifically the one written to her the day before his death.

I love your smile, my angel, so sweet. Do you remember the day I found your bed frame? We lay on the mattress together laughing in that old secondhand store when they told us we couldn't be on the furniture. Your laughter warmed my heart then as it does now. I am blessed to have you for my granddaughter.

She loved that entry and she would always treasure it. A part of her wanted to frame it and hang it on the wall of her bedroom. She remembered that day they'd shopped together. Her grandfather had been the king of looking for old furniture. No one had found better pieces or better bargains. He'd promised her a "magnificent" bed, one she would want to keep her entire life. The frame he'd found was unique, one of a kind, and she'd fallen in love with it.

She ran the pad of her finger over the entry in a little caress, blinking back tears. She missed his booming laugh. She missed everything about him. The way he'd loved his wife and daughter. He'd been so close to her father, treating him as a son, and he'd been so proud of Ania. He hadn't cared that she wasn't a boy. They'd raised her to take over the business, as if she'd be fully accepted by their clients. Now she knew better. Most wouldn't have accepted her, but it was what she wanted—and needed—from Mitya. It shouldn't matter that she was a woman.

She traced the little sketches her grandfather had made around the entry with her finger. Naturally, it was the bed frame. He'd done a much more complex drawing than he usually did, and although he wasn't the best of artists, he was good. She recognized every twist and turn in the intricate artwork adorning the carved frame. Vines and leaves ran around the spindles in the headboard, continued along the thick, wooden sides and around to the footboard. The lianas and plants continued to spread across the wood and into the small drawers that couldn't be seen because the carvings hid them so well. That had been the biggest selling point to Ania at the time.

She sat up straight, tapping the drawing. Looking at the entry. Was her grandfather trying to tell her something? Could the package be so small that it could be hidden in one of the little drawers in her bed frame?

The kitchen door opened and Vikenti carefully carried a mug of hot chocolate with whipped cream swirled artfully on the top. "Here you go, sweetheart. Josue has a small plate of cookies for you."

Josue placed them in front of her. "Enjoy."

"Who made them?" she asked. "They look delicious."

"I think it was Evangeline," Vikenti said. "If Mitya tells you he did, don't believe him. He'd burn down the house if he tried to cook." Vikenti stepped back and then frowned down at her. "Are you all right?"

"She's fine," Mitya answered from the doorway. "Thanks for bringing her the hot chocolate." His voice was barely restrained.

Ania flicked him a glance. His face was an expressionless

mask, but those eyes of his were telling her there was a lot going on beneath the surface.

Vikenti shrugged. "No problem, Mitya. We're heading back out on patrol." He led the way back into the house.

Mitya stepped out of their way and closed the door after them. "It's a little chilly out here, Ania."

"I like the cool air. It helps clear my head when I feel like I'm going a little crazy."

He came to her slowly, his gaze fixed on hers. She didn't look away, needing to see him. Needing to trust herself and her decisions.

"I hurt you in there, didn't I?" Mitya asked.

That startled her. Had Sevastyan talked to him? She doubted it. Sevastyan was too busy prowling around, scaring off anyone stupid enough to try to attack Mitya. She didn't answer him. What was she going to say, when he already knew the answer?

"I'm sorry, Ania. I don't know Joshua. He isn't a part of our family. I don't know who I can trust and who is risky for you to be around. I'd hoped the meeting would be finished and he'd be gone before you got up. You needed sleep."

Her stomach knotted, and she pressed her hand there. "I suppose had I stayed asleep I wouldn't have even known they were here."

"I would have told you. I asked my cousins who they thought we could trust. What you're not aware of, Ania, is, yes, we have taken over a crime lord's territories. Since we've formed our coalition, we've reduced hard drugs in our territories by a third. Guns by a little more, but human trafficking is cut by almost fifty percent. It isn't easy, and we're constantly having to do a balancing act. We have the cops breathing down our throats. I have my father coming here to kill me. He would torture and kill you in front of me if he could get his hands on you. If the other bosses find out we're undercutting them in hopes of taking them down or at least keeping them from getting too far out of hand, they would hunt us to the ends of the earth. Now we've got a new enemy and we don't know why."

He just said it all. Quietly. His voice so low she barely heard him. She couldn't believe she was hearing him. She stared at him, blinking, trying to focus. Had he just given her everything? Handed it to her without a fight? An argument? Anything? He'd just stood quietly, asking if he'd hurt her and then given her everything. Shared. Like she was really a part of him and not something he kept in his bedroom.

Ania stared up at him, shocked beyond measure, still not certain of what he'd just told her. She tried to process it all very fast. Twice she started to ask questions and stopped herself, wanting to make certain she understood what he'd just said. He was head of a crime family. Had a territory, but the goal, with a group of others like him, was to reduce the amount of criminal activity. Did that even make sense?

"I didn't want to tell you because . . . well, that's obvious. The danger to us will be even more than it would be if I was simply doing business like every other criminal. I don't like putting your life on the line, but living with me, you're always going to be in danger. Polite society is going to shun you, or whisper behind your back. It isn't as if I'm offering you the greatest life. On top of that, Dymka is dangerous, moody and rough. That makes me the same way. So, again, I know I'm not standing here offering you a fairy tale."

Ania put down her grandfather's journal. She smoothed the pages before she closed the book, her mind racing the entire time. He was really doing it—handing her the gift of a lifetime—a partnership with him.

"That being said, I'm not man enough to let you just walk away from me." His hands lifted to his wild mane of hair and he shoved his fingers through it, making it even wilder. He looked like his leopard, feral and dangerous, a force to be reckoned with. "I'm not certain how we're going to resolve this, but we have to find a way to do it, Ania."

She stood up and took the two steps to stand in front of him. "I needed you to share the truth with me, Mitya. I'm not a woman to stand on the sidelines. I was raised in a household where we participate, we aren't kept in the dark. My family had me learning self-defense at a very early age as well as learning to handle a variety of weapons. Clearly, I have superior skills when it comes to driving. I can be of use to you—"

His palm curled around the nape of her neck. "First, *kotyonok*, before you say another word, you need to know you are of use to me, you always will be. You're my partner. My choice. Always. Second, I'm not giving up sex in the car. Not now. Not ever. When we have children, it's probably the only place I'll be able to have sex with you uninterrupted. You can drive part of the time, but not all the time. I know you're worth your weight in gold as a driver, but you can't seriously expect me to give up back-seat sex."

She couldn't help but laugh. "Miron, and I'm so glad he's going to be okay, does not have skills, honey, and you need a driver with skills."

"You did fine. Any driver who gets shot can be yanked out of your way and you can show off, but most of the time, you're in the back seat with me."

She didn't roll her eyes, but she felt like it, not that she wanted to miss the sex in the back seat either.

"You saved our lives," Mitya said. "None of us would have survived had you not taken control of the car, Ania. Sevastyan gives you the highest praise possible. All I care about is knowing you're safe. I've put you in a terrible position . . ."

"I believe a good part of this mess is because of my grandfather and what he did. I'm the one who put you in danger. And I think I know where the missing package is. I might be reading more into it than there is, but I think he left me a clue."

Mitya tipped her face up. "I have to know that we're good, Ania. Before anything else. I'm not going to change who I am. I will always insist that you are protected. There will be times I order you into the safe room. I will expect you to go. I will always expect that you do as I say in front of my men. That you have my back. I will give you every consideration, and treat you as a partner, but when it comes down to danger, I can't move until I know you're safe." He tipped her face up to his. "Can you live with that?"

His eyes searched hers, looking for an answer. Almost desperate for one. Ania smiled at him. "Absolutely I can."

"Tell me what you'd like to do besides wait for me without a stitch on and give me every fuckin' thing I want or need. One thing I can do for you, give you. Something that matters to you."

"You said I could drive. That matters." Because it did. So much.

"Kotyonok."

The way he said it, that voice. One word. She still hesitated because this really mattered to her, and if he shot her down, she would be devastated.

"Baby. Just fuckin' tell me."

"You know that huge garage you have? The one for collecting cars? It's temperature controlled and there's nothing in it."

He shrugged, watching her face. Never blinking. Never taking his eyes off her. She forced herself to continue.

"I want to use it to design and build custom cars from the ground up. I know I can do it. I can use the money from the sale of my family business to start my own. If I never sell a single car, it won't matter. I just need to do it. I know I'll be good at it."

She was trembling. Inside. Outside. She could barely force herself to look at him.

He went still and then a slow smile softened his hard features briefly before he kissed her, taking her to that place she was becoming familiar with and craved.

He lifted his head. "I think that's the best idea I've ever heard. You tell me what you need, and I'll help you any way I can."

Ania put her arms around his neck and lifted her mouth to his.

18

THE house was cold. It shouldn't be. Ania had kept the heat low, but she couldn't stop shivering as she stepped inside. Mitya circled her waist with his arm, locking her to him. His body always felt warm to the point of being hot, and immediately his warmth seeped into her.

"It's too cold in here. I thought I'd left the heat on."

"Baby, it isn't that cold. You have a problem coming back to this house. I don't blame you at all, but maybe you should wait in the car. I can look through the drawers and see if you're right."

He kept her tightly against him, even when she reacted, nearly jerking out of his arms to glare at him, because how in the world would she ever have a problem being in her family home?

"That's not true," she denied, pushing at his arm.

Mitya didn't seem to notice she was struggling to get

free. "*Kotyonok*, you do. You become extremely emotional and now it's affecting you physically."

Ania took a deep breath and let it out. Her stomach was tied up in knots and she was nauseous. She didn't want to admit that he could be right, but she was afraid he spoke the truth. She glanced at Sevastyan. He had that same speculative look in his eyes she'd caught a couple of times. He even, if it was possible, looked compassionate.

"I'm all right," she assured. She didn't know who she was talking to, the two men or herself. She pressed a hand to her stomach and was grateful for Mitya walking in sync with her. She hadn't realized she was trembling until that moment. She was a mess just being in the house.

Mitya seemed to understand her mixed feelings, the confusion ruling her mind. She loved her family home, and yet now, she could barely stand being inside it. She could barely breathe and recognized the beginnings of a panic attack.

"Ania, did you always live here with your grandparents?" Mitya asked suddenly.

She saw Sevastyan flick him a quick glance and something passed between the two men, but she had no idea what it was. She forced her mind to concentrate on the question. "Yes, they built the house with my parents and had their wing attached."

He ran his hand along the polished banister. "I suppose that grandfather of yours would sit you on the banister and hold you while you slid down it as a little girl."

She suddenly recalled the memory. Mitya was right. Her grandfather had done so, starting from when she was in diapers, and her mother would object, half laughing and half serious, a little scared that her adventurous baby girl would try it on her own. He'd continued to sit her on the banister until she was five and then he'd let her slide on her own with him running next to her. She told them the remembrance.

Sevastyan flashed her one of his rare smiles. "I'll bet you loved that."

She nodded, the memory adding to her warmth. "I did. As I got older, Mom always pretended not to see us, but we made way too much noise for her not to know."

They had reached the top of the stairs. The long landing overlooked the first story. Mitya kept his arm around her as they walked to her bedroom.

"I love hearing the stories of your childhood, *kotyonok*. If we're going to learn how to provide our children with such a thing, it will have to come from you and your experiences. Your grandparents and parents knew how to love." He brushed a kiss on top of her head. "I'm thankful you do too."

Sevastyan slid in front of them smoothly, so smoothly that Ania hadn't realized Mitya had slowed their steps in order to allow his cousin the time to get around them so that he was the one in front of the door. Her heart clenched. Sevastyan was so willing to risk his life for Mitya—and now for her. She didn't want that for him. She didn't want him to feel as if his life wasn't worth as much as theirs.

He opened the door cautiously, although his leopard had to have told him the room was empty. Still, when he stepped inside, he did so alone, sweeping the room and the impressive bank of windows Ania had always loved. She wasn't certain how she felt about them now. Anyone could be lying up in the hills with a sniper rifle and easily see into the bedroom if the lights were on. Clearly, Sevastyan thought the same thing.

"You didn't put blackout screens on the windows?" he inquired.

"The remote's in the nightstand drawer," Ania offered. "I rarely used the screens, so I almost forgot they were there."

Sevastyan held up his hand to stop them from entering the room, stalked across it, found the remote and lowered the screens before beckoning them inside. Mitya went first, his hand in hers, tucking her close to him.

"Beautiful home, Ania," Sevastyan said. "You can actually feel the joy here."

It was the first time Ania had ever heard him with expression in his voice, other than command or reprimand. She glanced at him curiously. He was a difficult man to understand. All of the Amurovs were.

"I loved living here," she admitted. "We laughed all the time. That's what made it so difficult after I lost Mom and my grandparents. Then my father was shot, and he became bedridden. He could barely speak most of the time. Until we just now started talking about it, I think I'd pushed all the good memories aside and focused on losing them. Thank you both for giving those memories back to me."

Mitya hugged her. "I think Sevastyan's right, Ania. I think this house has so many good memories filling it, that when you go into each room, you can feel the happiness. I want that for our children, to fill our house with so much laughter that when anyone comes in, they can feel it." He stood in the middle of the darkened room. "Sevastyan's right. We need to keep the two properties together."

Sevastyan snapped on the small lamp beside her bed. "It doubles the size of the area the leopards can run. It isn't only our leopards that need to run. Our men have to allow theirs out as well."

Ania hadn't thought of that, and it made her feel a little selfish, especially when the men were there to guard Mitya and her. "I don't necessarily want to sell it," she admitted. "I'm just not ready to live here, especially alone."

Mitya glanced at her sharply. "I think we've established that you're living with me."

She rolled her eyes. "You're such a goof, Mitya. I wasn't

implying I thought I'd be living alone now. Sheesh." She tried to let go of his hand, but it was impossible.

Sevastyan smirked at his cousin. "I think that's a very good word to describe him, Ania. *Goof.* I'll let the others know."

Mitya pulled her tight against his chest, forcing her to tilt her head up to look at him. "Woman, you *never* talk to me like that in front of my men." He glared down at her, clearly trying to intimidate her.

"Sevastyan is family," she pointed out. "It isn't the same."

Sevastyan turned away, but not before she caught the pleased expression on his face. It occurred to her that he wanted to be acknowledged as family. By her? By Mitya? Their relationship seemed complicated. Sometimes they acted more like brothers than cousins. It seemed an impossibility to figure them out.

Mitya's large hand cupped the back of her head and then he was kissing her, and everything fell away but the feel of his mouth taking hers, the electricity arcing between them, the fire running like a river in her veins. Once kissing him, it was impossible to ever stop. She was completely addicted to him.

When he kissed her like this, almost tenderly, his hands gentle on her, it made her heart turn over and set butterflies fluttering in her stomach. The build was slow, a smoldering heat that burst into low flames, spread and then raged out of control. She loved the hot, out-of-control wildfires they shared, but this—the slow burn—got to her heart immediately. Sometimes love for him overwhelmed her.

She slid her hands up his chest and then circled his neck with her arms, melting into him. She hated the feeling of the material separating them. Skin to skin was better. She could feel the hard length of his cock pressing against her, telling her she wasn't alone in her desire. That always was a wonder to her—that Mitya reacted so strongly to her.

When he lifted his head, his mouth roamed over her face. "I love kissing you," he admitted. "And it's a good thing. Your mouth is going to get you out of a lot of trouble."

She laughed. She couldn't help it. "Yours is going to get you *into* a lot of trouble."

His eyebrow went up. "Seriously? Is that some kind of a challenge?"

"Only you would take it that way," she said, rolling her eyes.

Mitya kept his gaze fixed on hers and he looked positively wicked. Her stomach did a slow roll and she would have backed up a couple of steps, but he kept his arms around her.

"Sevastyan. Can you give us a few minutes?"

"No problem," Sevastyan said, ignoring Ania's quick shake of her head.

Even before the door closed, Mitya had picked her up and tossed her onto the bed. He followed her down, reaching for her shoes, pulling them off and then stripping her of her jeans. Ania couldn't help the laughter bubbling up.

"You're so crazy. I think you'd have sex in the middle of a mall."

He yanked her legs apart, licked up her thigh, and then his tongue was sliding over her lips and his teeth bit down, tugging, first one side and then the other. Her laughter turned into a gasp. Already her body was slick with need. He could do that, get to her so fast. She tried not to squirm, but his mouth was too sinful, his tongue too wicked.

He went back to her thigh, kissing his way reverently up and down both inner thighs. He nipped occasionally, sending a shocking dart of fire through her body, then eased that ache with his tongue. His kisses went higher and higher and she found herself holding her breath in anticipation. Waiting. Heat coiled inside of her. Need tightened her body.

He finally reached her straining clit, but instead of giving her some relief there, he traced around it with his tongue, occasionally giving the engorged button light flicks. Once he flicked hard enough to send shock waves rolling through her body, so she was gasping, arching off the bed. His hand came down on her belly, fingers spread to take in a lot of territory, putting just enough pressure to keep her in place and at his mercy.

Mitya used the flat part of his tongue, stroking and laving until she was squirming in need. The second hard strike was all the more shocking when his tongue had been so gentle. Ania felt the flick through her entire body each time. Her breasts ached. Her nipples peaked and became almost as inflamed as her clit. The muscles in her belly tightened, rippled and clenched with need.

Without warning, he changed his rhythm, suckling on her engorged, pulsing clit. She cried out as sensations nearly sent her careening over the edge. His gaze jumped to her face and he lifted his head.

"What do you have to say about my mouth now?"

She couldn't talk, but she would have said it was sinful. Wicked. The best, most perfect mouth in all the world.

He didn't wait for her answer. He used his tongue to dance over her sex, wiggling from side to side and then pressing hard, flicking and slapping and then suckling strongly. His teeth grazed her gently and she nearly came off the bed. She would have if it wasn't for his hand pinning her down.

His mouth was everywhere. His kisses soft. His tongue had a rhythm that sent fire dancing through her body, but she couldn't keep up with where the flames were going next. The intensity built and then receded, fast and then slow, kissing and then a shocking nip of his teeth.

He was killing her. The care he was taking. This may have started out as a joke between them, but he was loving her with his mouth, and she felt it. She felt it in his touch. In his kiss. In his tongue, even his teeth.

When he sent her crashing over the edge, she found herself with tears running down her face. She'd lost her family and thought her life was over. She had planned revenge and knew she would most likely die or end up in prison, but Mitya had given her life back to her. He'd stopped his car in the rain to help her and he'd somehow fallen in love with her.

"Baby. *Kotyonok*," he whispered the endearments as he rubbed his face on her thigh. "Why the tears? Tell me what's wrong." He sat on the edge of the bed and tugged until she was in his arms.

"Everything is right." Her response was muffled by his chest. "You just make me feel very loved sometimes. I convince myself you want me because of Dymka, or because the sex between us is amazing. Then you do something like that."

He held her tightly to him. The way he did that made her feel safe, even though their world seemed very unstable. He nuzzled the top of her head. "I love you more than anything, Ania. You have to always remember that. You're my world. I would give up everything for you. Believe me, I wish I'd never taken this position. Had I even an inkling that you were somewhere in the world, I wouldn't have done it. I keep urging Sevastyan to get out, but he won't listen."

He reached down for her shoes and jeans. Ania reluctantly caught the jeans to her and stood up, making her way to the bathroom to clean herself before pulling on the stretchy material. Mitya followed her, washing his face and rinsing out his mouth.

"I hate letting go of your taste. Nothing tastes as good as you."

She sent him a small smile, although color washed her

pale skin. "You say things that are so wrong and yet sound as sexy as hell. I think you might be the devil, Mitya, tempting me straight into sin and damnation."

He threw back his head and laughed. She loved the sound. Mitya didn't laugh often, and it was even rarer for a full-blown laugh to escape. "I could be that, my beautiful Ania. If so, you're my angel I love to corrupt."

She put her shoes on and went straight to a little drawer hidden with the others in the intricate carvings on the footboard. "When I was young, these small drawers were filled with rocks. I was fascinated with every type of rock there was. I drove my mother nuts bringing rocks home and leaving them everywhere. If the vacuum was being run, sooner or later, a rock would suddenly mess up the motor. Eventually, she said it was the rocks or her. It was a tough decision, but I chose her, and my precious collection of rocks was thrown into the yard."

Deliberately she sounded pouty, and Mitya laughed again. "How terribly sad for you." He spoke into his radio, calling Sevastyan back.

His cousin must have been standing right outside the door because there was no hesitation and he was back. Ania opened each of the drawers. The third drawer held a small unfamiliar notebook, and her heart nearly seized at the sight and then began to pound hard and fast. She took it out slowly and handed it to Mitya.

"This isn't mine. It isn't anything I've ever seen before."

"Shit. It's really here," Mitya said. "I honestly didn't think we'd ever recover it." He sank down onto the edge of the bed and opened it.

Sevastyan moved in close to him, and Ania crawled around to the other side of the bed so she was behind Mitya and could kneel up, her arms around his neck, chin resting on his shoulder, so she could read the contents as well.

"Amory wrote this," Mitya said. "I recognize the handwriting. He does that half print, half cursive kind of style, and he always puts a curlycue on the letter *g*." He glanced at his cousin. "You concur?"

Sevastyan took his time, studying the writing. "Definitely Amory."

Mitya read the first entry, frowning. "He's talking about following Joshua to the States. Joshua said he'd never met him."

"Keep reading," Ania urged. "Just because he's following Joshua doesn't mean he knows him. Maybe he has another reason."

"Says Joshua will lead him to Drake."

"Anyone can find Drake," Sevastyan said. "I heard his name when we were still in Russia. Pretty much if you knew he was on to you, word was, don't bother to continue, just walk away. He has a reputation."

"So, Amory's ultimate goal was Drake Donovan. Why didn't he just find him and kill him? He resides in New Orleans. He's not difficult to find," Mitya said.

He turned the page and began to read more. Ania read over his shoulder, and Sevastyan could read as well. Amory wanted to work in all the places Joshua had worked. He had trained at the Donovan training facility and then he'd gone to work for Jake Bannaconni. Drake visited often. Amory was always respectful, but he kept a close eye on both men. While he was there, he recruited one man to their cause. He had to be careful and go slowly so as not to raise any alarms.

"What cause?" Sevastyan asked. "And he writes 'their' cause. Whose cause?"

"Why follow Joshua?" Ania asked. "Any number of men have come here from Borneo. Why single out Joshua?"

"There doesn't appear to be an explanation," Mitya said, "but from those entries, it goes to dates and times Donovan and Bannaconni met. Amory said twice he heard them discussing taking down businesses specific to the Anwar family. He states he believes the Caruso family is their ally."

"This notebook was being delivered to the Anwar family," Sevastyan pointed out. "To start a war between them? To make it look as if Donovan and Bannaconni were in league against them?"

"And don't forget, my father delivered a package to the Caruso family. Was it a copy of this notebook?" Ania asked. She frowned. "Something wasn't quite right, but I couldn't hear an outright lie when the Carusos spoke to me."

"That's a possibility. It does seem as if someone is trying to sow the seeds of distrust among all of us," Mitya said. "They're succeeding with me. I've gotten to the point that I don't trust anyone but the people in this room."

"Fyodor and Timur would never, under any circumstances, betray us," Sevastyan said.

Mitya reached up and rubbed his palm over Ania's hand before thumbing through the notebook. "Amory had times and dates that Donovan met with Joshua. He went to work for him. It says he established himself and is becoming even more trusted within the security company. He thought Joshua had killed Rafe Cordeau for his territory. He mentions he hopes he has the satisfaction of killing him."

"Who is this bastard working for?" Mitya demanded.

"It has to be someone in the Borneo area," Ania said. "Nothing else makes sense."

"But who? Here's an entry about Elijah Lospostos. How clever he is. How he can't possibly know the treachery Drake Donovan and Joshua are capable of," Mitya said. "That's really strange. Of anyone, Elijah has the worst reputation. Well, other than our fathers, but Lospostos is a name to be feared. Amory writes that Elijah is unaware of Donovan's treachery. What does that mean? What has Donovan done that is so treacherous?"

"What is that?" Ania asked. She could see where a name had been written but then was crossed out multiple times and then erased. She could make out a few letters. "It looks like a name. Right there in the corner, Amory wrote it out and then tried to erase it."

Both men studied the letters.

"Looks like Carrieri or something close to that. Does that mean anything to you, Ania?"

She shook her head. "I've never heard the name before. Could that be what they were protecting? A name? Because they clearly wanted everyone to be afraid of everyone else."

Mitya sighed. "We can ask the others. They need to be told."

"Has anyone searched Amory's room?" Ania asked. "Maybe he left something there that would tell you why he despises Drake and Joshua."

"I looked. Thoroughly," Sevastyan added. "He lived like a monk. But he's planting the seeds here that Joshua and Drake are against the Anwar family. He also seems to be suggesting several times that they've met with the Caruso family."

Mitya nodded. "He's mentioned every crime family in Texas that has met with Elijah. He's grown to suspect that Jack Bannaconni is working for Drake, taking apart the companies Drake is pointing out to him. Two of those companies belonged to the Anwar family. One was dismantled; the other, Jake hasn't begun to go after. Amory was definitely stirring up trouble between all the families. He suggests that Elijah is seeking to take over Fyodor's territory or that he already runs it. Again, he's sowing seeds of doubt."

Sevastyan nodded. "Already several of the bosses are afraid of Elijah and the fact that he controls so much territory, both here and in other countries. Suggesting that

Elijah is actually the one calling the shots for Fyodor expands his holdings and power. None of them will like that at all."

"Amory has really concentrated on bringing Joshua to the forefront," Mitya said. "He's got his two recruits in place. They both came from the rain forest to work for Rafe Cordeau and stayed on after to work for Joshua. What they're really doing is reporting to someone else. Possibly this Carrieri. He doesn't give names, but Joshua will know who they are. What is his beef with Joshua?"

Sevastyan shrugged. "More than likely it isn't Amory's beef. It's someone else's."

Ania frowned and rubbed a finger along her bottom lip. "I was led to believe that there are very few shifters left alive. Like pockets of them scattered here and there. Is that wrong?"

"Very few," Mitya said. "Shifters are a dying breed. Many have found men or women who aren't shifters and married them, leaving the lairs altogether. Then others are like my father, so shortsighted that they're destroying the lairs from the inside out. Instead of embracing marriage and finding their true mates, they want to show their loyalty to other criminals."

"Then if we keep killing their leopards, they're going to run out of them," she pointed out. "Why keep coming at us like that?"

"She's got a point," Sevastyan said. "One of the men attacking us wasn't a shifter. He was human. We treated him like a shifter, but there was no evidence that he was leopard. Whoever is behind this is going to have to rethink their plans."

"They'll employ snipers," Ania said. "Mercenaries. They won't keep sending their shifters if they're going to try to kill us."

"I don't even think that's going to be necessary,"

Sevastyan said. "They want to disrupt all of us, break up the alliance, and they aren't even certain we have one. Mostly they seem to want everyone to go to war."

"And turn against Drake," Ania said.

"And Joshua," Mitya added. That really bothered him. Joshua seemed a very easygoing man, not at all like someone who made enemies. "Once they suspect we have the notebook in our possession, they're going to disappear. There were either of two reasons for retrieving the notebook. That was their original goal, not because it mattered to them to get it to the Anwar family so much as to keep us from figuring out that someone is very angry at Drake and Joshua. Or, they didn't want this name, Carrieri or whatever, to get out. Amory must have realized it could still be read and he was desperate to retrieve the book. That would also explain why there were no digital copies made."

"Everything in this journal is inflammatory, geared to get each of the families stirred up against the others. At the very least to throw suspicion on each family so no one trusts the others. The worst is bringing Bannaconni into it. He isn't part of any crime family," Sevastyan said. "This casts enough doubt on him to make it look as if he and Drake are partners in trying to take everyone over."

"Burn it now," Ania said. "Really, Mitya, just burn it. No one else has seen it, and those last entries are pure fiction. Amory made up his mind to send it to the Anwar family, and he wants war."

"The others need to see it," Sevastyan said. "Give Fyodor a call and ask him to have Joshua and the others meet us at his house tonight. They can drop everything and fly in. We need to let them see this and talk about it. I suggest we go straight there."

Sevastyan and Mitya exchanged a look she couldn't quite interpret, but whatever it meant, Mitya nodded immediately. She didn't mind because she wanted to see

Evangeline and Ashe. She was a little worried about Evangeline.

"No one is going to follow us there, are they?"

Mitya tucked the little notebook into an inside pocket and took her hand. He brushed a kiss across her knuckles. "Even if they try, Ania, who has the best driver around?"

She flashed a grin at Sevastyan. "You heard, I get to drive."

"Only if we get into trouble," Mitya hastily qualified. "We have things to finish. I need to be inside you. If feels like forever since I last fucked you, *kotyonok.*"

She glanced at Sevastyan. He always acted like he couldn't hear what Mitya said, but leopards had acute hearing. His cousin was walking ahead of them, making certain there was no danger in front of them. She tried not to react to Mitya's raw declaration. He was all about sex, and he didn't try to hide it. She liked it. She did. Okay, she loved it. But . . .

"Has it occurred to you that I could be like Evangeline and have problems, being sick? Or like Jake Bannaconni's wife and have trouble carrying?"

They were halfway down the stairs and Mitya stopped abruptly. "What does that mean, baby? What are you trying to say?"

Sevastyan was at the bottom of the staircase and he stopped as well, glancing at her and then looking away as if that would give them privacy.

"We wouldn't be able to have sex, Mitya. And then what would you do? You can't go more than a couple of hours before you want to start all over again."

Immediately he framed her face, his thumbs sliding along her neck. "Is that what worries you, Ania? I want sex with you as often and in as many ways as I can have it, but not at a cost to you. You're tired, or sick or having trouble carrying our baby, then we don't have sex. If we can't find other ways to take that edge off, then I'll look forward to that moment when we can. There won't be sex without you, Ania. No other woman. Believe it or not, I went a lot of years without when Dymka made it clear he was getting to the point he would wait for my release, so he could leap out and kill my partner."

She made a face. "That leopard of yours needs a good clout to his ear."

Sevastyan made a noise that sounded suspiciously like a snicker, but she couldn't be certain. He never changed expressions.

"You understand what I'm saying to you, Ania? Never worry about that. And never worry if you aren't feeling up to what I want to do. Just say so."

"I can't imagine that happening," Ania admitted. She was *so* up for anything, especially in the car, where he seemed to be just a little out of control. And she loved it.

THE small notebook was passed around the table, and each man skimmed it fast. Drake and Joshua were the last two to read the contents. Mitya watched them closely. He'd had his woman in the car on the way to his cousin's home. It wasn't a great distance, but he'd managed to make the experience spectacular for both of them.

The drive to Fyodor's wasn't a huge distance for Elijah or Jake either. To Mitya's shock and maybe horror, the two men had brought Eli Perez, the former DEA agent, with them. He worked for Jake Bannaconni now, but Mitya was extremely uneasy in his presence. The others seemed to trust him in the way they did Jake, as if he were a part of their partnership.

Joshua and Drake had to take a small plane from New Orleans to get there, so it gave the others an opportunity to read the notebook before they arrived and just skim it again at the table. Timur and Gorya read it thoroughly, and

Sevastyan went over it one more time before the meeting was called.

"This looks very personal," Drake said. "Aimed at me. I've got an enemy, and he's after all of you and our coalition in order to get at me."

"What about the name that's been crossed out. Carrieri? Do you know someone by that name? Someone you or Joshua crossed that could be out for revenge?" Mitya asked.

Joshua and Drake looked at each other, frowning, obviously trying to remember. Joshua shook his head. Drake answered. "I had so many clients over the years, and so many kidnappers. I'll look over my records, but the name doesn't ring a bell."

"Amory didn't realize we've formed an alliance," Elijah said. "He's guessing that Drake and Jake might be co-conspirators, but he doesn't know for certain. Mostly he speculates in order to cast suspicion."

"We discovered items on the men we dispatched that would make the world think that Mitya had shot Antosha. There were other items that would cast suspicion on others of us here at this table. Any friend of Drake's or Joshua's is being targeted," Sevastyan said.

"Why?" Jake asked the two men.

Drake shrugged. "I could have any number of enemies, but Joshua, not really. This had to have begun some time ago, so it isn't any of Nikita Bogomolov's crew. Sasha, Nikita's son, is included in our association, although loosely at this point. He still has to prove himself in order to come fully into the circle. So, for us to have a common enemy, that would narrow it down significantly."

"Is it possible Joshua was just a convenient entry to follow into the States?" Fyodor asked.

"Anything is possible," Drake conceded.

Mitya shook his head. "It feels too personal. Joshua? Any ideas? Who do you have for an enemy?"

"As far as I know, no one," Joshua said. "But I do originally come from Louisiana and the lair that Drake runs. I can't imagine that anyone there considers me an enemy, since I left when I was a toddler, but I suppose it could happen that someone harbors resentment."

Mitya shook his head. "This originates in Borneo." He said it with absolute conviction because he believed it. "Something happened there."

Joshua raked both hands through his hair. His gaze shifted to Drake. Mitya fought to keep his features an expressionless mask. There was something that neither man wanted to say or admit. He waited to see if Joshua was really with them or if they were all being played. His gaze shifted to Sevastyan. His cousin had caught that look as well, and he was waiting. Mitya had the feeling Sevastyan could turn violent in a heartbeat—and would.

"The only thing I can think of, I'm not very proud of," Joshua said. "No matter how I explain it, I'm not going to come out looking good on any level."

"It isn't necessary to explain anything," Drake said.

"I disagree," Joshua said. "If everyone is in danger here, and it's because of something I did, they need to know about it."

Drake shrugged. "It's up to you, Joshua."

Joshua reached for his coffee cup and turned it around idly as he searched for the right place to start. "We had come to know most of those who made it a practice to kidnap tourists or members of very wealthy families. We knew which ones would give back the victims the moment the ransom was paid, and which ones wouldn't. For most it was simply a business, like any other. We negotiated, paid the ransoms and retrieved the victims. A straight business transaction. If it was a group who preferred killing the victim, we raided and took them back."

Mitya knew Drake still ran a crew in Borneo for that purpose, and another in South America. Just because he wasn't there didn't mean the practice of kidnapping had ended.

"There was a rumor that five strangers had entered the rain forest. They hit a village and took two young girls. They set fires in the village, an unusual thing when they were going to ask for money to get the girls back. I tracked them, but I was a couple of days behind. As I followed them, I began to have suspicions that they were leopard."

He took a sip of coffee and when he looked around the table, there was rage in his eyes. "What they did to those girls were some of the worst things I've ever seen. I'm not going into details, but by the time I found them, the girls were in a catatonic state. I lost it. I'm not going to lie. I completely and utterly lost it. Those five leopards are dead, burned and buried so deep no one will find their ashes. I took the girls back to their village, but honestly, I wonder if both might have been better off buried with those men."

There was silence. Mitya frowned, going over Joshua's short rendition of the encounter, trying to find something that didn't add up. "Only those in that village knew you went after the girls, is that correct?"

Drake shook his head. "There were men in my organization who knew I sent him. The villagers certainly knew. As for those leopards' families, we didn't know where they came from. We had no idea. Questions weren't asked. They were killed."

Mitya was watching Joshua when Drake was explaining. Those blue eyes held so much rage that Dymka reacted. Those leopards hadn't just been killed. There was more to it than that. Five men to his one. Joshua was no pushover. He appeared cool and easygoing. He had a killer inside of him that struck when called on. Mitya hoped the others realized that.

Jake drummed his fingers on the table. "That doesn't give us a lot to go on. Drake, can you make inquiries as to what happened to those girls? What happened to the families of those girls? Where is everyone now?"

"This is fuckin' thin," Mitya said. "You have no idea where those five men came from, whether they were related, or anything about them."

Joshua shrugged. "They had accents that would have put them from South America, but they spoke perfect English to one another. All five of them used those little girls, but two of them were the ones that did the torturing. The others didn't so much as look up when the girls were screaming, so it was a common practice. Clearly, they'd seen it done before. None minded that the girls were bloody and broken, they used them anyway. That suggested they'd been together for some time, doing similar practices."

"You didn't get the impression they were related?"

"They could have been, but I didn't stop to look to see if they had similar features. I took them apart. To me they weren't human, shifter, or anything but vile scum. I might have been a little insane," he admitted, and rubbed at his temples as if he had a headache.

"I would have done the same," Fyodor admitted. "They would have died slow, and they would have died hard."

Timur nodded and looked at Gorya. Gorya turned away from them. Sevastyan didn't make a statement, but he looked at Mitya. Mitya knew Sevastyan would have done far worse to those men than Joshua could ever conceive of doing.

"We aren't saints here, Joshua," Mitya said. "Any of us. The bottom line is this: We have an enemy, all of us. He wants to sow suspicion between us, which, I'll admit, I was buying into. They have infiltrated Joshua's family. Jake's as well. We have to be very careful now, because when we bring anyone new in, they could be a potential Amory."

"Ania pointed out that he doesn't have an endless supply of shifters," Sevastyan added.

Mitya nodded. "She's right. They don't, any more than we do. We'll get it out there that we found the notebook. That way, they won't have a reason for continuing their attack on Ania or her house. I think they'll back off for a while and then come at us from a different direction."

"That makes sense," Drake agreed. "And it gives us some time to investigate. This thing with Joshua is the only tie that is between us that I can see. I did help with the investigation into the Bogomolov family, but I had little to do with it. I can't see that being a connection, especially when these sleepers have infiltrated a couple of years ago."

He looked at Jake. "I'm sorry we brought you into this. I thought I could keep you away from the worst of it."

Jake shrugged. "We knew there was that chance. In any case, we have the notebook, not anyone else. No one's seen it, so at least for now, my name is still not connected, more than loosely as your friend, to any crime family. Eli is in the clear as well. He's nowhere in there, because Amory left my house before he came on board. He had a recruit, he clearly states that, but the recruit hasn't figured out what's going on."

"Most likely because you're a paranoid son of a bitch and you don't let anyone near your office. Amory was patient and worked his way up to security in the house," Drake said. "Be careful not to let on that anything is different, Jake."

"That may not be true," Mitya said. "There's a possibility that a copy was made of this notebook and sent to the Caruso family. Antosha drove from New Orleans to Houston and made a delivery. Most likely he glanced at the notebook and didn't read it. Whether the Caruso family read it or it was stolen before they could, who knows, but we have to assume they read it."

"Great. We'll have to figure out a way to do damage control," Drake said. "Watch your six, Jake."

19

"GET the women in the safe room!" Fyodor shouted and hit the button under the table so that the wall opened up to reveal an array of weapons as well as gas masks.

Mitya got to his feet, wishing he could see his woman. "Need to know she's all right," he said. "Sevastyan?"

Sevastyan stuck his head out of the room. The hallway was pure chaos. Through the doors opening to the great room, they could see a hole in the outside wall. Surprisingly it wasn't as big as it had sounded, about four feet high and three feet wide. Smoke poured into the room along with dust and debris. Wood splintered, and great jagged pieces pointed toward the inside of the room like giant spears.

"Can that safe room stand up to explosives?" Mitya asked his cousin.

"Damn straight," Fyodor said. "Made certain of it." He was tossing weapons and masks to his cousins and the others in the room. "This has to be dear Uncle Lazar. He likes to make a big entrance."

"Classic attack," Mitya agreed. He'd seen his father do it a million times. He liked a big explosion to shock everyone, to kill as many as possible and then calmly follow up by entering the home and shooting everyone in sight.

The shock of the explosion would paralyze those Lazar attacked, making his appearance dramatic as well as terrifying. That wasn't going to be the case. He thought he'd caught the cousins together and that they would be with their women. He had no way of knowing they weren't alone, and each ally had brought their bodyguards with them.

There had been no one in the great room, so there wasn't a single death. Timur was already directing his troops. He had the shifters all stay back, circling around. He wanted them to quietly take out any of Lazar's soldiers they came across. Then they looked to Mitya. He knew his father and his methods better than anyone else.

"He will go after any woman or child. They'll make certain you hear their screams. If possible, they'll draw you out by dragging her in front of you and hurting her. Even raping her," Mitya explained. "There will be another explosion soon. They'll lob in gas, and he'll come behind that one with his men. Do we have eyes on them? We need to stay away from the walls. If there are masks anywhere else in the house, tell our men the locations so they can get them. They'll need them soon."

He spoke to them as he slid weapons and ammunition into the loops on his coat, adding to his arsenal, but his gaze was on Sevastyan. He'd sent Vikenti and Zinoviy to check on Ania. Sevastyan gave a small shake of his head.

Mitya's heart dropped. "Where the fuck is she?" he roared.

"She wasn't with the other women when the explosion went off. She'd gone to the kitchen to get whatever had been prepared for refreshments. Vikenti and Zinoviy headed that way after her."

The words were barely out of his mouth when another explosion ripped through the house, the shock wave even stronger this time. Mitya grabbed the heavy table for stability as the walls undulated and shook all around him. The blast was so loud, for a moment he could hear only ringing in his ears.

He felt desperate. He knew what Lazar was capable of. Worse, he knew Lazar would make Ania's death slow and ugly, most likely uglier than anything Joshua's killer shifters had visited on those little girls. Mitya had seen so many vile, depraved acts, so many types of torture in his lifetime, that the idea of his woman falling into his father's sick hands made him crazy. For a moment he couldn't think, and it had nothing whatsoever to do with the blast and ensuing chaos.

Sevastyan bumped him hard, and automatically, Mitya turned to follow him as his cousin led him out of the meeting room into the hall. The moment they stepped out into the hall, Kiriil and Josue fell in behind Mitya. Timur led Fyodor out, with Gorya right behind him.

"I put a tracker on her, Mitya," Sevastyan said. "Take a breath, we'll find her."

"If that fucker touches her—" Mitya snapped.

"He won't get to her," Sevastyan assured over his shoulder. "She's too smart for him, and she takes this shit seriously."

The smoke bombs began hitting the floor, lobbed through the holes in the walls and broken windows. The men inside spread out, their gas masks protecting them as they slid into the shadows of Fyodor's house. The room turned gray with fog and gas. The men were still. Waiting. Knowing Lazar's men would come in shooting, expecting to find everyone inside disoriented, dead or dying. They thought they would have easy targets.

Mitya didn't give a damn about them. He didn't want to be stationary; he wanted to be running to protect Ania. He hissed at Sevastyan, who seemed to be staring down at his watch. He pointed up. Mitya slid the tiny but very powerful bud into his ear. It could pick up his whisper and deliver it to Sevastyan and any others who thought to use their radios.

"Where the fuck is she?" he demanded.

"I think on the roof. She's definitely above us. Vikenti said the wall cabinet was opened and she must have armed herself and taken a mask. At least, there were several weapons missing, ammunition and a mask gone. He closed it back up just in case."

Mitya took a breath, breathing in clean air while the room filled with tear gas. Fyodor was going to have a time cleaning the room. The blinds and furniture he could replace, but scrubbing all that wood and redoing the floors wasn't going to be so easy. He tried to make himself think about that rather than the fact that his woman was out there somewhere and if she was spotted, Lazar would send every leopard he had to retrieve her.

Ania. Baby. Stay hidden. For me. I'll let him skin my leopard alive if that's what it takes to get you back. No self-respecting shifter would ever allow their leopard to take the brunt of torture or death. He meant it, though. He would give up his life in a heartbeat. He would take any torture Lazar wanted to hand out to him, and he would sacrifice his leopard for her. Dymka had already indicated willingness. The two of them would allow Lazar to do anything to them to keep Ania and Jewel safe. Mitya could barely breathe knowing Ania was out there somewhere unprotected. Dymka could barely restrain himself knowing Jewel was just as unprotected.

"She's extremely intelligent, Mitya," Sevastyan reiterated. "She didn't defy you, she was caught off guard and she kept it together. She recognized the panel and she opened it. How, I don't know, but she did it. She's armed, and she's got a mask. Her grandparents and parents trained her for any situation, and she knows we'll come for her. She knows she just has to hold out long enough for us to get to her."

Mitya couldn't do anything about it yet. Lazar's front team, his sacrificial pawns, were already moving toward them, coming in through the door that was down and the two holes in the side of the house. As a rule, Lazar sent that first team in to mop up. There were always five, and there were five now—crashing into the great room, guns blazing. These men weren't aware of the fact that Lazar sent them in first because he considered them the most expendable.

Mitya shot the one bursting into the room and rushing toward the hallway. The man went down, gas mask and all, but twisted and rolled on the floor for a moment before rising. "They're wearing vests," he informed the others.

Calm had settled over him. Combat calm. He wasn't the kind of man to yell and scream or get so agitated during a firefight that he lost it. Mitya was very centered, and the more chaos reigned around him, the cooler he was under fire. That stood him in good stead when directing his men. They were just as steady, following his lead. He took aim a second time, this time going for the head instead of the heart. As his enemy rose, trying to spray bullets into the shadows, Mitya squeezed the trigger once and watched him go down, this time to stay.

Sevastyan took aim at the second man nearest them. This man used his leopard to propel him to the center of the great room, his automatic spitting fire from one end to the other. None of those invading took aim at individual targets; that wasn't their purpose. First, they mowed down everyone, wounded or not, and then followed up with a single bullet to the head to make certain.

Sevastyan's target hadn't hit a single person. There

were no dead or dying in the great room. The room appeared empty. Sevastyan took his time, aiming at his opponent's head and squeezing the trigger. The bullet went right through the gas mask and into his target's eye. He went down, crumpling onto the floor, the automatic quiet. Timur shot a third intruder, while Drake and Joshua killed the other two.

Immediately, Mitya was on the move, rushing down the hall toward the kitchen, Sevastyan in front of him, Kiriil and Josue behind him. The kitchen was empty, but Dymka rose fast, catching her scent. She was at the end of her heat, but due to the continual interruptions, the cycle was lingering, drawn out a few more days. Jewel's potent pheromones remained, calling to her mate. That meant every male leopard would be able to scent her as well.

ANIA didn't like that Evangeline looked so pale. She was showing, the twin babies finally making their presence known. It wasn't that Evangeline was big; she wasn't. The illness had rendered her nearly unable to keep down food. Sometimes even water made her terribly sick. She'd lost weight rather than gained. Still, she never complained, not when Ania was around her. She looked tired, and Ania could see the worry on Ashe's face.

"I made refreshments for us," Evangeline insisted. "I really don't want to miss visiting with Ania." She objected to Ashe's insistence that she lie down.

"If they're in the kitchen, I'll get them for us and bring the tray back to your bedroom. Ashe can help you get ready for bed," Ania volunteered. "Where do I find the yummy stuff?" Because if Evangeline made it, whatever was waiting had to be excellent.

"I left the tray for us right on the counter. It's covered, although I have to admit, if the boys see anything out, they're like vultures." For the first time since Ania had gotten there, Evangeline smiled. "There's a pitcher of strawberry lemonade in the refrigerator. The glasses are set out by the tray."

Ania was so going to learn to be a great hostess the way Evangeline was. Her mother had been. Her grandmother had been. She hadn't taken the time to really learn those skills from either of them, and she regretted that. Everything her grandfather and father had taught her had seemed much more exciting. Now that she had lost her mother and grandmother, the things they had valued and were so good at seemed much more important.

"Evangeline's strawberry lemonade is the best," Ashe declared, already taking Evangeline's arm and leading her toward the bedroom. She mouthed "thank you" over her shoulder.

"Since I've had her pastries, and know they are, I'll look forward to drinking the lemonade," Ania said as she hurried out of the room.

For a moment she wished she could talk to Mitya. Fyodor loved his wife, and she couldn't imagine that Evangeline didn't have the best of care, but she looked pale and drawn, and it was worrisome. There was something very special about Evangeline. Anyone could see it.

Ania got turned around in the unfamiliar big house and had to backtrack to take the right hallway leading to the kitchen. The kitchen was quite large. Her grandmother, when helping design the interior of the house along with her mother, had designed a kick-ass kitchen. It was spacious and had a butcher block island that could be used on either side if more than one person was working, but this kitchen was something out of a magazine.

She couldn't help herself, Ania found herself examining the overhead light fixtures that shone down brightly on the counter work surfaces. The flooring was tile, a soft wheat color, intricately cut, adding to the beauty of the room. The uneven tiles added to the appearance of the room being right out of Tuscany, with a wide expanse of windows so that the cook could feel as if he or she were outside in the fresh air. The tiles also prevented anyone slipping should liquid be spilled on the floor.

The herb and vegetable gardens were right outside the windows. Ania couldn't help but stare at them. Dim lights shone outside the kitchen, illuminating the gardens. She hadn't turned on the lights in the kitchen because with her increased night vision she didn't need it. She could see one of Fyodor's guards pacing back and forth just beyond the gardens. It seemed that all of them had to live with body-guards.

She turned her attention away from the outside and back to the textured walls. They looked like wood, a light-colored wood, almost blond, with knotty rings scattered here and there. It was an unusual choice for a kitchen, but combined with the tiled floor, they gave the room an exotic, Italian feel. She had to run her hands over the walls in order to feel whether it was real wood or just looked authentic. Immediately she felt the difference from one panel to the next. The panel in the middle was slightly raised. Eyeing it, she couldn't visually see the variance, but it was there.

It took only a moment to find the hidden spring. The wall panel contained enough weapons for an army. She wasn't surprised. The walls in her house hid a few revelations as well. She had to smile. Didn't everyone's home have similar panels in the wall?

She turned back to the counters, looking for the tray of pastries. It was right beside the refrigerator. Of course, it would be close to where she could easily pull out the pitcher of strawberry lemonade. Evangeline would have everything ready so there would be the minimum amount of work when she had company. That was her secret. Great preparation. Ania remembered her mother and grandmother were the same way. She opened the fridge and found the pitcher immediately, pulled it out and placed it on the tray with the pastries and glasses.

She glanced up to take one last look at the gardens just outside the window and her heart nearly stopped. The guard was no longer pacing back and forth. He lay in the dirt, his automatic some distance from his hand. She didn't wait but whirled around and hit the spring for the panel in the wall. She grabbed a gas mask, three guns, a rifle and ammunition for each weapon. She wished there was a button to raise the alarm. She was going to have to mention to Fyodor and Mitya that alarms were good things to warn people when there was trouble. She spun around to head back to the bedroom to protect Evangeline and Ashe.

The explosion knocked her off her feet. She hit her head on the wall as she went down, opening a cut just above her temple. It hurt like hell, but there wasn't any real damage done. While she was on the floor, she took the time to load each gun and then she slid one weapon down into her boot, one into her waistband and the smallest into a pocket of her sweater. The ammunition went into the other pocket. She loaded the rifle and got cautiously to her feet.

The hallway leading back toward the interior of the house had debris in it. She wasn't absolutely certain she could find her way back to the bedroom anyway with the walls bowing in. She was fairly certain Fyodor would have a safe room for Evangeline, and Mitya would want her to go there, but peering down the hallway, she pulled back. Too much of a mess. It looked as if part of the hallway had caved in.

The other entrance led to the great room, and that seemed to be where the explosion had come from. Ania wasn't taking a chance heading in that direction. She glanced at the door leading outside to the gardens. If she could get outside, she could make it to the roof. It was a huge house with a very big roof. The covering above was fraught with gables and steep pitches as well as ridge-poles. There had to be places she could hide and yet still see what was happening below.

Once she made the decision, she moved fast. They were under attack, and it didn't feel the same as the other attacks. This was a well-thought-out battle plan. Mitya had said his father wanted to kill him as well as his cousins. Lazar seemed most likely to have orchestrated the explosion. She peered out the window cautiously, but it didn't seem as if anyone was close. She opened the door very slowly, giving herself just enough room to slip out.

Need you, Jewel, she whispered to the leopard as she crouched just outside the door.

She felt the leopard move closer to the surface. Heat banded. Her hair snapped and cracked. She used the information the leopard was helping her gather. A man was very close to her, facing toward the great room. He was definitely leopard. Jewel wrinkled her nose in contempt.

Ania moved farther back into the shadows as she crept through the garden toward the side of the house. The wraparound porch had a low-hanging roof. The moment she was certain she wouldn't draw attention to herself through movement, she slung the rifle around her neck and jumped for the porch. She caught the edge, slipped and dug her fingers in deep. Her hands had curved and long, wicked claws had sprung free, scrambling for purchase on the unfamiliar surface.

She swung there for a moment, heart in her throat, waiting for a hundred bullets to strike her. Swallowing fear, she pulled herself up, using a leopard's strength to swing her legs onto the rooftop. Once there, she lay flat and listened to her wild heartbeat. Mitya would come for her. She had no doubt that Sevastyan would come too. She just had to hold on. Hide. That was the sane thing to do.

Ania crawled across the roof to the next story jutting up into the sky. She needed to keep going upward. She eased her body slowly up the roof toward the ridgepole. Movement drew the eye, and the intruders were leopard. She didn't want anyone to spot her.

MITYA and Sevastyan exchanged a long look of total comprehension. It was impossible not to inhale and smell the female leopard in heat. Every single one of Lazar's leopards would catch that scent as well. The two men threw caution to the wind and openly hurried toward the kitchen door leading outside. Sevastyan had taken two steps when a bullet whined through the glass, shattering it and lodging across the room in a wooden panel of the wall.

Kiriil flung himself at Mitya, tackling him, bringing him down, while Sevastyan and Josue hit the floor too. The four did a hasty crab-walk to the safety of the island where they sat for a minute, breathing hard, getting the adrenaline under control. All four had removed their shoes and all unnecessary clothing in preparation for shifting. What was left could be removed fast. Shirts tore off and jeans stripped down easily. Their feet didn't like the debris the bombs had left behind, and none of them wanted to be in the great room where the tear gas had gone off. That would soak into their bare feet and burn like hell.

"You're going to get everyone killed, Mitya," Lazar's voice intoned. "You know I like a good bloodbath. Just walk out here and give yourself up. You know you have no chance. Be a man for once. Don't go running, curling your tail between your legs to hide the fact that you don't have any balls."

"I've heard that same speech dozens of times but with different names inserted," Mitya whispered to Sevastyan, Kiriil and Josue. "He can't even be bothered to get new material."

"Is that slut we all smell yours, Mitya? Or is she Fyodor's? She ran to us, wanting real men—not the poor substitutes she has here. She's begging for real men to give it to her. We'll bring her into the house, and you can watch as we all use her the way she's meant to be used. She's in heat, a real whore, willing and eager to please in the hopes that we'll relieve some of that burn for her."

Mitya had heard the crap his father often spouted, especially about women. How they were only good for fucking. How he would command them to do anything he wanted, and he often gave them to his men and watched them get fucked to death. That was his favorite, he'd declared, a woman dying of the very thing she begged for.

It was one thing to have his father shout ugly things about him, but he realized he wasn't quite as calm as he thought he could be when Lazar talked about his woman. "He doesn't have her," he whispered, needing to say it aloud to Sevastyan. Needing to hear Sevastyan confirm it.

"Not unless he's on the roof with her," Sevastyan said. "She's stationary at the moment."

Mitya couldn't help the sigh of relief. Ania was resourceful; he had to have faith in her. "She won't do anything crazy. Her parents saw to her survival training." Again, he found himself needing to hear the reassurance aloud.

Sevastyan sent him a small smile. "That woman is intelligent, and she's good with a gun. She's armed to the teeth. I wouldn't want to be on the receiving end of her wrath."

Mitya knew everything his cousin said was the truth, but he needed to find her. He needed to be with her, shielding her from the vile depravity of his father. He didn't even like her hearing the things Lazar said about her.

"She's got a temper," he said. "Don't want Lazar to set that off."

Again, Sevastyan flashed a faint grin. "That she does.

She kicked the holy hell out of me." He said it as if he was proud of her.

A thump was the only warning, and then a leopard dropped straight down on Josue, slashing his jugular with terrible claws, as his teeth simultaneously drove at Sevastyan's neck. Sevastyan threw himself sideways. Mitya shifted, ripping the jeans from his body, barely getting them off before Dymka was there, encased in the tee, which he shredded with one swipe of his claws. He sank his hooked nails into the leopard's back and ripped him away from Sevastyan, nearly throwing him across the room.

Dymka recognized the leopard instantly. Mitya had grown up with him, a man by the name of Artem. He had always done Lazar's bidding, as well as any of the lieutenants', no matter what was asked of him. He did it willingly and eagerly, no matter how demeaning or monstrous. He and Mitya had fought on numerous occasions. Artem despised Mitya because he was Lazar's son and therefore in a position of power, and because he'd wiped up the floor with Artem when they'd fought with their fists.

Clearly, Artem thought he had the experience, and that somehow, during the years Dymka and Mitya had been away from the lair, they had lost their ability to fight. Artem attacked with a terrible roar, a battle cry, meant to intimidate his opponent. Dymka charged so they met in the air, both leopards rearing up to slash at bellies.

Behind him, the kitchen was suddenly filled with fighting leopards as four more leapt through the window or came through the open door to join the battle. Sevastyan's big brute was in his element, snarling and driving a smaller golden male into a corner while another tried to ram him from the side. Another leopard and Kiriil came together in midair, slashing at each other with teeth and claws. The fourth leopard jumped from the butcher block straight down onto Josue, where he slumped to one side, struggling for air while his blood ran like a river down his body. The leopard blasted hot air in his face and then bit down, delivering the suffocating bite of their kind. He raised his head, his evil yellow stare finding Dymka.

Artem backed away warily as Dymka tore strips from his leopard's belly, leaving him bloody and injured. Just as suddenly he sprang forward almost triumphantly. That was all the warning Dymka needed. The big male managed to whirl out of the way as the fourth newcomer abandoned Josue's body and charged.

The leopard was a mixture of dark fur over gold. The rosettes were surprisingly small for an Amur leopard, a very distinctive mix. Mitya recognized him instantly. Where Artem was a show-off and an ass-kisser, Damir was an altogether different proposition. He had held out against the corruption going on in the lair, working, like Mitya, on his education. He was the son of one of Lazar's inner circle, so he was subjected to beatings when he refused to do the things required of them, like torture anyone Lazar didn't like.

Mitya was sorry to see that over time, Damir had conformed rather than left the lair. Once, he'd been a decent human being. The real attack would come from Damir because he was no coward. Artem was. The man would hold back, allowing Damir to take the most dangerous point. Dymka kept an eye on the golden leopard but watched the darker one, readying himself for the attack.

Damir's leopard pulled back his lips in a snarl and then rushed, using his speed to try to drive Dymka off his feet. Dymka leapt, using his flexible spine to turn back in midair and slash a deep furrow from nose to eye as Damir shot past him. Momentum took Dymka right into Artem, where the leopard was crouched, waiting to run in and join the fray if Damir knocked Dymka off his feet. He sent Artem tumbling when his larger, solid-muscled body hit the leopard hard.

Dymka followed him, ripping and slashing, tearing great chunks of fur and skin from the cat as he tried to scramble to his feet. Dymka didn't allow it, landing on the cat's back, his teeth sinking into his neck in an effort to sever the spine.

Damir snarled a warning and then came at him again. This time he was much leerier, watching for Dymka's re-action. Mitya knew Damir had to smell Jewel's scent all over Dymka. He would know that the female Lazar was scouring the grounds for belonged to Mitya. They knew she'd left the kitchen and that she was outside somewhere.

The sound of gunfire was loud on the surrounding grounds. Fyodor was running the battle. This was his home, and he knew every single nook and cranny of his estate as well as every place a leopard could run.

Lazar had not caught the cousins alone. He thought he'd been so clever because he'd caught them all together. He hadn't considered that the others, their friends, were all leopard, or that they had brought personal bodyguards with them.

Artem's leopard collapsed, sides heaving, but Dymka didn't believe the leopard was finished. He spun to face Damir, jumping sideways away from Artem, just to be safe. Artem wouldn't attack face-to-face, but the moment Dymka's back was to him, he would try to take advantage.

A leopard screamed not two feet from them. Damir made the mistake of turning his head to check on his friend. Instantly, Dymka was on him. Mitya had had that particular mistake beaten out of him by the time he was twelve. Nothing could interfere with a leopard's fight to the death. Dymka was taught, as was Mitya, to keep his entire focus on the fight until he had made certain his op-ponent was no longer breathing.

Dymka took full advantage, locking his teeth into Damir's neck, holding him there in the suffocating bite. All the while, he watched Artem. The cat slunk away rather than trying to help Damir. The years hadn't changed him much. He was still the coward he'd been back then. Mitya despised him. So did Dymka.

Damir's cat refused to submit. Mitya hadn't expected it to. Very slowly the life drained from the eyes and Damir slid all the way to the floor. Dymka held him a few more moments, all the while watching Artem. Rather than try to help Damir, the golden cat pushed backward toward the door.

Sevastyan had killed the smaller cat and was now in a fierce battle with the larger one, along with Kiriil. There was no way to help Josue. He was already dead, slumped over on the floor as well. Mitya felt regret for the loss of life, *both* lives.

There had been a time Damir had been a decent human being. He had held out for a long while, but looking back, Mitya realized, Damir had held out because he had. It had been Mitya's strength that had carried the two of them, and when Mitya was gone, Damir had crumbled.

Artem moved again, drawing Dymka's attention. The moment the golden leopard saw he was the focus of the larger cat, he turned and ran, leaping up to the window and pushing through in spite of the shards of glass still in the frame. Dymka was too large to fit through that particular window, but the door was still cracked open and the cat sprinted outside after the golden leopard.

Artem stopped at the edge of the vegetable garden, but when he saw Dymka burst from the house, he turned tail and ran. Dymka rushed past one of Lazar's lieutenants, who gave a startled shout and then turned his automatic toward the big leopard. It would be impossible for any of them not to know Mitya's cat. They'd all participated in beating him and fighting with him on the pretense of training him.

He lifted the automatic and the sound of a rifle was

almost simultaneous with the bullet that took the back of the lieutenant's head. He went down to his knees and then he fell forward, his face in the dirt, his nerveless finger never finding the trigger.

Dymka put on a burst of speed, launching himself in the air, extending his front legs to hook his claws in Artem's hindquarters. He dragged the cat to a halt and slammed him to the ground, refusing to let him go. His hooked nails pierced deep as he bit down on the spine. The cat screamed, the sound reverberating through the night.

Another of Lazar's most trusted men rushed up to the two leopards, putting the barrel of his gun almost right at Dymka's head. Dymka had no choice but to release Artem and throw himself sideways to avoid the shot. A rifle sounded again, and a hole blossomed through the back of the man's neck and out his throat. The spinal cord was severed instantly. Mitya knew him. He had been Lazar's friend for over twenty years. He was just as perverted and corrupt as Lazar.

Artem was off and running again, determined to get away. Dymka refused to let him, not even when he rushed between two of Lazar's soldiers. Before either could react, one was down, and the second shot was almost on top of the first. The second soldier went down hard. Dymka just had a glimpse of the spray of blood across the leaves and dirt. Artem had stopped to look back to see if the two men would shoot his pursuer.

Dymka hit the golden leopard in his side with enough force that it had to feel as if a freight train had struck him. The blow drove through the cat, breaking bones. Artem let out another scream and tried to get up. He managed to make it to his feet, but staggered, trying to turn. Dymka hit him from the other side, the blow just as vicious, breaking more ribs.

The leopard's cry was a steady shriek now. Dymka had
no mercy. He snapped the right back leg and then the left
one, so that the cat couldn't walk. Artem tried to drag
himself away, but Dymka wouldn't let him. Artem hadn't
helped Damir, and Dymka had always despised the golden
cat anyway. He caught hold of the neck to deliver the suffocating bite and silence the shrieking for good.

As he held Artem in that death bite, waiting for the kill,
a shadow emerged from the trees, yellow eyes staring ma-
levolently. The eyes focused completely on Mitya and then
the big cat swiped at the leaves and debris with his paw,
indicating his contempt. He let out a roaring challenge.

*There will be another someone close. Perhaps more
than one,* Mitya cautioned his leopard. Dymka had fought
three cats. He'd run a distance. He had to be growing
tired, which was what Lazar had counted on.

*I smell them. They think to hide their stench from me
by staying downwind, but it shifts every few minutes and
I caught their scents. Lazar has two of his favorite partners stalking me.*

Mitya could feel his leopard's wrath, the rage that
swirled in his gut and welled up like a volcano. Dymka
wanted to rush Lazar's cat. He was eager to meet the experienced fighter in a battle and see who emerged the vic-
tor. Mitya held him back.

*Let him come to you. Take this opportunity to rest. He
wants to issue a challenge, to intimidate and rile you up
so you aren't thinking in battle. He's older, Dymka, but
he's experienced. You need to settle down and remember
every battle technique. What he favors.*

*He favors having his lieutenants cheat and fight
with him.*

Dymka was not wrong. Lazar would fight, but he didn't
like to get ripped up. The moment a younger leopard
looked as if it might score on him, he signaled to his allies

and they rushed the leopard and delivered a savage retribution.

Lazar's leopard rushed at them and then broke off before he got too close. Mitya had seen this type of challenge hundreds of times. Many male leopards used it, particularly when there was a female in heat they wanted to claim. Whether they liked it or not, the males were affected by Jewel's heat. Lazar didn't have as much control over his leopard as he used to, or he wouldn't have allowed that particular challenge. Kazimer, Lazar's leopard, knew Dymka was Jewel's mate. The leopard had his own agenda for fighting Dymka that had nothing to do with Lazar's agenda.

Kazimer wants Jewel for himself. Dymka snarled it.

Ania is sitting up there on that roof with a sniper rifle picking off anyone coming near us. She's not going to let Kazimer or Lazar near her, Mitya assured. *Stay in control. Fight your fight, not his.*

Mitya had learned discipline in a hard school, and he was determined that his leopard stay controlled. They'd practiced daily for just this occasion. He wasn't about to let Jewel's pheromones make his leopard insane enough to make mistakes and lose this fight.

Take him down fast. Don't challenge him. Just kill him.

Dymka watched Kazimer get closer and closer with each swipe of his paw, his sawing challenge filling the air. Bolstered by his own adrenaline and rage, and the need for the female, Kazimer grew bolder, coming once more at Dymka to issue his very vocal challenge.

Dymka went from absolute stillness to blurring action in the space of half a second. He rushed the other male, taking him in the side, smashing into him and driving him off his feet. Kazimer was fast, faster than Mitya thought he could be, but he wasn't a match for Dymka's speed. He couldn't get out of the way, nor get to his feet in time to keep Dymka from ripping long streaks into his side. When he rolled to try to get to his feet, the vicious claws hooked into his belly and ripped there as well.

Lazar's two lieutenants burst from the trees, each coming in from a different direction. They ran full out to get to their leader; as his personal guards, they had profited from his leadership and had enjoyed whatever they desired for years. Mitya recognized both leopards. These men had enjoyed hurting him for Lazar, forcing Dymka out to protect him when he was a boy. They were both cruel and vicious, determined to kill him and keep Lazar alive.

Guga was a big man with huge hands. He liked to cuff children, knocking them off their feet as they ran for school or to stores. He laughed when they were hurt. He was always the first man to enjoy the rape of a female, pushing all the others out of the way. All that translated into a leopard that was huge, with enormous claws and a vicious, cruel temperament.

Dymka held Kazimer down easily, found his spine through the loose fur and bit down. He held steady as Guga charged. Mitya could see the snarling, malicious animal getting larger and larger, his eyes twin pinpoints of light in all those spots. He kept coming, but Dymka refused to relinquish his hold on Kazimer.

Shockingly, the big cat suddenly plowed to a stop, his back legs dragging in the dirt as if he'd put the brakes on. Mitya was looking right into his face. He could actually feel the blast of hot air the leopard wheezed out as he neared Dymka. The cat looked as if he'd smashed head-first into a brick wall. Red blood poured from his snarling face as he stared at them, uncomprehending. The blood originated from right between his eyes, running down his nose and dripping to the ground. He shook his head. Stared at them. Tried to take a step.

Mitya registered the second shot when it came. He hadn't heard the first. He'd been too focused on Dymka and his bite, severing the spinal column of Lazar's big male. His leopard still refused to let go, even when Lazar's cat went limp, submitting. Dymka refused to accept his recognition of defeat. He wanted Lazar and Kazimer dead and wouldn't accept anything less.

Fidel, Lazar's second-in-command, rushed them from the other direction. He had slowed his attack, leery once he saw Guga go down. Dymka shook Kazimer, his gaze on Fidel, hatred and a cold fury in every line of his body. He dropped Kazimer onto the ground, swiping contemptuously with his paw and roaring a challenge at Fidel. To Mitya's shock, Fidel, that invincible leopard who had always been monstrous and seemed undefeatable, turned and ran. Dymka was on him in seconds, bringing him down as if he were a small deer in the forest.

ANIA didn't have a clear shot at the big leopard fast approaching Dymka as Mitya's large male delivered the killing bite to Lazar. Her heart had been pounding out of control, but now, seeing Dymka's complete confidence and the other leopard turning to run from him, she breathed a sigh of relief. That didn't stop her from keeping an eye to the scope, just in case she needed to aid Dymka, although she was fairly certain the big leopard wouldn't appreciate any interference. No one was going to kill that leopard, or her man, Mitya. Not when she had a rifle in her hands.

A whisper of sound had her turning, and her blood ran cold. A leopard had managed to climb onto the roof and was stalking her, already too close. Almost on top of her. She tried to turn toward him, dropping the rifle because he was too close, and pulling the smaller Glock from her waistband as the leopard's hot breath blasted in her face. Malevolent eyes stared down at her, nose wrinkled, lips pulled back in a snarl.

Jewel rose fast, looking to protect her, but she fought back the change, knowing her little female had no chance against the male. She kept the gun down by her side, out of sight, hoping the male would want to force her to shift rather than kill her outright.

He thrust his head closer, the warning sounds rumbling from his throat, his eyes never leaving her face. She'd have one shot. If she didn't kill him, he'd kill her. Without warning, he hooked his claw into her leg and ripped down from her thigh to her calf. Pain was bright hot and excruciating. She heard herself scream and hastily shut it off in midcry. That would only divide Dymka's attention, and she knew he was fighting the leopard he'd chased down.

Tears flooded, blurring her vision, but she hung on to the gun as the leopard dragged her across the roof by his claw. The tiles scraped at the skin on her back, but she barely felt it, not with the rake mark down her leg and the hooked nail embedded in her calf.

She took a breath, forced calm into her panicked mind and made the decision to shoot. She wasn't going to survive with him dragging her around, and he was strong enough to do it all day. He was definitely trying to force her to shift, in order for his leopard to get at Jewel.

She took another deep breath. He was staring at her with that same malicious stare, his claw hooked into her leg, basically telling her the next swipe was going to hurt even more. She brought up the Glock fast and fired two rounds in rapid succession. The first one struck the leopard as he jumped to the side, clipping his ear. The second missed altogether.

As he leapt away from her, he slid on the tiles and nearly went over the edge of the roof. Ania threw herself forward, headfirst, trying to get another shot as the leopard's back legs went into the air. He dug his claws into the tiles and heaved, throwing himself forward and almost on top of her.

As she fired, she heard the sound of at least two other guns unloading. The big male's momentum carried him forward and then he dropped right on top of her, his weight indicating he was dead. There was no movement. Nothing.

Ania could barely breathe with the heavy weight on her. She tried pushing him off, but it was impossible. Then, suddenly, he was lifted off her, and she was staring up at Vikenti and Zinoviy. The looks of fear turned to grins.

"You're alive."

"Just barely. He was crushing me."

Vikenti crouched down to examine her leg while Zinoviy casually removed the weapon from her hand.

Vikenti whistled softly. "He got you good. This is going to be one ugly scar."

She glared at him. "Very funny. Did Dymka manage to kill that last leopard?"

"He made short work of him," Zinoviy assured. "They're on their way back, just making certain they've got every one of the bastards. Fyodor, Timur and Gorya along with everyone else have thoroughly wiped them out. No one will be going back to the lair from here."

"Is everyone okay?"

"We lost two of our men. Four wounded severely and two more with not-so-bad injuries, from what Fyodor is reporting. Mop-up is still going on." Vikenti reached down and lifted her easily. "Let's get you inside where the doc can take a look at you. Leopards can give you a very nasty infection."

Zinoviy shoved the leopard carcass from the roof and watched it drop to the ground below. "Your man isn't going to be happy that one's already dead. He'll probably skin it and use that for target practice."

Ania shuddered. "I'd rather he not do that."

The two men grinned at each other and then Zinoviy leapt to the ground and looked up, holding out his hands.

"Don't you dare drop me," she commanded, grasping at Vikenti's shirt.

Vikenti laughed and made the leap with her in his arms.

20

"COME here, *kotyonok*," Mitya said, his voice gentle.

Ania turned from where she was staring out the window of their bedroom to look at him. He sat on the edge of the bed, his hand held out to her. Just looking at him sent butterflies winging like mad in her stomach. He was handsome in his rough way, and that appealed to her. There was never going to be a boyish quality to Mitya. He was a man, and one who was always in control of what was happening around him.

She loved him. Really loved him. The last couple of weeks had really made her see there was far more to Mitya than the wild lover she knew. He was gentle and sweet, caring for her while the injury from the leopard healed. He waited on her, bringing her meals himself. He spent time with her, playing chess and watching movies that made her cry. Well, he watched her, and she watched the movies.

Mostly he pored over her plans to redesign the garage for her work. He made suggestions when he thought they would help, and it surprised her that almost every suggestion was an excellent one. She loved that and loved that he seemed every bit as enthusiastic about her new venture as she was.

It was amazing to be able to sketch ideas and show them to him, watch his face light up as if he really appreciated each drawing. Sometimes he liked them so much he wanted to frame them. She already had several ideas for cars, but they had to get the garage pulled together first, so she'd tried to keep her mind on all the details needed to get her business up and running. Mitya helped her with staying on task. Even Sevastyan was on board, although he mostly thought in terms of security and how best to protect her when she worked in the huge, temperature-controlled garage.

Ania crossed the room to take Mitya's hand. He pulled her onto his lap, smoothing back her hair and wrapping his arms around her. She was learning all kinds of things about him. He liked her close to him when they talked. He listened when she had something to say. He laughed more without Dymka's constant raging. The male leopard was calmer, which gave Mitya more time to relax.

"I know it's been difficult to stay cooped up, Ania," Mitya said. "Doc said it was necessary until that rake mark closed and there was no chance of infection."

She leaned into him, inhaling his scent. She loved the way he smelled. "I didn't mind, I caught up on my reading and managed to sketch and design and lay out the garage the way I think will work best. It worked out."

He nuzzled her shoulder, then his teeth tugged at her earlobe. "Did you learn anything I might need to try on you from those romance novels of yours?"

She laughed and turned her face up to look at him. "I think you know more than enough to keep me satisfied for the next hundred years."

He kissed her chin and nibbled his way up to her lower lip, teeth catching and tugging gently before letting her go. "I'm always willing to learn more."

"If you know any more, honey, you might kill me."

Mitya laughed. She loved it when he laughed. It was still so rare that when he did, she felt like he was giving her a gift. She touched his lips. Traced them with her fingertips. Lightly. Barely there. Just touching him sent a tremor through her body.

He had added privacy screens to the windows of the garage, because he'd already planned out, very vocally, that he should be able to visit often and who knew what would happen? If there were cars and back seats lying around . . . He made her laugh so often with his outrageous suggestions she found herself smiling most of the time.

"I just want you to know, Mitya, that I'm so thankful I'm with you. I look at you and melt inside. I can't possibly ever tell you how much you mean to me. When I saw Dymka charging after that leopard, uncaring that Lazar's men were everywhere and they had guns, my heart was in my throat. I thought you would be killed, and I never would have the chance to tell you how much you matter to me. That I love you more than anything."

Maybe she hadn't known until that exact moment, when Dymka had burst out of the house chasing a leopard through Lazar's armed soldiers, just how much he mattered. She had been upset that she wasn't in the safe room where he would have wanted her. Until that moment. Until she knew she wasn't going to let anything, or anyone, take Mitya from her. She had skills, and they'd been put into play. She hadn't missed a single shot.

His rough features softened. "I'm so in love with you, Ania, sometimes I can't breathe. I always worry that I'm too rough with you. A leopard's heat is difficult at best and sometimes brutal. We got brutal. I would start out trying to be careful of you and then the wild was there. No, more like savage. I couldn't keep control like I needed to. I was afraid you'd want to run from me."

She framed his face with her hands. "It was the same way with me. Fortunately, whatever you were feeling, I was too. I like when we're wild like that. I like when you're gentle and I can feel love when you touch me."

He frowned. "No matter how I'm touching you, Ania, I'm loving you. I don't care if we're playing with cuffs or I'm in the car standing over you, my cock in your mouth, I'm loving you. You say no to anything and mean it, at any time, and we stop. I want you to always feel loved."

She leaned into him and kissed him. His taste was always that little bit feral. Part of the excitement with Mitya was that feeling of loss of control. His arms tightened around her and then he took over the kiss, pouring fire into her so that her panties went damp and her breasts instantly ached.

When he lifted his head, Mitya stared down into Ania's eyes, shocked at the depth of feeling she always managed to wring out of him. She said she loved him, and he could see it in her eyes that she did. She was his world. His reason for existence. For getting up in the morning and for trying to weed out the worst of the criminals.

Sevastyan called him whipped, and he knew he was. He didn't care. He looked forward to going to bed, just so he could hold her, watch her sleep, wake her up with his mouth between her legs, devouring her honey that was meant for him alone. He loved that. Loved holding her down with one hand on her belly as she woke up, her hips bucking, his face right where he preferred to be.

He loved her lips stretched around his cock while he moved in and out of her mouth, her soft hands cupping his balls, eyes liquid and looking up into his. That was such a turn-on, and the feeling was exquisite. Unbelievable.

He loved his body moving in hers, surrounded by fire, by a fist of hot, wet silk, so tight she was strangling him, dragging his seed right out of him. Most of all, he loved her company. Watching her laugh. The way her face lit up. She could light up the world. She was intelligent and talented when it came to her work. She had compassion in her when he didn't, but he was learning from her.

"I never want you to think I'm not loving you," he repeated. "Even when I get harsh with you." He wished he could feel remorse for those times. He often thought about having her at his mercy, his hand on her bottom, his cock surging in and out of her while she was helpless in cuffs. Every time he thought about it, he grew so hard he was afraid he might shatter.

Her soft laughter was unexpected. "You liked it."

So, she knew. And she didn't mind. "Yeah, baby, I liked it. A hell of a lot. I would have done more of the same for you not making it into the safe room, but since you might have saved my life, I thought I'd let it slide." He loved teasing her. Loved seeing the mock frown on her face and the way she gave him her princess-to-peasant haughty look.

"*Might* have saved your life?" she echoed. "I totally saved your life. It seems I have to do that quite often. That should get me out of trouble for the next few years."

He raised an eyebrow. "Next few years? Are you expecting to jack up for the next few *years* and get away with it because you *might* have saved my life a time or two?"

"Well," she hedged. "Maybe not years."

"I think you've forgotten you damaged my property."

She looked puzzled. "Your property?"

He lifted the hem of the shirt she was wearing. His shirt. She wore her favorite, a button-down flannel that she'd found somewhere. On her it looked sexy. On him, not so much. He slid his hand lightly down the rake mark that ran from the top of her thigh to her calf. It had been very deep and would forever leave a scar.

"My property," he reiterated.

"Well, that's true," she agreed reluctantly. "Maybe not years," she repeated. "A few months."

"Now that I look at this, it makes me angry again." It made him feel sick to his stomach. He hadn't been there. Thankfully, Vikenti and Zinoviy had done their jobs.

Ania slipped off his lap to the floor, right between his legs, and his cock instantly reacted to the sight of her like that. She covered his growing cock with her palm, rubbing gently, all the while looking up at him innocently, as if she wasn't trying to distract him.

"I don't think I want you angry with me, Mitya."

There was no way to be angry with her, even if he really had cause. Not when she could make every nerve ending in his body come alive the way she did.

"Sit with your back to the ottoman," he instructed. He liked that the ottoman was low.

She did so immediately.

"Unbutton that shirt and take it off, your panties too." He stood up, towering over her.

Ania slid each button free and shrugged out of the too-big shirt and then slid the panties from her body. The sight of her breasts added steel to his cock. He went to the end table drawer and retrieved his favorite toys. He loved playing with her. They'd spent nearly the last two weeks in the bedroom, and he'd been a gentle, considerate lover, so conscious of her injury.

The threat of Lazar was over, and in his place, a new enemy had risen, but their coalition would always have new enemies. This one would be no different than all the others. Now that the doctor had told him the wound on Ania's leg was well on the way to healing and out of danger of infection, he could relax. And he could play. He could have her any way he wanted her.

He crouched down, licked at her nipple and then sucked hard, using tongue and teeth to get her ready. The clamp pinched hard enough to simulate his fingers when he was being rough. He clamped both nipples, smiling wickedly at her hiss of breath as he did so. The double-looped chain hung down, swinging slightly, causing that same sexy hiss. He flicked it once and then moved his hand between her legs to feel her slick heat.

"You like your jewelry, don't you, *kotyonok*?"

She couldn't very well deny it when he had the evidence right there. He waited for her nod before he showed her the vibrator. It was large, thick and shaped very much like his cock. It had bumps on it to rub along every sensitive nerve ending. He held it to her mouth until she opened for him. Once it was wet, he pushed it slowly inside her, fucking her with it for a stroke or two before turning it on low. She gasped. He took her hand and curled her fingers around it.

"Just like that, baby."

He stood and shed his clothes, watching her the entire time. She looked so sexy, sitting just exactly as he'd placed her, waiting for him. Waiting for his instructions. He dropped his hand on her head and caressed her scalp and then applied pressure until her head tilted all the way back, exposing the vulnerability of her throat to him. The leopard in him appreciated that submissive pose.

He straddled her, one leg on either side of her body, his cock and balls hanging over her head. "Open your mouth, Ania and turn the vibrator to medium."

She licked her lips and then did as he said, opening her mouth for him. He waited a heartbeat, shocked at the anticipation, at the way his cock jerked and pulsed, so eager to feel that hot, wet mouth closing around him. Her body shuddered again, and he knew she'd obeyed and turned up the vibrator.

His fist guiding his cock, he slid between her lips, watching her struggle to take the girth of him. He went as slowly as possible, the sight so erotic he knew he would wake a million times dripping with need because he'd never lose that image. He was careful, sliding an inch in, sliding back out, going in a little farther and retreating. He got a gentle rhythm going and reached for the chain dangling between her breasts. Using one hand at the base of his cock, he used the other to tug on her breasts, raising them toward him, watching her face, loving the look as she gasped and moaned around his cock.

He picked up the pace, sliding deeper, feeling that tight tunnel massaging his shaft, her tongue working the head.

"Fuck yourself with that vibrator, Ania. Keep working it."

She did so, her hands on it, pumping it in and out of her while he fucked her mouth. Each time he went deeper he had less control, the fire threatening to consume him. She struggled to swallow him down, to not panic when she couldn't breathe. The vibrator distracted her as did the way he tugged at the chain. His cock was already swelling. His balls, hitting her chin with every pump, drew up tight.

"On high, Ania." He could barely snap out the command, barely wait for her to comply. He was almost too far gone. "Swallow me down, baby. Take all of me."

She had no choice, his cock pinning her to the ottoman, but he felt her swallow, her muscles tightening around him. Then her throat convulsed as she orgasmed, a long, wicked wave that sent his seed burning like molten lava, boiling out of control, rocketing out of him. Flames raced up his thighs to his cock. Fire consumed him completely.

He was barely aware of anything but that euphoric place somewhere between heaven and hell.

His cock was still jerking, still semihard, probably as shocked as he was. He became aware of his heart pounding and his legs shaking. He pulled back immediately to give Ania air and heard her swift inhale. He tugged again on the chain, and that sent her into another frenzied orgasm. His cock still in her mouth, he watched the wave take her, rippling through her body, her breasts, her belly, even her thighs.

Her gaze jumped to his and he read the plea in her eyes. She wanted the vibrator off. He would have liked to give her another orgasm, but she was shaking her head. He nodded and she switched it off before she bathed his cock with her warm, wet mouth.

He helped her to her feet and laid her on the bed to remove the clamps, using his mouth immediately to alleviate the rush as the blood flowed back. When he had them off, he rolled over and lay looking up at the ceiling, his heart pumping hard. But it was his soul that she'd stolen from him. He didn't mind anymore. He was damn grateful he had her. His hand found hers.

"I love you so much, Ania. The things you do to me, the ways you make me feel are beyond description." He rubbed his chest over his heart. He meant the physical, that was so obvious, but it was so much deeper, that feeling. So overwhelming, and impossible to convey to her how she made him feel inside.

She turned onto her side. Her nipples brushed his arm and she gasped, sensitive from the clamps. He turned to her and gently sucked first one, then the other, to soothe her. Her fingers settled on his scalp, massaging. He loved that. He loved the way she always touched him.

"I love everything you do to me, Mitya. I don't know how I would ever live without you."

412   Christine Feehan

He still couldn't believe he'd found her out there on that
rainy, wet road, but he was very glad he had. They would
find their way; they already were. It was going to be a
good journey, this first one for their leopards and for them.
He looked forward to every moment, the wild ones, and
the beautiful ones, like the one they shared right then.

Keep reading for an excerpt from

VENDETTA ROAD

The next novel in the Torpedo Ink series
by Christine Feehan
Available January 2020 from Piatkus

SOLEIL Brodeur had never actually used the main entrance to the hotel. She used a private entrance and always had a concierge waiting to give her any little thing she wanted or to direct her to wherever she wanted to go. There was a private car to take her places. She had wanted to walk around the Strip like a normal tourist and just enjoy the day. Was that asking too much? Did she always have to dress right and talk only to the people Winston dictated she talk to? They were supposed to be having fun. Make that whatever Winston ordered was fun.

She wiped at the tears on her face and stopped to look around. There were people everywhere. She hadn't used the private entrance because she hadn't wanted the concierge to see her crying like a baby, which was so ridiculous there were no words. She had no idea where to go, which elevator to take or even if she could get one to her room from the main lobby. She'd traveled the world, stayed in hundreds of hotels, but she couldn't find her way to an elevator? She was *such* an idiot.

No one could force another person to marry them. The idea was ludicrous. She'd brought this entire mess on herself. There was no one else to blame. She might let everyone else do everything for her, but she always took responsibility for her own screwups. This was the worst of the worst.

She took a quick look around and caught sight of a woman's bathroom, tucked behind an alcove filled with gorgeous plants. She hurried across the gleaming marble-tiled floor and ducked into the alcove. The door was opened for her by an attendant in a hotel uniform. She went on through, wondering how many people couldn't open a door. Probably only her. A fresh flood of tears ensured her makeup would be a mess.

As with everything else in the hotel, the bathroom was the epitome of luxury. The door opened to a sitting room with faint music, comfortable but elegant chairs, and a sofa, giving women a place to relax if they wanted to hide for a few minutes. A soft fragrance spread through the room, and large, lacy plants in various shades of green added to the peaceful ambience. Once the door was closed, all noise from the outside lobby ceased.

A tall woman with dark hair stood in the midst of the greenery, dragging a dark tank top over a lacy red bra. She was beyond beautiful. Her face was flawless, with her dark eyes and inviting mouth. If Soleil hadn't been crying, she would have stopped and stared. She couldn't stay in the sitting room, not with the most gorgeous woman on the face of the earth casually changing from what looked like a sultry afternoon dress—*not* a girl-next-door sundress.

Soleil went past another concerned attendant to the sink, needing to splash cold water on her face. She had to stop crying, but all she seemed to be able to do was stare at herself in the mirror with tears running down her face.

She didn't look at all like the beautiful woman with gold at her ears and a flawless body to go with her flawless face. That woman probably looked gorgeous when she cried, not all splotchy and red.

There was a faint bruise on her left cheek where her fiancé had slapped her because she'd insisted on a prenup. There were bruises on both upper arms where he'd grabbed her hard and shaken her, as if somehow, by him threatening her, that would make her go through with the marriage.

She'd always had a ridiculous fantasy about being with someone a little rough, although they would never *hit* her. She never could quite feel that tingle with the men she dated. That spark. Winston hadn't appeared rough. He had soft hands. He always wore a business suit, and his shoes were gleaming with polish. In the weeks she'd known him, he'd never had a single hair out of place. She realized having the real thing wasn't at all what she'd dreamt about. No one had ever put their hands on her like that before.

It was ridiculous anyway. She had known better than to come to Vegas. She'd reluctantly agreed even though, in the back of her mind, she feared Winston Trent was going to try to get her to marry him. They'd argued about it several times before coming. He wanted to marry her quickly to "take care of her." She needed breathing room. She'd told him, and he hadn't listened.

Winston switched tactics, saying they didn't have to go through with a marriage, but she needed some fun. He planned the entire trip and "surprised" her. She should have refused to go. That would have been the adult thing to do. The intelligent thing. She did what she always did. She drifted. She let him talk her into it because she wasn't a fighter. She'd never been a fighter. She liked peace. She liked creating peace.

Her longtime lawyer and guardian, Kevin Bennet, had died unexpectedly in an accident just a month earlier. He had always managed her affairs, looked after her trust

fund and been more like a father to her, although she
didn't really know what a father was supposed to be like.
She was grieving. She'd told Winston that repeatedly, but
his answer was to get married and let him take care of
things. He had rushed out and hired a lawyer, but she was
uneasy around the new lawyer, a man by the name of Don-
ald Monroe, and felt like she wasn't ready to move on.
Again, Winston's answer had been to get married and let
him handle the lawyer.

She touched the bruises on her arm and shook her head,
knowing she was at her lowest point. She'd lost the one
man she could talk to and figure things out with. Everything felt so tangled, and she had absolutely no real idea of
what to do next.

"Honey, he's not worth it. No matter how much money
he's got, no matter how big a ring he puts on your finger,
if he puts his hands on you, you should run the opposite
way as fast as you can."

Soleil lifted her gaze in the mirror to see the woman
standing beside her. She had been the one in the sitting
room changing. She looked at the woman and then
dropped her gaze to the ring. "You're so right," she murmured, and pulled it off her finger to shove in the pocket
of her dress. "Thanks for the advice."

Up close, the stranger was even more gorgeous. Really,
really beautiful. It took some doing not to stare. The
woman rinsed her hands in the immaculate bowl and Soleil couldn't help glancing down to see if she wore a ring.
She didn't. She wasn't quite as tall as Soleil had first
thought but looked it because, although she had curves,
she was on the slimmer side. She wore skinny jeans, mo-
torcycle boots and a leather vest over a dark tank. She'd
gone from glamorous woman to hot biker babe in about
three minutes. Who could do that?

"You all right, honey? I could get you a room if you
need it for the night." Even her voice was sultry.

A perfect stranger in the women's room of a hotel was nicer to her than her fiancé, the man who had sworn he loved her. "Thank you, I really appreciate the offer, but I have a room. I'm going to pack and get out of here fast." The problem was, she was going to have to face Winston. They shared the room.

"Good for you," the woman approved.

"Did you hear all those sirens?" Soleil asked, trying to change the subject so she didn't look so pathetic. "It sounded like half the police force were going somewhere."

The woman nodded. "Around the corner, a couple of streets over. I heard there was a shooting in a massage parlor. Someone said everyone inside is dead."

"What is wrong with everyone these days?" Soleil asked.

The woman shrugged. "Most likely someone didn't pay when they should have." She picked up a small tote, started out and then stopped, turning back. "You have a cell phone?"

Soleil nodded.

"I'm Lana."

"Soleil."

"You here alone?"

"With him." She held up her bruised arm.

"Where's your family? Maybe you should give them a call."

Soleil looked down at the floor. It was absolutely clean, just like everything else. She sniffed and wasn't at all shocked to find even the bathroom smelled good. That citrus fragrance from the sitting room had drifted right in.

"I don't have a family," she admitted in a low voice.

"Friends nearby?" Lana stepped closer to her, concern in her voice. In her eyes.

Soleil struggled not to burst into tears at the obvious sympathy. The few friends she'd had, Winston had managed to alienate. She shook her head.

"Sometimes these things get ugly. You have any trouble at all, you can call me. I have friends. They'll come get you out of any situation." Lana snapped her fingers and held out her hand. "Give me your cell."

Soleil had no idea why in the world she would allow a perfect stranger to take her cell phone, but she did. She pulled it from her pocket, keyed in the code and handed it to Lana.

"I meant what I said. He's already proven he's willing to put his hands on you, so when you break it off, make certain you're not alone with him. Have your cell handy and call the cops. If you can't, you call me, understand?" Lana turned and pointed to her vest even as she programmed her number into Soleil's cell. "It's under 'Lana.' Don't you forget it."

On the back of her vest there was a very cool tree with ravens in the branches and skulls in the roots. A rocker above the tree proclaimed her Torpedo Ink. The one below said Sea Haven-Caspar. Soleil had heard of Sea Haven but not Sea Haven-Caspar and had no idea where that was, or what Torpedo Ink was other than a club. But it was cool as hell and Soleil's first time ever talking to a woman who rode motorcycles.

"We're in Vegas celebrating our brother's wedding to his woman, but you call, you understand? He lays his hands on you again or does anything that frightens you, lock yourself in a room and call." She handed the phone back to Soleil. "Someone will come for you, I promise."

"Thanks." Soleil wrapped her hands around her phone as if it were a lifeline. Maybe it was. At least, it was the first truly nice thing someone had done for her since Kevin had died.

Lana gave a friendly wave and walked out.

Praise for Christine Feehan's Leopard Novels

"Punctuated with plenty of danger and delicious tension . . . a wild ride with a sizzling, passionate romance at its heart."
—BookPage

"A really steamy, can't-catch-your-breath romance."
—Fresh Fiction

"The premise is raw and gritty; the romance is spirited and provocative; the characters are flawed, colorful and energetic."
—The Reading Cafe

"Heart-stopping action. Crazy sexy-time scenes. Tender emotions. . . . [A] little bit of something for everyone who enjoys a solid paranormal romance."
—Harlequin Junkie

"With a Feehan novel you know you will get well-developed characters and an engaging plot, so when you add a dose of sizzling sexuality, you have an unbeatable mix."
—RT Book Reviews

"A bloody good time."
—I Smell Sheep

"Heady, passionate, seductive. . . . Ms. Feehan does a fantastic job of building up to the climax for a smashing finale that leaves you breathless and satisfied."
—Smexy Books

"Readers . . . will be seduced by this erotic adventure."
—*Publishers Weekly*

"Another wild ride . . . enter the lair of the shapeshifters."
—Romance Reviews Today

"A passionate, jam-packed adventure."
—Fallen Angel Reviews

"The passion runs high and the sex is hot!"
—The Romance Readers Connection

"Sizzling and exciting . . . surprises erupt at every turn."
—Fresh Fiction

"A phenomenal story. . . . Christine Feehan knows how to weave a tale of action, suspense and paranormal passion that has earned her so many fans and keeps bringing new ones."
—Romance Junkies

Do you love fiction with a supernatural twist?

Want the chance to hear news about your favourite authors (and the chance to win free books)?

Keri Arthur
Kristen Callihan
P.C. Cast
Christine Feehan
Jacquelyn Frank
Larissa Ione
Darynda Jones
Sherrilyn Kenyon
Jayne Ann Krentz and Jayne Castle
Lucy March
Martin Millar
Tim O'Rourke
Lindsey Piper
Christopher Rice
J.R. Ward
Laura Wright

Then visit the Piatkus website
www.piatkus.co.uk

And follow us on Facebook and Twitter
www.facebook.com/piatkusfiction | @piatkusbooks

piatkus